The Rusty Years

Book One:
The Remembrance of Being Young

Alberta Sequeira

This is a work of fiction. All names, characters, places, and events are the work of the author's imagination. Any resemblance to a real person, place, or event is coincidental.

Evaluation: The Editorial Department, LLC, Tucson, AZ

Cover Design: Cindy Bauer

Authors Without Borders
ISBN: 978-1733284622

Published in the United States of America

Other Works by Alberta Sequeira

Fictional:
The Rusty Years
Book One: The Remembrance of Being Young
Book Two: Secrets Revealed

Memoirs:
Someone Stop This Merry-Go-Round: An Alcoholic Family in Crisis
(Sequel) *Please God Not Two: This Killer Called Alcoholism*

Narrative Non-Fiction:
The Mindset of the Alcoholic and Addict

Upcoming Books:
A Sample of Heaven: Our Last Call (Memoir)
First the War - Then the Flashbacks (Memoir)

Contributor:
The Speaker Anthology, VOL. 1 (page 98-100) - Dr. Kent Gustavson
and Sally Shields

All books are available at Amazon

Alberta Sequeria

Sophie Gramm

Now That's Class!

A special dedication to my mother, Sophie Gramm, who passed away on February 5, 2007 at ninety-two years old. I remembered many of her sayings about getting old. My memories of our long talks will always be treasured. This book is dedicated to her.

Alberta Sequeria

The Truth Be Told

I couldn't believe what I was hearing. I wanted to block my ears. My head was spinning and I felt faint.

"What do you mean you had a one-night stand with Cathy Greco before she left for Paris? You said it was over and that I had nothing to worry about with the two of you. We're getting married in two weeks and you're telling me now!"

Todd continued. "Last week, her mother, Sharon, called me saying her husband, Tony, wanted to talk to me. I honestly didn't know Cathy was back, Jenny. I swear. It wasn't until I went into his office and saw her sitting on the couch."

"Why did they call you? What was this so-called meeting about with her?"

"Jenny… Cathy's pregnant. She's claiming I'm the father."

"What?" Suddenly, I felt like someone kicked me in the stomach.

"She knew we were engaged when she pushed herself on me."

"Really, Todd, she pushed herself on you? You have a mind of your own to say NO! You either wanted it or didn't. After two years dating her, and breaking up, I guess she still has a hold on you.

"Did I ever come to mind during your sex, Todd? You made love to me a few months ago. My first time. I saved myself. Did that mean anything to you? Tell me, who was the lucky one to get laid first, her or me?"

"Jenny, I love you. Please, don't talk like that."

By now, tears were mounting and my eyes were watery. I tried to control my lower lip from shaking. It didn't seem real that we were having this conversation. I felt numb, in shock.

I took a deep breath. Cheating is one thing to accept loving someone, but Cathy was carrying his baby.

"How do you know you're the father? She's been gone three months. Cathy would never go that long without having sex. Anyone could be the father. She sleeps around as if she needs sex to survive. It doesn't matter if the man is married or not. It's not surprising she got knocked up. Why are you taking her word?"

"Mr. Greco had one of his gangsters take us to a hospital for a paternity test."

"You can't get one that fast."

"You can when a man is holding a gun to you."

"How sweet, Todd. Are you going to be a daddy?"

"I'm 99% the father. All those years dating Cathy and nothing happened. What timing."

For a moment, I stood in silence. What actions could be taken in a situation that I couldn't change? I was about to lose Todd. Cathy won again, taking the love of my life. There was no way I could compete. She was gorgeous, seductive with no flaws. She was picture perfect.

Cathy was returning to claim what was once hers. He was now mine. You could also use the word—breathtaking. At nineteen, she was the most famous and rich model for Coco Chanel known all over Europe and the world. She was Nina Mae.

Cathy was also filthy rich. Why did she need Todd? Farm-life was not her style. That's what she would get with Todd. She's used to being waited on and pampered. Her hardest work was probably lifting up a pen and signing her name on checks or autographs for her followers.

What was happening? Today, Todd and I met because I had something special to share with him. This crushing news took all my excitement away from the announcement. All the enthusiasm left me. How could we be happy I was carrying his child?

In a few weeks, we'd be saying our marriage vows. We were so close. I was going to be Mrs. Jenny Costa. These were my happiest moments. I was in love. My dreams were surrounded by Todd...by us. The one and the only threat that could take it all from me was at my doorstep.

Meeting Todd

I started to tell my story at the worst time of my life with an intense crisis that had to be faced. The physical pressure was either going to shape my life better or break me. There were high and low moments with hanging on to hope. Waiting for a resolution was so difficult that I couldn't move ahead. Whatever decision Todd and I made would affect us the rest of our lives. There was no progress because the problem wasn't mine to solve. I could only react to the choice Todd settled on with his action. I lost myself in Todd. He was the love of my life. What was I going to do with all these feelings?

I met Todd on a Sunday morning taking my mother to the Costa Farm to get our vegetables. We made the trip monthly to stock up on our produce. It was the hotspot in our small-town. They had a family business that grew from hard work to serve the community. Families would bring their purchases home to find a few extra greens, potatoes or apples that had been thrown into their bags. Every item was fresh and picked that day. The trip led into a social hour once you arrived with greetings and conversation about the updated news.

The Great Depression hit everyone. Money was scarce and the Costa family never charged what they should have for their laborious undertaking to give us the best from their fields. Budgets were carefully watched for only what was needed. You bought what could be stretched into numerous meals. Vegetables and fruit were usually served as snacks.

I took our chestnut farm-horse used for plowing the fields out of the barn and hitched him to the wagon. Mom got onto the passenger seat while I took the reins. I loved the ride through the dirt roads along the ponds and seeing nature with deer in the fields.

"How you feeling today, Mom?"

"I woke up excited going for our drive. I think this is the only time I leave the house." She looked over and smiled.

"I look forward to it myself. The Costa family keeps their farm so clean. I love watching the children getting tractor rides and going through the apple orchards. They light up when the tours start going through their barns to see the animals, especially the babies that were just born.

"Fall is a beautiful time. Thanksgiving is coming in a few weeks. They usually have the pumpkins with painted faces on them. We should get one of their homemade pies. What do you think, Mom?"

"It won't be easy choosing which one to buy. They have such a variety."

We arrived with the sight of children of all ages running from one end of the farm to the next. They had all different events going on for the youngsters. Homemade pies were showcased on the top shelves out front at the stand: salted caramel apple, ginger pumpkin, pecan, sweet potato with cornmeal crust, triple berry pie, and a delicious chocolate chess pie. The aroma was a delectable concoction of fresh scents of cinnamon spice toppings. I could feel my mouth watering as I passed each one.

Rita Costa and I were friends since high school. My cousin, Kathleen Perry, hadn't arrived yet to help out as she usually did for them. We were all in the same grade and the three of us became inseparable. We went everywhere together.

I spotted Rita waiting on a customer. "Hi Rita."

"Jenny. Nice to see you. Hello Mrs. Rossini. How are you?"

"I'm doing fine, dear. Your place is busy."

"This is the most active season for us. My mother lives in the house baking. It's wonderful going home and having the aroma of pastry. What would we do without you, Mom? Rita gave her a hug."

"This is why I love our farm," Judy said. "I'm glad Rita offers to help or I wouldn't be able to keep up. Our sons are a great help. Thank God, we all have the same dreams for this farmstead. That's why we have children, right Mary?"

My mother smiled. "Wish I had a son to help around the farm, Judy." Rita followed my mother as she picked out the vegetables to be bagged.

I watched as Judy welcomed their buyers with warmth and a friendly smile. She seemed to have a twinkle in her eyes. Judy had a solid body and muscle in her arms from all the lifting she did with heavy baskets and picking the vegetables in the garden. She had sandy brown hair below her ears keeping it off her face. Her family came first and their business was the soul of the household.

Her husband, Cory, was close to six feet tall with red hair. His descendants came from Scotland centuries ago. He was always by Judy's side, unless he was operating the equipment in the fields. Cory was never embarrassed to show his affection openly for his kids, including his sons. He loved them all. Sometimes, I'd catch a private glance or smile with Judy. I prayed to have a man like him. There's something sexy and soft about a gentle man.

This wasn't their only business. They ran a landscaping company and built a carpentry business along with the produce sales. Cory's father had been the fifth generation to keep the woodworking side going. They were on demand for houses and repairs.

As I waited on the side struggling with which pie to indulge in, I heard a tractor pulling up next to me. A strong smell of gasoline came from the hot engine. The heat from the motor hit me standing next to the rig. A large cart was hitched in the back with fresh tomatoes, cucumbers, string beans, potatoes, and fresh cut flowers.

I looked up and saw a slender man wearing a lightweight red t-shirt that had dirt over all of it and wearing dungaree overalls with a bib front. He was sweating, causing the shirt to stick to him showing the strong muscles in his chest. His hair was red like his dad's, with strong carrot tints. It fell into his eyes as he leaned down to pick up a basket of apples. His eyebrows and lashes were a light shade of red, almost fading into his facial skin covered with freckles that traveled along his arms. He jumped off the wagon and smiled. His caramel eyes went through me as he passed with a soft, "Hello."

I noticed his hoarse voice when he spoke to his mother. My heart skipped watching him move. He was handsome and manly. He started to pull baskets off the cart and brought them inside the stand. When he came out, Rita had finished filling all the bags for my mother.

A young woman got out of a 1930s pale-yellow convertible Mercedes and went into the stand. She was gorgeous. She even took my breath away. Her blonde hair was pulled up with a pin letting loose hair fall down by the side of her face. Her clothes were fashionable, wearing a white, floppy hat, a white full-length skirt with a black and white checkered top, finished with a black belt on her tiny waist. She wore white gloves. Someone like her stood out. She was too stylish to be at a farm stand.

She walked over to Todd. He looked down at her and seemed glued to her every move. She whispered something in his ear and squeezed his cheek. He carried a basket of mixed vegetables to her car and placed them in the trunk. She got into the driver's seat and waved out the window as she left the homestead.

My cousin, Kathleen, arrived to help Rita.

"Hey, Kathleen, who is that girl in that gorgeous yellow car taking off?"

"Cathy Greco. Someone not to be friends with...ever! There's gossip that her dad's a boss in the Italian Mafia."

"You're kidding?"

"No. She's trouble, Jenny. Beautiful, but spoiled rotten by her parents. Men—single or married have been involved with her. She loves stealing boyfriends away and then dumps them."

"She seems friendly with that boy in the stand."

Kathleen looked at me for a second. "That's Rita's brother, Todd. He dated her for a short time."

"How long?"

"I think two years."

"Two years! That's long. Are they a twosome?"

"No. He broke up with her because she cheated on him numerous times. I don't think she can stay with one man."

"No wonder she has a Mercedes. The family must be rich. Her clothes are to die for."

"She's a well-known model in New York and California. Why do you ask?"

"I think he's a hunk."

"Todd is a great guy. Anyone who gets him will be lucky. I'm glad Cathy's out of his life."

Rita was ready to total my mother's purchase when Todd walked over to us.

"Todd, I'd like you to meet Jenny and her mother, Mrs. Rossini."

"Nice to meet you both." He grabbed our bags and put them into our wagon. "You have a great-looking farm horse, Jenny."

"Thank you. We'd be lost without him. We have another one in the barn. They go crazy when one is left behind. He runs around in his stall."

Judy came over to us holding tickets in her hand. "Mr. Jackson stopped by today and gave me four tickets to the Cape Cod Playhouse in Dennis. Artie Shaw is coming for a one-time appearance in three weeks. Why don't you kids go to the event. Do you like jazz, Jenny?"

"I've never been but I love music. Can I go, Mom?"

She put her arm around me. "I think you're due for some fun."

"I'll ask Frankie. Todd, are you free to join us?" Rita asked.

"How can I say no. I'll polish my shoes. We'll pick you up that night, Jenny."

"I look forward to it."

"I'll call you with a time. We'll talk before then." Rita walked back to the stand.

Part of me was uneasy after seeing how Cathy had a hold on Todd. It couldn't be missed. How could any man walk away from her? I never laid eyes on someone as stunning.

We got into the wagon and I pushed those warning signs in the back of my mind and was excited beyond words. I finally met one of Rita's brothers. Where was she hiding him? The Costa's had another son, Samuel. He was called Sam by the family. He was finishing his last year in college in Boston. Rita said he had been away from home for four years.

That was my first meeting with Todd Costa. I hoped to see him often. When he jumped off the tractor, my heart raced and my knees were weak. I melted when he looked into my eyes, and his smile turned me to jelly. Seeing him dirty and sweaty turned me on instantly. Maybe I'll have a dance with him Saturday. I floated home with no conversation with my mother. I was glad she was enchanted with the sounds of the birds in the trees and the scenery surrounding her. This gave me a chance to stay in my trance.

Family Life

I grew up in Manhattan, New York on a farm. The city was electrifying. The lights filled the night, along with the entertainment and movie stars. I prayed to meet the man of my dreams in that exciting city.

A year ago, our lives changed for the worse when everything crashed from the Great Depression. Dad was out of work for months and mom struggled to make ends meet. I never heard her complain. I wasn't ashamed of being poor because everyone was at that time.

My cousin, Kathleen Perry, had moved from Manhattan a few years before with her parents to live in Chatham, Massachusetts. We kept in touch by mail. She had no siblings and either did I, which formed a tight bond between us.

In 1936, the final decision to move came last summer when my parents followed our relatives to Cape Cod.

My father died six months after our move from a car accident. Dad had little warmth. He wasn't afraid to show his coolness by being unfriendly and walking out of a room and leaving people alone in the middle of a conversation. Some folks turned away forever from his ruddiness. He was Italian with a bad temper. He loved to try to control everything and everyone. He also loved liquor.

I grew up not knowing the personal side of my father, never saw my parents spend time together, laugh, or even showed affection. He emotional abused me a few times. I envied families that were blessed having love for each other and showed their affection.

My mother, Mary Rossini, was thirty-five years old, a thin woman, who had been born in France and her maiden name was Boucher. She was blessed with an open personality. Her life revolved around me.

Lucky Dad left us enough money to survive.

My mother's sister, Dorothy Perry, was a full-figured woman and her husband, Joe, was easy-going and found humor in any situation.

Kathleen was fifteen years old with jet-black, straight hair down past her shoulders. She gave me a cushion for knowing at least one person in Chatham. Her life revolved around her drama classes when she was in high school. She got the staring parts, not only for her talent but for her beauty. Kathleen had a bubbly personality that took on its own magic, and therefore, charmed people.

I, on the other hand, had auburn hair with highlights. Freckles covered my face and arms. Todd and I could have passed for twins. I had my mother's beautiful emerald eyes and prayed to inherit her spirit to keep going no matter what roadblocks came my way.

My mother and I have been on our own for a year. With no siblings, I had farm work and my mother handled the cooking and cleaning.

Rita, Kathleen, and I searched daily for work. The positions were gone before they were even advertised. Men traveled by train far from home to apply for jobs. They were gone for months. Many came home empty handed and moved to another state trying to get out of the depression.

Entertainment Night

The weeks couldn't go fast enough for the dance plans to arrive. I rushed to get the animals fed and out to pasture early in the morning. I shortened their time to roam free by bringing them back to the barn earlier than normal for the night.

I chose a two-layered mauve skirt fully flared with a petticoat to dance with ease. I wore a cream, silk buttoned down blouse with black two-inch pump heels with a strap crossed in front. I kept my hair down with tight curls.

A knock came on the front door. As I opened the hatch, Todd stood wearing black pants, a red shirt, a light gray vest, and his attire finished with a tan, straw hat showing a wide silk black and white ribbon tied with a tiny buckle on the rim. He looked handsome, carefree, and ready for fun.

Todd had flowers behind his back. Once we got into the living room, he handed them to my mother. She was pleasantly surprised and took the bouquet. "What a beautiful arrangement. Thank you, Todd." She bent to smell the fragrance of purple lilacs mixed with yellow roses.

"I personally picked them from our field."

"Let me put them in a vase for you, Mom." I arranged them and put them on the mantle.

We talked about Todd's farm, his family, and his wishes to take over his parent's business when they passed. My mother studied him as he spoke and the gaze didn't seem to bother or fluster Todd. I felt confident he could handle himself.

"I won't keep her out late, Mrs. Rossini."

"You two have fun."

We got to the car and Rita and Frank were missing. "Where are they?"

"They took their own car. We'll see them there."

I was going to my first dance, alone with Todd. Swing, no less. As the country coped with the Great Depression and the war years, the big bands thrived and swept the land. I was witnessing the sounds of one of the greatest groups. I would be hearing the instruments live instead of reading about Artie Shaw's appearance in our newspaper.

The playhouse had a large backroom used for dancing while the front had been kept for famous actors and actresses in plays.

Out tickets were reserved at a front table on the floor. Rita and Frank were sitting when we arrived.

"You two are early."

"Can't wait to hear this band," Rita said excitedly. We sat and mixed in with conversation.

The famous jazz singer, Artie Shaw, stood facing me when the full, red curtain opened from each side. A full thirty-six-piece band appearing on stage. The music echoed and bounced off the walls with the first song, *It Don't Mean a Thing, If it Ain't Got That Swing*. People immediately jumped out of their seats doing the jitterbug and Lindy hop. My feet bounced under the table with each beat.

"What do you say? Want to swing? Todd asked with a teasing smile."

"Think you can keep up with me?"

The floor filled in seconds with eager dancers. Frankie and Rita were living it up on the floor. Women were lifted up by their dancing partners. To my complete amazement, Todd took control and heaved me around like a feather. He twisted and spun me fast, raising my skirt to show my thighs. I was circled in every direction and thrown up and down. Artie Shaw added some of Benny Goodman's songs and skipped into *Sing, Sing, Sing*.

The four of us never left the dance floor. The last song *Stardust* began. Todd held me tight against his body moving in a smooth, slow rhythm. I could feel the muscles in his arms while he held me. Our cheeks were glued together and I sunk in his hold. His finger pulled my face up, looking deep into my eyes. He gave me a soft kiss. Our first kiss! I had no idea how my legs kept me standing.

We returned one more time to The Cape Cod Playhouse to see the musical *The Major and the Minor* with Ginger Rogers and Fred Astaire. They were magical together. I never moved sitting in my chair. Todd and I held hands during the whole show. There was comfort with him; a natural belonging.

We pulled in the yard at 11 pm. Todd walked me to the front door. The lights were out. My mother was sleeping. He gave me a long, soft kiss, and leaned against me. His hardness caused me to give a moan. My knees felt weak. I knew at that moment, no one would complete me like Todd. He made me feel good about myself, loved, beautiful, and secure. An affection beyond my dreams.

As he looked down at me, he ran his fingers through my hair. "I'll call you." Smiled. Then walked to his car.

A New Car

Todd and I had been dating six months. I was on cloud nine. He borrowed his father's Ford pickup truck most of the time for our dates. One afternoon, I heard a car horn out front. There was Todd sitting behind the wheel of a 1929 Ford A Roadster convertible. You couldn't miss the vehicle. It was a bright, cherry red. Not many people would purchase a car during the Great Depression. Todd saved every penny through his high school years working for his parents and any other job he could find in-between.

I ran outside. "Oh my God, Todd! When did you get this?" My eyes widened.

"Yesterday morning. I wanted to surprise you."

"You certainly did."

"It's not new, but it shines! Get in."

"White leather seats."

He put his arm around me through the open front window, pulling me in for a long kiss. "It was worth the surprise on your face. I love you, Jenny. There's comfort when I'm with you. I can be myself."

I hugged him followed by a kiss on the cheek. "I love you, too."

"Get in. Let's go for a spin."

I jumped in and sat next to him with no separation to breathe.

We went through the back roads. I put my head back and let the wind blow through my hair. I felt free. How could I have found such a man?

"I'm happy for you. Congratulations on a gorgeous car."

"Thanks, but it's our car, Jenny. Not just mine. Someday, we may get married and have kids. I noticed you way back when you used to come over with Kathleen to see Rita. I'm surprised she kept quiet with me asking her all kinds of questions about you. My sister usually can't keep a secret."

He looked down at me. "Jenny, I knew you were going to be special when I held you in my arms on the dance floor."

"I felt the same, Todd. You make me happy. Every moment with you is treasured."

He pulled over to the side of the road. We kissed passionately. My heart pounded in my chest.

He touched my face. "I don't want to stop when I kiss you. I think we better get back before something happens."

We pulled into our driveway. He walked me up the steps, and my Aunt Dorothy opened the door. Her features resembled my mother. Both had the gentle expressions of kindness on their faces. My mother didn't have the natural beauty as my aunt, but she had the same rosy cheeks. Aunt Dorothy would come over to help when she could with my father gone. My mother enjoyed her sister's company.

"Todd, where did you get that car? That can't be yours!"

"It certainly is, Mrs. Perry."

"Who wouldn't want to ride in that car?"

"I'm glad you're home, Jenny. Your mother doesn't seem well. She has a low-grade fever. I'm going to stay over for the next two days. If she isn't better by then, I think we should call the doctor. I don't like her being weak. She's developed a continuous, hard cough. We all know how active she has been. She should be checked."

"She kept saying she was run-down."

I walked to her bedroom. She was sitting up with a pillow behind her back. She looked gray and weak.

"Mom, Aunt Dorothy is going to stay a few days to help out. If you're not better by Monday, I'm calling the doctor. Why didn't you tell me you were sick?"

"I thought it would pass. It's taken all the energy out of me."

"You rest. Tomorrow, Todd and I will go and get some light food for you."

I walked back to the kitchen and my Uncle Joe came with my aunt's clothes for a few days.

"Todd, maybe we can go to the store to get some special food that won't upset her stomach."

"I can get off work for a few hours. I'll be here in the morning around nine o'clock."

I walked him to the car and kissed him goodbye.

"I'll see you tomorrow."

Announcement

When Todd arrived home, he went directly into the carpentry shop. "Hi, Dad."

Cory Costa took over the lumber business after it had been passed down by his father twenty years ago. Families who had occupations worked hard hoping to leave their children their trade. From 1929 until 1934, millions of workers lost their jobs. The government fought to bring back private building industries after realizing it was necessary if the construction industry was to play a major part in leading the country out of depression.

Building and repairing homes helped their business explode near the end of the Depression. Todd's grandfather never gave up expanding his business for Cory. He had developed one of the largest industries in the area.

"Hi, Todd. You've been riding around showing off that Ford Roadster?"

"I surprised Jenny by giving her a ride. I wish you could have seen her expression."

"Make sure you save up again. It isn't easy putting money away these days." Cory threw lumber on the pile in the corner.

"Dad, Mrs. Rossini has been sick. Her sister, Dorothy, is staying with her to help. I'm going to leave in the morning and pick Jenny up to go grocery shopping. Is that going to be a problem?"

"No. We have Bob and Ray to help for the weekend."

Both men graduated from high school and worked for the Costas for over ten years.

"What time will you be back?"

"I was going to ask for the full-day off. Jenny's aunt will be there. I promise to make the time up."

"I can always use your help, but you deserve some time for yourself. You never take any."

"Dad, I love Jenny. I want to marry her."

Cory stopped throwing the boards on the stack and looked at his son. "You're serious."

"Yes, I am. No doubts, Dad."

"I think you better brace your mother on this matter.'

"I will. Where is she?"

"As usual, up at the house cooking and cleaning."

"Guess there's no better time to tell her. How do you feel about her, Dad?"

"I see her mostly when she comes to the stand with her mother to get vegetables. Rita has known her for a three years. They're close. She seems like a fine woman. Glad you dumped that Greco girl. She's a wild one!"

"I was infatuated with Cathy. She's a beautiful girl but someone who will never be faithful."

"Take your time with Jenny. Don't jump into marriage right away."

"I'm going to see Mom."

Todd walked to the house. They owned a two-floor, white farmhouse with black shutters. The huge wrap-around front porch had a swing on it. The red barn and the landscape and carpentry businesses were behind the home. The horses and cows roamed the fenced-in fields.

"Hi, Ma." Todd gave his mother a kiss on the cheek.

"I was getting worried about you. Dinner's ready."

Judy Costa was a worker, not only in the house but at the lumberyard if they needed another hand. She had the strength to do men's work. She had a heart of gold.

"I want to talk to you about Jenny, Ma." Todd hesitated. "I'm in love with her. I'm thinking of asking her to marry me."

"Are you sure, Todd? She seems like a sweet girl. Jenny is the complete opposite than Cathy. You thought you were madly in love with her."

24

"You're right, Ma. She's nothing like Cathy. That's why I love her."

"Do you think you should think longer on this?"

"If we get engaged, we won't get married right away. I want everyone to know her like I do."

Judy dropped the kitchen towel on the sink and ran over to hug him. "Oh, how wonderful!"

I'm sure we can give you some backland to build a house. Maybe you and the men can start building the home so the place will be ready for you when you set a date."

"Let's take one thing at a time. I want everything to be perfect. I'm taking Jenny out for the day tomorrow. We haven't spent a full day together."

"The family's going to be thrilled." Judy hugged her son again.

"Ma, keep it quiet until I have a ring on Jenny's finger."

"I promise."

Todd and Jenny's First Intimacy

In the morning, Todd picked me up to go grocery shopping. Chatham wasn't a big town, but everyone knew all the townspeople. Families came once a month to fill their pantries. I went down the aisles choosing light meals.

Before we left town, we went to Dr. Graham's office. He gave us a bottle of Piso for my mother's cold, along with vitamins. He scheduled a morning house visit on Monday.

We packed the car and headed back. Aunt Dorothy helped me put away the groceries. She spotted the medicine.

"Where did you get this?"

"We stopped at Dr. Graham's office. He said to start my mother on them. He's going to stop by Monday morning to examine her."

"Well, that saves me from calling him. You kids go before the day's over. We'll be fine."

The two of us went into the living room to see my mother before leaving. She looked worse. Her coloring seemed to have left her.

Aunt Dorothy, are you sure about us leaving? Maybe we should take her today to the doctor instead of waiting until he comes Monday. She doesn't look well." By now, I was concerned. "I'll start her on the medicine. We'll see how she is tomorrow."

I tried not to show the excitement with the thought of a full day being alone with Todd. I put my bathing suit on under my red shorts and put on a white and black polka dot shirt. I grabbed my pocketbook and beach items. Todd said he had his trunks underneath his dungarees.

He opened the passenger door for me to slide next to him.

"I want to spend every second with you. No distractions." Todd seemed delighted as I was with a full day together.

We rode through dirt paths that led nowhere special. We laughed talking about events. The warm air felt thick with the windows down. It was wonderful knowing no work faced me with the animals when I got back home. Uncle Joe offered to do my chore. How I wished it could be that way every day with a brother in the house.

Todd stopped and parked the car on a small incline facing a wide lake going through a section of the property.

"What a beautiful site looking at all this open space. It's not often you find land like this on the Cape."

"This is our back property."

"I didn't know you owned this much land."

"I've done a lot of fishing back here."

We got out and Todd opened the backdoor to the truck and took out a basket of food and a large blanket.

"Where did you get all this?"

"My mother. She wanted to do something special for us."

Todd spread the blanket out under a shade tree and placed the food down.

"Look at this! She has chicken legs, a salad—and let me see." I dug deeper into the basket. "Apples and bananas—and homemade sugar cookies."

"There should be some root beer."

"I haven't had soda pop in a long time."

Once we sat, I took off my shoes to enjoy the soft sand under my feet.

"What a wonderful breeze. This feels great, Todd."

While we ate slowly, I felt the urge to bring up Cathy. I wanted no surprises in case Todd still had feelings for her.

"Todd, why didn't you tell me about dating Cathy?" I looked straight at him, as I sipped on a bottle of pop.

"How did you find out about Cathy?"

"I was wondering who that striking woman was that came to your stand the day I met you. I couldn't miss her flirting. Rita told me you dated her a few years."

"I don't like being associated with Cathy. When you're a boy growing into manhood, you dreamt of getting a date with her. I was no different. We make foolish decisions being young. Cathy's father fulfilled her dreams and spoiled her. His money started her modeling career. She doesn't know how to love. It's sad for a woman to have everything going for her and, and at the same time, have nothing."

He looked at me. "She can't get close to who you are. I'm lucky to have you."

I put my arm around Todd and kissed him. He held my face.

"I'll never want anyone as I do you, Jenny. I want to talk about marriage. We can build a beautiful home on this lake."

Tears filled my eyes and fell down my cheeks. "How I longed to hear you say that to me. Todd, I can't see myself spending my life with anyone else. I love you so much."

We kissed, and it lasted longer than the embrace should have. The heat of his body against mine caused an arousal that traveled through my body. I craved more of his fondling. Todd kissed me softly, again and again, rubbing his hands on my legs, up to my thigh. My heart raced and my breathing got rapid. I lost where we were.

"I want you, please, Todd. Make love to me. I want you to be the first and only man in my life."

Our desire overruled sound judgment. I had never had a man touch my flesh, and I could feel my body reacting. He slowly undressed me. We lay naked on the blanket in the sweltering breeze. It was the first time I saw a man undressed. We made love and the fire between us exploded. It was a sexual encounter that left me knowing I'd be wanting more of him.

"I never knew making love could be this wonderful." I gave him a soft kiss. "I'll hold this moment in my heart forever."

I was content feeling like one. We stayed in each other's arms for a long time.

"Do you want to go for a swim? Let's cool off." Todd was putting on his trunks.

I slipped mine back on and ran after Todd as he jumped in the cold water. It was heaven with him holding me and kissing me. He teased dunking me under. We spent a half-hour in the water.

We dried off and sat on the blanket. We finished the sugar cookies.

"Do you want to announce our plans for marriage to our family?" he asked.

"Yes." I was in ecstasy.

"Let's get dressed and head back home." Todd gave me his hand to help me up.

When I arrived home, I returned a different person. Todd asked me to marry him, and we made love. I had lost my innocence.

"Hi, Mom. I want to tell you something." I walked over to her. "Todd and I are going to set a date to get married."

"What great news." She looked over at her sister. "Did you hear that, Dorothy? Our Jenny's getting married."

"Well, I just made a marble cake. It's still warm. I'll start the coffee. We need to celebrate," my aunt stated. Your Uncle Joe will be here soon. He had to pick some things up at the house for me."

We all sat around the table when he arrived, and we talked about our future plans.

Lover's Lake

Dr. Graham came on Monday and examined my mother.

"Your fever went down from the pills you took. How do you feel? You're still coughing."

"I feel better but no energy."

"Mary, I want you in bed another week. If you're not better, we'll talk about what we can do next."

"Okay, Dr. Graham."

"Jenny, if you need me, call."

"I will."

"Mary, I'll be back in a few weeks unless you get worse."

I walked the doctor to the door and thanked him for coming.

I returned to the Costa Farm to get our monthly supply by myself. Mom was getting up and around but not with energy. She was not herself.

Rita started packing my groceries in a large bag. "Hey, Jenny. Kathleen and I are going Saturday for a swim on our private pond. Want to join us?"

"I have to get my work done getting the animals fed and out to pasture first."

"I'll help," Kathleen offered as she waited on someone else.

"I hate to get up early but I'll try to come," Rita replied.

Saturday, at 4 am, I woke up before sunrise and put my feet into my black knee-high rubber boots. I started my daily farm work. I shoveled cow, chicken, pig, and goat manure. I hauled it off in a wheelbarrow to the compost pile. My next chore was grabbing a low stool and milking the animals. I leaned under each cow and goat pulling on their udders, dripping the milk into the steel containers.

How did I ever get this responsibility? This is man's work. I was starting to tire of the daily job.

At 6 am, I heard Rita and Kathleen walking up to the barn.

"Well, look at you sitting *udder* a cow looking like a pro," Kathleen laughed at her own joke.

"Please, don't ask me to pull on those things. I don't even want to touch them." Rita had a disgusted look on her face.

"If I don't do this, our family won't have cheese and milk."

Kathleen grabbed gloves from the table. "What can I do?"

"You can take the buckets of milk and put them into that large refrigerator in the corner. Rita, since I can tell you don't want to dirty your hands, let the chicken out of the barn into their fenced area. You can spread their feed on the ground. The bag is by the gate. I've finished milking the cows and goats. They can go out to the pastures. You can throw the hay into their stalls. The pitchforks are by the door.

"I'll brush down White Christmas." My father bought her for me from a farmer before he died. I went over to my pure white mare and lifted her front leg. With a pick, I took all the stones out from under her shoes on each foot. I used a currycomb and a dandy brush to remove her loose hair, along with brushing her tail. I finished using a fly spray on her coat, around her eyes, and the face to keep insects off. I did the same to the other two farm horses. I led them all out the gate to the pastures for the day.

With Rita and Kathleen's help, within two hours, everything was cleaned in the animal's stalls, all of them were fed, and led outside to roam the enclosed pasture.

"We have an outside shower around the barn. I placed towels for each of us on the stool outside the gate."

I got a laugh looking at Rita. After caring for the farm animals, she acted as if she couldn't get her soiled clothes off fast enough. I think she would have felt better being sterilized from head to toe.

"Glad I don't have a date after this! I could never care for the animals. I hate the smell." Rita tried taking the top layer of dirt off her hands.

I looked surprised. "You own a farm, don't you?"

"Yeah, but my brother and father do that work."

Once we scrubbed ourselves and put our bathing suits on under our clean outfits, I brought them into the house to say hello to my mother.

Kathleen walked up to Mom giving her a kiss. "Good Morning, Aunt Mary."

"Hi, Kathleen." She turned to Rita. It's nice to have you here. How did you get a day off?"

"Ray and Bob are helping Todd cover for me. They'll probably blackmail me saying I owe them."

"Sit down; I'm about to make waffles and scrambled eggs before you take off for the day. I packed a basket of snacks when you get hungry. Keep the box in the shade. I wrapped some ice in a bag to keep the drinks cold. You'll find peanut butter and jelly sandwiches. That should keep you satisfied until supper."

"Are you feeling better, Ma?"

"I seem to have more strength. It must have been a bug."

We chatted with her while we gulped the breakfast down. Getting up early to tend to the animals gave me a huge appetite. It was the biggest meal of the day for me.

Kathleen and Rita hopped on their bikes and headed towards the lake. I pulled mine out that had been leaning against the back of the house. We peddled down to Lovers Lake laughing and racing. The path was beautiful with only the sounds of birds. Once we got to the water, the area opened up with no trees. The soft sand had no rocks. I liked swimming in freshwater more than the ocean. I hated the sticky feeling of saltwater and sand clinging to my skin.

"What a secluded place. How did you find this location so deep in the woods, Rita?"

"No one can come here except family or if you're invited. We own this section. Todd and Sam built that raft floating. Usually, Todd comes every morning for a swim, but he's working."

"I wish he was here," I remarked.

"Not me," Kathleen shouted. "This is *girl time*. Who needs boys?"

We all jumped into the water screaming from the shock of the coldness. It took a while for our bodies to adjust to the frigid temperature. Once we reached the raft, we climbed on top. We laid on our backs and continued our talk.

"Don't you two want to date? I'm sure you've been asked out." I gave them a side look waiting for an answer.

"When I can, I see Frankie," Rita replied. "It's usually a Saturday night. I like to keep some time to myself to go where I want and with whom." She looked over smiling at us.

"You see other guys?" I was shocked. "Isn't that cheating?"

"Why? He hasn't asked me to be his girl."

"What about you, Kathleen?"

"I've been asked out, but I spend my spare time at the Monomoy Theatre. I spend all summer staring in plays. Someday, I may be at the right place, at the right time, with the right scout looking for actresses. They offer great training. I don't have time for a relationship."

She laid her head back looking up at the sky. "My goal is to become a famous actress. Besides, I'll meet leading men in the plays." She closed her eyes with a sly smile. "I'll be able to pick and choose."

We dove off the raft and joked in the water swimming backward splashing each other and going underwater to grab each other's legs in a playful way.

After two hours in the lake, we swam back to the beach. We grabbed our towels and dried off.

"Anyone hungry?" I opened the basket my mother made us.

The peanut butter sandwiches slid down fast with our lemonade. The oatmeal raisin cookies were devoured.

Kathleen licked the peanut butter off her fingers. "Boy! I was hungry."

"It's 3 pm. I'm going to have to leave soon."

"Jenny, I can't believe you have to do the same chores tonight with the animals," Rita remarked.

"I tell myself it has to be done."

"No. Really. That's a man's job."

"It would have been nice to have had a brother to do this, but I don't. My mother helps when she can, but it's mostly me. We need animals for our food. I learned how to kill and clean the chickens. The larger animal, we pay someone to slaughter them. The butcher cuts and packs them for us."

After our clothes dried, we placed our things in the side saddlebags on our bikes. We all departed in different directions.

"Give Aunt Dorothy and Uncle Joe a hug for me," I said to Kathleen.

"Thank your mom for the food," Rita yelled peddling down the path.

Finding Jobs

Rita called me Sunday morning. "Kathleen told me that the *Nelson News* in Orleans will be looking for an editor and a reporter. Those are two great positions for us. I would love to report the news, and you took up editing in school."

"I didn't see the ad in tonight's newspaper."

"It isn't in there. Kathleen heard about the positions from Julie Evans, who's one of the reporters. Julie's a friend of hers. The positions will be advertised in two days. Why don't we leave first thing in the morning? I'll meet you eight. Think you can make it?"

"Of course. Finding jobs is almost impossible. There'll be hundreds leaving off their resumes. How are you going for a position in journalism? You didn't take that course."

"I can learn anything. Do you realize how rare human resources check on people's diplomas and their studies?"

"How do you have the guts to fake something like this, Rita?"

"Anyone can learn a job. They can put a notepad and a pencil in my hands, and I have the brains and tongue to ask people questions to write an article. Give me a camera and I can take pictures. How hard can the position be?"

"It would be great having a job before Todd and I got married."

"Okay. I'll pick you up."

"See you then."

****

The next morning, Rita and I walked into the building of the *Nelson News* dressed professionally in dresses and high heels. We wore our white hand gloves with a shoulder purse.

When the receptionist heard we wanted to apply for the two upcoming positions, she looked up at us. "We're supposed to advertise these two positions tomorrow. How did you hear about them?" The girl at the desk sounded upset.

A well-dressed man walked over to us. "I'll take over, Jackie."

"But, Mr. Nelson, the positions aren't listed yet."

"Beverly and Victor are leaving tomorrow. Replacing them right away would be a bonus. I don't like positions open long."

He looked at us. "Come into my office."

He led us into a corner room surrounded by glass windows on two sides of the room from floor to ceiling facing the city of Orleans. We were on the seventh story.

"My name's Mr. Nelson—George Nelson. I'm the owner. Have you two had any experiences with a newspaper or a media position?"

Rita spoke right up. She offered her hand. "Nice to meet you, George. My name's Rita Costa from Chatham. I graduated with a diploma in journalism."

I closed my eyes for a second and took a deep gulp from her lie.

"I like being out-front and meeting people. I covered all our newspaper's events and interviewed students for their stories. I went outside the high school to write about some incidents." Rita continued smoothly with one lie after another.

Mr. Nelson seemed glued to Rita. I couldn't believe she called him *George*.

"You realize that this position may have you in different states covering the news. You may be traveling outside the United States?"

"I think traveling would be interesting. I'm not involved in any relationship."

He turned towards me.

"And you Miss…I'm sorry, what's your name?"

"Jenny Rossini. I had a four-year course in editing."

"We're in need of these placements being filled as soon as possible. I think I'm good at judging a person's character. I'm going to give you both a two-week trial. If you aren't perfect in these positions, I'll let you go. There are too many experienced people looking for jobs. I can be picky. You'll be on trial to prove yourselves. Do you think you can handle tons of work being thrown on your desk? If so, I'd like you to start on Monday."

"Yes, Mr. Nelson." We both replied at once.

"Good. See you at 7 am…*sharp*. I don't put up with excuses for being late." He stood up to show us out of his office.

We left in shock. "How could we have been so lucky to get these two positions?"

"They call it fibbing, Jenny. Did you see Mr. Nelson's expression, when I called him *George*?" Rita laughed uncontrollably. "Men love attention from women. Remember that while you're working here, Jenny. If they can't get you to notice them, they fall all over you. Keep them guessing."

"I won't be looking for a man's attention."

"You may not be but take my word; men don't care if you're single, engaged or married. Always keep them guessing."

"You sound like a pro, Rita."

"No—smart, Jenny!"

****

The next day, Rita called Kathleen to thank her for the information about the upcoming positions at the *Nelson News*. Mr. Nelson interviewed us himself.

"We both got the two jobs, Kathleen. We want to thank you for letting us know about them before they got posted in the newspapers."

"I thought of you and Jenny right away."

"Why don't the three of us get together for lunch Saturday? It's been a while since we sat and talked."

"Rita, I was going to call you. I'm going with my parents to Santa Rosa in California to see my dad's brother. My mother and I never met his family. They have two daughters my age. I've only talked to them on the phone.

"On the way, Dad has to stop in Detroit, Michigan for business. I thought I'd take advantage of this trip and travel to Los Angeles to apply for an acting position. I'm tired of searching for a job in the Cape area. By the time I hear about one, it's filled."

"If you find something there, would you take it? I can't picture the three of us separated."

"Rita, we'll be gone for three months. I'll call when we're due back. It won't be the same without you and Jenny, but there's no reason why we can't stay in touch. I'll send you their address and phone number."

Kathleen got excited. "I have to share this with you or I'll explode. A few months ago, I made a call to the *Selznick International Pictures*. You know, David O. Selznick—the producer."

"Really. Did you hear back from them?"

"His secretary answered and asked me to send my photos after hearing about my background with acting in staring parts in plays. A week later, she said they were impressed with my photos. I have an appointment in a month for an interview. Santa Rosa isn't too far from Los Angeles. Mr. Selznick is working on a film *Gone with the Wind* with Clark Gable and Vivien Leigh."

"Wow, what a chance Kathleen. This was great timing for your trip."

"Tell Jenny I'm sorry for not having a chance to say goodbye."

"I'll tell her. Have a safe trip. I hope you get into the movies. What do they say, '*Break a leg*?'" They both laughed.

"I'll miss you both, Rita. Love to everyone."

It was the first time the three of us were separated.

Mom's Health

I noticed my mother was constantly cold one moment and then hot. She was on the couch covered with a blanket wrapped around her. "You okay, Mom?"

"I got a chill. Thought I'd cover up with the afghan and lay down to read."

I walked over and felt her forehead. "You seem warm again."

"Do I?"

"Mom, you've got to be seen by Dr. Graham. You canceled his last appointment to examine you. This has been going on too long."

I couldn't brushed-off my mother's symptoms returning every other week anymore. It was amazing she had the energy to keep up with washing clothes, cleaning the house, and preparing the meals.

"I miss sitting on the swing," my mother said.

"When you get better, Mom."

The only thing I remember Dad doing that brought any excitement was when he came home with a swing for the front porch. Someone was tossing it out. He threw it in the back of his truck. If the item had cost money, he never would have taken the bench. Mom loved sitting out in the fresh air while she swayed back and forth in the swing.

"Where did you go with Rita the other day?"

"We applied for a job at the *Nelson News*. I'm going to be an editor, Ma. Rita will be a journalist. Now I can bring money in to help with the expenses."

"That's wonderful, Jenny."

"I don't want to go to work and worry about you being alone. Let me get you some chicken soup I made last night. Then, I want you in bed. I'll clean up."

I was concerned with her going to bed at 6 pm. It was unusual.

I called Dr. Graham. "I can't get there until the end of next week. If it's really bad with her health, leave me a message."

The Train Wreck

My mother bounced back again. Monday morning Rita and I started our jobs. It was as if the positions were made for us. Within days, we knew our responsibilities without needing training. Mr. Nelson had been impressed.

We were there a few weeks when Rita was called into Mr. Nelson's office to cover a breaking story. It would start her career off big and make her their top journalist.

"We got news of a train that went off the tracks in Detroit and crashed into some cars at a railroad crossing. I want you to cover this story. Rick is ready to take you to Logan Airport in Boston. The tickets are reserved for you at the gate office."

"I don't have any clothes!"

"I threw in some extra cash to buy outfits you need. I don't care how long you have to stay. Keep your receipts and I'll reimburse you. Stories with train wrecks don't happen often. I'm sure other newspapers are trying to get their reporters to the scene. That's why I'm flying you instead of taking a train.

"When you get to Detroit, Ben Robinson will meet you. The accident is not far from where he's staying. He'll drive you anywhere. Jack Goodman will be your photographer. Call me when you get there."

Rick Bettencourt, another reporter from the Nelson News, waited for Rita at the door. They got into his car and he didn't offer any conversation.

"Is there something wrong, Rick?"

"I don't know why Mr. Nelson didn't send me. I've been at this newspaper for ten years, and he throws this great assignment at you after a few weeks."

"I'm sorry you feel that way. I don't ask for any special treatment."

He dropped Rita off at the airport. She went to get her tickets at the gate. Mr. Nelson had her signed up as a first-class passenger. Rita was in a section with full-meal service.

She grabbed a newspaper before boarding. The New York Times had a front-page write up. Four passenger cars were wiped out. The train went off the tracks and rolled over onto the main road. Some had burst into flames killing numerous passengers.

In a short time with her position, Rita had time to get to know the ropes handling events for the newspaper. Now, she was on her way to Detroit to cover the biggest story.

When Rita stepped off the plane, Ben Roberson was there waiting with a sign reading, "Nelson News."

"Hi, Ben. I'm Rita." She shook his hand and jumped into the backseat of his car waiting outside the station. The photographer, Jack Goodman, was sitting in the front passenger seat and introduced himself.

"Where're we going first?" Rita sat on the edge of the backseat and leaned closer to them.

"This train accident happened right down the street. Some roads are blocked, but I've had time to find the ones open. Reporters are all over the place. Luckily, Mr. Nelson reserved rooms for us. The hotels are full."

They arrived at the pileup scene with train cars smashed to pieces and thick, black smoke filled the air as if the incident had just happened. Ten train cars were derailed from the track lying on their side. A few dropped down a slope.

The policemen and ambulance crews were still recovering bodies. The railcars couldn't be moved because the accident was being investigated. The vehicles that had waited at the railway crossing were all towed away. Any survivors who had been injured were transported to the nearest hospitals.

"Hey, Ben," a voice called out. He looked and saw Steve Stone, a reporter from the Hyannis Daily News, covered with blood.

"My God. What happened to you, man?"

"They discovered passengers that weren't removed from the train. One car had people who had fallen between the seats. I was at the location and helped. What an awful scene."

"Steve, this is Rita Costa."

"Hi." He kept his eyes on the scene and the commotion, ignoring her.

"How many were taken to the hospital?" Rita asked as she tried to step over the scattered, bent iron pieces in the street. The thick pollution and dust in the air left everyone choking on the soot flying around them. The fumes from the flames reeked of carbon monoxide.

"They were taken to the Harper Hospital downtown."

"I can't believe anyone survived this." Jack ran his camera to capture the devastation.

Rita wanted to get to the emergency room. "Ben, can you take me to the hospital? How long ago did the ambulances take the patients?"

"Most were transferred a half-hour after impact. Maybe ten were taken today. Some didn't make it."

"Jack, can you give me the pictures you've taken? I'm going to call Mr. Nelson and mail the film to him."

Ben turned to Rita. "Why do you want to go to the hospital? The news is right here at the accident scene."

"I don't think so. The people are the news. They experienced this horrible event. I want to get over there before the other reporters think the same way."

Jack ran by Rita with the camera on his shoulder. "Before we go, I'd like to get a personal interview on camera with Steve while he has blood on his clothes. That would be dramatic. Let me get the camera setup."

Having Steve interviewed would show his bad shape. What a gripping effect for the Nelson News. It would also exhibit the depth of this horrible accident.

Jack started shooting the train's surrounding area with debris. After they were taken, Steve told his story from the beginning of his arrival of what he experienced.

"We'll send this to the newspaper as soon as we get to the hospital." They rushed to their car.

****

As soon as Rita arrived at the hospital, she telephoned Mr. Nelson.

"Jack took a lot of pictures and interviewed Steve Stone at the accident scene. Steve is a reporter for the Hyannis Daily News. He was covered in blood from helping move the injured. Jack's going to send them to you. I'm going to try to interview some survivors at the hospital."

"Great work, Rita!"

She hung up and said goodbye to Jack and disappeared around the corner. The hospital was dealing with confusion from doctors and nurses running in every direction in the emergency rooms. They were trying to save the remaining victims.

"Excuse me." Rita tried to get the attention of a nurse pulling an IV stand. "Are there any survivors that I can interview?"

"Who let you in here?"

"Please, I won't stay long."

"You have to leave." The nurse ran down the corridor entering one of the emergency rooms.

Rita saw a doctor in white clothing rushing down the hallway. "Excuse me. My name's Rita Costa from the Nelson News from Orleans, Massachusetts. I would appreciate an interview with a patient from the train wreck if they're up to talking."

"Were you called to come to the hospital?"

The doctor was a handsome, distinguished, older man with pure white hair.

"I was told by the owner, Mr. Nelson, from the Nelson News."

"I'm not sure if any of the patients can talk now. What's your name again?"

"Rita. Rita Costa."

He looked at her, "If you come back tomorrow, I'll see what I can do. Right now, I have to take someone into surgery."

"Your name, doctor?"

"I'm Dr. Richard Blair." He rushed through the open elevator doors to surgery.

A young woman was wheeled passed Rita by a medical team. They stopped to get some further information at the nurse's station. Rita took a look at the girl and got sick. The patient was unconscious, and her face was completely torn up. She was unrecognizable. Rita felt sorry for her. If she lived through the tragedy, she'd be facing years of operations.

The nurse at the station gave the medical team some files. "Dr. Blair just went up to get ready for surgery. He's in operating room four. Here are the woman's records. Her name is Kathleen Perry."

Rita turned with absolute fright on her face. "Kathleen!"

"Didn't I tell you to leave? I'm going to call the police to remove you."

"Please, I know that girl. She is a friend of mine."

The nurse gave the eye to the police officer at the door. He walked up to Rita, "You have to wait in the family room."

"Where are her parents, Dorothy and Joe Perry?"

"We can't give any information out."

Rita was forcibly removed from the corridor and led to the waiting room. She sat anxiously with two other families. If she had not been employed with the Nelson News, she wouldn't have known about Kathleen being a victim.

Rita had covered many upsetting news events, but this train wreck was the most emotional one. The accident involved her closest friend. This was the life Rita craved: the action, the pain of people, and the raw news. How was she going to get the strength to give Kathleen support?

****

The next day, while I was editing, the phone rang.

"Good Morning. Nelson News. This is Jenny Rossini. May I help you?"

"Jenny?"

"Hi, Rita. I heard Mr. Nelson sent you to cover the train wreck in Detroit."

"Oh my God, Jenny. Kathleen's car was hit by that train. I can't get any information on your aunt or uncle."

I felt myself go weak.

"I saw this woman being pushed to the operating room. I would never have recognized her. She had so many facial injuries. Our beautiful Kathleen." Rita broke down sobbing. "She'll never be the same again."

"Are you sure it's her? Maybe you made a mistake."

"The nurse said her name. How many Kathleen Perry's are there? She told me that her father was going to stop in Detroit because he had a business meeting there before continuing to California."

"Oh, my God! My mother's going to be devastated." I was in a panic.

"Dr. Blair's going to try to get me in to see some people who had been in the wreck. I want to interview them. Now, I have to stay to see Kathleen."

"When you talk to her, call me. Please find out about my aunt and uncle's situation."

"I'll try to call you tomorrow, but I'm not going to see Kathleen for a few days; besides, I'm not immediate family."

"Call me if you hear anything or need me, Rita. Please, I maybe her only family member."

I needed to know everyone's condition. I hung up and put my head in my hands and fell apart.

Mr. Nelson came over to me. "What's wrong, Jenny?"

I told him about the conversation with Rita.

Mr. Nelson looked charged with excitement. "This may give Rita a real personal interview with someone injured."

"Are you serious, Mr. Nelson? My cousin may die, and you're talking about getting an interview first-hand!"

"I'm sorry about your cousin, but this is a newspaper in

competition with others. If we can get an inside story, this could go big."

"You'll have to excuse me, but I am going to take my break."

I walked by Mr. Nelson to go to the lunchroom. A small corner seat was available. I sat alone fearing the worst. How was I going to tell my mother? Before leaving for California, the Perry family had put money down to buy a farm in Chatham to be near us.

Bad News

Rita sat in the family room waiting for Dr. Blair's return. Seven hours later, the doctor walked up to a dozen or so people waiting to hear the conditions of their loved ones. He was carrying a patient chart.

"I'm looking for any relatives to Dorothy and Joe Perry from Chatham, Massachusetts."

No one answered. He spotted Rita.

"Oh, hello, Miss Costa.

"No family members?" he asked. He turned and left the room.

"Dr. Blair, wait!" Rita ran down the corridor to catch up to him.

"Yes, Miss Costa."

"Please, call me Rita. Your patient, Kathleen Perry, is a dear friend of mine. Her parents, Dorothy and Joe Perry are relatives of my brother's fiancée, Jenny Rossini. Kathleen's her cousin. Can you tell me about their condition?"

He pointed to an empty room. "Why don't you have a seat." He waited for her to get settled. "I'm sorry, Rita. Kathleen's parents died two hours after being brought in from head trauma."

Rita started to choke up. "How am I going to tell Jenny that her aunt and uncle got killed? I really need to know how Kathleen's doing."

"You won't be able to see her. The surgery was extensive on her face. Their car was the first one to stop at the train gate. Her face smashed into the side window and broke the glass. The impact was disastrous. I'm surprised she survived. This poor girl's going to need multiple surgeries."

"Oh, my God!"

"I was going to speak to Kathleen's relatives if they were here."

"Kathleen's an only child, Dr. Blair."

"I guess you're close enough to family. Can you inform her cousin?"

"Yes." By now, Rita was coming apart emotionally.

"If you need more information, call my office. I'm sorry. I have to go back to the operating room. There are others who need my help."

****

Rita made a call to the *Nelson News* office.

"Jenny, I'm sorry to give you bad news." Her voice broke up. "Your aunt and uncle died on the same day of the accident. Kathleen's out of surgery, but not out of the woods. She's going to need more procedures."

I felt faint. "How do I tell my mother? She's going to be so affected by her sister and brother-in-law's deaths. They were her only family. I have to go home before someone confronts her by telephone. The train wreck's all over the news."

"Their names have not been given out yet. Take care of yourself, Jenny. Tell Todd and my parents what's going on with Kathleen."

"I'm going to call Todd. I don't want to tell my mother alone."

I dialed Todd's number. My hands were shaking. I had to redial twice.

"Hello, Costa Lumberyard."

"I'm glad you answered, Todd."

"You okay, Jenny? You sound upset."

"I've had terrible news. Your sister was sent to cover the train wreck in Detroit. She had discovered my aunt and uncle's car was hit by the train at the train rail. They were both killed." I sobbed.

"Jenny, I'm so sorry. I pray Kathleen wasn't hurt."

"Her face had been disfigured from injuries. They operated on her, and there'll be more surgeries facing her."

"Such a beautiful girl. How can something like this have happened? I'll be right over to bring you home."

I turned to go into Mr. Nelson's office, and I bumped right into him turning the corner.

"What's all the commotion?"

I told him that I had to leave and tell my mother the news.

"Aren't you going to finish the editing tonight? This is big news, Jenny. Rita will be sending more details. You can't just walk out."

"I have to go home, Mr. Nelson. This news is going to shock my mother. She's very ill. I don't want her hearing my aunt and uncle got killed from anyone else."

"I'm sorry but the accident is top news. You need to edit this work."

Monica Phillips, who had been a part-time worker and my assistant, spoke up. "I'll be happy to stay all night to cover for her, Mr. Nelson." She had mentioned numerous times how she'd like a break to get a position like mine.

"I like people doing their own work."

"Why don't you give Monica a chance to prove herself? We should all have backups for an emergency."

"If she's good, I may replace you, Jenny. I want employees who are dedicated to this newspaper."

I couldn't believe how heartless he was acting towards me.

Todd walked into the office. "Are you ready, honey?"

"If you need to replace me, Mr. Nelson, do so."

Todd walked me out. "What's that all about?"

"It's a long story."

"Don't worry about your job. We'll be married soon, and you won't have to work. I'll take care of you and your mother. I plan on asking her to move in with us to our new home."

"Really! She'd love that. I can't wait to tell her." I squeezed his hand.

****

A few minutes later, we pulled up to my house.

"Before I go in, let me get my thoughts together. What news to give her on top of being sick. I thank God you're with me, Todd." I couldn't hold back tears.

"Do you want me to tell her?"

"I have to do this. Let's go I while I can."

We walked through the kitchen into the living room. My mother was laying on the couch covered with a blanket.

"You're both out of work early," my mother said looking surprised.

"How you doing, Mom?"

"I felt weak all day. I miss your Aunt Dorothy spoiling me. I can't wait for her to return. It's going to be a long three months without them. She deserves some vacation time with her family. Did you know they're buying Johnsons' farm down the road? They put a deposit on the property before they left. We can be together every day."

Todd spoke up. "Mrs. Rossini, there has been a terrible accident."

"Is that the train wreck in Detroit? I have been listening to it on the radio. How awful. The locomotive hit at least five cars, went off the tracks, and then down an embankment."

"Yes, that's the one, Mrs. Rossini."

I sat next to my mother and held her hand. "Mom, Aunt Dorothy, and the family were in one of those cars at the rail gate." I started to unravel.

My mother didn't move a muscle. She started to brace herself. "Oh no! Please, don't tell me they were killed!"

Todd got on the other side of my mother and put his arm around her shoulders. "I'm sorry. Your sister and Joe died from their injuries."

"Oh, my God, no!" Every part of her body shook.

"Mom, Kathleen's alive, but she had to have surgery on her face."

I didn't want to go into more detail. I wanted my mother to remember the beautiful girl Kathleen had been.

My mother broke down, while I embraced her. The news made her collapse.

"Todd, help me get her to bed."

He picked my mother up. Since she had lost twenty pounds, she wasn't heavy. He placed her head on a pillow after I adjusted the support.

"I'm going to call the doctor. You stay with her, Jenny."

My mother and I cried holding each other. I heard Todd's conversation with Dr. Graham.

"I know you came a few weeks ago, but I think it's an emergency to see her. On top of her not getting better, we just gave the sad news her sister, Dorothy, and brother-in-law, Joe, were killed in the train accident in Detroit.

Todd hesitated. "Yes, Dr. Graham, Kathleen was with them. Her injuries were serious. Today, she had been operated on for facial injuries—Thank you. See you in a while."

An hour later, we heard Dr. Graham pull-up in his Ford station wagon. He took out his black medical bag and started toward the front door.

Todd greeted him. "Thank you for coming. Mrs. Rossini is in her bedroom."

He walked down the hallway to her room. "Hello, Mary. I'm so sorry for the loss of your family. Dorothy was very close to you. I pray Kathleen comes out of this. Let's take a look at you. Can you sit up?"

She tried to but fell back onto the pillow.

"Mary, you're very weak. I don't like this. You should be in the hospital. I need to run some tests."

"I hate hospitals."

"I think most of us do. It's Friday and the beds are full. Monday, patients are let home. I'll get a room for you."

He looked back at Todd. "Do you two think you can bring her in or do you need an ambulance?"

"I can handle her. I'll pick her and Jenny up Monday morning. What time do you want her admitted?"

"I'll have a room for her at 10 am. The nurses will be waiting with my paperwork."

Dr. Graham faced my mother. "You take care of yourself." He turned and whispered, "I don't want her out of bed. Here's more medicine for the fever. Until you bring her in, administer these pills every four hours. If she gets worse, call an ambulance."

I tucked the blanket around her. "Mom, you rest. I'm going to walk the doctor out."

When we got to the door, I asked, "What are you looking for? Is this serious?"

"I'm not sure, Jenny. I don't like the weight loss, her weakness, high fevers, and now she's starting with a heavy cough. She's not showing any signs of improvement. After the tests, I'll have more to tell you."

"Thanks for coming. I hope we can solve this so my mother can bounce back to her old self."

I returned to my mother's bedroom to give her a pill to relax her.

Mom looked at us. "I can't understand why I don't feel better being on medicine. I hate this weakness. I hope you two don't get this." Her coughing started.

"It's the weekend. Jenny, you take care of her. I'll do whatever needs to be done for your animals."

"Don't you work on Saturdays?" I asked.

"I'll tell my father this afternoon. He'll understand. I hate to leave you alone, Jenny, but I have a job that has to be inspected today. I was going to ask you to come with me, but I guess that won't be possible." Todd gave me a hug.

"I would have loved the ride with you, but my mother needs me."

"I understand. I'll call you tonight. Saturday's a busy day. I'll see if I can sneak out early. The stress-level is sky-high with not enough hands. I don't know what we'd do without Ray and Bob helping."

"How can your business be booming with the Great Depression going on affecting everyone?"

"We have President Roosevelt to thank. He passed some breaks with government agencies to get Americans back to work. One program referred to construction companies. We're blessed. None of us want to turn away work for families. They'll only find someone else."

"Where are you going for the inspection?"

"My father was supposed to go, but there's no way he can take time out, especially with me taking Monday off."

"Who is it?"

"Mr. Greco called for a quote on a new barn for some heifers he bought."

"Heifers! Since when has he gotten into raising animals?"

"That's what I wondered."

"I hate you going over there. I'm sure Cathy's home."

"I gather she'll be there. Mr. Greco said they have a party for her tonight. He wanted me there early so he wouldn't miss the celebration."

"What kind of party?" I wasn't feeling uncomfortable with him in her home.

"I didn't ask. Don't let your mind go crazy. You know I love you."

"I guess I have to trust you. I wish your dad was going instead."

"Come here. Give me a kiss." He pulled me into him. "I'll give you a call when I come home. I doubt if it'll be late."

I said goodbye. I wasn't confident this was going to be a good situation.

Cathy Greco's Going Away Party

When Todd pulled up in front of the Greco's gate, a guard came up to him.

"What's your name? Is Mr. Greco expecting you?"

"I'm Todd Costa from the Costa Lumberyard, and yes, he's expecting me."

The gateman got on the phone. "A Mr. Todd Costa to see you— Will do, Sir."

He leaned into Todd's open window. "Go around the backyard. Mr. Greco will be waiting."

Todd came to another section of their home with open fields. He got out of the truck and stood facing Tony Greco wearing a navy suit with a white dress shirt and a bright red tie. He was already dressed for the party.

"Hello, Todd. Glad to see you again."

Todd had known the Costa family dating their daughter for two years.

"Likewise. Where do you want the two-story barn? Is this the location?"

"Yes. In two months, we have two dozen heifers coming."

Todd started asking Mr. Greco what he wanted for size and design and started measuring the footage. It took an hour to finish. "I'll get a quote out to you next week."

"Why don't you stay for a drink? Sharon hasn't seen you in a while. Come in and say hi."

"I really have to get back to help out my father. We're short-handed this weekend."

"It's seven o'clock and the sun is due to go down. I doubt if you'll be open for business."

"What's the occasion?"

"You didn't hear? Cathy's going to Europe to model in Paris. It would be an insult if you didn't say hello.

Tony's wife, Sharon, was dressed in a red print summer dress fitted tightly to her body.

"Well, hello, Todd." Sharon kissed him on the cheek. "How are you? Happy you could join us."

Tony put his arm around Todd's shoulder. "Now, that's what I call a woman! What do you think, Todd?" Tony's eyes were on his daughter standing on the top stairway.

Cathy moved slowly down the winding steps. There stood a girl who was beyond her years. Her blonde hair was pulled in an upward style with curls falling alongside her face. Her beautiful, blue eyes went right through Todd as her stare locked into him. Her gown wasn't something a nineteen-year-old should have wrapped around her alluring body.

Being a model, her scarlet-red dress clung to every curve with a noticeable low cleavage which revealed luscious, desirable breasts. With her tiny waist and small rounded hips, the dress fell smoothly over her frame with a slit opened to the middle of her right upper, firm thigh. She was a miniature of her mother.

She moved like an experienced, bewitched serpent with confidence going down each step. Cathy was a tease. Her every movement was hot and seductive. She was way beyond her years of experience with erotic charm. Once she turned on her sexual magnetism, her wants were impossible for the man to get out of her hold.

When she reached the last step, Cathy went right up to Todd and pushed her body against him, giving him a long kiss while she felt his hardness as she leaned into him. Cathy was delighted Todd was aroused by her. He still had it for her. She was a woman for getting satisfaction. Men were all her victims. Todd was no different. Cathy lived for control.

She put her arm around Todd's waist. "What a wonderful surprise, father. I couldn't have asked for a better gift for my party."

"I don't mean to disappoint you, Cathy, but I can't stay."

Tony came up to Todd with a shot of whiskey. "Here Todd, relax."

"No thank you, Sir."

"I insist." He gave a long demanding look at Todd, holding the glass.

Cocktail waitresses, in short, black skirts up to their middle thighs, wearing white-laced aprons, and netted, black nylon stockings stood out with their high-spiked heels while they passed the liquor around with no limit. As soon as the tray was empty, full glasses were added. An hour went by, and the mixed drinks flowed non-stop.

Feeling the buzz from drinking, Todd took his keys out of his pocket and went out the backdoor. He got down the steps when someone grabbed his arm.

"There you are." Cathy faced him. She pushed him against the house with her body. "Where do you think you're going?"

"Look, Cathy. I need to get back. Sorry if you want a playmate. I don't belong to you. We're not a couple anymore."

She looked up at him while unlatching the two top buttons on his shirt. "I don't care who's in your life. I want, what I want….and right now, it's you. Remember those days, Todd?" She kissed his hairy chest. "You can't tell me you don't want me. I was the best you ever had. You told me yourself."

"That was a long time ago." He felt his body quiver with her lips on his skin.

"What we had was not forgettable."

"It was just sex and nothing else." Todd pushed her away.

She grabbed his shirt and pulled him back. "Yes…and it was wonderful! That's all I want right now. You know how to please me, what excites me, what makes me scream for more."

Cathy reached up and kissed him hard and long. Being intoxicated, Todd started to cave in, instead of walking away. She was offering the forbidden fruit on a silver platter. His strength for rejecting her was gone.

She led him around the corner to the barn and pushed open the door. Hay was scattered on the floor. Cathy laid on the straw. She yanked Todd down to her. The slit to her dress opened and exposed her seductive, red panties.

"Touch me, Todd, and tell me you don't want this."

He had over-drank his limit and stayed too long. Maybe deep down, he wanted Cathy as soon as he saw her coming down the stairway. After all, there were no rules with her.

Todd kissed her back. His hands started to explore every inch of her solid body. There wasn't a part of Cathy that Todd didn't know where to touch to arouse her.

"I know you like this, Cathy?" He started to undress her.

"You know me so well, Todd. I love you." Cathy wrapped her arms tightly around his neck and clung to him as if she owned him. They became one instantly, and she gave a loud moan.

After a half-hour of numerous sex acts, Todd panicked as soon as he got satisfied. "This shouldn't have happened."

"Don't say that. You know how I feel about you."

"You don't feel any emotions for anyone, Cathy. You want to conquer. If you tell Jenny, I swear, I will deny this mistake until I die."

"I don't need a commitment. Marry Jenny if you want, but you'll be coming to me when she becomes a boring sex partner. You'll be the one making the moves for sex, not her. She doesn't have the animal in her. Jenny's too ladylike. Remember, I belong to you. I'll always be waiting."

"You're going to have some fun trying to look innocent with hay all over you."

Cathy reached up to kiss him.

He pushed her hand away. "Tell your parents I'm sorry I couldn't stay."

"Todd, please, I don't want you to leave."

"There's nothing between us, Cathy. How could I have been so stupid to cheat on Jenny? I love that girl."

Todd pushed the barn door open and rushed out front to the family truck without saying goodbye.

****

"Cathy? *Cathy?*" Mr. Greco yelled coming through the backyard.

"I'm here, Dad."

"Where?

He found her coming up the stairs to the deck.

"Where have you been? Everyone's looking for you. Did you forget you're the guest of honor?"

"I was talking to some friends."

"In the barn? You smell of liquor."

"I had some like everyone else that's present."

"Get in the house, and act like you're excited about going to Paris tomorrow."

Once Cathy came into the light in the kitchen, her father noticed how disarrayed she was with hay and a wrinkled dress.

"Look at you!"

"What?"

"*What?* You have hay all over your dress and in your hair. Were you rolling in it with Todd?"

"Dad!"

"Don't *dad* me. Here you are becoming a model for Coco Chanel at nineteen years old. A dream any girl would die for, and you don't know how to be a lady. You have beauty, the figure, and the money. Act like a star."

Sharon walked up to them. "Do you two realize that everyone can hear you yelling?"

She took one look at her daughter and started pulling hay out of Cathy's once beautiful up-style hairdo that had become limp. "Where have you been?"

"I don't want to talk about this anymore. You're both treating me like a child."

Tony had no patience. He grabbed Cathy by the arm. "I've spent millions of dollars to get you to the top with our family name. Don't tell me what I can and can't have from you. Grow up. You're going to Paris and stop thinking you need men in your life. Now, go freshen-up in the washroom off the kitchen—and I mean in minutes," her father demanded.

Girls wanted Cathy completely away from their boyfriends. Men looked at her from the outside. No one wanted to stick around long enough to truly know her. Cathy was now reaching her twenties with a hunger for making the men have an uncontrollable desire for her.

"Cathy?" She turned and saw her mother standing in the doorway of the powder room.

"How long does it take for you to get ready? You're putting us in an embarrassing situation."

"I'm sorry. I'll be right out."

Cathy walked into the living room, and all eyes went back on her. "Well, here's our woman of the day. Welcome back Cathy," a man replied drunk, who she didn't know. Everyone clapped.

The night went into midnight and the guests were told the party had to end so Cathy could get her rest for a morning flight to Paris.

Tony's Guests

Once the party ended, Tony walked Sharon to the stairway. He kissed her goodnight.

"I'll see you in the morning."

Sharon was aware of Tony's routine with his meetings and who attended them. She tried as much as possible not to ask him questions involving the Mob. She climbed the stairs to take the bath that the maid had prepared for her. Sharon emerged herself in the tub of hot, steaming, strawberry-fragranced water, allowing the bubbles to reach her neck. Quiet time was rare.

When the water-cooled, Sharon got out and dried off. The wall mirror showed an older woman. Still attractive, but her youth faded.

Sharon wrapped a white robe around her and went into the bedroom and sat in front of the mirror on her makeup stand to brush her long blonde hair. Even with her makeup off, she was stunning.

She had all the money a woman would want, a beautiful home, a daughter she loved, cooks, maids, chauffeurs, landscapers, but her life was hollow.

****

Tony walked into his den and pressed a button behind the bookshelves. It opened up to a large meeting room. A table of seven Mob bosses and other gang members from New York, Boston, Detroit, and Chicago waited for him.

"Sorry for the delay," Tony said, getting a drink at the bar. "The party lasted longer than expected. At least, we have witnesses who saw a party for Cathy tonight."

The room filled with cigarette and cigar smoke. Half-empty glasses of liquor sat on tables. Tony had a bartender serve the gangsters who filled the room. All the people in the meeting were wanted by the FBI for crimes. These were high profile convicts.

Tony was the head of the Mob from the Cape Cod area. His home was one that the authorities wouldn't think of criminals being since it was outside the large cities.

"Let's get down to business," one of them said. "We have to catch the last plane out of Boston in a few hours."

They put all the maps on the tables to see where the other gangsters were located trying to take over their territory. Reports came in on who killed which one and where the bodies were buried.

Laughter filled the room. Killing became an everyday occurrence. It was their occupation to grab all the money from business owners monthly. If not, their family members were beaten. The mafia wanted their share from private sales. They robbed banks and stole liquor to sell to their clients. Money was hidden in locations no one would think of looking.

They were about to end the meeting when the unlocked doors flew open and thirty police officers with shotguns stormed the room. No one had time to get to their firearms.

"Hands up and get against the wall!" The law enforcement officers were at every corner of the room. Tables and chairs were being thrown in every direction.

The mob members were hit with the barrel of a gun. Others tried to get out the backdoor to only have the police waiting outside shooting in the air to get them to lay down on the ground.

Tony had no time to react. How did the police and the FBI know about this meeting? The members knew that if you talked, they would never see daylight again.

"I'll kill the person who squealed," Tony yelled out, yanking his arms trying to get out of the grip from an agent.

Hearing the commotion, Sharon and Cathy rushed down the stairs to only find the house full of law enforcement officers. The sirens were blaring and the police car lights were flashing outside.

She pushed through the cops to get to her husband. "What's going on?"

"Don't say a thing. Keep your mouth shut. Do you hear me?" Tony was wild.

"Cathy, go back upstairs," Sharon demanded.

"What's happening?" She was frightened.

"I said go upstairs. Don't let me repeat it."

Before Tony could react, he was handcuffed. There was no way of defending himself or the others. The police force hit a gold mine with the most wanted criminals. It was a huge bust.

Tony looked back yelling at Sharon, "Call Phil."

****

When the last criminal was led out of the house, Sharon called their lawyer. "I'd like to speak to Phil right away."

Phil's girlfriend answered. "Oh, hello, Mrs. Greco. Hang on."

"Hi, Sharon. How are you?"

"Tony wanted me to call you, Phil. He's been arrested."

"Arrested. For what?"

"I'd rather you come over here to talk instead of discussing this matter on the phone."

"I'll see you in an hour."

Sharon was left picking up the mess that Tony left scattered in the room. This wasn't the first time he had been pulled into a police station. Phil would have to come back with a huge defense to get him off.

Cathy was about to leave for Paris, and Sharon feared the news was going to come out. It wouldn't take long to reach France with this mob arrest. The world was aware of these hardened criminals and murderers.

A knock came to the front door.

"Hi, Phil. Come in." Sharon had left the heavy, black-iron door open behind the flowered glass entrance.

"No one here?"

"I gave the workers extra pay to go home until Monday. Cathy's upstairs."

Sharon took him into their guest living room. One side contained a bookcase from ceiling to floor with multiple shelves with books from travel guides to law manuals. Tony had studied long and hard on the law.

"Have a seat." Sharon pointed to the green, satin couch. "How about a martini, Phil?

"Am I going to need one?"

Sharon walked over and placed Phil's drink on the coffee table after putting a coaster from the bar under his glass.

"None for you?"

"I had one before you came. I need to stay alert during our discussion."

"Who was at the meeting this time?"

Phil was well attuned to Tony's involvement with the mob. He was one of the bosses. Phil got Tony off every conviction, which frustrated the police and FBI. Tony paid a large chunk of money to get Phil's services handling any crime against him.

"I hate to tell you, Phil, but over half the mob bosses in the group were in attendance."

"*Mob leaders*?"

"Yes." She started to name them one by one.

"Oh my God. This is going to be impossible to get him out of this."

"Please, Phil. Think of something."

"Sharon, I may not be able to bail him out."

"Don't say that."

"Look at me. They caught every person in the room. It's like hitting the lottery! What a gift to the FBI. All in one location. I told Tony to never do that. There'll be no defense. It's not like the FBI tried to get a member to confess to his whereabouts. They witnessed the event and have all of them in custody.

"I have done a lot to get him out with every arrest, Sharon. There's no excuse to be made with all these criminals in your home! What defense can I give the Feds?"

"Our daughter leaves tomorrow for Paris for a modeling position with Coco Chanel. Tony has to be home to see her off. Can you arrange that?"

"I might be able to get him out on bail. It's going to be costly. This isn't something small. It may be in the millions! I hope this doesn't have an effect on Cathy. Coco doesn't allow any scandal in her business or with her models."

"Do you know her?" Sharon asked.

"I met her twice during a case in Paris. One of her girls needed a lawyer, and Coco requested me to defend the model. Someone told her I was the best. The girl was sexually abused and beaten by a well-known politician. It's a miracle she lived."

Phil got up to leave. "First, let's work on getting Tony out on bail. Be prepared for a million dollars."

He drank the rest of his martini in one gulp and put the glass down. "I thought I'd need this."

"Thanks, Phil. I appreciate you coming over."

"We're just starting, Sharon. Pray for a miracle, because that's what it'll take to clear Tony."

"What are the chances?"

"Slim. I'd say impossible." He started to walk to the front door. "I know my way out."

****

Cathy and Sharon were finishing their breakfast when Tony walked in the backdoor.

Tony threw the newspaper on the table. "Well, this is going to cost me a few pennies. Next week, we have to give a million and a half back to Phil for my bail."

"How much? Where do we get that amount of money? Have you forgotten banks in all 48 states had restrictions placed on how much money depositors can withdraw? How are we going to get that amount out?

Sharon was frustrated and got up to clear the table. Cathy grabbed the dishes and silverware out of her hand. "Mother, I'll do this. You and Dad go talk."

They walked into Tony's sitting room. Sharon continued, "How can we afford that amount of money?"

"I knew the banks were going under before they announced it. We were told President Franklin Roosevelt might take action. That's what we do in our group...keep on top of money issues. I have our cash hidden. I moved our money before the crash."

"You moved it? Where?"

"When it's necessary, I'll tell you."

"Don't you think I'll need money while you're in jail? I'm getting tired of not being a partner with you."

"Do you feel mistreated?"

"I feel like an outsider. I haven't seen any warmth or affection from you in years. Your whole world is the mob. Cathy and I are left to fend for ourselves. You show no excitement being around me."

"Didn't I get you butlers, maids, cooks, and gardeners?"

"What about giving you?"

"What's going on, Sharon?"

"Tony, your freedom is about to be taken away from you. The fear of being locked up doesn't do a thing to you? What motivates you besides money, fame, and women?"

"What do you mean *women*?"

"Do you honestly think I'm stupid, Tony. Perfume reeks on you coming home. The length of time depends on who you're entertaining."

"You don't know what you're talking about."

"Oh, yes, I do. If you go to jail, don't think I'm going to rot at home like an old maid and watch my life go by me. I'm an attractive woman. Getting by will be no problem."

"Not without money."

"You'd do that to me and Cathy?" She went right up to his face. "Let me tell you something, darling. We'll survive without your money. I'm not stupid. Through the years, I've banked whatever I could in case something like this happened. I have a lot of life left in me and a solid body for a woman in her forties.

"Cathy's on her way to fame. She'll be able to stand-alone. Working for Coco Chanel will place her in the richest atmosphere in the world."

"If she doesn't blow that fame with sleeping with men in Paris." Tony had a grin on his face.

"Don't worry. She'll learn how to handle herself. Coco will teach her. She's young. I guess your absence molded us into being independent women. You can work your way out of this mess with Phil. I'm having no part in these procedures. Cathy will leave tomorrow to be as far away from these criminal problems as possible."

Sharon walked up to the stairs and left Tony pouring himself a martini.

Cathy's Trip to Paris

Tony yelled upstairs. "Cathy? Are you ready? Bill's here waiting in the limo."

"I'm ready, Dad."

She came running down the stairs wearing a pair of black Levi jeans and a black and white tweed wool sweater. She flung her Victorian striped black and brown scarf around her neck. Cathy never had a problem keeping up with the newest styles in clothes. She wanted it—she got it.

Bill Sherman was their chauffeur for the last ten years. He took Cathy's three bags in the hallway out to the black limo in the circular driveway. He got behind the wheel and waited.

Sharon hugged her daughter. "Do good. Your father worked hard to give you this opportunity. He loves you."

"He doesn't act like it, Mother. Why do you have to say it for him?"

"He never shows emotions. You're his life. Everything he has worked for has been for us. Remember that in Paris. You're going to live a wonderful and exciting life.

Her father came out of the den. "This is your future. Don't blow it. Get selfish and get a name for yourself. Don't let anything or anyone get in your way." He gave her a sincere squeeze and kiss.

They walked her to the limo. Bill had the backdoor open for her. She got halfway into the backseat and faced a young man. He looked to be in his late twenties with shoulder-length blonde hair. He was wearing an ensemble of black and white pinstripe pants with a matching double-breasted pinstriped jacket with a black shirt with pointed collars. He had on white elastic suspenders and a bright red necktie.

Cathy backed out went up to her father. "Who's this man?"

"It's your first time out of the country. I want you to be protected."

"Are you telling me, I have to take him every place I go?"

"Let's say, he'll be close by."

"Is he one of your mob men?"

"Don't question what I do, Cathy."

Cathy looked in the backseat. "Excuse me, but I'd rather you sat upfront with Bill. I'll sit alone."

The gentleman got out of the car and then leaned back in with one hand on the rooftop. "By the way, my name is Dan Spencer, but you can call me Danny."

"Mr. Spencer will be fine."

Dan gave Tony a thumb up sign getting in the front seat.

"Remember—she's my daughter," he said with authority.

They reached the airport and walked into the Imperial Airways for International flights. Bill took her luggage out of the trunk and gave Dan her bags. Cathy had no idea where to go or what to do.

"Follow me. In a few months, you'll become a pro at traveling."

Cathy had no choice but to depend on him.

Dan went up to the counter to get their tickets for the assigned seats and checked their bags.

"I'm scared to death to fly. I think I am going to be sick."

Dan handed her a pill. "Take this."

"What is it?"

"It will keep you from getting airsick. Relax, Cathy. You'll have a great experience."

"Is this going to be a big plane?"

"It should accommodate 20 passengers. It has a steward's pantry and two lavatories. We'll be on the Empire Class airplane. Since we're flying at night, we'll have beds."

"We're going to sleep on this plane? I heard it can be bumpy."

"It might be. They play movies. Maybe the film will take your mind off the rough ride. I can always hold your hand." Dan gave her a sexy smile.

Cathy ignored his remark. "Do you travel a lot?"

"I wouldn't say a lot, but I've gone to Europe a few times. Imperial Airways is the most luxurious way to travel. All their planes are heated and air-conditioned... and there's no need to worry about noise. It wasn't that way years ago."

He looked at her face noticing her beauty. Cathy's hair was down flowing freely around her face. "Don't worry. I'm here to take care of you."

They walked out to the landing strip and climbed up the stairs to their plane. Once they got seated, she started to relax.

"Do you want the window seat?" he asked.

"I don't want to see how high we go."

"If you change your mind, we can switch. It's really beautiful above the clouds."

"I feel like I can't keep my eyes open."

"It's the pill. Close your eyes and take it easy."

Cathy lasted until the plane took off. She experienced the sudden take-off and climbing high in the sky.

Cathy Arrives in Paris

Cathy walked through the doors of Gabrielle Bonheur's modeling studio and stared at the stunning suits and dresses. Coco Chanel's famous black designs hung on the clothes racks against the wall; gorgeous fur jackets and shoes a woman would die to own.

Becoming one of her models seemed like a dream. She was now among the richest and distinguished women in the fashion circle. She couldn't wait to meet the famous French designer in the world. Actresses were fighting to wear her dresses in the movies. Cathy now had the opportunity to become well known all over the globe.

"May I help you?" A woman with a French accent greeted Cathy as she came into the main studio.

"Yes. I'm Cathy Greco. I have an appointment with Miss Chanel today."

"Have a seat, Madame, and I'll let her know you have arrived."

Cathy took in every area of the room. It contained 18th-century oriental screens in a wallpaper-like fashion. Coco was known to hate doors so every room was wide open.

Cathy stood still as Coco walked towards her. She had a short hairstyle, with black straight hair below her ears, and wore a maroon, long-straight flowing dress down to her shoes. There were five rows of pearls surrounded by diamonds falling down her neck to the front of the dress to her waist. Her pearl earrings were encircled by matching gems. Coco wore dark, ruby lipstick, which looked rich against her fair skin. Her deep brown eyes stood out with mahogany eye shadow and eyeliner. Her eyebrows were defined with a long, thin swipe of fawn coloring going over them to the end of the eye area. Coco was stunning. The only way to describe her—classy. She walked tall with a slim figure. Cathy faced a legend.

"Hello, Miss Greco." Coco held out her hand.

"It's an honor to meet you Madam, Chanel."

"Please, call me Coco. You're even more beautiful than your pictures. If you present yourself well, I'd say you might be my most enchanted model."

Coco's voice was like music with her clear, French accent with a rhythm with each word.

"I'd like you to try on a casual outfit for me, darling, and see how you walk." Before Cathy could respond, Coco raised her hand with a gesture toward her assistant to help Cathy into her clothes.

"Bring Miss Greco into the dressing room and help her into the black sweater and white skirt attire."

Cathy felt her nerves starting to surface knowing she had to model for the most recognized woman with her famous clothesline. Modeling in New York didn't come close to this world.

Cathy stood in the doorway wearing a fashionable outfit. Coco's arms went up in the air. "Come, don't be shy. That doesn't work here. Shoulders back. You need to hold yourself up with absolute confidence."

Cathy took a deep breath and walked towards Coco with long strides trying to show her secure and positive self.

"I like what I see. Where have you been hiding, my dear? You're not only stunning, but you're talented with your walk. How long have you been modeling?"

"I started at thirteen. It's been six years."

"I'll teach you the ropes, and you can go to the top if you work hard. I'll save you to model my new ensembles. Let's try on more garments."

Cathy modeled for a few hours and felt sure of herself the longer she performed wearing expensive garments that weren't shown on the runway of Paris. *She* would present them. *She* would become the famous model who unveiled Coco's new, unknown attire. *She* would be the one in the headlines.

"Tomorrow, you'll showcase my new dresses. No one has ever

seen or worn these outfits. We also need to drop the name, Cathy Greco. You'll now be *Nina Mae!* It's more French.

Cathy's insides roared with pride and excitement. *Nina Mae* was going to become Coco Chanel's number one model.

Kathleen's Awakening

"Kathleen, open your eyes."

The head nurse was trying to get Kathleen to wake up after the twelve-hour surgery. Glass had been embedded into her facial skin and skull.

The nurse kept whispering, "Kathleen?"

A whimpering sound came out of her as she woke in a daze. She put her hand up to her face and felt bandages wrapped around the top of her head. Only her eyes, nose, ears, and mouth were uncovered.

The nurse grabbed her hand. "Don't touch your bandages, Kathleen. You can contaminate them. You came out of surgery."

"My parents. Where are my mother and father? Tell me they're alive."

"They're being taken care of by the doctors. You need to get yourself well." The nurse had been given strict orders not to tell Kathleen of their deaths coming out of a serious operation.

"I want to see them."

"Kathleen, you are in the ICU unit."

Dr. Blair came on the other side of the bed. "There's someone waiting to talk to you. If you don't want to, we'll understand."

"Who is it?"

"Rita Costa. She's been waiting for two days."

"*Rita, where are you?*" Kathleen came to life, trying to look around for her.

She felt two warm hands grab hers. "I'm here."

Kathleen started to cry.

"Don't cry, Kathleen. It'll be hard to wipe the tears under the bandages."

"Stay with me. Don't leave me. I'm so scared. The pain is awful. Did Jenny come?"

"No, she's back home with her mom? She's still sick."

"I don't remember that, Rita. Why can't I remember?"

"You were in a car accident with a train."

Suddenly, Kathleen blacked out.

"Oh my God. She's dead!"

"No, Rita, she's going to go in and out. I don't think there's an inch on her face, head, and neck that doesn't have stitches. She's got a long road ahead of her." The nurse tucked her blankets tightly under her.

Dr. Blair gave her nurse orders. "I want you to put the order of morphine on more frequently. The longer she's out, the faster her recovery will be."

"Yes, doctor."

"Rita, come with me," Dr. Blair said. "How long can you stay?"

"I have to ask Mr. Nelson when he wants me back."

"I'll check to see if anyone in the accident can talk to you before the other reporters. If you can stay, I believe you'll be a great help getting Kathleen back on her feet."

"How long are you talking?"

"A few months."

"I'm not sure Mr. Nelson will allow me to stay that long."

"If you keep sending him updates, I'm sure he'll be happy. I'll do my best to help you. Maybe if you have Kathleen in the spotlight at home with daily reports on how she's doing, the articles will bring a following. I'll allow your photographer to take pictures, that's if Kathleen agrees. She may be heavily sedated. If I need you, I'll have you paged. Do you have a place to stay?"

"Mr. Nelson reserved a room at the Teller Hotel. It's on Park Blvd down the street. Our other reporter, Jack, and my driver, Ben, are staying in other rooms on the same floor."

"Once Kathleen learns her parents are gone, I'm not sure how she'll handle the news. Here's a badge to let you in any room. You go and do your work."

"Wow, the tag reads, *Rita Costa, Reporter* for the *Nelson News.*

Thank you."

"Only a doctor can give this to you."

Rita clipped the badge on and went toward the elevators.

The emergency room had patients settled in rooms with closed curtains. The commotion was still high. Rita spotted a man sitting up.

"Excuse me, nurse. I'm Rita Costa from the *Nelson News*. Is that man from the train accident? I'd like to interview him if he's up to answering questions."

"He's the engineer. His name is Frank Foster." The nurse was surprised a reporter was given a badge by a doctor.

"The engineer!"

Rita couldn't believe she was about to interview the most important person in the wreckage. This interview would be the biggest break in the news.

She noticed Jack walk by and went out to get him. "I need you in this room. Bring your camera—Immediately!"

He followed her.

"Hello, Mr. Foster. My name is Rita Costa from the *Nelson News* in Orleans, Massachusetts. The photographer is Jack Goodman. Do you mind him filming you?"

"I don't know much. It all happened fast."

"Can we interview you?"

He shook his head yes.

"What do you remember the accident?"

"I felt the switch to the track turn on, but we went to the right instead of going straight. I had no time to react. The railroad-crossing bar was down and the red signal lights were blinking. I could hear the clanking of the alarm to warn drivers that a train was coming.

"Once the engine hit the turned switch, it went right off the tracks and fell to its side and slid down the embankment. My fear was seeing multiple cars at the junction. I must have blacked out."

Rita went closer and whispered. "Mr. Foster, I'm sure there'll be a large investigation. I don't want you to say things without your lawyer present."

He looked upset. "You can quote me on knowing the accident was the railroad's mistake, not mine."

"Will you sign a paper for our permission to quote you?"

"Yes."

Rita pulled out her official paperwork and wrote his testimony. He signed on the permission line and admitted to being awake and alert with his statements.

"I'll let you rest. I don't want you to get tired. We'll come back tomorrow."

"Thank you. I need someone to help me tell my story."

Rita pulled out her business card. "In case you want to share any information with me for any reason in the future. I'll be in the hospital for another three weeks."

"I'll call you for the exclusive story."

"The *Nelson News* would be honored to cover your side of the story."

Rita went to the hall to use the public telephones. She called Mr. Nelson and gave him the complete update with Kathleen—and Mr. Foster, the engineer.

"You talked to the engineer? *What a story!*" Mr. Nelson went crazy.

"I had Jack tape our conversation while I interviewed him."

"You got his testimony on the accident! I can't believe this. You did great. Better than I expected."

"Dr. Blair wants me to stay two months to help Kathleen Perry through all this. She's Jenny's cousin."

"The story needs to come from the people involved in the train wreck. Kathleen's from Chatham. The Cape Cod readers will want to know how she's doing. I think we'll get a lot of followers from the newspaper if you interview the engineer along with Kathleen's recovery. The townspeople will be interested in following Kathleen from this tragedy."

"You might be right," Rita answered.

"I felt you were going to be good in this position, Rita. Where's Ben and Jack?"

"Jack filmed the engineer talking, and I'm sure he went to send the

tape to you. Ben drove me here, and I haven't seen him."
"Okay. Keep me updated. Again, great job, Rita."

Mary Rossini's Decline in Health

"Jenny, I'm done with my soup. Can you take my tray?"

I had given my mother chicken broth for supper to keep her meals light until being admitted to Cape Cod Hospital in Hyannis. After cleaning the kitchen, I bathed her and got her comfortable in bed. I placed a small cowbell on her nightstand. "If you need me, ring this, Mom."

"I will, honey."

I gave her a pill to make her sleep for the night.

When I looked up at the clock, it was 10 pm. Todd hadn't called me. I wondered why Mr. Greco's quote for the new barn took this long. It wasn't like Todd not to call me at the end of the day to say goodnight.

I took a shower and climbed into bed. All kinds of emotions were going through my head with the deaths of my aunt and uncle from the train wreck. Rita was out of town. I was dealing with the sorrow of Kathleen and my mother being ill. Now, I added fear wondering if Todd was with Cathy. My mind had too much to absorb at one time. Before I realized it, I fell asleep from mental exhaustion.

Morning came, and Todd never called. He had mentioned the stress from too much work. I wanted to trust him. Not knowing what happened, I called.

"Hi, Mrs. Costa. I was wondering if Todd was there?"

"He's still sleeping. It's not like him to stay in bed this late. He had a lot of work yesterday at the shop."

"It's odd for him not to call me before going to bed. I finally shut the light off at eleven."

"I waited late myself and went to bed, Jenny."

"Did he tell you about my Aunt Dorothy and Uncle Joe?"

"Todd said they were heading for California."

"They didn't make it. They were in the train wreck in Detroit."

"No! Oh, Jenny, how awful. Are they okay?"

"They were killed." My voice started to break up. I needed someone to talk to about my pain and loss.

"Honey, I'm so sorry. It's odd that we didn't hear from Rita about this horrible news. Our daughter usually calls after her news coverage. How's Kathleen?"

I informed her of the whole surgery information that I had heard from Rita.

"If you need any of us for anything, promise you'll call."

"I will. "

"I'll let Todd know you called."

"Thank you, Mrs. Costa."

I hung up and had a sick feeling in the pit of my stomach. *What's going on with Todd?* When you love someone, you get to know all their actions. I couldn't understand Todd not being up at the crack of dawn to feed the animals and avoided calling me last night. *Did he spend the night with Cathy?*

****

In the morning, I went to see my mother in her bedroom. "I'm going to make you a light breakfast, Mom. You can't eat heavy with your tests tomorrow. How do you feel?"

"Still worn-out." My mother continued to cough. "I would like to go out to the porch today, Jenny. I love sitting in the rocking chair looking out at the pasture. It's so peaceful. I haven't done that in a long time."

"You're supposed to stay in bed."

"I want to go outside, Jenny." She looked firm.

I helped her to the porch, putting a cushion on her seat, and placed a pillow behind her back in the rocker. "Here's your shawl. I don't want you to get a chill." I wrapped it around her shoulders.

"Thanks, Jenny. Oh, the memories rocking you in this chair before bed. Do you remember?"

"The memories are embedded in my heart when I got older and you read to me. I clung to your embrace at night. I loved the way you ran your fingers gently and slowly through my hair as you told me stories. I always felt your love."

"God blessed me having you, Jenny. I wish the second child had not died at birth. You wouldn't be alone when I leave."

"Don't talk like that, Mom. You're going to be okay. When you've been sick this long, it's normal to think you're never going to get better. We shouldn't have waited all these months to get you to the hospital."

"Jenny, I might not make it."

"I don't want to hear anything negative." I could feel tears surfacing.

"I hate knowing I may not see you and Todd get married. You have yourself a fine man. I can see the love he has for you."

"We were going to save a surprise for you, but I'm going to tell you. Todd has ten acres on his parents' property that will be his. His father's building a home for us above Lovers Lake. He's adding a room of your own so you can live with us. Todd wants us all to be together. You'll never have to do any work again."

"Newlyweds need to be alone. You two shouldn't be tied down with caring for an ailing mother."

"Are you serious? We'd love to have you with us. How wonderful it will be for you to watch me do the cooking, cleaning…and you can enjoy watching your grandchildren play. We'll bring your rocker, and you can hold the kids on your lap and give them memories as you did for me in this grand old chair." I rubbed the top of my mother's hand that lay on the arm of the rocker.

"Wouldn't that be wonderful? You giving me grandchildren. That would please me, Jenny."

"Mom, you lived a life alone with no warmth or laughter with Dad. How awful that must have been. He was such a cold man."

Staring into space, my mother started to rock back and forth slowly.

"He knew no better, Jenny. His father beat him and his two other brothers. They grew up to be abusive to their wives. They lived with no love. His grandmother was the only one who showed them any affection. They adored her, but she died from pneumonia. One brother died from a heart attack and the other one was killed in a car accident from drinking.

"I knew your father when he was a young man with big dreams and a warm heart."

Mom looked over at me. "When you were born, he came alive. How he loved us. We were his world. He would hold you in his arms and rock you in this same rocker as he looked down at you for hours. He'd say, 'Mary, look at what our love gave us. I'm going to give Jenny the love that I didn't have.'

"Your father was the manager of the *New York Daily News*. He was proud of his work and made good money. When they laid him off, he became bitter taking his frustration out on us. The people he loved him the most.

"Instead of turning to me, he turned to the bottle. Liquor turned him into someone I didn't know. I clung to the man I once knew. Instead of leaving him, I kept you living in a horrible, confusing life. I'm surprised you turned out to be such a gentle, loving person.

"You saw me being mentally abused by your father too many times. I should have pulled you out of that life. Instead, I dragged you through the mud. I had no job or money to leave him. Women didn't leave their men. It didn't help when we moved here with high hopes and he could only get work for Mr. Jackson running his farm. A big difference from banking."

"Mom, you did the best you could at that time." I walked over and kissed her on the forehead. "I want to thank you for telling me there was a time Dad had been a loving father and husband. I wish I had known the good in him."

I put my arm around her shoulder. "What about you, Mom? What were your dreams?"

"I had the opposite life, Jenny. Your grandparents were wonderful. I wish you had known them. I remember dragging you to those horrid nursing homes for them to see you. I never went without a parent's love. My dream was to fall in love, get married, and have a huge family. I wanted at least twelve children.

"My parents were no different than most. They worked on the farm, raised cows, goats, horses, pigs, chickens, and a few ducks. We ate off the land of 40 acres growing corn, potatoes, and vegetables. Your Aunt Dorothy and I ran a vegetable stand along with our mother. The men handled the animals."

Mom stopped talking and choked up. "I can't believe she will never be with me again." She started to cry.

I held her hand. "Don't, Mom. She and Uncle Joe are in God's presence now. They're at peace. It's us, who are left behind that suffer. Pray for them so they can get to heaven faster."

Mom took a handkerchief out of her pocket to wipe her eyes. She went back rocking and smiled at me. "Dorothy was a beauty. The boys were always after her. I was a looker, but not as captivating as her. She was loaded with personality. I mixed in but had no confidence.

"I was so happy when Dorothy met Joe. He owned a trucking business in Eastham. His business was the biggest company selling farm and plow equipment. His parents loved Dorothy."

"Grandma never had any more kids?" I asked.

"No. She had four miscarriages. Pregnant women always helped on the farm and the hard work made us lose children."

"Your father was a handsome man. He came weekly with his parents to purchase vegetables from our stand. They would arrive in his horse-drawn wagon, like we do, and filled the cart up for months. My first date with your father was spent sitting down at Silver Lake in Manhattan."

"I can still feel the passion when he looked into my eyes or when he held my hand. I hold on to those fond memories. If only, he kept that intense love for me."

My mother stopped talking. "Oh, well, we can't go back."

"Maybe not, Mom, but we have those remembrances. No one can take them away from us. Thank you for sharing all of them with me."

"I'm glad I told you. Your father would want you to know the love he once showed."

We stopped talking and enjoyed the togetherness. Sitting there, I came to understand why my mother stayed with an abusive man. I couldn't respect him from the years of craving his love growing up.

Todd's Phone Call

The phone rang. I left my mother and ran from the porch to answer it.

"Hello?"

"Hi, Jenny. I'm sorry for not calling last night." Todd was on the other end. "It took a long time to give Mr. Greco his quote for the barn. He wanted more prices on items than I anticipated. It went from a barn to the field posts around the property to keep the heifers in one area."

"Was Cathy there?"

"Yes."

I got quiet and couldn't get another word out.

"Jenny, I got carried away. They had a party and I drank, which I haven't done in years. A few of my buddies from school were there, and we got talking for hours."

"Did Cathy drink with you?"

He started to stumble on his words. He didn't sound comfortable with the question. He was stuttering and couldn't hide the tension. Todd never bent the truth with anyone. He was as honest as one came. I knew that well.

"How's your Mom doing? Is she feeling better? he asked.

"She's very weak. I'm starting to fear the worse."

"I forgot the time you wanted me at the house tomorrow," Todd said.

"We have to have her at the hospital by 10 am. I'm sure there'll be a lot of paperwork. I'd say be here no later than 8:30 am."

"Okay. Do you need anything?"

"No, just you."

I was feeling insecure. I needed to see how he acted with me. His voice wasn't normal and he didn't sound relaxed talking to me. My heart raced. I wanted to know the truth, and at the same time, I didn't. My first thought was to bury what happened. I knew his being with Cathy would eat at me.

His conversation seemed forced. We had never had to explain our actions. If my mother hadn't been sick, I would have gone with Todd. The situation would have been awkward being on Cathy's turf. At least, there wouldn't have been that golden opportunity for her to move into a territory that wasn't hers.

"I have to attend to my mother, Todd. See you tomorrow."

We hung up, and I sat in the chair for a moment realizing that he didn't end by saying, "I love you." *Was I making something out of nothing?* I was doubting my own intuition.

I walked back out to the porch with my mother.

"Was that Todd?"

"Yes."

"Is he coming over?"

"No. He's taking tomorrow off to help admit you to the hospital."

While answering my mother, I tried to smile. She had enough on her mind without hearing about my fears and insecurities.

"I'm so happy you have him in your life. Maybe you'll have what I didn't. Don't give too much rope to a man. Love him, but be aware that they're men. They don't follow the same rules as women. They can get up and do anything at any time, while we're locked into responsibilities. We have to think of everyone else before ourselves."

"Did you feel that way?'

"Yes. I hated myself each time I had allowed myself to be used. Remember, we're treated the way we allow someone to treat us. If I had put my foot down with your father, when I first saw him going in another direction, maybe he would have thought of us before making decisions that were unhealthy for our family."

"Do you think Todd's that way?"

"I hope not. When you live day in and out with one person, stress can do a lot to a relationship that was once beautiful and strong. Our problems come from what we allow. Notice when something bad is happening and stop the actions in their tracks. Don't give lies or questions time to build up and get bigger. It may become too late to handle the problem. If the situation doesn't feel right, get the facts."

"Boy, you're full of advice today, Mom."

"It's been enjoyable talking together. Why didn't we ever have this closeness?"

"I'm not a young girl anymore. It helps us relate better." By now, I felt like a woman. Why not? Todd made love to me. I had experienced true love.

Mom looked over at me. "Let's promise each other to do this often when I come home."

I hugged my mother. "I promise."

Admitting My Mother to the Hospital

Monday morning arrived, and I jumped out of bed with excitement knowing I would be with Todd. I needed to hold him.

"Hello. Everyone up?" Todd opened the front door and walked into the kitchen.

Just hearing his voice made me weak in the knees. I greeted him with a hug. He kissed me hard and long. I knew at that moment, how much I loved him.

"How's your mom?"

"She's not doing well, Todd. We'll have to help her to the car." I looked at him. "I've missed you."

"I'm sorry for worrying you."

"Let's not talk about the Greco family. Today, my mother comes first."

We went into her bedroom. She was pale.

"I'm going to carry you out to the car, Mrs. Rossini."

"I don't want to be a bother, Todd."

He picked her up and carried her outside. I opened the front door to the passenger side. Todd placed Mom in the seat.

"Let me put the pillow behind your back, Mom. Does that feel better?"

"Much. Thank you, honey." She smiled at me. I sensed she might be scared.

I got into the backseat, and Todd started down the dirt road. The travel time had been about a half-hour when we pulled up to the entrance to the Cape Cod Hospital.

Todd went inside and got a wheelchair. I took the pillow out of the car and replaced it behind her back for comfort.

"Why don't you take her to the admitting room, Jenny, and I'll park the car. It'll save time."

"I'll see you there." I pushed her down the hospital hallway.

"Good morning. Can I help you?" A heavy nurse asked.

"My name's Jenny Rossini and this is my mother, Mary. Dr. Graham wanted me to admit her today."

"Let me see." She reached for a clipboard. "Oh, yes. Mary Rossini." She turned to the head nurse at the station, "Do we have a bed ready for her?"

"Yes. Room 316 on the third floor. We just have a few questions about her medical history."

Todd entered the admitting office.

"How's it going?"

"They have the room for her. I just have to answer these questions."

It took ten minutes to finish and the nurse came over to her wheelchair.

"Hello, Mary. My name is Rachel, and I'll be your nurse today. I'm going to get you settled. Dr. Thompson will see you at one o'clock."

"He's someone new."

"Dr. Graham will see the results of the tests. Dr. Thompson will handle your mother's health while she's in the hospital."

Todd and I followed behind the nurse holding hands while she was rolled into the elevator. We entered a large room with one bed placed by a window.

"A private room?" I remarked.

"That was Dr. Graham's request."

The window faced the rooftop. No beautiful view. A small bathroom was in the corner. Two nurses lifted my mother, put her down on the bed, and placed a light covering over her. Rachel tucked the edges of the top sheet under the mattress.

"Would you care for a drink of water, Mary?"

"That would be great. Please, add ice. I hate warm water."

Mom coughed harder and longer than she had in the past few weeks. She held a Kleenex to her mouth.

"There's a small coffee shop on the first floor if you two want to get something to eat," Rachel suggested. "We have to get your mother setup with an IV and different oxygen tubes.

"I could go for a good breakfast," Todd replied.

We went down the elevator and followed the signs to the cafeteria.

"The coffee smells good. Do you want one?"

"I'd like a corn muffin with it. I didn't get a chance to eat before we left."

"Are you sure that's all you want? "

"I'm too uptight to eat a full meal."

"Go find us a table."

There were only five left. I noticed three servers behind the counter. I was surprised at how many people were in the cafeteria.

Todd brought over a corn muffin with two coffees and a full serving consisting of two fried eggs, bacon, and fried potatoes. "I hope you don't mind me getting a large breakfast. I'm starved."

"Of course not," I took a sip of coffee.

"Jenny, I don't like the idea of you being alone at home with your mother here. I'd ask Rita to stay with you, but she's still in Detroit. My parents offered for you to come and stay with us."

"That's considerate of them. It wouldn't be proper for me to stay at your home."

"I want you with me."

"I'll stay until I can make other arrangements. Maybe when Rita comes back, she can come to my place. We work together so we can go in one car. Talking about cars, my parent's car is at the house. Maybe we can bring it to your place."

"I'm happy taking you places. Let's leave it this way. As long as Rita doesn't have to travel to another assignment when she comes home, this arrangement will work out. Have you heard anything else about Kathleen?"

"No. I can't believe something like this happened to her."

"She's lucky she wasn't killed," Todd said.

"Was she?"

"What are you saying, Jenny?"

"Don't get me wrong. I thank God, she's alive, but I look at what's facing her. She may never be recognizable. I can't imagine my face smashed with tons of scares and not seeing the same person when I looked in the mirror. I'm sure she's feeling the same."

"What's sad is that Kathleen and her parents had no control over the accident. Who would think, you stop at a crossing and railroad cars go off the track, and one smashes into your car." Todd shook his head in amazement.

"I only hope my aunt and uncle never knew what happened."

I put my head in my hands and started to cry. "I haven't had the time to even think about the loss of my aunt and uncle. They were such wonderful people. I know my mother loves me taking care of her, but there was a special relationship with my Aunt Dorothy spending the time with her."

"I'm so sorry, Jenny," Todd sat next to me and put his arm around me. "This has to be hard."

"I wish I could be with Kathleen like Rita has been."

"God works in odd ways, Jenny. Don't you think it's strange that Rita's sent to cover the train accident and discovered Kathleen being in a death situation?"

"It's like a bad dream."

Todd and I changed the topic to our future plans with his father, along with Bob and Ray, working on plans for a home for us. We got excited thinking about moving into a brand-new house facing the lake.

After eating, Todd and I went up to Mom's hospital room. When we arrived, Dr. Thompson was by her bedside listening to her heart.

We both stood by the door entrance. The doctor came up to us.

"Hello. You must be Jenny and Todd. I'm Dr. Thompson." He shook our hands. "I'm finishing your mother's physical examination." He looked to be in his forties, over six feet tall, with dirty blonde hair with overnight beard growth. He must not have had time to go home being busy with his patients.

The doctor looked at us. "I want her to rest. I'll check her again tomorrow morning. I gave her pills that will make her drowsy. She needs sleep with a day of tests scheduled."

"I love you, Mom." I blew her a kiss. I was trying not to fear the worse. She looked awful.

She looked back. "I love you both more." Her voice was weak.

Dr. Thompson walked us out into the hall.

"Did you find anything?" I asked.

"We won't know what she has until tomorrow when I do a ton of blood work and X-Rays. It'll be a long day for her. The full results will take two days to come back. I'd advise you to not come back until we can go over the full results."

"What if she asks for me?"

Dr. Thompson put his hand on my shoulder. "She'll be in good hands. Her nurse, Rachel, will keep her relaxed."

"Two days seem so far off."

"It is. You can use the rest yourself." Todd gave me a grin, squeezing my hand.

"She won't know what's going on tomorrow," Dr. Thompson said.

"I'll take care of Jenny," Todd replied.

"Dr. Graham told me that you lost your aunt and uncle in that horrible train accident in Detroit. I'm so sorry for your loss, Jenny. This situation with your mother has added stress."

"Thank you, Dr. Thompson. We'll see you in a few days."

Moving in With the Costa Family

Todd took me home so I could gather my clothes to stay with his family. I hoped not to be there too long.

"Tomorrow, I'll have Ray and Bob get the stock truck and bring your animals back at our place. I'll put your horse, White Christmas, in the back of the barn with my black stallion, Midnight," Todd said. "While you're packing, I'll go out and feed them all."

I gathered my items and looked around at our empty house. There was no life left inside.

Within an hour, Todd and I arrived back at his home.

"Hello, Jenny. I'm glad you're staying with us," Judy said. She hugged me coming into their kitchen. "How's your mom?"

"I won't know for two days. That's when all the tests will be completed. It'll be good to know what we're dealing with so she can recover faster."

"Let me have your bags. I'll take it up to the spare bedroom." Cory grabbed the handles.

I tried to relax, but I felt weird staying with Todd. If Rita was home, I would have been comfortable and relaxed. "I appreciate you doing this for me."

"Anytime." Judy put her arm around my shoulder. "After all, you'll be a family member soon."

"I can't wait for that." Todd gave me a loving look.

The four of us sat down to a welcoming meal that Judy had cooked. "I hope you two are hungry."

"I know I am, Mrs. Costa. I only had a muffin." I gazed at the homemade buns, pork roast slices, applesauce, fresh vegetables, and a fresh garden salad.

Before we ate, Judy said a blessing. As the food was passed around the table, I listened to the three of them laughing. Their jokes were about the day's events. Todd's parents were warm and loving. I could see how Judy and Cory wanted nothing but the best for their son.

"I can't wait for you to meet my brother, Sam. He'll be the best man for our wedding." Todd reached over for a second helping on the pork roast.

"What school is he attending?" I asked.

"Hyannis State Teacher's College in Barnstable," Mr. Costa answered. "He's in his last year, and he's taking advantage of the summer course. We're proud of him."

Mr. Costa sat back and looked at me. "Have you heard any more from Rita? How's Kathleen doing?"

"Rita's supposed to call me tomorrow when I go back to work. Mr. Nelson requires all reporters to call in every day."

"This may be her first big break as a reporter," Judy said.

"Yes, but what a terrible story to cover. She has to be emotional visiting Kathleen. I wouldn't want to be the one informing her about her parents dying," Todd said.

"If Rita calls you with an update, please let me know," I asked.

"Who wants brownies? There right from the oven." Judy brought the warm dessert out to the table.

"If it's no bother, I'd like some hot tea, Mrs. Costa."

After everyone was full of sweets, I helped clear-off the table along with Todd. I was happy to see he thought nothing of helping with women's work. In fact, the two of us did the dishes; I washed, and Todd wiped and put away.

"So, you always help, or are you trying to impress me?" I teased.

"My father told me that no job is only for a wife or husband. If you can help each other, pitch right in with the work."

"I think I am going to like your father." I leaned over to kiss him.

It was a long and stressful day. Todd and I sat talking for an hour on the front porch swing before calling it a night.

"Tomorrow, I have something special to show you."

"I love surprises. Can you give me a hint?"

"It won't be a surprise if I told you. We'll go for a ride."

"That will be fun. It's been a long day. I'd better get some shut-eye. It's already 9 pm."

He gave me a long passionate kiss. "That's enough kissing for tonight." We laughed.

****

The morning came and the sun traveled through my bedroom window. I could see the cows grazing in the pasture. Some were in groups; others were individually feeding on the grass. Todd was throwing grain on the ground for the hens. I lay there watching the chickens peck away into the dirt to collect the kernels. Their clucking sounds could be heard through my open window as their chicks followed every direction the mother hen took. I was fascinated by watching their action grabbing pieces one by one, non-stop.

My imagination ran with the thought of being married to Todd and how I'd be helping him with the farm responsibilities. Loving Todd was easy. He gave back so freely and was very tender and emotional with his feelings.

The smell of bacon and coffee traveled from the kitchen and found its way into my bedroom. I was surprised that the smell of food seemed to upset my stomach.

Todd knocked on my bedroom door. "Come on, lazybones. Mom made a great breakfast. We all eat at one sitting while the meal is hot. It's Sunday and we have to go to the 8 am Mass."

"Be right down. Let me jump into my skirt and blouse."

This was the family life I wanted. Being alone with my mother was a hardship. There was no father or a brother to start the farm chores that all became mine. The added burden came with helping my mother with the housework and cooking. I did the man's work to help keep the animals healthy to produce their food and worked the fields to pick the crops. I loved the idea of Todd taking care of me for a change. I now had an idea of how my mother must have felt struggling to care for a child alone.

"Good morning, Jenny." Judy was putting the hot corn cakes onto the kitchen table. "We never start our week without the Lord."

"I'm excited to go with all of you."

I sat at the kitchen table and loved how no one woke up grumpy. My father felt he had no reason to smile when we were together for meals. The room filled with laughter and conversations about who was going where and what chores had to be done for the day. I never had family time with love and togetherness growing up.

I thought of Rita and wished she had been sitting at the table with us. I hated our separation. I didn't have time to share with Kathleen, as we always had in the past. I felt like I had deserted her when she needed me the most.

Once breakfast was done, we all piled into the horse-drawn carriage.

"Going to church this way is exciting." I was looking forward to riding in a buggy.

"It gives us time to take in our surroundings that God has made for us, instead of rushing by the gorgeous scenery in the cars," Todd remarked.

They were right. In the fifteen-minute horse-drawn ride, we saw deer, beautiful brooks, and lakes along the roadside. The clean air was refreshing and started energy within me.

The church was what I expected...a small, white-sided building with close to fifty hardwood pews. The altar was small with only one altar boy. Everyone was saying their hellos, greeting the morning with friendships.

Once the Mass was over, the priest stood outside the door on the steps and spent time talking to the parishioners. Todd took me over to meet Father Rick.

"Father, I'd like to introduce my fiancée, Jenny Rossini."

He came towards me and extended his hand. "I guess we'll be meeting sometime to arrange the Mass for your wedding. Glad to meet you."

"Same here, Father Rick." I gave him a warm smile.

He was short in his late thirties with a dark, brown crew cut. The extremely short style stayed neatly in place. He wore a long, white linen liturgical vestment with tapered sleeves, a robe that's worn by the priest during the Holy Mass. It symbolized the innocence and purity that should adorn the soul of the priest who ascended the altar.

Judy and Cory joined Todd with the introduction. "We're so excited, Father, to have this wedding with Todd and Jenny. She's such a wonderful girl."

"It's a blessing to have new couples join our church. Welcome again, Jenny. See you all next week."

Before we got into the carriage, Cory turned and looked at Todd. "We'll be going back home with the O'Connor's in their car. Why don't you two enjoy the day?"

Todd helped me into the buggy on the passenger side and took the reins settling in his seat.

"I want to take you to a special place,"

"I can't imagine what this mystery could be," I remarked.

****

We headed back in the direction of the family's farmland and took a dirt road that had breath-taking scenery around Lovers Lake.

"This is beautiful, Todd. Can we stop and sit for a while?"

"Not until I show you something."

We rode further down a narrow path heading deeper into the woods. I spotted an old church with a high steeple. For an old building hidden away from everything, I was surprised how newly painted the outside structure looked.

The grounds had colorful, full-blooming roses and azalea bushes that surrounded the church. I got a whiff of their fragrances. Along the walkway, I noticed yellow daisies.

I couldn't name all the plants among the Dutch flower gardens with tulips of every color that filled the whole area. The aroma of the sweet-fragrances mixed with numerous flowers was quite strong but pleasant. Some late perennials were still trying to break out of the ground with their buds.

"Stop right here," I said. I looked over every inch of the grounds.

I got out and walked slowly into the flower gardens and filled my imagination with God's creations.

"I have never seen a place so private and captivating."

Standing motionless, I watched the flowers that were being covered with butterflies with their different colors and designs on their extensions. I heard the sound from the wings of hummingbirds vibrate as they hovered over Petunias dipping their thin beaks deep inside to get the nectar and bees hopping from one bloom to the next.

I turned looking to see where the sound of burbling water was coming from in the area. "Do I hear water?"

"Yes." Todd took my hand and led me down a footpath.

A cleared-out trail went down a small grade in the woods, and we came to an open area at a small incline where the rushing water came from a tiny rock formation that flowed from another section into Lovers Lake.

I turned to Todd with tears in my eyes. "I can't believe a place like this could exist."

"I brought you here for a reason. Let's go back so I can take you inside the chapel."

Todd led me towards the door.

"Maybe it's locked, and we can't go inside. The path looks like no one travels them," I remarked.

"Not for over thirty years."

Todd unlocked the heavy, carved, wooden door that gave a loud noise closing behind us. We stood in an undersized chapel with pews to fit maybe 50-75 people. The statues of The Blessed Mother on the right side of the altar revealed her holding baby Jesus and Saint Joseph by her side. The church walls were surrounded by vibrant colors on the glass-stained windows. The structure looked too kept to have been closed for years.

A crucifix showed Jesus' cuts and bruises from His beating before dying. It was on a stand on the side of the altar. The thorns on His head showed how deep they had dug into His scalp. Blood dripped from His Head, into His Eyes, down His Body, and onto His Feet. The statue had hair on his arms and legs to remind us that He was Human. It was the actual size of a man.

"I have never felt closer to God as I do at this moment, Todd." I felt the spiritual feeling go right through my heart.

"Do you like the chapel?"

"How did you get the key?"

"Father Rick gave me a key to show you. He said they used to have Mass here until they closed the church."

"Why?'

"The Vatican didn't think enough people came here to keep the doors open. My parents were the last ones to get married here."

"Really? How special!"

"Jenny, I would love us to get married taking our vows here in this special place. It's small, but you don't have many family members, except your mom, and maybe Kathleen will be better for the wedding. My family's small with a brother, a sister, and a few friends like you. It would be a perfect setting for us. What do you think?"

I stared at him. "I would love to get married here."

Holding a tiny box in his hand, Todd got on one knee and looked up at me. He opened the small container that displayed an antique style engagement ring with a white gold set with rounded diamonds. The center diamonds sat in a beautiful carved square setting graced by delicate leaves and blossoms carved on each side.

"Jenny, I want to ask you before God to marry me. Will you be my wife?" His eyes filled with emotion.

"Oh, Todd. How beautiful!" I looked at the gorgeous engagement ring. "I would be honored to become Mrs. Jenny Costa." I kissed him tenderly.

"Let me put the ring on your finger."

Todd's hands were shaking. He removed the band from the case and took time to admire the sparkle in the diamonds. He took my left hand and placed the ring on my finger.

I looked down at the circle band and then held my hand up high staring at the most spectacular ring I had ever seen. I swore the ring would never be taken off my finger.

"Oh, my gosh. This is the most exquisite engagement ring that I have ever seen. Look at the glitter and different colors when the light hits the diamonds."

"Now, our engagement is real, Jenny. We can set a date later."

He looked at my ring. "My wedding ring has a few diamonds with the same leaves and blossoms on the side matching your engagement ring.

"I feel like the luckiest girl in the world." It was overwhelming.

"I'm having something engraved inside the ring."

"Can I do the same for yours before our wedding?" I was lost in an emotional moment.

"Then the set wouldn't be a surprise."

"I want to do this for you, Todd. We would both have rings with our love engraved in them. How special would that be?"

"Okay, you can call the jeweler. I'll give you our ID number to the set. You can tell him what you want in mine. I don't want you to go and see the rings. It's supposed to be a special moment putting the band on your finger at our wedding."

We hugged and kissed at the altar with more love than either of us knew could be possible.

"If the church is closed, how are we going to be able to be married here?"

"Father Rick got permission from the Bishop to perform the service for us."

"I never knew I could be this happy."

"I think of us being together forever, and it takes my breath away, Jenny. You're my life. Without you, I'm nothing."

I couldn't stop kissing him.

"Maybe we should kneel and say a prayer to God to bless us. When we go to the hospital, we'll tell your mother. My parents and Father Rick knew I was going to ask you today," Todd confessed.

"They did? How sneaky!"

When we left, Todd locked the door to the church. I heard a loud click. I saw the name above the door: Joseph and Mary Family Church. The chapel on the side was named St. Therese The Little

Flower.

The structure was old but looked new. "How are the gardens outside kept so beautiful?"

"My mother did all the planting and hired someone to clean the whole inside from corner to corner." Todd hugged me. "Just in case, you said yes to this location."

"Yeah, like I wouldn't," I remarked laughing. I squeezed Todd's hand.

"Our house will be facing Lovers Lake. My father, Bob, and Ray have started on the framework. Dad wants me to wait until the house is done to show you. He hired my uncle from his construction company to help. Ray and Bob have a hand in the work when they get time. I wanted a dream home for you, Jenny. My father isn't telling me either about all the things they're doing."

"A home is where we make it, and as long as I am with you, I don't care where it's located, although, this area is spectacular!" I looked around and felt like I was in Paradise.

"My father designed a bedroom and private bath for your mom when she comes home. I want her to have privacy."

"She has struggled all her life alone. This is going to mean the world to her. She can walk to the lake, sit reading a book, or just putter around the house. I love you for offering her to live with us." I started to cry.

"Your mother doesn't need any more responsibility. We're all family, and that's all I want, except adding little feet running around to complete our dreams. I want you to stay home and be a mom with no worries."

"I can't wait for us to have kids, Todd."

The sunlight started to dim on the church. "We have to get going. It's getting late."

We climbed into the buggy. My heart was full of love.

****

When we pulled up to the house, Judy and Cory ran out to meet us.

"Tell me you said yes, Jenny," Judy was smiling with tears.

"How could I not be with a man like Todd? He's everything a woman would want and more."

"Let me see the ring." Judy held my finger.

Cory walked over and gave me a kiss. He smiled, shaking Todd's hand. "Congratulations, son."

Judy put her arm around us. "We have a great dinner to celebrate along with a toast of wine. Sam's sorry not being able to be here."

The dining room table was set with the finest linen cover and satin napkins. Berry colored wine glasses were filled with Burgundy wine. It was fruitier and not too strong to serve a young couple.

I could smell the food on a charcoal burner outside. A cook wearing a long apron stood near the grill barbecuing and two women were braising the rest of the meal in the kitchen. The Costas' didn't seem to be poor, but they never acted like they were above anyone. They thanked God every day for what they had in food and financial savings during the Great Depression. Like Todd, Cory felt the family was a gift to treasure.

His father started the meal with the toast. "Congratulations to both of you. Judy and I couldn't be happier. Todd's got a wonderful woman. We love you both and can't wait to officially have you in our family, Jenny."

"Thank you from the bottom of my heart. I only wish Rita and Kathleen were here to share this with us."

I held back telling them that I had an unloved life growing up with my father. It hadn't been until I had been invited to live in their home, that I came to realize how a loving family acts.

"My mother was a blessing with all that she had sacrificed for me. I can't wait for us to give her security when she comes to live in our new house. Thank you for the work you're doing for us. The location at Lovers Lake and near that beautiful chapel is amazing. I'm going to be thrilled having your first grandchild, and I hope it's not long after we marry."

"I toast to that." Cory lifted his wine glass.

The food was served by hired hands. Hot, sizzling filet mignon steaks on rich, white china plates with gold trim. That was a treat during the Great Depression. Cory had killed a young heifer. Judy served family-style string beans, corn, hot homemade honey buns, fresh garden salad, a melody of cooked vegetables from their garden and baked potatoes that were dug from their grounds outback.

I looked at all the food on the table and thought of how blessed this family had been with food. Our family ate leftovers until they were gone. Sometimes, the meal was a cooked chicken leg with a cup of tea. I couldn't wait for my mother to become part of this family.

The meal took an hour to enjoy, ending with strawberry shortcake with vanilla ice cream dripped on top. In those days, ice cream was not a daily treat.

My Wedding Dress

I felt full after the meal. I didn't eat that much at one sitting. "If I eat this way every day, I might not fit into a wedding gown." I rubbed my stomach.

"Talking about wedding gowns, we want to buy your wedding dress, Jenny. We can go shopping together."

"I can't have you do that. I have some money saved from working."

"We truly want to do this. It would be such an honor," Cory replied back. "In fact, Judy can pick her dress out at the same time."

Judy jumped in. "That would be a fun day for just us women. I haven't been out myself for a long time. We can go to Baxter's Boathouse in Hyannis for lunch. We can make a day of the event."

Todd leaned over and placed his hand on my arm. "My parents want to do this for you. Mom's right. She doesn't get out much. Let them do this for you."

"I don't know what to say, Mr. and Mrs. Costa, except thank you. I think Mom would enjoy a day out because she never went to town for enjoyment, only to buy food. Most of the time, she made the list, and my father went to get the items."

"Good. It's settled." Judy was firm.

Cory spoke up. "Since we're on this topic of the wedding, we would like to do one more thing for you and Todd. Let's have the gathering in the barn outback. We could have one heck of a dance party out there. The men can get the location in shape for the event.

"Our friends, Abe and Dave, live in Barnstable and have some instruments that they play. We can get some feet kicking with their band. Everyone brings a dish. That's how we do weddings. We believe in saving the money for the couple and not paying out hundreds to put a celebration on for them." Cory acted excited himself.

Tears surfaced again. "I don't feel right with you doing this much."

Todd cut in. "Jenny, your mom's too sick to plan a day like this for you. It's on our farm, the band will cost nothing, and people always bring the best food you ever ate. This is how our friends work together for an occasion. We'll be doing the same for others after we get married."

"Did you two decide on a date?" Judy asked.

"No, we haven't." Todd looked over at me.

Judy ran enthusiastically out of the room. "Let me get the calendar. We need a Sunday because we don't want to interfere with people working on Saturdays. We're in the first week of July. What do you think of Sunday, October 4th at 10 am, and the buffet can follow? It's a little over three months, and by this time, your mom will be healthy and strong. Kathleen might be home by then."

"What do you think, Jenny?" Todd asked.'

"I'd like a fall wedding. The leaves will be turning color and the air will be crisp."

"We'll get the invitations out in a few weeks and go looking for the dresses," Judy said excitedly. "I can call Father Rick and give him the date and time to reserve the church. Your dad and I were the last ones to marry in the chapel. How special."

****

The weather was beautiful in the low eighties with no clouds in the sky.

"Why don't we get our bathing suits and go for a swim at the lake?" I asked Todd. We put them on under our clothes, grabbed a blanket and towels.

"Where are you two off to? Judy asked.

"To the lake for a swim, Mom."

"Wait. I'll throw some leftovers and drinks in the cooler for you."

"Ma, we just ate," Todd remarked.

"You always get hungry by the water."

We gathered the items and headed out.

Todd drove through a thin forest of pitch pine trees, a species that highly adapted to the Cape's well-drained sandy soil. "Beyond this wooded section is a hidden beach," Todd pointed out. "It's a peaceful area."

He parked the vehicle under a large elm tree for shade and cracked the windows for ventilation. He took the basket of food and the blanket out of the car and took my hand. "Follow me down this dirt path. Sam and my father helped me clear a trail through the woods to make the walk easier to get to the lake."

The stride through the forest was silent, except for the crunching of snapping branches as we stepped-over them, and the sound of birds flying and chirping high in the trees.

"It's like hearing nature blending in with all the rustling sounds," I remarked.

"There're many different species of birds in the Cape Cod area. Along the beach, we might see red-throated loons, gulls, sandpipers, or wrens. We might get lucky to see some bobwhites, which usually group around West Yarmouth."

"How do you know all this?" I asked.

"I bought a book on birds in the area. I haven't named all of them that congregate in this one location. I have loved this backland of my parents for years. Sometimes, I come here just to unwind. My parents knew this and I think that's why they gave us this portion of their land."

"I can't believe this will all be ours, Todd. I never dreamed life would bring me a man I loved this deeply with in-laws so warm and loving."

"It's all ours, Jenny. This is another section of the lake we own. Wait until we can share this with our children. How great will that be? If we have a son, I can take him fishing. Our daughter can help you in the kitchen. I'll give you everything you didn't have in life."

We reached the open lake, and Todd spread the large, red and navy plaid blanket out on the sand. I helped him put everything out on top.

We walked toward the edge of the lake. He put his toe in the water to test the coolness.

I jumped in with a splash yelling, "The last one in is a rotten egg!"

Todd followed and swam pass me. "Beat you." He reached the floating dock. I wasn't far behind. Holding onto the two wooded arm rails, I climbed the two steps and sat down.

"A bit out of breath." I felt as if it was an effort to get air in my lungs. "I have to get more exercise. Lately, I seem to get tired easily. Too much sitting at a desk in the office, I guess. How come no one else is here to enjoy this gorgeous day?"

"No one will ever come here. This section of the lake belongs to our family. We built the dock."

Todd put his arm around me, and he looked in every direction on the lake. "Can you imagine us waking up and coming to this secluded lagoon?"

"What an education our children will have with the wildlife," I replied.

"How many kids would you like us to have, Jenny?"

Since I'm an only child, I'd love to have four or five. Does that scare you?"

"I only have Sam and Rita. I'd love a large family. I'd bring them up to be close and do a lot of things together. It won't matter what gender as long as they're healthy."

"Yes, that's what's important…healthy kids." I grabbed his hand. "By the time we plan the wedding, and help my mom get on her feet, time will fly by fast, especially with work. It'll go faster than we realize."

"When we go see your mother tomorrow, the doctor should have the test results. I think you should prepare yourself, Jenny. I don't think she's well. She looks so frail and pale."

"Let's think positive. For now, I want to enjoy this moment with you." I laid back on the dock and looked up at the sky.

Todd laid next to me leaning on his left elbow and started to run his fingers through my wet, tangled hair. "You have had a lot of tragic events. Try to get all the rest you can this week. Sometimes, I take my close family-life for granted. I won't again after seeing what has happened to you," He stood up and gave me his hand.

Todd dove into the lake and turned back waiting for me to dive. Instead, I climbed down the steps backward and swam to him.

"Are you sure you're okay, honey?"

"Just short-winded."

Todd turned onto his back. "We should relax and float back to shore."

"Sounds good to me." I couldn't understand why I would be so exhausted.

We reached the shore and wiped ourselves off with two thick, blue beach towels and then sat down on the blanket.

"How can I have eaten so much at dinner and be drooling thinking about the pastry your mom put into the basket."

We devoured the fudgy brownies and talked for over an hour about our wedding plans.

"They say the older you get the faster time goes. I hope every day is long for us." I reached up and kissed him, pulling him down on me.

It was a soft, loving kiss and I gripped his waist. Todd kissed me on my face and eyes.

"I feel like I can disappear into your soul when we touch. I had never felt so loved." I gave him another passionate kiss.

"Jenny, when you kiss like that, I'm not strong at stopping."

"Don't you want me? Did I disappoint you last time?"

"Disappointed? Jenny, I loved touching you."

"Then don't stop," I said.

Todd sat up. "If you get pregnant before we get married, I don't want people looking down at you. We know the love between us, but our families might not understand. I should have been in control with you the last time."

"I don't want to hold back, Todd. A month ago, you gave me a taste of making love and that's all I want when I'm with you. That's all I think about during the day. I can feel your touch and get aroused by recalling the things we did together.

"I think I'm going to have to lock you up, Jenny, until our wedding day." He sat up.

"I can't get enough of you, Todd. I leaned forward into his back and put my arms around his stomach, kissing the back of his neck. "I love you."

He grabbed my hands. "I want us to wait longer, Jenny. When you become my wife, we'll be together every night." He gave me a hug. "Let's put our things in the car."

I didn't know if his refusal was for the reason he gave or if something was wrong. His distance made me wonder if he was sorry for our past lovemaking.

We filled the vehicle with our belongings and headed back home.

The Newspaper Headline

Todd parked the car in the driveway and we headed for the back entrance to the kitchen. I could hear his parents having a loud conversation.

Cory hollered, "I had a strong feeling about Tony Greco's connections to the mob."

"What's the problem, Dad?" Todd walked toward him after dropping the empty basket on the kitchen table.

"Look at this headline on the front page of the newspaper... *Tony Greco's Home Invaded by FBI Agents. Seven Wanted Mobsters are Taken into Custody.* That was the day you were getting the quote. Did you see any of these gang members at the party?"

"No."

"How could you have missed them? Everyone has seen their pictures in the newspaper numerous times. Didn't you recognize any of them?"

"The guys and I were out in the barn."

"Was Cathy with you?" Judy asked.

I stared at Todd, waiting for him to answer his mother.

"She was for a while."

"I don't understand. If the party was for Cathy, why was she with friends in the barn of all places?" Cory looked as if he was trying to fit pieces together.

"I don't know. The people inside were mostly her parent's friends."

"My heavens," Judy stated. "Look at all the gang members they arrested at his home. It states they have all been wanted for committing a spree of robberies, kidnappings, and other crimes—God, some are wanted for murder! What were they doing at Cathy's party?

Why would so many criminals be at one location? Someone must have tipped the officials off."

Todd spoke up. "Maybe the party was supposed to distract guests away from the meeting!"

"That would make sense," I answered.

"The guests who came to the front door where dressed in formal wear and led into the sunroom for cocktails. That's why the rest of us went outside. I didn't feel clean with dirty clothes on after working."

"Todd, whatever happened to the quote that Tony Greco wanted for his barn? You never presented the plans to me," his father asked.

"Tony wanted a new barn built to hold a few dozen heifers and walked me through the property. I left him a quote and have the copy in my pant pocket upstairs. You would never believe what this man owns outback. It's all hidden from the house."

"Does he want us to do the work?"

"Cory, why in God's name would you want us to still do work for this man? The newspaper says he was arrested for questions about his involvement. I want nothing to do with him. I don't care how much profit we would make." Judy had a panic sound to her voice.

"We left with the understanding that I would put another quote together for him for planting new shrubs, trees, and flowers around his barn."

"Get the paperwork?"

"Dad, I got side-tracked having the weekend with Jenny. Besides, Mr. Greco said there was no rush on the quote. I'm sorry for forgetting something minor." The remark was said in a sarcastic tone. Todd looked irritated.

"Don't talk that way to your father! You know our family made that a number one rule to work on a deal as soon as we got home from the job. That's our livelihood, and it's not a minor deal," his mother snapped.

"What more can I say about this event? I don't know what Cathy knew or didn't. I was asked to stay for dinner, and I refused. I had no interest in sitting at the Greco's black-tie dinner! I can't stand high-class people acting stuffy. I saw my buddies and went outside to talk to them."

"How did you end up in the barn?" Judy asked.

"Cathy came out and suggested that we all go in there so we wouldn't be around the guests. Maybe she did know something was happening and didn't want us to see it?"

I cut in, "You said you were drinking. Where did you get the liquor in the barn?"

"Cathy came out with a bottle in her hand. We already had a few drinks in the house. She stayed a while and then went back. Us guys stayed talking for about another hour and left."

"What time was that?" his dad asked.

"I wasn't keeping tabs on the time, Dad. I hadn't seen my buddies for so long and we tried catching up on the summer events. I haven't had a drink since my graduation night. You'd think I was one of the gang members the way you're all asking me these questions. I'm just as shocked seeing the headline. In fact, more so, knowing I was there with no idea who had been in the house. Do you really think I'd stick around if I knew all those dangerous men wanted by the FBI were at their home?"

"I'm sorry, Todd. I find it odd that so many were there and no one saw them," his father said.

"Dad, Mr. Greco is known to be involved with the mob. Don't you think he had a plan to have the party for Cathy so there wouldn't be any witnesses to confirm something was going on after they left that night? He might have had a hidden room. After all, the mafia's known for that, aren't they?"

"Where's Cathy going?" Judy asked.

"She's going to Paris to be a model for some designer named Gabrielle Bonheur."

"Coco Chanel! Wow, that's the highest you can go in the modeling world." I was amazed she had that connection.

"I hope the FBI doesn't come knocking on our door looking for you to ask a lot of questions." Judy acted scared. "Anyone giving information about the Greco's would be signing their own death certificate."

"I'm sure the boys who were with Todd and Cathy will tell the truth that they all knew nothing that had been going on with these hoodlums," his father said. "You stick to your guns, son. You had no idea what was taking place. I'm sure your buddies can testify you were there with them the whole time."

"Let's change the subject. How did you two enjoy the day?" Judy asked.

"It was great, Mom. I took Jenny to Lovers Lake across from the property you and Dad gave us."

"Couldn't wait to show her, huh?" Cory said with a wide smile.

"She didn't see the house, Dad."

Cory went over to his son and put his arm on his shoulder. "Don't bring her near to the house until you're ready to move into the place. I want both of you to see the finished work after the *I do*."

"Come sit down and eat. Today, I felt lazy and sent your father to get some pizza in town." Judy placed the cutlery in front of us.

"We could have picked it up for you, Mom."

As we ate, there wasn't the happy laughter we usually had with family. Rita was the one who got the flow going with her jokes and interesting events.

After eating, Todd and I went to sit on the swing on the porch. "I bet Cathy looked stunning dressed for her party."

Todd held me close to him. "You have nothing to fear from her. Soon, we'll be together forever."

I hugged him, but couldn't shake my worries. "I'm more tired than I thought. I'm going to go upstairs and pick my clothes out for work tomorrow. Wednesday, we go see my mother and get the results of her tests."

I kissed Todd and turned towards the stairs. "See you for breakfast."

****

The next morning, I heard Todd and his father speaking as they went down the stairs to the kitchen. I wasn't far behind them.

Good Morning, Jenny." Judy placed a scorching, covered skillet full of warm

blueberry pancakes on a hotplate in the middle of the breakfast table.

"Good Morning, Mrs. Costa. It smells yummy in here."

"Hum, Hum!" Cory said, as he came behind his wife and wrapped his arms around her. He pulled her tight against him. "You sure do know how to get to a man's heart, woman!" He kissed the back of her neck.

She looked up at him. "I'm not stupid. A good meal is a bait for wheeling in the fish my mother used to say!" They laughed.

Todd walked over and gave me a fast kiss. "Good Morning, honey. Did you sleep well?"

"That guest bed is too comfortable. I wish today had been a Saturday. Might have slept longer."

"No time off with this line of work, except Sundays," Todd replied. "I need to feed the animals and work at the stand."

"Yesterday, the lumber for Benjamin's home was delivered," Judy said. She leaned over Todd to drop a few more pancakes on his plate.

"Don't be shy, Jenny. Take more," Judy remarked

"I think I have my mom on my mind, Mrs. Costa, and I don't feel hungry. For me, eating four of your thick pancakes was a lot."

Ring, ring! Our conversation stopped.

"Who can be on the phone that early?"

"We won't know until we answer it, "Todd joked. " Hello?"

"Hi, Todd. It's Sam. Is Mom still at the house?"

"Sam, it's 7 am. She doesn't go down that early. Did you forget?"

"Stop giving me a hard time. Let me talk to her."

Todd looked over at his mother motioning it was Sam.

"Hi, Sam. You're calling bright and early."

"I wanted to bring someone special home for you and Dad to meet Sunday. The weather's going to be good, and I thought we'd take a ride down."

"She must be special."

"Yes."

"Did you just meet her? Where have you been hiding her?" his mother teased.

"I wanted to make sure she was the one."

"Does she have a name?"

"Her name is Faith Hamilton. I met her in the library. She's from Kentucky and her parents own a horse ranch. They breed thoroughbreds. The rest you'll have to find out when we come."

"Is this serious?"

"It is. We're getting married next year. We didn't want to take Todd and Jenny's day away from them in October. Plus, being together a little longer will give our parents time to meet.

"I asked her to marry me last Saturday."

"Why do I have to pull information out of you?"

"Are you upset?" Sam asked.

"No. I'm thrilled. Dad and I will have two daughters-in-law by next year!"

"Daughter-in-law!" Cory yelled. "Don't tell me Sam has a girlfriend?"

Judy turned to him and said, "No, a fiancée!"

Cory took over the phone. "Congratulations, son. Can't wait to meet her."

"Please, don't everyone smother her when she comes through the door. I don't want her to be uncomfortable."

"We'll treat her no different than family members, Sam. Knowing your mom, she'll go out of her way with cooking. Looking forward to meeting Faith and seeing you. It's been a while. Going to attend Mass with us?"

"We're going to St. Mary's. We should be at the house by 1 o'clock.

"Drive carefully."

"Will do. See you then."

****

"Todd, it's close to 7:30 am. I have to get to work. I start at eight.

The *Nelson New* is about a twenty-minute ride."

"I'm all set if you are."

"I'll get my pocketbook. Thank you both for a great weekend." I hugged Judy and Cory.

"We'll see you tonight, and don't feel you have to keep thanking us."

Todd pulled the car up by the door. I sat in the passenger seat feeling tired before the day started.

"You look washed-out. Are you okay, Jenny?"

"I didn't fall asleep until 2 o'clock and had a hard time going back to sleep."

"Are you going to be able to do your work?" Todd was concerned.

"Yeah. Work has to get done. I'm looking forward to calling Rita and seeing how Kathleen's doing? She didn't call your parents, did she?"

"No. That isn't like her. She always keeps the family updated on Kathleen."

"I'll let you know her condition when I talk to Rita."

Her Parent's Death

Rita arrived at Dr. Blair's office at 9 am. "Glad you're here, Rita. I appreciate you being in the room when I tell Kathleen about her parents."

"I was up all night sick thinking about this."

"Families don't realize how doctors feel inside informing them a loved one died, never mind two."

They walked into the room and Kathleen was sitting up.

"Hi, Kathleen." Rita tried to be upbeat.

"My bandages come off soon. I'm so nervous."

Rita grabbed Kathleen's hand. "You're going to come through this. Jenny and I will help you. She sends her love. I spoke to her this morning."

"Rita, I'm not going to look the same. I'll be a stranger to myself and to all of you."

"You will always be you. The rehabilitation center will help you adjust. You have to take one step at a time.

"I have some good news for you. Jenny and Todd got engaged. Most likely, you'll be one of her bridesmaids so you have to get on your feet for October. That's in a few months."

"Let's not jump ahead of ourselves," Dr. Blair remarked. "I don't want to get Kathleen's hopes too high on something that may not take place."

"Has anyone called my relatives in Santa Rosa? Our arrival date was a month ago. My parents and I were on the way up there to meet my dad's brother, Dick, and his wife, Phyllis. If they call the house, there will be no answer which will worry them.

"No one had information on who to contact. Do you have a

telephone number?"

"It's in my handbag. Rita, will you go into my locker and get it? The piece is in the zipped section. There it is, Rita. See the red paper sticking out? I copied their telephone number on the slip."

Dr. Blair took the paper. "I would like to have your permission to call and update them on your condition."

Kathleen looked over at the doctor. "By the way, Dr. Blair, I want to see my parents today. I haven't seen them since my two procedures. Can I be put in a wheelchair to go to their rooms? It'll be wonderful to see them. They don't have serious injuries, do they?" Kathleen hesitated. "Oh my God! If they're still here this long, they must be in bad shape. Are you holding something from me?"

She looked straight at Rita. "Have you seen them? Why are you looking at me that way?"

Dr. Blair went up to Kathleen. Her eyes filled up and Rita got a Kleenex out of the box on the side table.

"Kathleen, we couldn't tell you in-between the surgeries, because you were weak. Your parents had life-threatening injuries and we tried to save them, but they died that night."

All they could see was Kathleen's eyes through the opening of the dressing. At first, Kathleen tried to absorb the horror of the news.

Rita took Kathleen's hand again. "I'm so sorry, Kathleen."

"NO. I DON'T BELIEVE YOU! TELL ME THEY'RE ALIVE!" She started to scream at the top of her lungs. "They died that night? I'm sitting here thinking they're alive."

"Rachel!" Dr. Blair called out in a controlled voice, not to upset Kathleen more than they had.

"Yes, Dr. Blair."

He whispered. "Give Miss Perry another small dose of sedatives in her IV."

Rita couldn't hold Kathleen in her arms to comfort her.

The nurse injected more tranquilizers into the IV. "This will help you calm down." Her nurse smiled trying to comfort her.

"I don't want to calm down. I don't want to live. There's no reason. I'm all alone. Oh my God! I never said goodbye to my parents. I can't go on without them." Kathleen was hysterical. She sobbed while Rita held her hand. Rita had tears coming down her face seeing her dearest friend in such pain.

"I wish I could comfort you, Kathleen. What a terrible way to lose them."

"Oh, Rita. How do I go on without them?"

"You take one day at a time. You have to think of getting well."

"Were they buried?"

"You're their only immediate family. At eighteen, you're at the age to make the decision. They're in the morgue."

"This long? My poor parents. I don't know what to do."

"Why don't you let the Nickerson Funeral Home take them back to Chatham and lay them to rest at the Bethel Cemetery in South Chatham? They loved that area. I can start the arrangements, and I know Jenny would help plan the Mass."

"How am I going to go?"

Dr. Blair stood next to her bed. "You can't travel, Kathleen. The bandages are still on you. You're not close to being healed. Going outside could cause an infection."

"I can't go to my parent's funeral?"

"Your parents would understand. As soon as you come home, I'll take you to the cemetery." Rita didn't know what else to say.

"You need to rest so you can build up your strength," Dr. Blair insisted.

"Right now, I don't care about anything." Kathleen turned on her side and faced the wall.

"That's normal. You're in shock. It's an awful way to find out."

"I never got to say goodbye to them and now, I can't go to their burial. One minute they are alive and suddenly, I'm informed they died." She turned to look at Rita. "Stay with me. Don't leave me alone."

"I can stay until tomorrow and then I have to return to work. I've been calling in your condition to the newspaper and the other people who were hit by the train. You'll need more time to restore your health. Dr. Blair's son, Peter, will take good care of you once his father retires. Jenny and I will try to come back together."

"Why did this happen to me?"

"There's never an answer for tragedy," Rita replied. "The engineer of the train only knows what happened. It's sad when the decisions and actions of someone else affect the lives of the innocent. The police and railroad investigators are working to get the facts on this incident."

The nurse must have given Kathleen a large dose of sedatives because Kathleen went into a deep sleep.

Dr. Blair's secretary, Debbie, came into the room. "I talked to Mrs. Perry myself. They're in complete shock. They made numerous calls to their home. Their family won't be able to travel the distance for the funeral down the Cape or visit Kathleen. Mr. Perry isn't healthy. He has diabetes and lost a leg. In fact, they're trying to get him into a nursing home."

Rita spoke up. "If the hospital will allow it, I can call Jenny to make the arrangements for Kathleen's parent's bodies to be taken to the Nickerson Funeral Home in Chatham, Massachusetts. I'm sure Jenny will have the legal right being the only family member to make the decision."

"I'll have the hospital release the bodies within the hour," Dr. Blair stated.

****

I picked the telephone up on the first ring and heard Rita's voice. "Hi, Jenny." She was crying on the other end of the phone.

"What's the matter, Rita?"

She told me every step that had taken place with Kathleen; the shock of hearing about her parent's death, and the need to have their bodies taken to the Nickerson Funeral Home in Chatham without her attending, tore her apart.

"Jenny, could you take over and make the arrangements for the wake and funeral. I'd appreciate you handling the Mass and burial plans. I'll be back tomorrow."

Rita gave me all the information with the next steps for Kathleen's recovery. I was happy she didn't need to endure any more suffering with surgeries.

"She hasn't had the bandages taken off. Kathleen will be lucky if she has normal features. I'm sorry. I know it sounds cold, but she had serious structural damage. I don't think she'll ever lose all the scars. She's going to lose her dream of acting."

I cried hard hearing such horrible news. Kathleen wanted to be a movie star for years. She had an appointment with David O. Selznick who produced *Gone with the Wind*. She was ninety percent there. Having a date to be interviewed in California was so close to filling her wish. She had been a stunning woman. Her fantasy was fading.

"Don't cry, Jenny. It's no one's fault. It's sad a tragic accident turned Kathleen's life into dealing with a badly damaged face and her parent's death. I'm glad you're not here to see her in this condition. I'll see you tomorrow. Hold on until I get there."

"I will."

"I'll call the story into the newspaper with the names of Kathleen's parents dying from their trauma," Rita stated. "Their bodies have waited too long to be put to rest. I'll write up a short story with an update on Kathleen's condition. Mr. Nelson wants me to end this coverage of the train wreck and get back to work at the office. "

"I'll be glad to see you, Rita. I'm staying with your parents until my mother comes home. Hopefully, we'll have her results when you return."

"We'll talk when I get there."

I hung up depressed. My cousin had her life turned-around into a catastrophic nightmare and my situation was uncertain with Todd. I tried not having my thoughts run out-of-control to only find out later Todd did nothing wrong. The nerves in my body were jumping from too much stress with one bad report after another.

Rita was gone for over two months, and I felt lost without her. We needed each other more than ever with Kathleen's accident.

The world had stopped for us, three friends. Our lives would no longer be carefree and full of laughter. I should have been on cloud nine with my engagement and my plans getting married. Kathleen had a black future. Rita filled her days drowning in her job.

I made the call to the Nickerson Funeral Home and spoke to the director to have a one-day wake and the burials on the same day. It was rare to have any under three days. They agreed to Sunday, which was five days away. They had to wait for the bodies to arrive. I arranged things at the church. Late in the day, I called Rita with the final arrangements.

I went back to finishing the editing with other reporters calling in their news. Lunchtime arrived and the Joan knocked on my door

"Are you joining us for lunch at the Chatham Fish Pier?" Joan had her purse in her hand. Every Friday, we went out of the office to have lunch with the women at work.

"I guess I could use a break."

Becky from Accounts Payable joined us as we rode together in Joan's car. We talked non-stop about the train accident. Rita had called into the office daily giving the updates. Everyone knew and loved the Perry's and were heartsick over Kathleen.

Arriving at the pier, the smell of the fish outside the shack seemed strong. We sat down and studied the menu. I usually loved the haddock fish sandwich, but nothing on the menu hit my stomach.

Everyone looked at me after they placed their order. I hesitated, while the waiter looked down at me waiting for an answer on my choice.

"My stomach has been upset all day. I'll have a small bowl of clam chowder."

"That's it?" Joan asked. "Are you sick?"

"With all that has happened to me, I'm not hungry."

I didn't want to complain, but when the chowder arrived and I started to eat, my upset stomach got worse. I could hardly get the pieces of seafood down my throat. After sitting with the girls, I wished I was back at the office, alone.

Once we arrived back at work, I closed my door.

Becky peeked in. "Are you sure you're okay?"

"I'm uptight waiting for the results on my mother's tests tomorrow. I think her condition is serious."

"Let me know if you need anything."

"That means a lot, Becky."

"I mean it. Call me."

"I will if need be."

I pushed to get my work done. I felt exhausted from doing no real physical work. Five o'clock finally arrived to end the day.

Alberta Sequeria

Mary Rossini's Tests

I walked out of work and Todd was waiting in his car. I fell into the passenger seat.

"You look beat?"

"I feel exhausted."

Todd bent down to kiss me.

I told him Kathleen's reaction to getting the bad news about her parent's deaths, calling the funeral home, Fr. Rick scheduling the Mass, and the plan at the cemetery burial. On top of my personal responsibility arranging it all, Mr. Nelson kept throwing tons of faxes on my desk from the reporters.

"All this doesn't seem real to me."

"Jenny, at least Kathleen doesn't have to face more procedures."

"Todd, I want to visit my mother. I feel something's wrong."

"I'll stop at Jack's Market. They have a pay phone outside, and I'll let my parents know we're heading to see her. Knowing Mom, she'll hold up supper for us if I don't call. We're close to the hospital."

We pulled up to the grocery store, and Todd went to use the payphone against the building. Within minutes, he came out of the glass booth.

"Okay. I told them we may be home late." Todd continued the drive.

The Cape Cod Hospital was a fifteen-minutes ride. We arrived at six. The visitor's hours were over at eight.

We walked down to my mother's room. When we got there, two nurses were with my mother along with Dr. Thompson. He turned and noticed us standing in the doorway and walked towards us.

"I'm glad you're here."

124

"Is my mother okay? Why are you all around her?"

"Let's go into the waiting room." The doctor led us to the empty cubicle.

I felt my heart skip fast and felt faint. Todd grabbed my arm to balance me.

"The two of you have a seat." He pointed to the chairs and looked serious.

"We got all the tests back this morning. Your mother's worse than we thought, Jenny. She has Tuberculosis in the last stage. Usually, I recommend a sanatorium, but with my years of dealing with this disease, I'd say she only has days left. We can make her comfortable instead of moving her. She has lost more weight since you brought her to the hospital. I'm sorry for such bad news. I'm afraid she won't be coming home."

"Does she know?"

"Your mother has to know she has a grave illness seeing every nurse wearing gloves and sterilized outfits. She's coughing up blood. The nurses had to put her on a breathing machine. If we give her antibiotics, they won't cure her. The illness is too advanced. We're giving her sedatives to help relieve the awareness of her condition."

I couldn't believe what he was saying. I wanted to block it out.

"Your mother had to have this disease for two years. She should have been seen right away with her symptoms. I can't believe she continued doing her daily responsibilities."

"My mother never stopped doing housework until a month ago. She only complained about being tired."

"Is it possible we can see her?" Todd asked.

"No one can go in except the medical team."

"I can't let my mother die without seeing me!" I put my face into my hands and tears started to roll down my face. Todd put his arm around me. I felt smothered. I couldn't go forward or backward in my thoughts. Hours ago, I had made arrangements for a Mass and burial for my aunt and uncle, and now I had to add my mother.

The excitement of my wedding faded. I wanted to go to a dark corner and hide from the world and rot away. My mind felt too tired to make a decision with anything.

Doctor Thompson looked at me. "Tomorrow morning, come back around ten. There isn't anything you can do. Go home and get a good night's rest."

"Jenny, he has a point." Todd was trying to be reasonable.

****

Before leaving the hospital, the doctor allowed us to go up to the window of my mother's room. There were two nurses by her side injecting an IV in the top of her left hand and a machine was hooked up to help her breathe. There was no color in her skin; only a grayish, pale-tone. Her thinness showed the outline of bones, which looked like death.

Sobs started to pour out of me to the point of shaking. Todd held me close.

"She's so alone, and I can't hold her hand. It's not fair with her suffering trying to get air and feeling weak. Why does God let good people endure so much pain before dying?"

"We'll never know why we suffer, Jenny. You can go crazy trying to understand life and death. We go to a better place with God. As long as we love and believe in Him, we'll live forever."

"I want her to see me so she's aware that I didn't abandon her."

"Your mother's in a state of not thinking about you or anyone else. I'm sure she's too weak to worry. You're in more pain than she is right now. Death leaves the ones behind with the torture. What she needs from you are prayers. God will take care of the rest."

"I believe that, but right now, my heart's being torn out of me. What am I going to do without her? She won't see us get married."

Todd pulled me tighter into his arms. "You're going to go on living. On our wedding day, she'll be looking down at us, smiling. Believe in the good and think positive."

He took my hand. "Let's go home and return tomorrow. We can't do anything since she's sedated. All you're doing is putting yourself through agony." Todd kept his hand around my shoulder walking me down the corridor and out the hospital doors.

He drove slowly down the dirt path to his parents and he could only watch me go through my sorrow. I looked out the side window making soft whimpering sounds. I felt the excruciating hopelessness of not being able to stop the death process of my mother.

It was after 8 pm when we got back to the house.

"Hi kids. Supper will be ready in a half-hour. Having an easy and fast meal; just spaghetti with meatballs with a salad. I have some garlic bread in the oven. Wash up and relax."

She turned and saw my puffy eyes from crying. "How's your mom doing?"

I let the last of my sobs roll out of me. My shoulders shook.

Judy placed the box of spaghetti on the counter and came over to me.

"Honey, what happened? What did the doctor say?"

Todd spoke since no words would come out. "Mary has tuberculosis, Mom. They give her a few days."

I fell completely into the welcoming and comforting arms of Judy.

"My mother won't see us getting married."

"You're going to be stronger than you think because your mom would want it that way."

"I don't know what I'd do if I didn't have Todd and all of you."

"You're not going to be alone with this. We'll help you."

Cory walked in and found the commotion with everyone. Todd gave him the bad news.

"I can't imagine what you're going through right now, Jenny. Maybe we can close the business and go see your mother with you."

"They won't allow you in her room. She has no awareness of our presence. We're going to see her in the morning."

"Todd, you take care of Jenny and we'll take care of the orders and customers."

"Why don't you go upstairs, Jenny, and take a nap? We'll call you when the meal is ready." Judy's eyes filled.

"A rest sounds good."

Todd put his arm around me. "I'm going to take her upstairs. I'll be back down."

Todd and I climbed the stairs to the bedroom. I was ready to collapse physically and mentally.

****

Judy became sad. "Oh, that poor girl. Right before getting married. She has no one in the family, except Kathleen. Her aunt and uncle are not even buried yet. How much can she take?" Judy started weeping.

Cory held her. "She's such a sweet girl. I hate seeing her in pain, and we can't do anything for her."

"I hope she knows how much we love her?"

"Of course, she does, Judy. Right now, her mind is on her mother. Jenny's going to need us when Mary dies. We'll be the only ones in her life. God had a reason bringing us all together. We're lucky He chose us to have Jenny in our family. She'll never go without love."

"I want to go sit outside a while, Cory. This has shaken me more than I realized. We'll give Jenny an hour to rest." They went out to their porch and sat on the swing. Cory held her hand as they swayed slowly back and forth.

"It's like the world stops when a loved one's dying." Cory looked out at the open fields.

"Somehow, we seem to pull things together, Cory. This isn't one of them."

Todd walked down the stairway looking drained. He joined his parents.

"I'm sure Mary has no life insurance. The poor woman had nothing. I want to cover the expenses. We can have people up here after the funeral. It would be a good idea to get started on these arrangements before she dies.

He looked at Todd. "Did Jenny say where she wanted to put her mother to rest?"

"Jenny has made funeral arrangements for her aunt and uncle to be buried at Bethel Cemetery in South Chatham next to her father. Maybe we should have her mom buried at the same location. I'll talk to her about the idea and see how she feels. She's in such an emotional state. There hasn't been any private time for her to deal with all these deaths.

"We'll discuss these plans after supper. I want to make sure she can handle making decisions."

Judy went into the house to put the water on again for the spaghetti. Twenty-minutes passed, and she dropped the pasta into the boiling pot. She added a small amount of salt and olive oil stirring the water. "If Jenny's sleeping, we should leave her be. I can heat hers later. It's best she rests."

****

Within the hour, Todd came upstairs knocking on my door.

"Come in."

"I wasn't sure if you were hungry."

"I never went to sleep, but it felt good to rest and be alone."

Todd sat on the edge of the bed. "Do you feel up to eating something? You can't afford to get yourself rundown."

"I'll try." Deep down, I didn't want to get out of bed. I wanted to spend my time separated from the family.

Judy placed the meal on the table. Spaghetti was my favorite, but the spicy aroma of the meatballs and Italian sauce upset my stomach. I didn't want to hurt Judy by refusing to eat.

"Did you get any sleep?" Cory asked. He reached for the freshly grated cheese.

"Not much," I answered. I sat with my hands folded on my lap. There seemed to be no energy to lift them.

"Emotions from stress can do that, Jenny." Cory continued to pour the parmesan cheese over the top of his spaghetti sauce. The more cheese he put on the pasta, the more upset my stomach got from the strong scent. I wondered how I was going to get the meal down me.

Judy filled a small plate halfway for me. "If you want more, don't be shy." She placed a hot cup of tea next to my plate.

I felt a deep love looking up at her. Todd's mother knew my likes and what comforted me in the short time staying with them. I had been blessed having her come into my life while I was losing my mother.

"Thank you, Mrs. Costa.

She smiled. "Take your time, honey."

I tried to eat as much as my stomach could handle. I felt sick. The spicy meal was battling to settle in my stomach. I excused myself and got up with my hot tea and went outside to the porch.

It was peaceful by myself. I wasn't being forced to make decisions or answer questions being thrown at me. I looked out over the property the Costas' owned. It had to take them years to build this business for their family. I sipped my hot brew. I hoped to achieve what Cory and Judy had with their family. After being by myself awhile, Todd came to sit next to me.

"How are you feeling?" He reached for my hand.

"Todd, I'd like my aunt and uncle to be buried with my mother, but not at Bethel Cemetery in South Chatham. Can you see if Fr. Rick could arrange for them to be buried at the St. Theresa Little Flower Cemetery in the back of the chapel?"

"They haven't buried someone there in decades. I can ask him tomorrow."

I continued. "We're going to be married at the location. I'll feel like they'll all be with us when we say our vows."

That's a good idea. Maybe the burials will bring people back to our little church."

"Thank you, Todd. I feel at peace with this decision."

He wrapped his fingers around mine tighter. We slowly rocked in the summer night. The shooting stars crossed the sky like fireballs leaving a colorful trail behind them. I was mesmerized by the action in the silence of the night.

"Up there, way above the clouds and stars is Heaven." I didn't look at Todd. I was in my own world with my eyes looking up. "It must be peaceful in God's company."

Todd put his arm around my shoulders. "When we're with Him, I can't imagine anything else mattering. There's no more pain or suffering. He has a reason to take our loved ones from us. After all, we're His. Your family members are with Him and Our Blessed

Mother. They're at peace."

"I miss Kathleen. We were so close. Now, she's cut-off from me."

"She'll be coming home soon. Kathleen will need our help to recover."

"I'd like that." I cuddled into Todd and felt safe.

"We better get some sleep, Jenny. It's been a heartrending week for you."

Todd helped me to my feet and my body trembled. We walked into the living room to say goodnight to his parents.

"If Fr. Rick would allow the request, Jenny has decided to put her whole family to rest at the St. Theresa Little Flower Cemetery."

"I feel it's the right resting place for them."

"What a wonderful idea; at the chapel where you'll be married, Judy said."

"I'm going to say goodnight and get some sleep," I turned to go up the hall steps.

"See you in the morning." Cory gave me a hug.

The Fearful Call

Ring, Ring. It was 4 am, and the phone woke me up with the fear of bad news.

Todd went from his bedroom out to the upstairs hall to a corner table to answer the phone. I was right behind him wrapping my robe around me.

"Hello?"

"May I speak to Jenny Rossini?"

"Can I ask who's calling?"

"This is Wendy, the head nurse at the ICU unit at Cape Cod Hospital. I'm calling about her mother."

I heard the conversation on the other end. I grabbed the phone from him.

"Hello. This is Jenny."

"This is Wendy. Your mother is taking a turn for the worse, and we think you should come over as soon as possible."

"Yes, we're on our way." I was in a panic and started to cry. At the same time, my body trembled. I felt faint.

Cory and Judy came rushing out of their bedroom. "Who was that?"

"It's the hospital, Mom. Mrs. Rossini is failing. I'm taking Jenny there now."

"Why don't we come with you?" Cory turned to get his clothes.

"No, Dad. Stay home."

I put my dark blue jeans on and pulled an oversized, gray sweatshirt over my head and ran a comb through my hair without styling it. My hands shook rushing to put on lipstick.

By the time I got downstairs, Todd was waiting for me.

"I'll get the car."

"No, I'm ready. I'll go with you."

As we went through the kitchen to the backdoor, I grabbed my handbag off the spindle of the chair. The sun wasn't up and the early morning air smelled clean and refreshing.

The travel time seemed like hours. Being extremely early caused no problem getting a parking spot.

We rushed by the receptionist with her yelling, "Wait!" Her request had been ignored when we ran to the elevator for the ICU unit. Arriving, we met a nurse and asked for Wendy.

"Wait here and I'll get her."

Wendy came walking down the corridor wearing a white uniform and white shoes. A serious expression was on her face.

"Jenny?"

"Yes. Can I see my mother?" I asked.

"I can take you to the window, but not into her room. Who's this?" The nurse looked at Todd.

"He's my fiancé, and I'm not going without him."

Wendy looked back at me. "I guess it'll be okay."

She led us down the same walkway we had traveled the day before.

Wendy took us up to the big, wide window to my mother's room.

"She's so far away from me. I want to hold her." I was anxious about our separation.

Wendy hesitated and then said, "Let me see what I can do."

She went into my mother's room after putting on infectious clothing and spoke to the nurses surrounding my mother's bed. They turned and looked at us.

The three nurses grabbed the IV stands and tubes connected to my mother's arms and began to roll the bed right up to the wide window.

My mother had aged from the trauma her body had gone through. Her dark, brown hair had numerous gray strands running through and her eyes were sunken. My tears flowed non-stop. I put my hand on the window near her face.

Without any warning, as if my mother had felt my presence, she turned and looked up at me. A beautiful smile came on her face as her lips pronounced, "I love you." Her eyes closed, and the heart rate on the monitor went flat. Rachel called the doctor.

As they worked to bring her back, I watched in horror. The doctor looked up at me and shook his head that she was gone. They closed my mother's eyes, and she seemed to be at peace. I couldn't remember a time she had that tranquil look.

My family's deaths all happened so close together that the events were like a bad dream. I felt the emptiness knowing the opportunity of that mother-daughter talk we spoke about on the porch was never going to happen. Mom wouldn't be holding her future grandchildren. It would have been my time to take care of my mother in her aging years. In a single moment, my loved ones were gone. A family wiped out.

Wendy walked up to us in the corridor. "Let me take you to the family room. Dr. Thompson will be in to talk."

As we were led around the corner to the room, I felt numb. Two women sat quietly with no conversation between them while a television played softly. The elderly women had the same blank expression as mine. Maybe her husband died, and her daughter was there to give comfort.

I wanted to be all alone to lie in bed with my head on a pillow, a blanket over my body, and sink into depression.

Doctor Thompson came into the waiting room and sat down on a couch next to me. "I'm sorry for your loss, Jenny. Losing your mother is painful. We have to know where to take her body. Do you have a funeral home we can call? We also need your written permission to do so."

His voice confused me. I wanted to get a grip on what happened, instead of him throwing questions at me on what I wanted to be done.

Her body. His words described my mother as a body; that shook me. *Give her a name,* I thought, *even say my mother, Mary Rossini. Not body.*

Todd spoke, "We're going to make funeral arrangements today. You can call Nickerson Funeral Home in Chatham to take her mother. Jenny's aunt and uncle are there waiting for their burial."

134

"How awful. You poor thing, losing an aunt and uncle at the same time," Dr. Thompson said with sincerity.

I was too stunned to look at him.

"I'd appreciate it if you'd inform the funeral home that I'll call them in a few hours. I have to call a priest to get permission for a location for burial." Todd took over the next steps for me. "Come on, honey. I think you need to get home to rest."

On my way walking down the corridor, my knees got weak, and I stumbled.

"Can someone get me a wheelchair?" Todd asked the doctor.

"Rachel, get a wheelchair," Dr. Thompson requested.

I didn't fight the suggestion. Todd made me comfortable, and Rachel insisted on pushing me to the door.

"We'll wait for you to get the car, Todd." The nurse put a hand on my shoulder.

The car pulled up, and Todd helped me into the passenger seat. He smiled down at me and gently squeezed my hand. While he drove, he didn't push for conversation. I wanted to be mentally alone. I was trying to absorb the tragedies in my life in such a short time. I couldn't understand losing so many at once in a few weeks. I needed Kathleen and Rita. We always comforted each other.

When Todd's parents saw his car pull up, they came out the front door. They noticed the sorrow on my face. Todd nodded that my mother had died.

Cory took me by the arm. "You go park the car, Todd. We'll take her from here."

"We're so sorry, Jenny." Judy cried.

Todd's parents got me onto the couch and covered me up with a blanket. August wasn't cold, but I was shaking. Cory put another lighter blanket around me and grabbed the couch pillow to put under my head.

"Lay down and rest. We'll get you some hot tea." Cory looked up at Judy for her to prepare the brew.

Todd went to the phone and dialed the Nickerson Funeral Home. He gave them all the information. He explained that my wishes were now for Joe and Dorothy Perry to be buried with my mother behind the chapel.

Once Todd completed talking to the director, he called Fr. Rick. He explained my request to have all three members of my family to be buried at the Little Flower Cemetery.

"Wow, it has to be at least thirty years since we buried anyone there," Fr. Rick replied. "I'm going to have to ask the bishop for permission to do so. It may take me a few days."

"Jenny's staying here with us, so you can call me back when you find out. Since we plan on getting married there, it would mean a lot to her."

"I understand how special the plans would be for her. I'll get back to you."

"Thank you, Fr. Rick."

Todd hung up and looked at his parents. "I'm going to call Rita and let her know what happened and the funeral arrangements.

More Bad News

Rita was called at the nurse's station and a telephone call was waiting for her. "Hello. How are you, Todd? Some surprise hearing from you." She listened until her brother finished the news about Mary.

"That's awful, Todd. Jenny must be crushed. Both of my best friends lost their parents who are related. What are the odds?"

"Will you be back for the funeral? We're planning on Sunday. We don't want to drag this out any longer. I'm waiting to see if Fr. Rick can allow the burials at St. Theresa Little Flower Cemetery."

"That's a great idea. I'm supposed to come home tomorrow. I want to say goodbye to Kathleen before I leave."

"Take care of yourself. We'll be happy to see you. It's been quiet without you running in and out of the house gabbing about your upcoming assignments." They laughed together.

Rita hung up and started to pack her belongings. She had a ticket for the noon flight back home. It had been two months since she had arrived to cover the train wreckage in Detroit. She took a taxi to the hospital to see Kathleen one more time. Kathleen's door to her room was halfway open when Rita knocked.

"Come in."

Rita found Kathleen sitting up in an armchair.

"I wasn't sure if you were here."

The nurse smiled at Rita. "I just washed Kathleen and changed her bedding. Sitting too long in bed isn't fun."

"How do you feel today? It looks good seeing you out of bed."

"It feels good," Kathleen replied energetically. "I met Peter Blair. He's really friendly. He's taking the head position in the Trauma Unit as the Chief of Plastic Surgery. I have to go into two months of rehabilitation."

"Are you still considering moving in with your Uncle Dick's family in California?"

"I can't picture living far from you and Jenny. I'm going to need you two. Besides, Uncle Dick's going into a nursing home. I'm going to call David O. Selznick and see if I can reschedule an interview in six months. I need to see how my surgeries are going to do with scaring. Pray for me, Rita."

"Your parents put money down on a home in Chatham. What will you do?"

"They were purchasing Johnson's farm. I'm going to wait until I get back home to decide whether to move or not."

"I came to tell you bad news, Kathleen."

"Nothing can be worse than losing my parents."

"Yesterday, your Aunt Mary died."

"Died! I didn't know she was that sick when my mother was caring for her."

"It all happened within weeks. She had Tuberculosis. I guess she had the disease for years and never went to the doctors to get checked. By then, the illness was too progressive."

"I loved my Aunt Mary. She was like a mother to me." Tears filled Kathleen's eyes.

"It's one death after another in our family. We were all happy, and now, Jenny and I have no parents. It doesn't seem real." Kathleen wept from too many losses. Rita put her arm around her.

"Jenny decided to have all of them buried together at the St. Theresa Little Flower Cemetery. It's located in the back of the church where they're getting married. Will you be all right with that decision? I know you were thinking of having them buried at another cemetery in Chatham."

"I think that would be wonderful. I haven't seen the location, but I'm sure it's better than the cemetery near the main road."

"I have to catch a flight at noon. I can't stay any longer, Kathleen."

"I understand. I'm going to miss you." She grabbed Rita's arm.

"We have room to take care of you until you get on your feet. After recovering, you can decide. Jenny and Todd will be married soon and they said you could use the room they had built for her mother."

"I'm not sure, Rita."

"Think about it."

Dr. Peter Blair walked into her room. His father had already retired.

"Rita informed me that my Aunt Mary died. She was my mother's sister. They're all going to be buried together."

"What a tragedy," Dr. Blair said.

Kathleen started to cry.

"Don't, Kathleen. Your parents wouldn't want you to hurt like this. You've had enough sadness without going to a funeral for the three of them. You'll see their resting place."

Rita hugged Kathleen the best she could with the bandages around her head. She looked at her watch. "I have to go and catch my flight. I want to get there a couple of hours before takeoff."

Rita and Kathleen hug for a long time. "I'm going to miss your daily visits."

"You'll be home soon. Think seriously about staying with us."

"I'll take good care of Kathleen," Dr. Blair replied.

"Give my love to Jenny."

Rita turned at the doorway and waved, throwing kisses to Kathleen.

Alberta Sequeria

Rita's Return Home

Rita handed over her small luggage at the gate to a male crewmember and went up the steps to get on the plane. She sat in a window seat. Numerous times, she had stated how scared to death she was to fly.

The 1930s were known as the "Golden Age of Flight." However, traveling by railways and sailing by steamships had developed a standard of luxury and economy that was impossible for air travel to beat.

Rita was a reporter and considered a businesswoman. Her travel would be paid by the *Nelson News* and fell into the position of a high-class clientele. Plush, upholstered seats, wet bars, smoking lounges, and wooden paneling gave the impression of luxury, despite the non-benefits of engine noise and turbulence. Air travel was perceived in the 1930s as dangerous, and insurance rates for air trips were four times higher than the normal price. Horrible turbulence in airplanes occurred even on a clear day. The plane would drop hundreds of feet in minutes. It was a continuous bumpy ride until they landed. It was like riding a rollercoaster.

The flight wasn't rough as it usually was during her trips. When the plane landed, Rita took a deep breath of relief, swearing to never fly again.

When the plane taxied up to the gate, Rita spotted Todd waiting for her. They had been together every day of their lives until she took the job at the newspaper. She lit-up seeing him and ran to give a bear hug.

"Wow, where did you get this strength?" Todd asked. He lost his balance.

"I missed you, Todd."

"I missed you, too." He lifted her up into the air, swung her around a few times and kissed her.

Todd picked up her bag, and they walked towards the terminal holding hands.

"I didn't eat much when I was in Detroit. I was on the go. Every day, I worried about Kathleen. I don't know if the doctor made a miracle happen. She has to wait until the bandages are off."

"We have to keep Kathleen in our prayers. Let's go home, Rita. Everyone can't wait to see you."

They chatted all the way home. Being with Rita was never a dull moment for Todd. There was no problem trying to find something to talk about with their conversations. Rita was bubbly and outgoing. They laughed at crazy things.

****

Rita walked in the front door and met her parents with open arms and passed kisses from one to another. "Oh, how I have missed everyone."

She came to the kitchen table and wrapped her arms around me. "I'm so sorry, Jenny, about your family, especially your mom. What an awful time you're going through."

"I'm glad you're home. I need you." We hugged tightly.

After catching up on the latest news, Cory pulled out a chair from the kitchen table for Rita. "Okay, let's sit down to the great meal Mom made for us. I may even pull out a bottle of wine. Let's see. I have either California Burgundy or a Zinfandel. What are your choices?"

"Where did you get the bottles?" Judy asked as she placed the mashed potatoes on the table. "We don't serve alcohol often."

"Believe it or not, Tony Greco gave me them when we did his front yard."

"That criminal?"

"Judy, we can either throw the bottles out or enjoy the drink."

"I'll have a glass." Rita grabbed five wine goblets. "With the two months I had, I deserve a drink."

"I think we all could use one," Cory replied, pouring their choices.

"Let's say a blessing first." Judy looked over at Todd.

"Thank you, Lord, for our family being together. Bless Jenny's family members who are in your loving arms. Get Kathleen strong, and as always, thank you for our food, while others go hungry."

It was a wonderful home-cooked meal that Rita had not had in months. We passed the vegetable soup, followed by fried chicken legs, string beans picked from their garden, mashed potatoes, fresh garden salad, and sweet corn cut from the field early in the morning. If it wasn't for their animals and gardens, they would be struggling like most families. Laughter filled the house with Rita home. The bad experiences and losses disappeared for a few hours. Everyone was excited trying to get their story out first.

When our stomachs were full, and the wine had relaxed us, the atmosphere became more somber as we talked about Kathleen and the loss of my family.

"I have good news," Todd said smiling. "Fr. Rick talked to Bishop Feehan. He has approved the burials at the cemetery."

"That's great news, Todd." I got excited for the first time in weeks. "The service will be beautiful."

"Rita, how's Kathleen doing?" I asked. "You said that she won't be needing surgery."

"Isn't that great? She was heartbroken not being able to come to the funerals. I told her that Jenny and I will take her there when she comes back home. She had decided not to go to her uncle's in Santa Rosa. She tried getting her interview scheduled later with the producer. Kathleen isn't sure if she should buy Johnson's property. She may want to stay at her parent's home.

"I was wondering, Mom and Dad, could we take her in until she's healthier and stable to be alone. Jenny and I can take care of her when we're home."

"I don't see why not. We have an extra room."

"Todd, you and I can take her in when she comes home. We'll have the extra room in our new home. You know; the one we were going to give my mother."

"Let's see what she wants to do. She has a place with any of us."

"Tomorrow, we'll go to church and say a prayer for her." Cory took his last sip of wine.

"By the way, Mom, why did you call Mr. Greco a criminal?" Rita asked, returning to her mother's remark.

"There was a huge bust at their home about a week ago. They found mafia bosses at his house, including a couple of murderers. Everyone's talking about the arrests."

"Why did they go to the house in the first place? Was there something going on or too much noise from a party?"

Cory cut in. "There had been a going away party for Cathy leaving for Paris for a modeling position for Gabrielle Bonheur."

"Gabrielle Bonheur!"

Cory shook his head. "Tony Greco's the most powerful man around, not only in the Cape Cod area but more in New York and Detroit. They played his actions down with his position in the Senate. I'm sure the job will be gone."

"So, tell me more about the arrests. Did they take Mr. Greco in with the others?"

"We still have the newspaper article somewhere in the living room. I'll go get it." Judy pushed her chair back from the table to get up.

I looked at Todd and he seemed upset with this bad event being brought up again.

Cory continued. "In fact, your brother was there that night."

"You were? How come you never brought the subject up driving home?"

"I figured there would be a huge possibility of the topic being brought up here tonight, so I let the story slide. Besides, I never saw anyone there except the guests who attended."

"How did you get invited to Cathy's going away party without Jenny?"

"I wasn't. Mr. Greco wanted Dad to give him a quote on shrubs in the back, which led to a new barn for heifers. Dad was tied-up with work, so he sent me. Lucky me! Jenny was taking care of her mom."

"Did you see the police come?"

"Police!" Judy was still shocked. "Try the FBI."

"Are you serious?" Rita poured herself another glass of wine.

Judy slapped the newspaper in front of Rita on the table.

"WOW! Look at the police cars in his driveway. They even show the people being handcuffed."

"Look at the second page." I didn't want her to miss any news.

"Talk about a close-up of Mr. Greco. Is he still in jail?"

Cory got up to grab the front page again. "He's out on bail. Money's no object for him. The others are being held without bail. Why not. Look at their records."

"I leave town and the hottest news happens. What reporter covered the story?" She looked and saw Rick's name. "He finally covered the best story of the year. He had to be thrilled that I was out of town."

"Did you get scared seeing the police and FBI coming in the house, Todd?"

"I left before everything broke out with the raid."

"I'm sure Cathy must have been upset seeing her father being arrested the day before she was going out of the country. Did she say anything to you, Todd?"

"I didn't spend that much time with Cathy. What happened after I left had nothing to do with me."

"I wonder if they'll be questioning everyone who was there. Do you think they'll call you?"

"Asking me questions will be a waste of time. I can't testify to something I didn't see or wasn't even aware was going on with their meeting."

"If you were with Cathy, I hope she'll stick up for you," Rita wondered. "I have confidence that you had nothing to do with the incident.

"Todd had two buddies that were with him, so there are two other witnesses to back him up being in the barn." Cory had confidence with a backup.

"Maybe you should call them, Todd, and get the stories straight just in case," Rita mentioned.

"Why do I get the feeling that I'm the one being questioned? I'd like to drop the subject."

I jumped in. "How could so many wanted criminals and murderers, who are so well-known and wanted by the FBI, be in the company of guests, and no one recognized them?"

"First of all, you have to see them so you can recognize them. I didn't. End of story!"

Todd got up from the table and walked outside.

Rita looked at her parents. "How come he's so sensitive with all this?"

"I guess we have thrown a lot of questions at him. The poor guy was at the wrong place at the wrong time, as they say." Judy started to pick up the dirty dishes off the table and headed toward the kitchen sink.

Rita stood up and wiped her hands with her napkin. "I'm going to talk to him."

I started to help Judy clean up. I knew Rita wanted to be alone with her brother.

****

Rita found Todd sitting on a huge log outback that had been cut down years ago. She sat alongside him and put an arm around his shoulders. Todd was looking down as if he had been defeated. "Are you okay? Did I say something that hurt or upset you?"

"It's not you, Rita."

"You must have something eating at you. Getting this upset with a conversation, and then walking out, isn't like you."

"I want to share something with you, but at the same time, I don't want to involve you."

"We have always shared everything that happened to us."

Todd put his head into his hands and bent down crying.

Rita never saw Todd this emotional. She got on her knees in front of him and took his hands, "What is it, Todd?"

"Rita, I did something absolutely insane. It's even hard to tell you, but it's eating at me to the point of being sick. Let's walk down to the lake. I don't want anyone to see us."

Rita held his hand, and they walked down the path.

"If Jenny asks why we were here, tell her you wanted to talk about Kathleen. See. Already, I'm asking you to lie for me."

"Todd, what happened at Cathy's? Did you see the men? Did you know they were there?"

"It has nothing to do with the men. It has to do with Cathy."

"Cathy?"

"I went there to get a quote for Dad. After Mr. Greco and I came to a decision on the work, he asked me to come to the house since a party was going on for Cathy. I wasn't comfortable going and felt it would be a mistake. Little did I know how much. No one says no to Tony Greco.

"I walked in when Cathy was coming down the stairs. She was gorgeous, Rita. I hate saying it, but she was. I couldn't take my eyes off her. She stared me down until she got to the bottom step. Without any shame, she came directly over to me in front of everyone and kissed me. I mean a long, hard kiss."

"She loves wrapping those octopus' arms around men, doesn't she?"

"Rita, I got so turned on, but I walked away from her. Waitresses were passing liquor out one after another. I knew I had too many. I walked out the backdoor."

Todd took a moment and looked into Rita's eyes. "I knew if I didn't leave, I was going to do something stupid. I was intoxicated. I haven't got drunk like that since graduating from high school. I started to leave and was going to Dad's truck when Cathy stopped me outside and pushed me into the barn. She became physical by touching me all over and put my hands on her breasts and other places."

Rita looked at her brother without moving a muscle or blinking an eye.

"Once I got to the point of being absolutely inebriated, I wanted to have her. Not from love. I had been turned on from the beginning."

He looked at his sister. Her expression showed the shock of knowing what she heard.

"Say something. I'm feeling bad enough without you not talking to me."

"Were you out of your mind? Your actions are going to have a disastrous effect on Jenny."

"I love Jenny with all my heart. I'm sick that I did this out of lust from being drunk. I don't want a thing to do with Cathy ever again. I'm glad she left for Paris. I'm sure she'll find another man to grab on to who will most likely belong to another woman."

"I gather you haven't told Jenny."

"Told Jenny! Are you crazy? How do I do that? This would crush her, and she'll end our marriage plans. I can't lose her!"

"Todd, women who are in love swallow a lot of pain from a man hurting them, especially cheating. Jenny might forgive you, but I'm sure she won't forget. If you tell her now, you won't have to live in fear that Cathy can threaten you with this anytime. Don't let one lie lead to another, or no one will believe you when you're telling the truth.

"I have no doubt how much Jenny loves you, but living with deceit is worse than telling the truth. If you two broke up, our family would be crushed. We love both of you. I know the love you have for her, but Jenny has to be told."

"You want me to tell Jenny that I cheated with Cathy on top of her losing family members in two weeks? Now, she'll have added hurt and pain."

"You have a point, but honesty is the best move. Otherwise, Cathy's in control."

"To make things worse, Jenny and I made love a few months ago for the first time. Now, I had this sexual encounter with Cathy. It was beautiful and loving with Jenny. How do I explain my actions? I can't make sense out of them myself."

"You and I find answers for each other. This is a mess, Todd. I think you're living in hopes that Cathy keeps her mouth shut, but we both know she's a witch. You should come clean with Jenny. Confess this cheating before you say your marriage vows."

"What if I lose her? I'd rather die than live without her. I mean that,

Rita. I'm torturing myself over my bad choice. No one can hate me more than I do. I'd do anything to take that moment back. I get sick thinking that I gave into Cathy. I wish I could blame Dad for not going in my place. I even asked Jenny to come with me, but she couldn't leave her mother who was sick."

Todd broke down with hard sobs. "Oh, God, what have I done?"

Feeling bad for her brother, Rita held him in her arms.

"We better get back to the house before someone comes looking for us. Since we haven't been together for a long time, we'll say that we wanted to talk about everything I covered in Detroit."

"Here goes our first lie."

"It's up to you, Todd, on telling Jenny. This was your decision. Like it or not, you have to pay for your actions. I wish you could hide it, but telling Jenny after taking your marriage vows, will be worse. You can't start a marriage out with hidden secrets. Cathy's not one to protect you. I wouldn't put it past her to have done this purposely.

Introduction to Faith

While everyone was eating breakfast, the phone rang. Todd was standing next to the receiver and picked it up.

"Hello? Hi, Sam. How are you?"

"Good. I wanted to make sure everyone was going to be home for Faith and me to drop by tomorrow."

"Tomorrow, we're having the wake and funeral for Jenny's mother, aunt, and uncle."

"All three!" I forgot. Rita called me last week and told me about their deaths. Who would think three in a family would pass close together? That's sad, Todd. Weren't you talking about taking Jenny's mother in when you got into your new home?"

"We were in the process of having Dad build an extra bedroom for her. Jenny's in a state of shock."

"Listen; tell Mom and Dad that we'll come tonight. We want to attend the funeral. It's not the greatest time to meet Jenny. I want to know my future sister-in-law, and this will give me time to introduce Faith."

"We're both gaining a sister-in-law. Are you happy, Sam?"

"You're going to love her, Todd. She's so sweet and a family person. Her parents own a horseracing farm in Kentucky. I've met them, and I know Dad and Mom will love Faith and her family."

"Can we plan on you for supper? Say, around five?"

"That's good. Tell Mom and Dad, I'm looking forward to them meeting Faith."

"Will do. See you then. Drive carefully."

"Who was that?" Judy asked. Her hands were holding a load of clothes in a large basket coming from the laundry room to hang outside.

"It's Sam. They're coming tonight and staying over for the funeral services."

"How wonderful. It'll be a sad day, but on the other hand, Jenny will be meeting another part of our family. The two future sisters-in-law's can talk and get to know each other."

"Did I hear the phone ring?" Cory asked. He came into the kitchen from cutting the shrubs out front. He noticed the big laundry basket in Judy's hands with clothes overlapping. "Looks like you were busy." He picked the load up to bring it outside to the clothesline.

I walked into the kitchen. I slept later than usual. "What's everyone doing today?"

"I washed clothes."

"I should have helped you, Mrs. Costa."

"It's more important you get your rest for the funeral tomorrow.

By the way, Corey, I had to use the washboard because there's a problem with the wringer."

"I'll look into it."

"Today, Sam's coming home, and he's bringing Faith. They plan on attending the funeral."

"I can't wait to meet her. Maybe I can ask her to be my bridesmaid. Kathleen won't be home in time."

"What a good idea." Judy perked right up.

"I'll help you hang the clothes on the clothesline. I want something to do." I followed behind her.

****

The day was spent with me helping the family selling the flowers and vegetables from their stand. The time went fast, and I helped Judy get supper ready.

Honk. Honk.

"Who's making all that noise?" Todd looked out the kitchen window. "It's Sam and Faith."

"Wow! Look at his car." Todd's eyes lit-up.

He ran out the front door to greet his brother, who he hadn't seen for four years.

Sam opened the car door and hugged Todd. "Long time since we saw each other."

"It's your fault. You had to go to college. Trying to show me up?"

Sam was a muscular man at twenty-six years old. He was tall with dark brown, tight curly hair that hung down his face. He wore a gold, weaved, straw boater hat with a wide, black ribbon around the rim. He looked the part of an Ivy League college boy.

"Let me introduce Faith." Sam ran around the passenger side to open her door.

"Faith, this is my brother Todd."

She was a slandered woman with beautiful, ash brown, wavy hair, halfway to her shoulders, parted down the center. Faith wore a pink dress with a black, spotted design throughout. The front had a high V-neck, closed with a large white and blue flower pin.

"Hello, Todd. Nice to meet you."

Todd went over to hug her, followed by a light kiss on the check. "Hi, Faith. Welcome to our mad-house."

Her voice was sexy with an accent.

"Where're you originally from, Faith?" Todd asked.

"I was born in Kentucky, but my father had a job in Sweden for ten years, when I was a young child. I guess I picked up their drawl. I'm trying to shake it." She laughed.

"No. Don't change. I could listen to you talk all day. Did you fall in love with her accent, Sam, or her?"

"When I saw her in the library, I was blown away before she said one word. I knew I had to meet her." The three of them chuckled.

Todd walked around Sam's car. "You have got to be doing something right. What's this; a 1931 Auburn Model 8-98 Brougham Chassis?"

"Pretty sharp, huh? It's a 4-door, 5 passengers. It's a large roomy car. The rear door's wide allowing the passengers sitting in the back to enter without disturbing those in front. I hated those two-door cars. It's also an eight-cylinder."

"This is sharp." Todd examined every inch of the car. "Can I ask what you paid?"

"It was $1,395."

"What! Are you crazy spending that much? How are you going to pay for it?"

"I've had a part-time job at the campus for four years running the school newspaper. They pay well. I'll give you a ride after we eat. First, I want Mom and Dad to meet Faith."

They walked up to the front porch steps, and Judy and Cory were standing in the open doorway.

Sam kissed his mother and gave a bear hug to his father with a firm hold. "Boy, have I missed all of you."

"You look mature, son. I guess college agrees with you."

Sam turned back and took Faith's hand. Mom...Dad, this is Faith.

"We finally got to meet." Judy gave her a warm squeeze.

Cory was next to give her a gentle embrace. "Let's go inside and relax.

Rita came running down the stairs missing a few steps and jumped into Sam's arms.

Her kisses landed all over his face. "Oh, I've missed you."

"I wasn't sure if you were going to kiss or attack me."

Stepping out of his grip, she walked over to Faith. "Hello. I'm Rita. I might not have given you a good first impression. This is a normal greeting when he has been gone way too long."

"It wonderful to meet you, Rita."

Todd went into the kitchen. "Jenny, Sam and Faith are here. I'd like you to come into the living room."

"Already? Let me wipe my hands."

Todd gave me a kiss. "You're going to be fine, Jenny. Relax."

Before they left the room, everyone walked into the kitchen and sat at the table. They could smell the coffee that Judy had already started brewing.

"Coffee smells good." Todd walked over to check to see if the brew was ready.

"Give it five more minutes," his mother stated.

Todd brought me over to meet Sam and Faith.

"Hello, Jenny. We're both sorry for your losses." Sam gave me an embrace.

Faith took me in her arms. "I'm glad to finally meet you."

"Glad you both came."

Sam hit Todd on his back. "It's not that long and you'll be walking down the aisle."

"It'll be the best day of my life. It can't come soon enough." Todd put his arm around me and pulled me into his side.

Judy put the cups out on the table along with the creamer and sugar bowl. She carried over club sandwiches on a large platter. She had prepared them ahead.

"Okay. Let's sit down and enjoy," Judy said.

Conversation flowed for an hour getting to know Faith and hear about Sam getting his Masters.

After the family ate, the girls started to help Judy clear the kitchen table. Dishes were washed, dried, and put away in the cabinets.

"Let's go out to the front porch and bring your coffee. Jenny here's your hot tea. Anyone want some?"

"I think I will," Rita replied.

They all grabbed their drinks and headed out the screen door to the porch. Sam and Faith went to the swing, holding hands. The others filled the two antique wicker sets consisting of one sofa and two lounge chairs. Todd and Sam bought them for their parent's 25th wedding anniversary that was coming up soon.

"This is a wonderful spot," Faith said looking around the farm. It reminds me of our horse farm in Lexington, Kentucky with the barns. I could never live in the city."

"We have all been brought up on this farm and worked hard. It's good to be back from Detroit," Rita said with relief.

Everyone was enjoying the fresh, summer, night breeze. They talked and laughed the night away getting to know each other.

Rita's Secret Man

Saturday night the Costa's sat at the supper table making plans for our wedding in October. We knew the season would make a beautiful wedding day.

"Jenny, we'd want to make sure you're comfortable with the wedding plans. After the ceremony at the chapel, we could take wonderful pictures. The flowers will still be in full bloom." I could see Cory wanted to be involved.

"I can pitch in to help, Mom," Todd replied.

"With all that planned, we can start outlining what flowers to use for the church and tables in the barn. It would be fun," Rita said.

"We need to talk about the gowns." Judy wanted everyone's attention.

Rita jumped in. "I forgot about the dresses. That's the exciting part. Why don't we plan to look for your wedding dress in a few weeks, Jenny?"

"That sounds like fun with all of us together," I answered.

Judy put her arm around me. "How selfish of me talking like I'm your mother. " I'm not trying to take her place. Cory and I love you like a daughter."

"I know you do. I couldn't wait for my mother to see us get married. It's wonderful having all of you." I fought back tears.

Rita stood up from her chair. "Okay, these plans are supposed to be happy."

"That's right, Todd said. We should think of happy thoughts about our special day coming. Monday, you girls take off for the day, and the guys will get things done around here."

Rita spoke up, "I'm going to grab Jenny for girl-talk."

We both got up and walked out to the front porch, and I headed for the swing. She grabbed my hand. "I'd like to go for a walk down the path toward the pond."

As we walked down the dirt road, Rita started the conversation. "There are a lot of people who have to travel far and wide to get to the sun, sand, and saltwater. We take Chatham and the surrounding towns down Cape Cod for granted living here.

"I remember as young kids my parents took us to the Bourne Bridge. At the time, it was a drawbridge that had to be pulled when a boat went through. That's where Dad taught Todd and me how to fish. We caught some big fish. We stood off the jetty, and Mom would be sitting on the blanket taking food out of her famous basket when we all got hungry, which didn't take long. I never knew there was a bottom to that wicker container of hers. Where did those years go?"

"I love this area myself. I can't imagine living anywhere else. I'd hate to move away, wouldn't you, Rita?'

"When we have lived in one spot a long time, I don't think anyone wants to move, unless they have bad memories or a job change."

"I can't believe your parents are building a house for Todd and me. We're so lucky. The area in the woods is so peaceful and quiet. What a great location to bring up our family."

We walked until we came to the pond on the other side of where our home would be standing.

"I never came to this side of your property before," I remarked.

"There are a lot of paths through these woods. We have traveled through them in our younger days. Todd, Sam, and I cleared them when we found out they led us to different areas."

"Are you planning on moving out of your parent's home, Rita?"

"I'd like to be on my own, but women are supposed to stay home until they marry. I've been looking around for a place for a few months."

"Do you think you'll marry? I never saw you with anyone or heard you talk about a special man."

"I dated Frankie long enough with no proposal. On my travels, I met another man."

"What happened?"

"He's married."

"Rita, you don't want to get involved with a man who offers no future."

"He's not in love with his wife."

"They all make you think that. You're too smart to be taken in with him."

"The sad part is, Jenny, I love him. I feel alive with him. I block the fact out that he might be seeing other women."

"How can you waste your time with him? Honestly."

"We can't help who we fall for, Jenny."

"Yes, we can. We have choices. You don't want to give him up so you use excuses for the relationship. I love you." I put my hand on her arm. "Don't throw your life away. There are too many good and available men out there. You must be around them day in and day out with your job."

"If this was you, Jenny, I'd be saying the same things. I tried three times leaving him."

"Don't go where he's going. It's that simple."

"You can't understand because you have Todd. I'm not that lucky."

"But you're worth more than being used. A married man having different women brings him excitement with a variety of sex partners. That's it. Nothing more. Don't make the situation out to be what you want it to become. Men who have multiple partners get bored with one woman.

"I'll never marry, Jenny."

"Don't feel that way. You have so much to offer a man. Someone's out there who can love you back and give you a family.'"

"It won't be the end of the world if I stay single. You don't miss what you don't have."

"You're right, but think of what you *can* have. I'd hate to die knowing I left no one behind to say that I was here."

"All that's important, Jenny, is that we live our lives loving and doing good things for others. God gives us life on earth and calls us home when our time's up. It doesn't mean we have to get married."

"Do you know the sin you're living in? How will God bless you sleeping with a married man who wants nothing else from you? Are you really that desperate?"

"Jenny, I don't want to get mad at you, but unless you're in my shoes, you wouldn't understand."

"I wouldn't want to be in your situation, because it's wrong. There's not one good reason your actions with him are right. Not one. Rita, he's not yours to have. He gave his vows to someone else."

I didn't want to tell Rita that I sinned with her brother. Todd made love to me after we swam in this very lake in front of us. My first sexual encounter with a man and I never knew how loving intimacy could be between two people.

"I want to change the subject," Rita replied. "I don't think I should have told you. I wanted to share this confusion with you because we always had that comfort to discuss anything."

I looked over at her. "I don't want us to stop being close. Disagreeing doesn't mean I don't love you. It shows I do. If I didn't care, why would I worry about your actions? It sounds like you want me to agree with you. Is that your only way for us to stay close? A lot of events affect relationships with others, and I don't want that to happen to us."

"Nothing will ever come between our friendship. Deep down I know you're right. I should leave him because I know it's wrong, but at the same time, I have feelings for him."

"I think you're mixing love with lust. If you were with him every day, you would see the bad side of him. Everyone shows their good side for a few hours. I'll tell you what. When you go to bed tonight, take a pad of paper and a pen upstairs and seriously write the good and bad about the relationship. Keep doing it for six months. Write about what you felt with each meeting. Then look to see which side is longer. Be honest with yourself."

"Maybe I'll do that." Rita smiled and hugged me. "I love you."

"I love you, too."

"Jenny, I'm so happy you and Todd are getting married. We have been close since high school. I'm glad you and he met. I saw the sparks fly between you two."

"So am I. He has brought more joy and love in my life. Look at your family I'm getting. I'm sad about losing my mother. She'll always be in my heart."

"I know she'll be looking down at you during your vows, Jenny."

"That's why I want to bury my family together at the cemetery behind the church. We'll get married in that beautiful chapel, and I'll feel them there."

"Todd loves you more than anything. Don't ever doubt his love."

"Why would I, Rita? He's good to me."

"Remember men are weak."

"Why would you say that to me?"

"Because I don't want you to put him on a pedestal. Too often, we expect the person to be perfect."

"He's perfect for me." I smiled.

The Funeral

"Is everyone ready to leave this morning? It's 9:30," Judy announced, finishing the breakfast dishes.

"I just need my pocketbook," Rita said. She drank the last drop of her coffee before washing the cup in the sink.

I got into the family car and we headed for the small chapel.

Fr. Rick walked out from the chapel and down the front stairs to greet us. "We're going to be celebrating the life of your family, Jenny."

The church was filled with friends of the Costa family, mine, and the Perry's.' Multiple flower arrangements sent a strong fragrance throughout the walls.

Fr. Rick walked onto the altar. "The Nickerson Funeral Home has arrived with the three caskets. Could you all stand please?"

I tried to brace myself while three coffins were rolled down the aisle to the front. Todd held my hand.

Tears couldn't be held back. One death was bad enough, but three wonderful, loving people from my family were being put to rest at the same time.

Fr. Rick gave a heartwarming eulogy individually. He knew them all and spoke from the heart about the good traits with each one. When he finished, he came down giving his sincere sympathy for my loss.

Pallbearers from the Nickerson Funeral Home rolled the three caskets out the side door of the church to the cemetery. The plots were already dug with a green rug covering the holes. There were chairs for the family members. Fr. Rick continued to give the last blessing with everyone crowded behind me.

We watched as the sand was thrown over the caskets. I kept trying to convince myself that they were dead and not aware of being buried. It was too emotional to witness such actions. Once they stopped, all the flowers from the church were laid on the graves.

Fr. Rick announced the burial arrangements. "The headstones will be ready in a month. If you come back the stones will be up. I want to thank Jenny for deciding on the funeral and burial to be held at St. Therese The Little Flower Chapel. Having her loved ones buried in this cemetery may bring this location alive again with parishioners. I have sent a letter to Bishop William Fredrick to rethink about me opening the chapel for regular Masses on Sundays.

"Let us all keep Kathleen Perry in our prayers for a full recovery. It's a shame she couldn't be here to say goodbye to her parents." He then turned to everyone. "The ceremony is over."

Cory stood up. "Our family would like to extend an invitation to everyone to join us for a light brunch at our barn."

****

Three twelve-foot brunch tables were decorated with centerpieces of seasonal flowers. Clear plastic cups were filled with apple and orange juice that had been placed alongside the hot coffee and tea.

Judy's homemade blueberry muffins were wrapped in a red and blue plaid towel placed in her large wicker basket. She served her outstanding apple pancakes and French toast with homemade strawberry syrup on the side. Scrambled eggs, bacon, and homemade bread, along with Anchovy & Chutney Rolls, Black Bean Soup, Sautéed Kidneys, and Indian Rice were added to the table. A large bowl was stocked with fresh cut-up strawberries, red grapes, cantaloupe, and blueberries. Four homemade pound cakes were sliced. The caterers made an orange Jell-O ring filled with peaches.

Neighbors looked amazed at the table full of food. Most likely, many didn't have this much in a month. They didn't realize that the Costas made every single ration placed in front of them from their gardens and fields.

The night before the funeral, in the early morning hours, Cory had killed and skinned one of their calves. He prepared the meat by rubbing it down with olive oil and salt. He then seasoned the cut with additional salt, pepper, garlic, rosemary, and wrapped the meat in a foil to simmer slowly in their oven.

He had the veal at a warm temperature in the oven. Once he brought the tenderized, seasoned meat out and placed it on a large cutting board, the first slice brought the juices flowing. Usually, this was a special cut of meat saved only for an exceptional event. Cory felt this was one of those days.

When everyone was seated, Fr. Rick blessed the food and gave a small prayer. "God, we ask you to bless this food Cory and Judy have arranged while others are struggling. Bless the caterers who are serving this delicious meal. Bring peace to Jenny and Kathleen with the loss of their parents. Welcome, Mary, Dorothy, and Joe into your Kingdom. Amen."

Everyone couldn't get enough in with the conversations on who was doing what and the event of our wedding coming up in October. The women welcomed Faith into their group. Faith told stories about her family moving to Sweden for her father's job and raising thoroughbred horses in Lexington, Kentucky. I talked about the disappointment of Kathleen not being able to meet with David Selznick from the MGM Studios."

"Kathleen never mentioned something so terrific," Judy said.

"Mr. Selznick wanted to interview her for a part in one of his upcoming movies next year."

"What a horrible thing to have happened to her with this opportunity," Rita replied.

Fr. Rick was about to leave and came up to the family. "Don't let this be a sad event. Great times are coming up. Todd and Jenny are getting married in the beautiful chapel. Cory informed me that their reception will be in his barn. Many things to look forward to this fall. I'm sure Jenny and Rita will bring Kathleen to her parent's resting place when she's home. Let's think of today as an important time together with shared losses and renewed friendships."

Father gave a last blessing to the group before leaving.

I was blessed to have God send me to Judy and Cory's family. They were going to be wonderful in-laws.

Women's Day Out

Monday morning came and the four women were up at six to eat breakfast and get ready to spend the day shopping for gowns.

Rita drove her car, and the four of us giggled with the energized reality that Todd and I were not far from our wedding day. She drove to the center of Orleans to the famous Cape Cod Bridal Shop.

Once we got in the store, each one ran up to the formalwear grabbing different styles of gowns. I spotted a gown with absolute elegance. The material was weightless tulle and metallic embroidered lace sheath. Swarovski crystals and beading accent the sweetheart neckline, adding whimsy and romance lacing on the short sleeves and back. It was finished with crystal buttons over the zipper closure. A detachable velvet ribbon belt was attached.

"Rita, look at this wedding dress!" I held the dress with a glow in my eyes. "I think this is the one."

Judy came over with one in her hand. After seeing what I picked, she returned hers to the stock. "Jenny, try on the gown for us to see."

The three of them sat waiting for me to showcase my dress. The store saleswoman took me outback. I walked out watching the expression on each one.

Faith looked at me without blinking. "You look absolutely beautiful. I'd love to look like that on my wedding day."

"I have the perfect headpiece for you. It's gorgeous!" The saleswoman remarked. She took the box off the shelf. She opened it and placed the piece on my head. "The ivory pearl and Czech rhinestones on the white velvet ribbon headband matches your wedding gown. Do you like it?"

"I love it. The headpiece matches my dress perfectly."

"Now you need shoes. Wait here. What size are you?"

"I'm a six."

Within a few minutes, the woman returned with an open shoebox. "Here we are. There were satin rhinestone and glass seed beads on the whole back of the white satin shoes, coming about a few inches to the side. It followed with peep toes.

I slipped into them. They fit like a glove. I twirled around and around looking in the full-length mirror. "I feel like a princess. I hope Todd will be blown away watching me walk toward him."

"How can he not be?" Judy put her arms around me. "You look gorgeous!"

"Okay, enough with Jenny. I'm the maid-of-honor. I have to shine." Rita ran back to the rack.

I went back to take my gown off and put the dress aside with the store manager.

"If you don't lose or gain any weight, there won't be a need to adjust one thing," she remarked.

I went out front to help with the search for Rita's dress. There were many to choose from on the stand.

Rita's eye went to the powder-blue dress mixed in tightly with the others. She pulled the dress out and gave a deep sigh. "Yes."

"What did you find?" Faith ran to see what she picked.

"It's from the designer, Nataya."

The dress was a delicate embroidered blue tulle dress. It had a deeper blue cotton muslin and a tea-length tiered hem with a beautiful gathered design. A sweetheart neckline met with delicate white dotted sleeves and a sinuously shaped A-line silhouette, complete with sweet rosettes. The blue satin wide belt had two white roses on each side of the tie. There were three layers falling down over each other to the end of the dress.

"I have got to try this one on before someone else grabs it." Rita ran into the dressing room.

"Okay, now I need one to offset Rita's blue," Faith said.

Judy held one in her hand. "This is lovely for the mother-of-the-groom," she said softly. The dress was an alluring dusty sand shade of romantic embroidered tulle and soft muslin. The sweeping layers offset with see-through-three-quarter length sleeves with the same embroidered tulle design, and a scalloped v-neckline, while the delicate sheer overlay rendered a radiant and vivaciously vintage style. The unattached muslin was hemmed with gathered tulle and a classic empire waist lined with lovely lace and cinched at the waist with a concealed side zipper.

"What a great choice," I said as I examined the dress. "That will be so feminine on you, Mrs. Costa."

"You like it?"

"I love it." I ran my fingers gently down the gown.

"My turn to try one."

"Faith? Where are you?" I yelled.

"I'm behind the second rack by the window wall."

"Find anything?"

"Not yet."

"What a pretty mauve color in this dress, Faith."

"Let me see." Faith held the dress up. "Where did you find this one?"

"At the end of the rack."

"It's by the same designer, Nataya, as Rita's."

The famed powder mauve Great Gatsby dress had a delicate airy look.

"It looks comfortable with no belt. The style looks to be designed to conform beautifully to the body."

The dress consisted of flexible chiffon upper and cotton under-dress. The gown was topped off with the same powder mauve off-center, a large rose that tied the two sides together with ruffles going down the sides to about five inches longer than the dress.

"You should try this one, Faith."

"Yeah. You like it."

"Put it on and let's see how it looks."

"Okay. I'll be right out."

I sat down and watched each one march in front of me all dressed up. Every dress fit the women like they were made for them. Within an hour and a half, all four of us had our dresses, shoes, and hats. All we had to do was pick them up a week before.

There was no doubt in my mind that my wedding dress was perfect. I couldn't wait to watch Todd's eyes as I came closer to him with each step. I was going to shine, and this was going to be my day. All my dreams would be filled by becoming Todd's wife. That was all I had lived for with every passing day.

House Near Completion

Todd worked at the flower stand, while Cory and Sam met Bob and Ray, to work on their new home.

The four men pulled up to the house, and Sam's eyes widened. "Wow, Dad! This is going to be beautiful! You have the whole place completed."

They walked into the house and Sam studied each room. The walls were already up and wallpapered. The oversized living room looked rich with the brown and yellow-flowered wallpaper with an off-white background.

Going into the kitchen, the room only needed the appliances. The main bedroom wallpaper was a reminder of where the house was built with soft pink flowers with hidden soft green and brown trees around a lake scene on a tan background.

"I could look at this paper all day, Dad. Good choice."

Sam was surprised to see the bathroom decorated with huge yellow and white flowers combined with a deep maroon background. He studied the wall.

"You don't like it?" Cory asked. His son looked around the room a few times.

"The more I look at the wallpaper, the prettier the print gets. It shocked me at first with the deep maroon."

"Let me show you the two other bedrooms."

The second bedroom was wallpapered with multiple cream-colored blossoms with an inner core of deep brown buds and a background of a tiny, thin striped design of tan.

The third and last bedroom had bright white, red, and yellow flowers raising vines on a golden lattice with a light beige background.

Sam looked at Cory. "This is different. Not something for a bedroom, yet, makes you feel alive."

"It was supposed to be Jenny's mother's bedroom. This wasn't what we picked out for wallpaper for her. She was going to live with them.

"What a shame, Dad."

"I had a reason for making this room busier. Rita told me that Jenny loves to draw and paint. She said Jenny did some great pictures in school for art classes. She won trophies numerous times for her work."

"She never talked about it, huh?"

"No. Rita brought her talent up. In fact, I'm not sure if Todd knows that side of Jenny."

"I think she's going to love this room."

Sam looked in the far corner and saw all the acrylic painting supplies set-up on shelves. He walked over to them. There he noticed paintbrushes, canvas, wood, palette, cleaning soap, varnish, easels, aprons, palette knife, scraping tools, sponges, toothpicks, masking tape, pencils, and charcoal.

"How did you know what she needed?"

"Your mother and I took a rare day to ourselves and drove downtown, and we went into an art studio. The artist told us what Jenny would need to start. I guess we both got carried away with supplies.

"I can't wait to see her expression when she walks into this room. It'll be worth every penny spent on her. Jenny's going to make a wonderful wife for Todd. He's nuts about her. She's all he talks about when we work together.

"You hardly have anything left to do here."

Bob walked over to them. "Ray and I are picking up the stove, refrigerator, and a washing machine today. I bet you didn't see the small room off the kitchen. She will have her own laundry space. Come on, we'll show you."

They walked into a large room. "In this corner, we're putting a Maytag washing machine. The top of the line. The side door is for her to walk right out to the clothesline that Ray will put up today. The six-foot table is for her to lay the clothes on when she brings them in from outside. Jenny will also have a laundry bag and a basket to bring the clothes out."

Cory brought them back into the kitchen. "We are putting a Tappan Gas Range with a GE Thrifty Six Fridge in this corner. Under the kitchen double-window, we're adding a refinished farm sink. It's a 42" cast-iron drain board. It'll be made of high-back porcelain. We ordered the basin with a large faucet and drain tops on each side of the washbowl."

"Today, our goal is for all of us to get the wrap-around porch on the house," Ray said, getting his hammer. "Bob and I are buying them a 6-foot swing that's a three-seater with a chain on both sides. We'll put that on when the porch is completed. Every time you look for both of them, they're outside on the swing at home. We heard that Jenny had one at her parent's home."

"Faith and I came up with a great wedding gift. We want to give them a Philco radio with a built-in Ariel tuning system with ultra-high fidelity, and the unit is able to pick up stations from countries around the world and police, air, and shipping. That should keep Todd entertained."

"By next week, the whole inside will be done," Cory said. Todd mentioned that he and Jenny will be picking out their furniture next week. He has been putting money aside for the past year.

"When you and Faith get married, I'll let you decide on the house style you want, and I have another lot on the other side of the lake that could be just as nice. You can wave to each other." They laughed.

"You were smart making all the extra bedrooms big so they won't have to move because of family growth."

"I hope you and Todd give us many grandkids, especially boys. I'd love to know our name carries on with the Costa family."

"It'll be awhile for us, Dad. Faith has to get settled into her work to be secure before a family. Once we are, I'm sure she'll want them. I need a place big enough with land for an animal hospital so the farm animals can roam after healing.

"You and Mom were smart buying all the animals before the depression hit us. We lost the Williams, Bentley's, Silva's, and too many to name. The poor families couldn't find work or afford food."

"The Lord was with us, Sam. He blessed us with the ability to have something left for all of you if something happens to your mother or me."

Sam tapped his father on the back. "You have a long time left with us, Dad. Don't think that way. Let's get going on this house. We can get this porch up in a day with the four of us working hard. After that, all it will need is the outside paint."

Sam took another look out the kitchen window. "Jenny will love checking out the views from this window facing the lake. What a sight! Dad, this is breathtaking. I can picture Faith and me living here."

"I'll let you decide on the paint for the outside. Let's go look at the exterior." They stood studying the section of the house. "What color do you think would be nice?"

Sam stepped back rubbing his chin. "I can see a light-blue that almost looks gray with cream trim. The color will keep the house hidden without standing out in the woods."

They joined Bob and Ray who were putting up the boards for the porch. For the rest of the day, all that could be heard faintly through the backwoods were hammers and lumber falling in place.

****

Sam and Faith were gathering their overnight bag to go back to Bourne to their college dorms.

"I really have enjoyed myself. It was wonderful meeting all of you." Faith hugged Judy.

"It was a wonderful day helping Jenny pick her wedding dress out. We don't have to run around the last minute. We look forward to meeting your parents at Jenny's wedding. If you can get the time off, why don't you stay a week after the wedding? In fact, Faith, two weeks would give you and your parents time to see important locations in the Cape Cod area."

"Where will you put us all up?" Sam asked.

"We'll have two empty rooms after Todd and Jenny get married. You and Faith can have a separate one. We have that spare room that's rarely used. Faith's parents can use that one. It's a good excuse for me to work on decorating the room and making everything comfortable for them. I can't tell you how long I've been wanting to tackle that job. This will make me start straightening the space."

Cory gave his son a strong hug and a kiss. Showing affection with his children was a natural thing for him.

Rita came in with her coffee after spending time relaxing on the swing. "It was fantastic having time with Faith."

"What about me?" Sam picked his sister up off the floor.

"Careful, I have coffee in my hand."

"I think you're next coming home with a special guy."

"Don't hold your breath," Rita said with a grin."

"The older you get, you'll be known as *Chatham's old maid*," Sam said tickling her.

"If she doesn't marry, she can be our babysitter when the kids start coming," Todd yelled coming down the stairs.

Sam hugged Todd and then slapped his brother on the back. "I'm happy for you two. Will you be going on a honeymoon?"

"No. I think Jenny's going to be in heaven going into our new house. We're going next week to pick out our furniture."

"I'm getting butterflies just thinking about it." I entered the hall coming out from doing dishes with a kitchen towel on my shoulder. "I want to thank you both for coming to the funeral. It was nice having your support." I spread my arms and hugged them both at the same time.

"We're truly sorry for your loss, Jenny." Faith gave me a kiss.

"Okay, I think we're set. Anymore kisses?" Sam looked at his mother."

"I think you forgot me," Judy said.

"How could I forget you? I saved the best for last." He gave her a peck on the cheek.

Everyone stood on the front porch waving as Sam and Faith drove up the driveway towards the main road.

****

"I love your family, Sam. It was an awful way to have met them with a funeral, but I think Jenny liked the commotion every day."

"I have to admit since I left for college, I didn't realize the importance of family days. Those four years were busy with my studies. I want to move in with my parents if you're comfortable with the idea?"

"I think we should. Our savings can grow faster being with them.

"When we visit again, Todd and Jenny will be husband and wife. How exciting. Wait until you see her dressed up, Sam. Jenny was absolutely breathtaking. I hope I look as good as she does when our time comes."

He held her hand on the seat as he drove. "I have no doubt you'll be gorgeous, my love."

She smiled. "I love you, Samuel."

"Wow, that's serious when you call me Samuel!"

"Better believe it. Why are we going down to the chapel again?"

"I want to show you Todd and Jenny's home. I worked at the house today with my dad, Bob, and Ray. We put the whole wrap-a-round porch up in hours. How I wish this was ours, Faith."

He passed the chapel and went down further towards Lover's Lake.

"What a beautiful area. How come we didn't ride down after the funeral?"

"Dad wants to keep the house as a surprise for Todd and Jenny. Otherwise, we would have driven down."

"Look at this lake!" Faith sat up straight to take the whole view in.

"This is Lover's Lake, Faith. I can see why."

"What a name?"

"Hold on. You haven't seen the best yet."

Sam drove deeper into the woods down a long dirt road and turned up a steep hill. They came directly to the house. Faith's eyes widened as she saw the home.

"Come on." He grabbed her hand. "I can't wait to show you."

Sam took her to the front that faced Lover's Lake. The house sat on a location that was higher than the tall trees in the forest and had a full view of the water. "Cory, Bob, and Ray had spent a month clearing the trees away with my father's truck to get this magnificent sight."

"This is remarkable. This place must have fallen out of heaven, Sam."

"You like the area?"

"How could I not? We have to take my parents here."

"Wait until a few weeks when the foliage comes with all the leaves turning color. We have to take pictures on our next visit.

"My father said when we marry he's going to give us a piece of land on the other side of the lake."

"Really! Oh, Sam, what a wonderful gift."

"We'll have enough land to have space for the animals you want with the hospital."

He turned and faced her. "I was going to surprise you, but I would have burst if I didn't tell you. Faith, it's everything we talked about building. Dad said he has a piece of land for Rita, too, unless she wants the family house passed down to her."

"How did they get all this land?"

"From my father's parents. He bought extra pieces that were aside his lots when they came up for sale. It's taken years, but the forest is coming alive again."

"Let me take you through the house."

"How can you get into the place?"

"Dad gave me an extra set of keys to show you, but I have to give it back to Todd on his wedding day."

Faith had the same expression looking out the kitchen window as Sam when he had faced the lake for the first time. "I would want to do the dishes all day long looking out at this view."

Sam went to the back of her wrapping his arms around her waist while looking at the scenery with her. He took her through every room, and they both fell in love with every inch of the house.

Faith looked around the rooms. "There isn't much left for them to do here."

"The only thing is painting the outside and putting in the appliances. They plan to do that next week. Dad let me pick the color."

"Sam, the radio we want to buy them will be great in this corner of the living room."

"I thought the same thing when Dad took me in here."

Before leaving, they sat on the porch steps looking out at Lover's Lake for a half-hour talking about what they can do when they're given the land on the other side of Todd and Jenny's property. They both agreed on flatland for the house and the animal hospital with hills and valleys for the animals to roam.

Sam kept looking over every inch his eyes could take in to remember the water scene and nature surrounding the home.

"We live in Bourne and never think of traveling this far down the Cape. When we come back, I want to travel through the towns of Dennis, Brewster, Orleans, Eastham, Wellfleet, Turo, right down to Provincetown," Faith said.

"I like that idea. We can take a few extra days to stay in different spots. After all, we'll have no more homework to complete." They laughed and kissed.

They walked to the car and started to pull out of the property, stopping to take one more look back. They both fell in love with the location and couldn't help envying Todd and Jenny for having such a dream home.

Jenny's Secret

Rita and I started to get our clothes together to go to work at the *Nelson News* the next day.

"I have been away from work for a week, and I hate going back."

"How do you think I feel being in Detroit for two months?"

"At least, you were on the go traveling. Your job isn't boring. I sit at a desk all day."

I opened the closet and took out a red, printed dress with a white lace collar. "You like this?" I held the outfit up for Rita to examine.

"Yeah. I like you in bright colors."

"I can't stop thinking of Kathleen being disfigured for life. If she isn't as stunning as before the accident, I don't know how she'll get in the movies."

"Jenny, we have to pray for her."

"It'll be wonderful being with her when she comes home. I'm so lucky, Rita, having your parents help me after losing my mother. What's Kathleen going to do? She lost both her parents. They were wonderful people."

"Funny how things change. One minute you're happy with loved ones all around you and then you're alone. Your loss and Kathleen's happened too close."

I sat on the bed, looking up at Rita, as she held her black skirt and a light-blue blouse in her hands. "I don't know what I'd do if my parents died.

"Rita, don't ever say something like that. It would be horrible. I've come to love them. I couldn't stand losing someone else. I've been thinking. You should be open to someone coming into your life."

"Yeah, but it's who. Men aren't interested in a woman on the go with a career. They want wives home, pregnant, and a babysitter for their kids. Keeping us busy, helps the husbands have all the freedom to go or do anything. Then, there are those who love the idea of a woman on the side coming and going so they can say goodbye to her, return to their wives, until she shows up again. As for you, Jenny, you have a gem of a man, and not because he's my brother."

Without warning, I got a nauseated feeling. It must have shown. Rita looked at me.

"Are you okay, Jenny?"

"No."

Rita threw the clothes on the bed and took my arm.

"How selfish of me. You lost so many loved ones in a month, especially your mom. I don't think any of us gave you a chance to absorb the reality of your losses. Then, we all dragged you around the next day to get your wedding gown. None of us even asked if you were up to the full day. I'm sorry."

"I loved every minute with the family. It's a day I will never forget. We all got to know Faith."

"Well, I'm all organized for the dreadful Monday to return to work. How about you, Jenny?"

"My clothes are hung on the closet door.

Nausea hit me again and I ran for the bathroom throwing up. I came out and flopped into the armchair.

"Jenny, why don't I take you to a doctor? You might have a stomach bug."

"I've been to him."

"Really. What did he say?"

"I'm pregnant."

"You're what!"

"What am I going to do?"

"You can't hide it unless you're lucky not to show when you get married."

"What's Todd going to think?"

"First of all, getting pregnant takes two. I think he had contributed to this event. Second of all, I think Todd will love you more."

"Your parents are going to be disappointed in me."

Rita stood in front of me. "Jenny, my parents are crazy about you. If they hear you're carrying their grandchild, they'll do flip-flops around the kitchen. They won't love you any less. As for me? I'm thrilled. Maybe a baby should not start before the marriage, but you love one another. Since the wedding's close, I'm sure people will think you got pregnant during your honeymoon. I'd love to be there when you tell Dad and Mom."

"Rita, let me handle this. Please. Swear to tell no one. I want to do the announcing, and I have to tell Todd first."

"Okay, when do you think?"

"I don't know. I have to feel the right moment. Maybe Todd and I can go for a walk tomorrow down by the lake."

"Girls, breakfast's ready," Judy yelled from the bottom of the stairs.

"Be right down, Mom. Are you up to eating?"

"Not really, but I don't want anyone figuring out why I'm sick."

We headed down the stairs to the kitchen and joined the family.

After breakfast, everyone went their own way. Todd was going to work at the stand and meet Bob and Ray at the carpentry shop. Rita and I drove to work, while Judy cleaned the kitchen. Cory joined the men.

Plans for a Day Out

Everyone gathered at the kitchen table for supper at the end of the day. Things were quiet until Cory spoke up.

"You know what, Judy?"

"No, what Cory?" She asked in a joking way.

"I have made plans for us to take Friday off next week and go for a long ride through the Cape. Maybe we'll buy lunch to bring to the beach and listen to the crashing waves hit the shoreline. It'll be our day to do anything we want."

"Cory, that would be wonderful. How can we close the stand?"

"We're not. I asked Bob and Ray to run the business for us."

Todd cut in, "I was going to ask for that day off for Jenny and me to pick out our furniture."

"We'll let Bob and Ray know. They have handled the business numerous times over the years. I'll have Bob put gas in the truck and check the oil. I haven't taken the truck for the long run in years," Cory answered.

"Dad, why don't you take my car? Give Mom a treat. Jenny and I can use the truck."

"Thanks, but I want to feel like I'm single again taking your mother out on our first date in my old, beat-up truck. Remember, Judy?" They gave each other a mysterious, private look.

"Those were the days, Cory. I remember going fishing off the Chatham drawbridge with you and your grandfather. I came to love fishing. I know what we can do," Judy started to get excited. "Remember that roadside shack that sold a large platter of fried clams? Where was that?"

"We ordered the meal in Orleans. They had good seafood. I think I can find it again."

I looked up at Rita while trying to eat my baked potato, hoping to hold it down without getting sick. "What will you be up to Friday?"

"South Dennis is having their summer pig roast. The mayor's supposed to be there, and I have to cover the story. The area is set up for the circus, games, horseracing, beer barrel riding, and more activities are planned to take place. While I'm running around, I'm sure I'll be eating bags of saltwater taffy."

"Looks like no one will be home," Judy said. "That's rare."

"We'll have a lot to talk about when we come home," Todd said. "Jenny and I will be able to describe our furniture, and Rita can talk about getting fat on the taffy."

"Help me clear the table and I'll bring out the Cranberry apple pie," Judy requested.

"How am I going to compete with your cooking when Todd and I get married?"

"You won't, Rita said. " You bring all your kids over for a visit during mealtime." She looked up at her parents smiling.

Judy looked back at Rita. "Can you get the dessert out? I want to talk to Jenny."

"What did you do Jenny?" Todd asked with a wide smile. "No dessert for you!"

Judy and Jenny sat in their favorite spot on the porch. "This is nice." Judy looked up at the sky lit with stars.

"Is there something wrong?" Mrs. Costa.

"Jenny, I feel old when you call me Mrs. Costa. Please, call me Judy and my husband Cory."

"Okay."

"Have you made any plans with your parent's home? It's been empty a long time."

"I have been avoiding going there, except when I feed the animals. The place seems empty with no life. I have been thinking when Todd and I get married, I'm selling the property. We could use the money to buy some farm animals. I could never live there again. I need a new life. That's why I'm so thankful for the home you're building for us.

Gosh, you're giving us a lot."

"Jenny, it was a sad reason for having you stay with us because of your mother's illness, but Cory and I had a great blessing getting the chance to know you before the wedding."

"I'm the one who has been blessed. Something really clicked when the four of us went shopping for my gown. Everyone was themselves, and we had private time with Faith. It would never have been the same sitting in the house talking to each other. You never seem to get special time to talk. Like we're doing now.

"I love this family. After losing Mom, the support from you and Cory has been a godsend. I'd be lost without both of you. I can see how your children look up to you both."

"Jenny, you're going to be a loving daughter to us. Once you and Todd have children, it'll be the frosting on the cake, shall we say." Judy laughed.

It was the perfect time to tell Judy that I was pregnant, but the timing didn't feel right before Todd knew. I held the news back.

"This house we built for you is from love. We can't wait to hear little feet running around on the floors."

"I promise Todd and I'll give you many."

Judy held me tightly in her arms. "We'd love that."

We both went on having small talk about the future. After an hour, I decided to go to bed early and relax.

I met up with Todd. "Hope you don't mind, but I'm going to say goodnight to everyone."

"That's okay, honey. We'll see you in the morning."

Cathy's Stardom

Cathy had her twenty-fourth runway show in Paris. She was a hit with every one of them. Flashbulbs came close to blinding her when the reporters took photo shoots of her in Coco Chanel's outfits. She prayed not to miss a step and fall. She was with the richest and most prestigious people at the shows.

Coco saved Cathy to walkout at the end with her newest and most breathtaking wardrobes. All eyes were on Cathy. She ate up the attention. The other models were already getting upset that Coco chose Cathy instead of them. They worked years to get to the fame and this blonde bombshell took over their spot. None of them tried to get close to her. A hatred had grown; not so much from being chosen by Coco, but the conceit Cathy presented after climbing to the top from her first show. She looked down at every model.

Newspapers and magazines worldwide started to write about this new girl modeling for Miss Channel. Cathy became the most glamorized model in years. Men buzzed around her like a swarm of bees and offered her drinks. Cathy could smell the money in the air with the atmosphere of fame; it came in clothes, stardom, hotels, the finest dressing rooms, and jewelry that had been given to her. The welcoming mat was set when she had attended and requested special seats at theaters and reserved locations to tables at restaurants. She had preferred entry at nightclubs and given the first-row seats at award functions.

Cathy became an idol. Teenage girls would run-up asking for her autograph. They begged hairdressers to give them the same hairstyle she wore. Her new name, *Nina Mae,* added to her stardom.

****

Within two months, Cathy started to feel tired and her nerves kept her from getting enough sleep to feel energized the next day.

After one show, Coco went into Cathy's dressing room. "I want to send you for a week to Bondi Beach, in Sydney, Australia. I own the island and you can rest. I think becoming a star hit you too fast. I have had you going from morning to night. You look a little rundown, and I don't want any bags under the eyes or anything showing being tired from a model aspect, especially you, my star. You have to look fresh every time you go out."

In a few days, Cathy packed her clothes to take a flight from Charles de Gaulle International Airport and get away by herself. Her father's bodyguard, Dan, was never seen once she moved into her suite. She looked forward to the time alone.

Within hours, Cathy's reserved driver delivered her to the most luscious house with its own beachfront to the whole island. When she looked out the glass door from the sunroom, she faced an Olympic size pool. The house sat on a tall hill.

Cathy put on her black, two-piece bathing suit. She grabbed a red, canvas shoulder bag and packed a beach towel, and sun lotion into the tote. She was amazed Coco had every item anyone would need in her beach house.

As she started to walk down towards the beach, a man in casual clothes came up to her. He looked to be in his late thirties, with jet-black, wild, greasy, windblown hair. He was short and stocky with a coarse beard needing a shave. He wore brown sandals with a pair of white and blue big-flowered shorts down to his knees, and a t-shirt with *Bondi Beach* written across the front.

He spoke with a strong Australian accent. "Hello, Miss Mae. My name is Georgi. You must not go anywhere alone. I'm following the orders of Coco Chanel to take you down to the beach or wherever you want to go. I'll keep watch over you." He got into a golf cart with double row seats and waited for her to get into the vehicle.

Cathy was now used to being called *Nina Mae*. No one had called her Cathy for a long time. The sound of Nina Mae kept her distance from being the girl from Cape Cod, Massachusetts.

In the few months of being in Paris, she wondered if she would ever be able to go back to a low-keyed, boring life with no meaning back home. And yet, she felt lonely. Cathy struggled to adjust to her fame which developed in just one runway show. Her private life was taken away from her.

They arrived at the beach that had lounge chairs under Palapa thatched huts. She pulled a chair out from under the hut to the open sunrays.

Georgi came running up to her. "No, Nina. You must not sit in the direct sun. It's not allowed for models of Miss Chanel."

"Why not? I'm here to relax. Unwind."

"You can get burnt. You're only allowed to sit under the hut. I have placed some books for you to read. If you like, I can get you a tropical drink. We have Caribbean Rum Punch, Frozen Rum Runners, Banana Daiquiri, or a Mai Tai."

"I'll take a Mai Tai." She wanted something to relax her. She loved watching the waves crashing on the beach and the sounds of the seagulls circling the air hoping to find leftover food scattered on the shoreline. When she closed her eyes, the sounds gave her a picture of Cape Cod. To her surprise, she felt homesick.

Georgi came down with her drink on a tray, this time barefoot, with his feet stepping deep into the hot sand. It didn't seem to bother him. Cathy figured the bottom of his feet must have looked like leather. She had no desire to find out.

The Mai Tai went down smooth and tasted good from being thirsty. The drink was what she needed. She looked back wondering where Georgi disappeared.

Cathy started getting aroused from the hot heat on her body. She was disappointed in Coco's taste of men to be her watch guard. She read about Australian men supposedly having sun-kissed, dark skin with an athletic build. Georgi seemed like a leftover; the runt of the litter. She could use a stallion about now. Coco had kept Cathy so busy, she forgot about sex.

There was a book on the side table she started to read. Halfway through the book, her eyes got heavy and she dozed off. When she opened her eyes, it had been the best sleep in two months. Cathy hated waking up sweaty from the tropical heat. The wet bathing suit clung to her. Her stomach was upset. She blamed the feeling from the drink. Maybe she drank the alcoholic beverage too fast. Cathy had to get out of the high temperatures that were now in the high nineties.

Georgi came out of nowhere each time she moved. "Can I get you something?" he asked.

"I need to go back to the house. The heat's getting to me."

"I'll get the golf cart. Let me get your book and drink."

Cathy climbed into the bright, red cart with tan seats. It had a passenger seat in front and a two-seater facing the back. She was starting to feel dizzy and faint.

"Are you feeling okay, Nina? You don't look well."

"I don't feel good. Maybe it was the drink."

"It's too hot to spend a lot of time on the beach. You were there for two hours. Take a cold shower; it'll make you feel better."

"I will. Thanks." She wondered where he had been to know she had slept two hours. Does he sit and watch her?

He helped her get inside the house. Do you want me to stay until you shower to make sure you're okay?"

"No. I'll be alright."

"Are you sure."

"Yes, I am."

"I'll be in the north end of the house. There's a buzzer in every room if you need me." Again, Georgi vanished.

The cool water felt refreshing running down her clammy body. Cathy wished Georgi was desirable. She would have invited him into the shower. She craved someone with a sexy smile, eyes with a hunger to take her while whispering nasty things in her ear, muscular arms around her, with strong, tight thighs between hers, while his large hands searched every sensual part of her body.

She started to picture Dan who came on the trip to watch over her, although she never saw him. He would fit the need right about now.

184

The one time she would have allowed him to have his way with her. *His loss.*

An hour later, George knocked on the door.

"Hello, Georgi. What's wrong?"

"I wanted to make sure you weren't ill before I went in for the night."

"I'm okay. Do they have any locations with parties or music?"

"Ms. Chanel gives me strict rules to not take anyone to other locations. This house is where she sends the models to rest. She must have a big event coming up for you."

"I don't know."

"Okay. I'll check on you tomorrow. You'll be served a wonderful breakfast at around nine o'clock. Get some sleep." He disappeared around the corner.

Cathy felt she needed to have a snack to settle her stomach, but didn't want to call Georgi. He'd be like sticky paper. The refrigerator had bottled water, orange and apple juice, and an assortment of freshly made sandwiches to satisfy anyone's hunger. The cabinet had peanut butter crackers and snacks. She took the crackers with apple juice. Eating made her feel better for a few hours, but nausea returned.

After two days of being at the beach house, she told Georgi she wanted to go back to Paris. There was no sense of staying alone for a week. Instead of enjoying the island, she felt caged. Georgi was getting on her nerves. No matter where Cathy went, she tripped over him. Wherever she looked, there stood Georgi. He wasn't even good on the eyes. Maybe Coco picked him for to keep the models in line with no sexual play. *Someone would have to be desperate*, she thought.

Within hours, he drove Cathy to the airport to return to her suite in Paris. Landing on the strip and seeing the people running around the airport made her feel alive. Her chafferer met her at the gate, but not in time before a group of teenage girls came screaming and pushing to see *Nina Mae*. Others watched to see who the crowd was running to and spotted the famous model. The crowd doubled. Cathy devoured the attention.

****

After a month of being back from Australia, Cathy had no energy and started looking more drained than when she left on vacation.

"Nina, darling, we have to find out why you're so exhausted. It's starting to show on your face. You haven't walked down the runway with the pep displayed weeks ago."

"I don't know why I can't sleep, and I'm not eating right."

"Maybe you should go see a doctor. I don't want to lose my best model. If you can't keep up, I will have to replace you. You're good as long as you're famous. If you don't keep up with the pace, you're left behind. As they say, 'One moment you're in, and the next you're out.'"

"Please, Coco, don't replace me."

"I'll have Millie call my doctor and set an appointment up for you. I have to know if you can keep up with this constant availability with nightly shows. There's not another model as famous as you or has your money. I've made you a millionaire in less than a month. Now, you make that weekly. I'd hate to see you fade out."

Coco held onto her carved, ivory-flowered cigarette holder in her right hand. She lifted her head, and blew out smoke from a Lucky Strike cigarette into the air.

"My secretary, Millie, will get an appointment for you today. I want you rested for the final runway show in two days. Now, go darling, upstairs, and rest. Millie will call you."

Cathy was tired. Her king-size bed felt welcoming as she fell on the mattress.

Within the hour the phone rang. Cathy woke up in a fog. She reached with her eyes still closed for the desk phone.

"Hello?"

"Hi, Nina. This is Millie. You have an appointment at 3 pm. Your chauffeur will be outback in an hour. Coco wants you to go as covered up as you can. She wants no one to see you. Dress down. Go through the office and out the backdoor."

Half awake, she answered. "Alright."

Cathy dragged herself out of bed and jumped into the shower. She combed her hair and put a headscarf on to hide her face. Before leaving, she filled her lips with a soft pink shade of lipstick.

When she got to the car, Millie was in the backseat. "Oh, hello, Millie. I didn't expect you to come with me."

"None of Coco's girls go alone to be examined."

They drove off with little said between them. Millie was the woman who helped all the models, but she was hardly seen or carried a conversation.

Millie and Cathy walked into the doctor's office, and the nurse rushed them through a private room.

After the examination, the chauffeur pulled into the parking lot behind the Hotel Lutetia. Millie helped Cathy out. "You okay?"

"Yes."

They headed to Coco's suite. When they got to her floor, Millie let Cathy go by herself to talk to Coco.

"Good luck." Millie disappeared into the elevator when the door closed, and Cathy stood facing Coco.

"Hi, darling. Come and sit next to me." Coco patted her hand on a blue mohair sectional sofa.

"Charlene, make some hot tea."

Coco puffed away like a steam engine with her cigarette dangling between her fingers. Her rooms always smelled of smoke, and the air was thick with the vapor. Cathy wondered why Coco never opened the windows to get fresh air into the rooms.

Cathy put her head in her hands and sobbed.

"Come, come, Nina. The news can't be that bad."

"Yes, it is. More serious than I thought."

The tea was brought and placed on the dark marble top of the coffee table.

"Thank you, Charlene. Leave us now."

"Pull yourself together, Nina. Tell me what the doctor found." Coco got angry. She had no patience for emotional or weak models. She wanted confidence and strength from them.

Cathy told Coco in detail what the doctor discussed.

"Can he take care of this?"

"It may be too late."

"Too late!"

"I don't know what to do." Cathy looked up at Coco.

"Do you think you're up to handling changing in and out of my fashion designs for three hours tomorrow night with our last line of clothing for the Fall? "

"I want to go down that runway. No one can model your line of clothes like me, and you know that for a fact. I'm not crippled."

"Don't get nasty with me, Nina. I made you, and I can break you. It's not my fault you're in this condition. My line of work is my life. I fought to get where I am today. No one's going to make me crumble because of their bad choices. I'll replace you first.

"I'll tell you what we're going to do," Coco stated, while she bent over to drop her long cigarette ashes in a tray. "I'm sure you'll be okay for one night. Don't disappoint me. I'll have a few standbys. Nothing and no one will tarnish my work or name."

"You act like all of a sudden, my stardom means nothing, and people will forget who I am. I'm in demand, Coco, and I can get a modeling job at the top with any designer in Europe. Many fashion designers have called me to model for them. I turned them down."

Coco stood up, faced Cathy, leaned into her, and put both her hands on the arm of the chair. "First of all, Nina—I *am* the top; you can't go any higher. You're not my first model that has been called by other designers to work for them. Don't make threats. You'll be out the door in a second. Models would give up their souls to be owned by me. Any model who works for Coco Chanel, and goes to another designer, loses fame within months.

"I invested in you because your father sent me pictures of your best modeling shows. They were wonderful, and you were a breath of youth." She stood up straight. "Besides, his money was hard to refuse. You're paid richly. I made *Nina Mae*. You're *Coco Chanel's* top model. I don't need *you* to make *me*. I'll always be famous."

Coco got closer to Cathy. "I already proved myself. Any model associated with my name and fashions goes to the top. Movie stars—

and the filthy rich from all over the world beg to wear my clothes at any of their events.

"Haven't I helped your name? Isn't that important to you? Weren't you happy to have me?"

"Stop bitching and whining, Nina. It's not becoming. Get a hold of yourself. You have grown to stardom, but not maturity. Maybe you got your way back in Chatham, but I'm the queen in Paris. You sound like you have been spoiled. Appreciate what you have without getting bigheaded thinking you became famous on your own. I made you, not your father. He gave you the start to open the door, I did the work.

"Let me tell you something else. Models are only as good as they are at the time. If you didn't have this problem to fix, you would continue being my model for years. I would pay you more. It's hard handling the money you have now. Imagine having more, Nina?

"This is my career. I can't keep a model because I like or feel sorry for them. When I hired you, I told you my decisions are not made from emotions. If I felt for every model who had problems, I wouldn't be where I am. Selfish or not—I come first along with my goals, not the models."

Coco walked to her huge window facing Paris, the busiest city, with her cigarette smoke encircling her head. She kept her back to Cathy. "I'm getting tired of this long talk. Since you can't make up your mind about your situation, I'll make the decision for you.

"Saturday is our last show for two months. After the show, I want you on a plane heading back home and talk about this problem with your doctor. Within a week, I want your ruling on what you're going to do to take care of yourself. Maybe they can help you."

Coco kept her back to Cathy. "If you wait too long, you'll be too old to model. The modeling world is for the young unless you're a supermodel. With your looks, Nina, you could be one of those models who go way into her forties or later. Don't throw your future away."

She turned facing Cathy. "You take my breath away when I watch you come out from behind the curtains and strut down the runway. You have beautiful, long legs. You're graceful for a girl of nineteen with no professional training. You're a natural."

Coco's voice got soft and sounded compassionate. "I truly hope you make the right decision, Nina, because I have loved watching you go to the top. I love making models. It would be a shame to waste your beauty and talent. A woman like you shouldn't waste their life trying to please a man when you can have no limits. You belong to the public. Nothing's more exciting than becoming famous in Paris."

Coco turned her back away, but not fast enough before Cathy was shocked to see tears filling Coco's eyes. "Go back to your suite and rest for your big runway show tomorrow. I'm sincerely sorry you have to deal with this situation."

The next night, Coco Chanel's final Fall runway show came and Nina Mae shined with everyone falling all over her after the show. Flowers of all sorts filled her dressing room placed on tables and the floor. The media pushed their arms over other reporters into her open door backstage and flashed their cameras hoping they got a good shot of this girl who was becoming a legend.

The next day, Cathy booked a late flight from the Paris Charles De Gaulle Airport back to Boston, Massachusetts to make a home visit.

Cathy Coming Home

"Hello?" Sharon answered the phone.

"Hi, Mother, it's Cathy."

"Cathy! Tony—its Cathy," she yelled out. "How are you?"

"I'm great. I'm coming home for a week, maybe two."

"How wonderful. Your pictures and write-ups have been all over the newspapers. You've been on the cover of Vogue Magazine so many times. The townspeople are so proud of you."

"I should be there sometime on Tuesday. I'll call you when I land."

"I can't wait to see you, honey."

"Me too. Talk later, Mother."

"Bye, honey. I love you."

"Love you, too."

Cathy hung the phone up sitting in the armchair. Her mother's voice brought back the turmoil in Chatham. Paris was her home. The past seemed like failure. She felt like everyone was beneath her after the fast-growing fame and wealth that had been bestowed on her.

Cathy prayed to have her problem solved. She'd be able to return to Paris and never go home again. She wanted to delete her history, even Todd. *Out of sight, out of mind*, she thought. She knew any man could give her what she wanted in Paris. They had money with no holes in their pockets. Never would she need money…or anyone.

A knock came on the door. Carl, her chauffeur, took her bags to the car. Coco never came to say goodbye. Cathy entered the backseat with the fear she may not see Carl again. He had been a dear friend.

He pulled up to the airport and got out to get her belongings.

"Carl?"

"Yes, Miss Mae."

She took his hands and held both. "Thank you for all you've done."

"Don't say that, Nina. You'll be back."

"I don't know, Carl. I can't picture you taking someone else everywhere instead of me."

"Let's not say goodbye, Miss Mae. I'll say until you return."

"I like that." She shocked him and herself by giving him a peck on his cheek. "Be careful and stay safe, Carl."

"You, too, Miss Mae."

"Say my name again."

"Nina Mae."

"Thank you, Carl."

She climbed the steps to the plane. Her seat was in the private section enclosed by a heavy, navy curtain to separate her from the others on board. To her shock, Dan was seated across from her.

"How did you know I was going back home?"

"I know everything, Cathy. That's my job."

"I never saw you once in Paris."

"Oh, I was around. I saw you plenty, Miss Mae. You were one classy lady in Paris. No one could have become more feminine than you in Coco Chanel's designs."

"I hate to end our conversation, Dan, but I'm going to rest."

"See you when you wake up." He had a confident smile.

Looking at Dan, Cathy knew she had gone way too long without being with an aggressive man in bed.

Cory and Judy Look Back

Cory went out the front door to get the newspaper while Judy made coffee. Once he got back to the table, she placed the hot brew in front of him.

"Good Morning," she said. "How did you sleep?"

"For once, right through the night."

Cory opened the folded morning newspaper.

"Well, look whose home!" he said to Judy. "Cathy's back from Paris. What reason would make her come home after all the excitement becoming famous? She made the front page."

"Really. Let me see." Judy looked over his shoulder at the newspaper. "Do you think she returned because of her father's trial?"

"I don't know. I think it's best we don't say anything. Jenny's not too sure of Todd and Cathy's actions that night. In fact, neither am I."

"Cory, what an awful thing to say about our son. Todd would never fool around with Cathy. He loves Jenny. He's not that kind of boy. He has morals."

"He's human, Judy. Right or wrong. Todd dated Cathy for two years." His finger pointed to the page, "Look at this woman. Drinks can do a lot to a man with this sex goddess in front of him. He admitted drinking too much that night."

"You sound like an FBI agent interrogating him."

"I've had bad vibes. When Todd tried to tell us his side of the story, he was a bunch of nerves. He stumbled for words. I've never seen him like that before."

"I don't like you saying anything against him." Judy started to walk away from Cory. "He needs our support, and you don't sound like someone he can count on right now."

"Never the less, the article would only get Jenny upset." Cory read the write-up further down. "It looks like she's only staying for two weeks. The further away that woman gets from us, the better I'd feel."

"I only hope the FBI doesn't come to Todd as a witness from Tony's arrest and the others. I'd hate our name connected to the Greco's for any reason."

Cory looked around the kitchen. "It seems quiet in the house with everyone gone. I didn't realize how much commotion was going on since the funeral."

Judy sat down and put her hand on Cory's at the table. "It was wonderful having them all together, but this is peaceful with the two of us. I'm looking forward to getting away. The day can't come fast enough."

"I should have made plans long ago and more often. You bust yourself with the housework and cleaning ending the day at the stand until dark."

"It's our business we have built together. If it wasn't for the flower and vegetable stand or our carpentry business, we wouldn't be able to build the house for Todd and Jenny. We have enough saved to do the same for the others kids. God has been good to us, Cory."

"You're right. Many of our friends lost their land and homes from the Great Depression. There aren't many of us left. Some customers have shown jealousy and some anger because we have the businesses running. We worked our fingers to the bone keeping this place and trying to grow grass for the animals.

"If it wasn't for the lake below to get the water, we would be in their shoes. Look how farmers came behind our backs pulling their trucks up to the lake and tried to steal water. Then, we were looked upon as enemies stopping them. I hated doing that, Judy. They were our friends."

"Cory, if you didn't, we might have lost everything. The water was ours. It's not like we took something from another person. We came close to losing all our money until our finances started coming back. We didn't have many customers because no one had money. Only the necessities were bought.

194

"Our food came from our animals. Our milk, cheese, eggs, and meat kept us alive. I don't want to hear any guilt coming out of you. The Lord provided, and we worked with every ounce of strength in us."

Judy faced Cory. "I remember crying at night wondering if we were going to have to move and give all this up. We struggled with plowing the fields trying to plant the seed. Our coughs lingered, we developed irritated eyes, and we could feel the dust in our lungs from lack of rain.

"I remember watching you and our sons working months without seeing any results. Remember sitting on the porch praying for rain? I do. I watched you come close to giving up, and me trying to give you the courage to go on when deep down, I didn't have any faith myself. I tried to keep everyone smiling when I was dying inside. I planned the day for games or programs to listen to on the radio for the kids. I'd go to bed mentally exhausted as well as physically.

"We had the Great Depression to handle. Thank God you took our saving out of the bank when you had a feeling this was coming. We couldn't even sleep thinking someone was going to find the money in the black box in the barn under the haystacks. Everyone lost their money in the banks. I'm glad I married a smart man who thought ahead." Judy hugged him.

She looked straight at him. "Don't ever let me hear you feel bad or guilty. At first, I did too, Cory, but I swallowed my emotions and turned my feelings off. I prayed for God to lead us, and He did. I believed when no one had faith in this family."

"Wow, that's telling me." Cory's eyebrows went up.

Judy grabbed Cory's face and turned it towards her. "I love you and don't ever forget it."

He smiled at her. "Judy, you have been the best partner, wife, mother, housekeeper, cook, and laundry person in the world. Did I leave anything out with your responsibilities around here?"

Judy smiled with tears in her eyes. She sat on his lap with her arm around his shoulders. "I love you, Judy. I don't tell you enough."

"You don't have to. You say it with your hard work for this family, caring for the animals, delivering plants, and building someone's barn or house. You put the food on the table for us all. Actions speak better than words."

They gave each other a long, passionate kiss. There was never private time for them to show their affection for one another during the day. He rubbed his hand through her bangs.

"I can't wait to have a full day alone with you. I want to see you with your hair down; the

way you wore the style when we met. I want to devote my attention only to you with no business facing us, no family, or people looking for answers. You and me, sweetheart."

"I think I can handle that for you, Mr. Costa." Judy got up after giving him a quick kiss. "Want another coffee?"

"That would be good."

"I'll start your eggs."

Cory went back to reading the news.

****

The phone rang at the flower stand. Todd picked it up.

"Hello."

"Hello, Todd. It's Sharon Greco."

Todd's heart stopped. Why would she be calling him? "Hello, Mrs. Greco. What can I do for you?"

"Come on, Todd. Stop being formal, you always called me Sharon."

He didn't say anything back. She continued, "Tony and I would like ten Rhododendron plants so we can install them around the barn. Do you think you can come today? You still have the job building the other barn. We haven't heard from you after the quote."

Todd was thankful that Cathy was in Paris. He could deal with her parents.

"I'm pretty tight with scheduled deliveries, Sharon."

"Oh, I'm sure you can squeeze this delivery in for us."

Todd took a deep breath. "What colors do you want? All one or a mixture?"

"You're the expert. What do you think?"

"White, pink, blue, and purple would be a good mixture around the barn."

"I'll leave the decision in your hands. See you soon."

Todd went to the stand and carefully picked out the chosen colors and threw in two yellow plants. He drove the truck over and put them into a few large crates in the back to secure them in place.

Todd needed an excuse to be out long, in case he got tied-up. He decided to fill the rest of the outstanding orders for Monday's deliveries. He placed all the other plants and shrubs in the back of the flatbed.

Todd went up the driveway without stopping to tell his father.

Judy was doing the dishes in the sink and noticed Todd passing the house in his father's truck. She stopped washing and stared out the window.

"What are you looking at, Judy?" Cory asked.

"That's odd. Todd's going out to the main road in your truck."

"Maybe he's delivering something."

"Yes, but don't you find it strange with him not stopping to tell us where he's going?"

"Judy, our son is a grown man. He knows this job inside and out. He does a lot of delivering without telling me."

"I find this unusual."

Judy continued washing but didn't feel comfortable. Her impulses gave the feeling something was wrong. Todd not stopping in to see his father first was different from how he did things. Now that Cathy was back, Judy prayed nothing would involve Todd.

****

Todd dropped-off all the plant orders to the other families before heading for the Greco house. He arrived later than planned, but he had built a good alibi for being home late.

All he wanted to do was drop the shrubs off and leave. To avoid any conversation with Sharon, Todd rode directly to the barn behind the house and placed ten shrubs down against the barn.

Tony and his extra men weren't anywhere to be seen. He had an eerie feeling about being called there. Something didn't feel right. After Todd unloaded the items, he left the invoice in an envelope attached to one of the plants.

Todd's truck was about to pass the house when Sharon came out waving her arms for him to stop.

He rotated his window down. "Hi, Sharon, I have six more deliveries. I left the shrubs at the barn. You can mail us a check. Have a good day."

"Wait, Todd. Tony and I would like to talk to you."

"Sharon, I can't stay, honestly. My dad's waiting for me to fill the orders we promised today. I squeezed yours in for you."

"This won't take long."

"With no disrespect, Sharon, I can't. Give me a call, or I'll come over tomorrow. We can discuss things."

Todd wanted to hold her off for one day and have time to talk to his father. He had no idea what was about to unfold, but his mind told him to leave fast.

"I'll see you tomorrow afternoon."

Todd put his foot lightly on the gas trying not to speed out. "He got to the gate and a black 1932 Ford Model 8 blocked the driveway. This wasn't good. He saw pictures of these vehicles that had been used as getaway cars with bank robberies for the Italian-American Mafia gangs.

By now, Todd expected to be threatened if he became a witness.

You hear about these things, but never think you'll be on the mafia's list. Todd started to breathe rapidly. He might not see his family again.

The driver came to Todd's side and tapped his finger on the glass. Todd rolled down his window.

The man talked slowly, and stared Todd directly in the eyes. "When Mr. Greco says he wants to see you, don't question the reason. Now get your ass back to the house, or I'll blow your damn head off and dispose of your body without thinking twice about it."

Todd turned around and headed to the backyard. Sharon stood there smiling with the door open for him to enter.

****

Sharon led him to the den. Tony was leaning back in his leather chair with his feet crossed on his desk, smoking a cigar. The smog encircled his face when he slowly blew the puff out of his curled lips. His eyes looked up and studied the flow of vapor.

"Have a seat on the sofa, Todd."

Todd turned as the door closed, revealing the couch. Cathy was sitting on the divan. She looked more mature. Her attire was expensive but casual. She didn't have that smug look as having something on him. She looked scared.

"Oh, hi, Cathy. I didn't know you were back home."

"My visit wasn't planned."

"You mean our daughter's picture hit the front page today and you missed seeing her photo?" Sharon asked.

"I'm up at 4 am to get my chores done. You called when I had finished, and I put the shrubs on the truck. I didn't have time to stop at the house and read a newspaper."

He felt his stupidity with the remark giving them the information that no one from home knew where he was going.

"I said, have a seat, Todd." Tony looked calm on the outside but Todd sensed that he wasn't.

He sat down next to Cathy and felt uncomfortable being close to her. He felt like a child getting ready to be reprimanded.

"Our daughter came home with a surprise visit with a problem she has to deal with and the complication affects all of us."

"What do I have to do with her dilemma?"

"Oh, *you* have everything to do with her complication," Sharon said, upset.

"I told you, Sharon, if you wanted to be present, keep your mouth shut. I'll do the talking. Now, sit down."

She sat in a black leather office seat in the corner.

"It seems, Todd, our daughter has got herself pregnant."

Todd's heart stopped.

"Again, what does her condition have to do with me? She leaves for Paris and comes back months later pregnant."

"The doctor's report shows how far along she is with the pregnancy, and the fact that you two had sex in the barn, makes the chances high on you being the father."

It took a few seconds for the remark to sink in Todd's brain.

"You can't be serious?"

"Oh, yes, I am." Tony wasn't moving a muscle but kept his eyes dead-on Todd.

"Your daughter has been gone for months, Mr. Greco, and I doubt she hasn't had time to fool around with plenty of men."

"That isn't what she told us."

Todd looked at Cathy upset. "You're not going to blame this on me."

Cathy looked calm and in a quiet tone said, "Todd, I swear, I haven't been with anyone, since our time together."

"Mr. Greco, I'm sorry Cathy has to handle this mess, but I'm not taking the blame. We all know, including you and your wife, that Cathy has been running around with multiple men. That's the reason we broke up. Now, you want me to believe that she has been innocent all these months being gone? She needs sex as one needs air to live."

"First of all, son, call me Dad."

"Don't ever call me son again, Mr. Greco. And, you're not my dad."

"Oh, but you will be."

"What are you talking about?"

Tony bent down in Todd's face. "You, Mr. Costa, are going to marry my daughter. If you think she's going to go around showing a huge stomach, and you're going your merry way, think again."

"I'm engaged to Jenny, and we're getting married in two weeks." Todd looked at Tony with daggers. "I love her, and I'm not marrying your daughter because she needs someone to cover up her running around in Paris.

"Yes, we had sex that night. Cathy was the one who pushed herself on me. My problem was having too much to drink, and I took what was offered to me, like most men have done in town with your daughter, married or not."

"Sharon and I know the remarks and name-calling going around about our daughter. We don't like gossip, but that's her choice. There was no physical damage to her passing herself around, except getting a bad name.

"We're not mad you had fun with her in the barn, Todd. Anyone being cornered by this beauty would fall for her trap. You're right, being drunk added to the desire and lust. Only satisfaction takes away those fits of hunger in us men." Tony sat with no emotion or movement.

"But, now she has the problem of a baby coming. Cathy can't hide she got knocked-up. There's no other solution. You have to pay for your rolling in the hay, shall we say."

"I'm telling you, I'll not marry Cathy, and give up my life with Jenny."

"If she was the love of your life, you wouldn't have been with Cathy." Sharon couldn't stay quiet.

Tony made a sharp turn in her direction. Now, he was angry.

"You're right. I shouldn't have been with Cathy. I know it, she knows it. Cathy has always loved the challenge of getting what doesn't belong to her."

Now, Tony was irritated, "I don't need to keep listening to what you want and why you did what you did with Cathy. I'm telling you both; you're to be married in a week. We don't want to wait until she shows, do we?"

"I'm not marrying your daughter this week or ever. She has a choice to have the baby or take another step. Once she does, she can go back to her life as *Nina Mae*. After all, Cathy's world has always been to think of only herself. She wouldn't know how to give love, even to her own infant."

Tony got up and pushed his chair away forcefully with one leg hitting the seat against the wall and came up to Todd's face.

"I've been damn patient long enough. You're marrying my daughter, come hell or high water. DO YOU HEAR ME?"

"I'm not giving up Jenny for anyone. No threat will make me."

Tony picked Todd up by the throat with one hand and pushed him against the wall. Todd's feet were off the floor. "You son-of-a-bitch! I'll break you in two."

Tony let go of his grip. Todd dropped to the floor, choking. While trying to catch his breath, he looked up at Tony. "I'll die by your hands before I give up Jenny. There's no proof I'm the father. If she never left town, and then claimed this, I might believe her.

"All of you, including Cathy, aren't going to pin me down for such a serious accusation, while she has been gone out of the country for three months. I know how Cathy works for the past five years. You all must have sat around asking yourselves *'What nice guy in town could be blamed for this? Oh, yes. Todd Costa.'* WRONG!"

Todd started towards the backdoor. "Since you have been a smart ass, I take the time limit back—this Friday. If not, there are going to be painful consequences you'll not be able to live with from your decision."

Todd went back to face Tony. "Don't you dare threaten me."

"Threaten you?" Tony laughed hard and loud. "We don't attack the person we're mad at, Todd. We go for the jugular vein where the person hurts the most...their family. Let's see if you can live with knowing your refusal to marry Cathy caused something horrible to happen to an innocent family member." He slowly blew a long, whiff of cigar smoke in Todd's face.

Todd went to swing at Tony when one of the triggermen grabbed his arm.

"Hum, you're more of a man than I thought. I don't think anyone in my lifetime tried or ever thought of taking a punch at me. They may have considered doing it but valued their life. My men will be watching you and every step your clan takes. I can crumble your bloodline business faster than you realize."

Cathy stood up and came between them. "Stop this Dad. He doesn't deserve to be treated this way. I can't believe you're such a cruel bully. How can you threaten his family? They're wonderful people. If something happens to them, I won't stand behind you."

"Are you softening up, Cathy? He got you pregnant! If you thought your pregnancy shouldn't have involved him, then you should have stayed in Paris and handled this like a grownup.

Tony walked closer to Cathy. "I'm sick of handling your problems. I got you the biggest modeling job in the *world* with Coco Chanel. You went to the stars with your fame and you're back here pregnant. You can't keep running home with your problems. I'll not let you walk around town showing you're single and pregnant. Everyone knows you're a tramp, you don't have to prove the fact by flaunting your condition."

Cathy went over to Todd showing emotions with tears forming, which he never saw from her. "Todd let's settle this right now with your doubts and all of us. I know you have reasons to doubt me. I can't believe I haven't been with anyone since you. Let's go and get a paternity test done.

"If the tests prove you're not the father, I won't bother you again. You can have your marriage with Jenny. I won't interfere. If the results come up positive, I'm not going through this alone. You owe me."

"I owe you? Cathy, you knew that I was engaged to Jenny when you pushed yourself on me. Yes, I never should have touched you. I'll take the blame, but that isn't going to take away my love or the desire to marry Jenny."

"Do you agree with the test?"

"Now?"

"Yes, why drag this on with fighting who's right or wrong."

Todd looked at Tony. "We need a doctor's appointment and this could take weeks for an answer."

"No, it won't. Eddie, you drive them to the hospital and go in to talk to the lab technician taking the blood. Make sure you have the results in a half-hour. If not, you know what to do."

****

They got into Eddie's car. Todd saw a rifle on the back floor.

Arriving at the hospital, they walked up to the receptionist's desk. Cathy requested a pregnancy test. A pretty nurse looked at the three of them. She smiled, "I'm sorry, but we have to have a doctor's order for blood tests. You can't just walk in and request one."

Eddie walked up to her, "Can I speak to you a moment—in private?" He gently took her by the arm, pulling her to the side.

He led her to a corner of the room. Eddie partially opened his coat and revealed a handgun. The Smith and Wesson Model 19 sticking up from his back holster wasn't something new to the attendant.

He looked at her with threatening authority keeping a stronghold on her. "There's no reason for anyone to get hurt. We need the result today. Do you think you can help us?"

"I think we can do that, sir." The nurse looked green.

"I want you to draw the blood, and we will follow you into the lab. I have to watch you."

"I can't allow you in the lab, but you can stand by the glass window and watch me. Following me inside will cause the workers to call the police."

She proceeded with his demand and took Cathy and Todd into a room to draw blood from both. Within an hour, the result came back. The nurse handed the closed envelope to Eddie.

"I thank you Miss, for your help. I'm sure you won't recall this event. I know where you work." Eddie gave her a sly grin.

"No, sir. I have no recognition of this matter."

Eddie ordered Cathy and Todd into his car. "You'll see the result when your father opens this envelope."

They walked into the house by the backdoor. Tony and Sharon were still sitting in the den. She jumped up trying to reach for the closed wrapping.

"Sit down, Sharon. I told you that I'll handle this situation."

Eddie placed the envelope on Tony's desk in front of him.

Everyone held their breath while he slowly opened the envelope. He read the outcome and then looked over at Todd. "You're ninety-nine percent the father of this child."

Cathy breathed a sigh of relief along with her mother. Todd stood traumatized. He was sick to his stomach.

"I can't believe this. All these years running around, you get pregnant while I have marriage plans. I want a copy of that report."

"I don't give out evidence that someone can use against me. I'll let you read the report. As for your marriage plans, I'll arrange for you and Cathy to get married under the gazelle outback. It's Wednesday and Friday would be too fast to tie the knot. I'm giving you ten days to let Jenny know you want out. You find an excuse, but don't tell her about my threats or more damage will be done. Jenny has to think you chose Cathy out of love. I will have the announcement of your engagement in the newspaper next week."

"If you put this in the newspaper and name us as a couple getting married, I will walk away. Everyone in town knows Jenny and I have a date two weeks from Sunday."

"I don't think you have any right to do anything, Todd. I'll wait for your answer. If you don't call within two days, your life will change forever. Whatever happens, it's from your decision."

"I'm sorry your daughter's pregnant, but I'm not giving my life up with Jenny because Cathy couldn't take care of this problem in Paris."

Cathy came up to Todd. "I tried. I saw a doctor. He said I was too far along to end the pregnancy. Taking the baby could kill me at this stage. Coco Chanel didn't want me seen in this condition. It wouldn't be good for my career. If I keep any baby weight on after the delivery, Coco may not let me model again."

"Hire you back? Are you telling me, after the baby comes, you want to go back to Paris? Do you expect me to give my marriage up with Jenny and take care of this baby alone? I'm sorry your precious future with modeling or a life of fame in Paris may be gone. You gave up your tremendous future when you wanted to get laid in the barn. That caused you to get knocked-up. If you had gone your own way that night and stayed with your guests, and had allowed me to go home, we both wouldn't be sitting here with this situation."

"Todd, I love you."

"You don't know how to love, Cathy. Now, you have a baby coming out of your fling. This situation might have happened in Paris sooner or later with another innocent man."

Cathy went up to her father. "Dad, let us work this out and promise me you won't hurt his family. You're facing a trial next week and any actions against Todd can make your jail time worse."

Tony pulled his daughter closer to him. He talked through his teeth. "Don't *ever* defend someone in front of me again and don't *ever* go against your family. You came here for me to handle this mess you're in, and I'm deciding your problem my way."

"Yes, the mob way." Cathy looked at her father.

He pushed her away. "Go sit down. Don't ever interfere with my talks with anyone again, and don't ever voice your opinion over mine."

Todd couldn't believe that Cathy stood up to her father.

Tony looked back at Todd, "I want an answer by Friday. You're not getting out of this having a happy marriage with Jenny and Cathy's life is over with the fame she had developed in Paris."

"Don't hold your breath, Mr. Greco." Todd walked out slamming the backdoor.

The two gangsters started to go after him, when Mr. Greco yelled, "Let him go."

****

Todd went through the shock of Cathy being pregnant; now the lab test proved he was the father. The visit ended with him being threatened to marry her. He got in his vehicle leaving the nightmare behind him. His stomach reached his throat and he stopped the car to throw up violently on the side of the road. Todd's world came to a dead stop. He began hyperventilating. His knees felt weak and his hands shook. His body was trembling as if he was trying to survive an earthquake.

Todd experienced the most horrifying news imaginable. All he could think of was being punished by God for breaking a commandment. He had put his manly desires over his love for Jenny. Less than fifteen-minutes of lust had caused serious threats from a Mob boss to harm his family.

He knew this was not over, even if Cathy wanted to deal with the problem herself. Her father was out for revenge. He was upset that she waited too long for an abortion. She could have taken care of the problem in France. If she had, no one would have known about her dilemma. Todd had wished Cathy had chosen this action.

He drove his truck to the beach. He got out and sat on the soft mound of sand. His body continued to unravel. *How am I going to handle this?* Fear and hopelessness engulfed him. *Jenny, what did I do to us?* He put his head down into his hands braced on his knees. Tears flowed down his cheeks with no sound coming out of him. He felt numb. How could one night have such a powerful impact?

Todd sat with the cool breeze from the ocean blowing on him. He couldn't imagine his life without Jenny and them going separate ways. Worse was the thought of Jenny marrying someone else and having his children. The possibility of that happening drove him insane.

Todd was the first man Jenny had been with sexually and their lovemaking was beautiful at the lake. How would she understand he had made love to Cathy a few weeks later?

He looked out at the waves crashing against the shore and thought of ending his life. The mafia didn't play around with an individual. They carried through with their threats.

Was Tony's actions a scare tactic? Would he really kill someone in his family because he wouldn't marry his daughter? It seemed unrealistic. Tony was already guilty of having his home occupied by numerous mafia leaders. It was an open and shut case. He was about to face jail time, maybe life. Tony might have thought there was nothing more to lose with another murder.

Why wasn't this Jenny? I would have been thrilled having a child with her.

Todd knew he couldn't stay away from home any longer. He had to face his parents and Jenny.

Todd's Return

At 5 pm, Rita met me at the front corridor of the *Nelson News*.

"How do you feel, Jenny? It must have been a long day for you."

"I can't get rid of nausea. I'm glad I brought one of your mother's cranberry apple muffins. I picked on the pastry all day with tea."

"Do you want to wait while I get the car?"

"I'm fine. It wouldn't take long for someone in the building to notice you pampering me."

"That's true."

We went to the side door of the building to get into Rita's car.

Orleans was a thirty-minute ride back home. "We were blessed getting a job together," Rita remarked. "People are still looking for positions after months of disappointment."

"I'll hate this ride in the winter. Glad I'll be able to stay home when the baby's born. I'm seriously thinking of selling my parent's home. We have 20 acres, and I should get a large amount of money for the sale. Todd and I can bank the profit."

"That would give you a solid foundation."

"I bet you couldn't stay home, Rita. Admit it; you love traveling and meeting people. I like having roots."

"You're right. I love kids, but there's no way I want my own."

"Why not? You're good with them."

"I think you and Todd are going to have a wonderful marriage, but it's not my thing. I need to be free. Staying in one place would make me bored out of my mind."

We drove letting the warm breeze come through our open windows blowing our hair.

"I love Cape Cod. Look at the views we see every day traveling past the beaches. I can't picture living anywhere else." I closed my eyes while the wind hit my face.

"Jenny, did you read the newspaper this morning?"

"You mean the bold headlines taking up the whole front page of Cathy being back home? I certainly did."

"I wonder what brings her back? It can't be needing money because she's a millionaire.

"Maybe she got a subpoena for her dad's trial?"

"She and her mother are protected from being witnesses. Cathy's too settled-in with the rich crowd to come home just for a visit. Imagine being known as *Nina Mae*? Her name's known all over the world. I don't like the girl, Rita, but it's a great accomplishment to reach. I think no one's surprised by her fame. I can't get rid of the feeling that Todd did something with her that night. Call it women's intuition. I want to believe he's telling me the truth."

"Jenny, you're getting married in a few weeks. Don't let your day be ruined by not trusting Todd. It's not a good way to start the rest of your life with a husband."

"I guess you're right."

"Besides, when he hears you're carrying his baby, he's going to be in heaven. Any idea when you'll tell him?"

"I think when we come back from getting our furniture. Your parents should be back from their day out. They need to spend time together with no problems from the family."

"That's true."

Rita pointed toward a building driving through the town. "Over there is the Myers Furniture Store. You and Todd should check it out."

"I'll mention the place to him."

The rest of the drive home was in silence. Rita finally pulled into their yard. "I can't wait to smell Mom's cooking. I don't know how she keeps up with all of us? I have never seen her do something special for herself. That's why I'm glad Dad's taking her out for a full day and have someone put a meal in front of her for a change."

Judy didn't disappoint Rita with the aroma of supper hitting her once the door opened. Her mother was like a time machine having everything ready when the family members walked in the door. They all had an appetite.

"You have the dining room table set already?" Rita asked."

"I started early. When we're done eating, you and Jenny can clear off the table and do the dishes. That's when I like to relax. Did you see your brother?"

"Isn't he with Dad down the shop?" Rita asked.

"Most likely," Judy answered.

Cory walked through the backdoor. "He went up to Judy and whispered. " Is Todd back yet?"

"No. I haven't heard from him."

"You're right. This is odd behavior from him. It's late."

"Dad isn't Todd with you."

"He had some late deliveries. We may not be able to wait for him with supper."

"He never misses your cooking." I was getting concerned.

Judy started to put the meal on the table. "Let's start with the corn soup, and maybe Todd will pull in before we finish."

"Did you two see the headlines in today's newspaper? Cathy's home. Not sure if we're supposed to call her *Nina Mae* now. I did a small telephone interview with Miss Chanel."

Cory looked at Judy. "How foolish of us not realizing both of them worked at the *Nelson News* and would have the ability to see the headlines. It wasn't as if the news on Cathy would be lost in some small article in the back pages."

"Did Todd know she was home?"

"I didn't get the chance to tell him, Jenny. He worked in the barn all morning doing his chores and then left with shrubs and flowers in the back of the pickup. He should be home soon." Cory stated.

"I'll clear the soup bowls, Mom." I could feel the tension in everyone with Todd being missing from the family meal.

Judy grabbed a plate and started to fill it. "I'll put Todd's meal back in the oven on warm until he gets home. I don't want this good meal to go to waste." She tried to keep a smile.

Once the family finished the main meal, I looked up at the clock.

The conversations were hard to keep going with Todd's absence.

Cory got up and moved around the room. Too much time had gone by, and he had no idea where to even look for his son. "This isn't normal for Todd. Where and who do we start calling?"

Rita got up. "Dad, I'm calling the cops. I need to know nothing has been reported."

"When he gets back, he's going to be told to never leave again without letting one of us know where he's going," Judy said.

Cory grabbed Judy's hands. "He's alright.

****

The family called all the people Todd had scheduled deliveries. The four of them finally heard Cory's truck coming down the dirt pathway. It was 7 pm and Todd had left at 1 pm. It was such a long span of time that they couldn't imagine what happened.

"Thank God!" Judy said leaning on the sink taking a deep breath.

Cory started for the door, and Judy grabbed his arm. "Give him a chance to explain."

Todd drove by the house straight down to the shop and parked the truck. He walked up the driveway and opened the kitchen door. All eyes were glued on him.

"I knew I'd be late for supper. The smell makes my mouth water." He walked over to me and kissed my cheek. "Sorry for being late."

"Do you know that we have all been sick with worry?" his mother asked.

"Why?"

Cory was upset. "What do you mean, why? Your mother's been sick thinking you got in an accident. Don't ever do this again."

"What are you upset about, Dad? We talked last night. I was going to try to do all of Monday and Tuesday deliveries today. That way, I'd be a day ahead so Jenny and I could go off Friday for our furniture without an overload for Bob and Ray. Don't you remember?"

"I honestly don't remember that at all, Todd."

"Dad, you were the one who put all the plants and shrubs in a pile by the door in case I decided to go. You even put the order slips on each one."

"I must be getting old or I have too much on my mind. How could I forget a double day delivery? I wouldn't let you go alone." Cory looked up at Judy, shaking his head.

"If I thought you forgot, I never would have gone off without talking to you before I left. I'm sorry."

"It's not your fault, son. Everyone was worried because I didn't remember." He apologized to the family.

"It shows you need a day away with Mom," Todd joked.

His mother warmed up Todd's supper and put the meal in front of him. She put her hand on the back of his shoulder and smiled. "Glad you're safe."

"Mom, you made such a great supper, but I can't eat right now. Do you mind if I take a shower? Maybe I can eat after I unwind."

I followed Todd upstairs.

"Can we talk?" I asked.

We sat across from one another in the two armchairs in his bedroom.

"Todd, what's wrong?"

"There's nothing wrong. Sorry everyone was worried." He looked around for his bath towel.

"That's not the problem, Todd. You're all uptight."

"I just delivered plants and shrubs all day until I reached exhaustion. I did the work so we could have a day together getting furniture without Bob and Ray being bogged down."

"Your home safe. That's what's important."

He turned and looked into my eyes, holding onto my shoulders. "Jenny, let's get married this weekend."

"This weekend? We have a planned wedding two weeks after Sunday. Your parents helped outline the menu and luncheon and sent out invites. It's wonderful you want to marry me, but why the hurry?"

"I don't want to wait, Jenny." He hugged me until I could hardly breathe. "I love you. I can't stand being separated anymore."

"We're not separated. Look at me, Todd." I grabbed his hand.

"We're living like husband and wife, except we're not sleeping in bed together. Two weeks from Sunday we take our vows. We only need to get Rita, Faith, and your brother a small gift for standing up for us. I thought we'd do that on Friday."

"That's just it, Jenny. We don't have to do all that if we elope."

"I can't do that to your parents. I can't picture you disappointing them either. Why would you hurt them with us running off?"

I stood up in front of him. "Todd, I don't know what's wrong with you, but you're not the same. My Todd would be out of his mind with excitement and happiness knowing we'd be saying our vows in that beautiful and blessed chapel you took me to with such love presenting my engagement ring to me. Remember our talks about walking into a home your dad built for us? The celebration is going to be spectacular!"

Todd looked at me. "We're leaving the day after tomorrow to pick out our furniture. Let's not wait. Dad said the house is completed. We can bring the furniture into the place and stay there."

"That action doesn't make sense. We can't live in the same house alone before being married. Todd. Would you really be fine with telling your family we eloped after all they have prepared for us? I want to marry you, but not like this. That's what couples do when the woman's pregnant before their wedding."

I felt this wasn't the time to tell Todd that I was pregnant. It would be an excuse to tie the knot before the arranged date. He wasn't acting rationally. I knew Todd was panicky for some unknown reason.

Todd put his head down like he was defeated.

I put my arm around his shoulder. "Honey, are you getting cold feet? A lot of men do."

"If there's one thing I'm sure of in my life, it's that I love you and want to get married."

"Something happened to you today."

"I've had a long hard day. I'm going to take a shower." He came over to me and squeezed my cheek. "I love you, Jenny." His eyes filled.

He walked down the hall to the bathroom. At first, I was too puzzled to move. After trying to get over the strange functioning of Todd, I went downstairs to sit on the porch swing.

Judy came out of the kitchen and joined me. She held my hand, as we slowly swayed back and forth. "Is everything okay?"

"I'm not sure. Something's wrong. He wanted to get married this Sunday.

"Sunday! This Sunday coming? Why would he want to do that?"

"He won't tell me why except he doesn't want to wait."

"Maybe since his father finished the house, he's anxious to move in with you."

"Judy, why wouldn't he be able to wait? It's only ten days away. It's not that I don't love him. I'd marry him tonight if the asking made sense, but his request doesn't."

Judy looked at me. "I told Cory that I had bad vibes with him not being home in time to eat."

I stopped the swing. "I hate asking … Do you think he was at the Greco's? Maybe he knew Cathy was there."

"Jenny, do you really believe in your heart that Todd has an interest in Cathy? I can't picture my son cheating on you. I know he loves you."

"I'm not sure if something happened that night when Todd went to her going away party and the cops arrested everyone. Let's face facts; at one time he was in love with her."

"He adores you. How can you even think he cheated on you?"

"I don't know, Judy. I pray my mind's just imagining things."

Judy put her arm around me. "Don't doubt him, Jenny. Mistrust can break couples up."

We continued sitting quietly, while each of us knew deep down that something went wrong with Todd.

Father and Son Talk

Todd went about his chores with low presence and few words. When the day was done, his father took him aside.

"What's going on with you? You're completely distanced from everyone."

"I have things on my mind, Dad."

"Get in the truck. I want to talk to you." They headed towards the lake.

Cory parked the vehicle and looked out at the breathtaking scenery. "You and Jenny are going to be doing a lot of fishing, canoeing, and swimming with this great clearance to the lake. What an area to bring up your kids."

Todd looked at the edge of the embankment and saw a small, short plank with a red canoe tied to the dock. Yellow oars were sticking up inside the small boat.

"Whose canoe is that?" Todd asked.

"Yours and Jenny's. Ray bought the kayak for you. It was supposed to be a surprise. He must have placed the boat here thinking you wouldn't come by until after your wedding.

"Todd, we have always talked. Nothing was ever too big for us to handle. Your mother and I aren't stupid or blind. When you love a child, you feel in your inner gut when something's wrong. Are you in some sort of trouble?"

Todd looked over at his father. "Dad, I'm in the worst mess any man can be in from doing the most inexcusable thing. If Jenny finds out, I may lose her."

"What are you talking about? Jenny would never leave you, she loves you. Why would she? Did you hurt her?"

"I don't know where to start. I'm so ashamed."

"Why don't you start from the beginning."

"It's a long story, Dad."

"We have time. I told your mother I was going to talk to you. She doesn't need another day wondering what's wrong with you. At this moment, she's making up an excuse for Jenny and Rita that we're having a father and son talk before the wedding.

Todd started by telling his father his mistake going to the Greco's to give Tony a quote for his barn, staying too long, drinking too much, Cathy pushing herself on him, and their sexual encounter.

"Oh, son, how could you do that being engaged to such a wonderful girl?"

"Easy, when you drank too much."

"There comes a time to make choices in your life. You caved-in with Cathy. Why?"

"I got weak, Dad. I love Jenny, but Cathy was stunning in this hot, red dress that fit her every curve. She took my breath away. It's still no excuse. Maybe there was this manly desire at the moment seeing her coming down the stairs and remembering back to the wild sex we had dating. When she was all over me, I wasn't in control of my morals. I let the sexual act happen."

Cory put his head down for a few seconds and then looked up at his son. "I'm disappointed that you would do this to Jenny. It wasn't right, but you shouldn't let this interfere with your relationship with Jenny. You can't tell her. The moment happened over three months ago. In ten days, you and Jenny will be married.

"You don't freely offer a confession to the one who loves you. No woman wants to hear the man she loves had the lust for another and then be asked to forgive him. It doesn't happen. Women don't forget the smallest thing we do when we hurt them. It's locked in their brain until they're buried underground. When we die, I wouldn't be surprised if they would be at the Pearly Gate with the same angry look on their face. Do you think Cathy told her parents about that night?"

"Dad, Cathy's pregnant. That's why she came home."

Cory looked shocked. "Oh, my God! She fooled around in Paris?"

"I went for a paternity test with Cathy at the hospital."

"You what?"

"Tony sent one of his gangsters with us and demanded the lab technician get the result right there and then. I was sure she fooled around in Paris. I wanted to prove I wasn't the father. To make matters more insane, I'm about to involve you in something that's dangerous. I'm petrified to tell you."

"Are you involved with the mob?"

"I'm not. Dad, Tony threatened me that if I didn't marry Cathy by this Sunday, he swore to harm a family member of mine."

"Are you serious?" Cory's face was red with anger.

"Dad, I'm not joking."

Todd went into every detail but held back being stopped at the gate with Mr. Greco's gangsters. "I promised myself not to tell you and I'd handle this myself."

"This isn't something you get to handle yourself. You need a lawyer. I'm going to call our attorney, Carl Miller, and file a complaint. He's on a pleasure trip this weekend with his wife, but I'll talk to him on Monday."

"Dad, I have no idea how to tell Jenny about this. I lied about being with Cathy the night of her party, but the news of her being pregnant will kill her. I'm going to be hurting the person I love. Without meaning to, I've ruined your day coming up with Mom. I'm sorry. That's why I was trying to hold out until Saturday to talk to you."

"Don't ever keep anything from me or your mother again. This is a criminal act. If you told me sooner, we might have had a meeting with Carl before he left. We can't discuss this with anyone. Does Rita know?"

"She knows I cheated on Jenny, but not this."

"When we go back home, we'll stick to the story that we had the father and son talk. From this moment, you don't go near the Greco compound. If they call, give me the phone. If you receive any more calls, you let me know right away. Do you hear me?"

"Yes, but there's still a problem with them wanting an answer by Friday. That's tomorrow. If Tony gets no call, he'll know I'm not going to marry Cathy."

"All of us will be gone Friday, so let the phone ring off the hook. I'll let Bob and Ray know not to tell them where any of us have gone for the day."

Cory turned the key to start his truck and headed back up the dirt path. Todd's eye caught the corner of the new house being built for him and Jenny on top of the slope.

"Is that our house?"

"I forgot you could see the home from here."

"Please, take me up to the house. Forget the surprise. I can get an idea of what kind of furniture to look at tomorrow."

His father drove up to the steep path.

Todd was speechless with the tour of the house and views from the steep elevation.

"I want to show you something." Cory led him into the third bedroom that was supposed to be for his future mother-in-law.

Todd looked around at the art material and was bewildered. "Why are art brushes and paint in here?"

Cory told him about Rita's story on Jenny's love for the arts and the drawings and paintings she did in the past to receive awards.

"I never knew that. Come to think of it, I did see some paintings on the walls of her home, but I thought she bought them. That's how professional they looked. Jenny's going to love this place. How can I thank you and mom for such a tremendous gift?"

Cory hugged his son. "Your marriage to Jenny will be our award."

"I wish I could take back my time with Cathy. There was no love there, Dad."

"That's the problem with men. When we want sex, we don't think with our heads. It's the aftermath of realizing how much our sinful actions will be hurting someone who loves us. We break their trust. That's the hardest to earn back."

They rode down the road talking about the business. Cory reminded his son that Attorney Miller handled his parent's will. "We'll go on Monday to talk to him together. You're going to have to tell Jenny. This has to come out in the open before your marriage."

Everyone's Day Out

Friday morning came and everyone was rushing for their full day away from work, except Rita.

"I envy all of you going somewhere. I have to work at the Barnstable festival. Where's Mom?"

Todd poured his coffee. "She upstairs. Jenny's helping her get ready for her day with Dad. You'd think she was going on a date."

"I think that's wonderful that two people their age and the years spent together that you can still feel that way."

Judy slipped into her summer dress and buttoned the front. It was a casual lightweight dress in a pale blue with deeper, navy, tiny, tiny flowers mixed in the design, with wide padded shoulders, short sleeves, a slim fitted waist with a matching belt, and a full bottom that whirled when she walked. To stay comfortable, she wore navy empire walking oxford shoes with a wide strap and a two-inch heel.

"You're going to blow your husband away when he sees you, Judy."

"Thanks, Jenny."

"I'd love to fix your hair for you. Something different than your usual everyday pinup style."

"Cory did ask me to wear my hair down. That's how I wore my locks when we met."

"How did you meet?"

"I remember that day like it was yesterday. I graduated from high school and was working behind the soda fountain at Dunnington Drugs. They had large Coke signs up, sold candy in jars, and small gifts to purchase. For some reason, the large, square black and white rubberized floor stands out in my mind.

"I made milkshakes and ice cream sodas. They called me the soda jerk. We sold all flavored ice cream. The little kids loved coming with their parents. Soda fountains were a social place. It was never quiet in the place because once anyone got into a booth they played the jukebox on the wall. Families came mostly on the weekends.

"We had a long counter where people sat for sandwiches, coffee, and dessert. I handled a lot by myself. This one Saturday, Cory walked into the store. Oh, he was a looker, Jenny.

"I saw him walk over to the medicine aisle. I heard him say to another guy standing next to him that his mother had been fighting a cold for days. Once he got the package, Cory came over to the counter and ordered a glass of cold Moxie. We had small talk, but I knew right away, he was the one. He was outgoing and mixed in with everyone eating in my section.

"I looked for him every day. In fact, I worked on my days off to see him. Then he asked me out. He picked me up in his truck. The same one he has today. I didn't care if he didn't have a car. I just wanted to be with him. We went for ice cream and sat on the beach talking for hours. It was a comfort that I never lost with him. I still have those deep feelings. Just talking about him gives me goose bumps." She laughed looking up at me.

"I feel that with Todd. We can sit without talking, yet, it's peaceful."

"If you two have that, you have it all."

"Let me see what I can do with your hair." I grabbed the comb.

When I took the pins out of Judy's hair, it fell to her shoulders with multiple waves. "Look at all the natural curls. I'd die for them. Why do you keep them pinned-up?"

"I have to keep my hair up working."

"You look different already. I don't have to make finger waves since you have them. I'd like to put this yellow flower pin in your hair." I pulled the left side of her hair up and fastened it tight. Once I finished her hairstyle, I looked straight at her face. "I'd like to do something wild. Let me put makeup on you."

"Oh, I don't know about that, Jenny. I never wore any."

220

"Judy, be different. Do something out of the ordinary. This is a special day for you and Cory."

I gave Judy pencil-thin brown eyebrows, a soft, pink lipstick, black mascara, with a touch of pink rouge on her cheeks.

"You look incredible, Judy. I never knew you had all this hidden beauty."

Judy walked over to the full-length mirror. "Wow, I don't recognize myself. How can I thank you, Jenny?"

"Don't. I enjoyed doing this."

"We're going to be a happy family. I hope you plan on lots of babies."

I suddenly developed a serious expression.

Judy took a double look at me. "What's the matter?"

"I want to tell you something. I'm going to tell Todd tonight, but you can't say anything until he knows."

"I'm excellent at keeping secrets. With all of you my book is full. What is it? Good news, I hope."

"Judy, I'm going to make you and Cory grandparents."

"I hope so. We plan on you giving us tons.'

"No…... I mean now. I'm pregnant, Judy."

She looked at me without any reaction for a moment. Tears filled her eyes. She walked over and hugged me gently and affectionately.

"Don't cry. I just put your makeup on!"

"Oh, sweetheart." She wrapped her arms around me tighter. "That's why you've been sick. Why didn't you tell us sooner?"

"I was afraid everyone would be disappointed in us because we didn't wait." We both cried holding each other from happiness.

"It's all your son's fault for being charming and handsome." We laughed. "I'm glad your family came into my life. When God called my mother home, I was lost. What would I have done without you and Cory? When I get married, I'm calling you, Mom. You can help me bring our baby up."

"Jenny. You have been a joy to us. I can't wait to tell Cory."

"Tell him when he's not driving. Maybe over lunch. Check to make sure I've told Todd today before you start congratulating him.

"Let me touch up the wet spots on your face from crying. There, you're new again. Let's go downstairs. Our men are waiting."

Rita was leaving through the backdoor. "Have fun everyone. See you all at supper. My treat. It will be ready at 6 pm. You should all be back by that time. No suppers. I'm making it tonight. Bye!" She closed the door behind her.

"Where's your father, Todd?" Judy asked

He took a double look at his mother and stopped in his tracks. "Wow, is that you, Mom? Honestly, you're beautiful!" He looked at his mother from head to toe.

"Thanks. You two are planning on picking up the gowns today?"

"No problem, Mom. That will be one thing you don't have to worry about getting done. The wedding's next weekend. Can you imagine, Jenny?" He wrapped his arm around my waist.

Bob drove the truck up to the house. "Cory, it's all been checked over. The breaks have fluid, oil change, and plenty of gas."

"Thanks Bob. I appreciate the work. I'll go in and get Judy."

"Have a great day, boss." Bob walked down to the shop where Ray was set up for the day's work.

Cory turned to go up the steps and saw Judy at the top. A smile came across his face. "My Lord, woman. Look at you! I almost didn't recognize you. You're prettier than the day I met you." He climbed to the top step and kissed her longer than normal in front of us.

Todd and I had grins watching his parents acting like teenagers.

"Okay, kids, we're off for the day. We'll see you at five tonight. Maybe sooner if your Mom gets bored with me."

The truck backed up and then headed up the dirt road. We saw Judy move closer to the driver's side.

"Guess it's our turn," Todd replied. "Let's find a quiet, little cafe for breakfast."

"I'll get the car. Do you have the slips for the gowns?"

"Yes, in my purse."

We drove out for our own day with excitement.

Picking Out Furniture

Todd opened the side passenger door and gave me a kiss. We rode the main drag that followed the beach and sand dunes along the way.

"I sure do love this place, Jenny. Soon, we'll have our own little hideaway in the woods."

"I can't wait, Todd." As he drove, I pushed closer holding onto his arm.

Within the thirty-minute ride, we came across a restaurant. "Here's Ma & Pa's Breakfast. Let's try this place," I said.

We walked to the front entrance. Todd took a good whiff. "Hum, smell the breakfast cooking and the strong aroma of coffee brewing?"

We picked a side booth in the corner. Todd ordered a cup of fruit and oatmeal, followed by broiled ham and poached eggs on toast. I had scrambled eggs with parsley, French home fries, toast, and a cup of decaf coffee.

I wanted to tell Todd about the baby but felt a breakfast place wasn't romantic. Too many people were laughing and talking at the counter, along with dishes clanking in the kitchen, orders were being yelled out to the waitresses, and the bell above the door rang each time someone came in or out of the diner.

"It's nice to get away from work. I guess we all get caught up with not taking enough time for enjoyment." Todd took a sip of coffee. "Wow! That's hot! Be careful with yours."

I started to feel how important it was to spend time together.

We ate with little talk because it was impossible to carry a conversation with all the noise from conversations. The cafe seemed like a truck stop.

Within twenty minutes, Todd asked, "Are you done?"

I took the last sip of my coffee.

"Let's go get all the gowns first so the day can be ours."

When we walked into the bridal store, Todd asked, "How did you ever choose a gown? Look at all of them."

"That's what was surprising. We all got ours within an hour."

"Hello. Can I help you?" A saleswoman walked up to us.

"I'm here to pick up three gowns and one wedding dress for the Costa party. Here are the slips for each dress."

"Oh, yes. Jenny, you're the bride. I'll get Jack to help me. If you want, pull your car up to the backdoor. It will be easier than carrying them out to your vehicle."

Todd went to get the car and pull the vehicle around the building.

"He's my husband to be, and I don't want him seeing the wedding dress. Is my gown in a clear plastic bag?"

"No, your gown is covered with a heavy, black bag. Once you get home, keep the dress in that bag and hang it out of the closet so the gown won't get squished. We have ironed every part of the dress. The other girls have to do the same with theirs. They're in the clear bags.

Todd walked into the bridal shop with his car parked in the back.

"Here's your signed receipt back. Mrs. Costa paid for everything."

She walked up to us. "We wish both of you years of happiness and thank you for choosing the Cape Cod Bridal Shop. If you have any questions, please don't hesitate to call us."

"It was a pleasure coming here. Your assistance was wonderful helping the four of us chose the dresses."

Jack and Todd took the dresses out one by one to keep them clean and without causing wrinkles.

I got into the car and leaned over to kiss Todd. "It's real." I took Todd's hand and placed it on my left breast. "Feel my heart. It's beating so fast with a thrill beyond words."

"Behave yourself," Todd said with a big grin.

"Now the furniture. What was the name of the store Rita had given you?"

"It was Myers Furniture Store. Right on Main Street. Oh, there it is. See the store on the corner?"

We walked through the front door and saw all the displays of furniture for every room. My most important room was our bedroom. We roamed in-between sets until we came across a carved French style set. It was a combination of maple and deep walnut wood. It included a bureau with a scalloped center mirror with two small ones on the side, tilting in. A tall chest with four deep drawers had beautiful French-designed handles, a night table with the same handles, and the double bed included a headboard with full French designs, footboard, rails, and slats.

"I like this bedroom set, Todd."

"I do, too. The others aren't as pretty."

We headed to the kitchen sets. Todd went right to a chrome kitchen dinette set with an oval top and four chairs that had black leather cushions."

A salesman finally noticed us looking through the furniture. "That's our best seller. We do have the same set in red. The table has a strong and durable surface and it's easy to clean.

"Do you like it, honey?" Todd looked at me.

I looked at the set and sat in one of the chairs. These are thick cushions. Yes, I do like this one."

"Would you rather it be red?" he asked.

"Let's go with the black because we're not sure what your dad picked out for wallpaper. The black will go with anything, plus the food spills won't show up so much.

"We'll take this and the French style bedroom set."

"I assume you two lovely people are about to be married." The salesman was giving his usual kind, flattering talk to pull us into a sale.

I looked up at Todd and smiled. "Yes, in one week."

"Congratulations."

"Thank you," Todd replied. "We want to look at the living room sets."

The salesperson walked us through another open door to a few backrooms with multiple sets. We were amazed at the choices.

"Why don't I give you a few minutes to look around at them. I don't want you to rush and not get the one you want." The salesman returned to the front of the store.

Todd went up to a light-tan, six-foot couch with tan throw pillows.

"This is rich-looking. It's a basic color."

The salesman could see that Todd zeroed-in on a set. Within minutes, he was upon us again.

"This comes with a matching set of two side chairs with dark, mahogany wood going down the front arms of the chairs to become the legs. You can add the high back chair to the set, and two end tables come with the couch."

I walked around the couch rubbing my hand on the material. Todd sat on the couch and went over to try the armchairs.

"You look like you're not sure," Todd said.

"It's not that I don't like the set. I do, but it's so light, anything will show up on it. Let's face it; we want a color for kids. This color would get dirty in no time."

"I didn't think of that."

"We do have this set in a chocolate brown outback."

"Now, that I would like to see," I said.

"Let me show you." He took us to a corner in another room.

"You're right with having kids. We should get this set," Todd said.

"I guess we have all the furniture for the house." Both of us were relieved to have it all picked out.

"When would you pick this up, Mr...?"

"Oh sorry, Todd Costa." He shook the salesman's hand. And your name?"

"I'm Brian Cooper."

"My dad and I, and a few other men will pick the furniture up next week. Can we plan on Wednesday? That's our slowest day."

"Let fill out the paperwork. Come to my office."

We immediately put a deposit down with the arrangements to come back Wednesday.

We walked out and sat in the car. "You're right. It's happening,

Jenny. We're going to be husband and wife. What more could I ask for in life? I've got the love of my life." Todd held me as if I was going to slip away.

"I don't want to leave Bob and Ray alone all day. It's 2 o'clock."

I wanted to tell Todd about our baby but couldn't find an opening with Todd talking about the business. I started to think maybe I should wait until we got home and go for a walk alone to the lake. I thought the location would be special. At the same time, I was scared he wouldn't be happy with my pregnancy.

"Your parents have done a lot for us, Todd. What would we do without them?

"They have always been there for all of us. That's why it's good for them to take off today by themselves. I don't think they ever did. It's a special day for their 25th wedding anniversary."

"Rita said she ordered a cake for them. We'll serve the pastry after we eat. They're going to be surprised. Rita's going to start supper once she gets home." I can't wait for the occasion.

"I hope they save room for supper after Dad was talking about eating a full lunch."

"We can go home and help Rita with the decorations. It's going to be a big surprise."

Todd's Confession

I moved closer to while he drove. "We have time, let's stop by the beach. I'd like to tell you something."

He looked at me with a wide smile. "You can't tell me now?"

"No, I want your full attention. Let's sit on the blanket."

We pulled over and Todd grabbed a blanket out of the backseat. Todd spread it out and we sat down.

"This is awesome, just you and me, Todd." He was watching the waves, as if he was there in body, but not mind.

"Are you okay, honey?" I put my arm around him.

"I've been depressed over something that I need to share with you."

"Well, I have been wanting to tell you something for weeks, and I think this will make your worries seem like nothing." I couldn't wait to share this electrifying moment.

"Jenny, before you tell me, I have something that needs to be said. I have tried to hide this situation hoping the problem would work itself out. In fact, my father was going to help solve it with me." He had a serious expression.

I took his hands and faced him. "Since when have you not been able to talk to me? We're too close to have secrets. Don't ever hold anything back from me. There isn't anything that we can't work out, no matter how bad the situation might seem."

"I need you to keep that remark in mind when I tell you something you're not going to like hearing." He looked down at the sand.

"Todd, you're scaring me." I was trying to brace myself. I couldn't imagine what had happened. I feared to face another disaster in my life.

Todd looked at me speechless.

"Honey, it's okay. You can tell me." I rubbed my hand on his back.

"Jenny, remember when I came home late because I had delivered the shrubs and plants to our clients?"

"Yes." I was still lost on why he was scared to share this event.

"Cathy's mother called me wanting some shrubs delivered that night."

I felt a knot in my stomach and let my tight hold on Todd's hands loosen and sat up straighter, making a wider separation between us; giving me a protective wall. My smile and understanding of trying to support Todd disappeared. I started to lose empathy knowing Cathy had returned and he went to her home. I had this deep fear that my love for Todd was about to be tested. I gave him my full attention and didn't interrupt.

Here I was about to tell him that I had a baby growing inside me. His baby. What a blessing. I wanted to see the same happy expression on his face as his mother's when I gave her the news. I would have been on cloud nine. I touched my stomach and braced myself for something I didn't want to hear.

"Jenny, Cathy isn't home for her father's court date. She's pregnant and claiming I'm the father."

"How can you be the father when she's been in Paris for months?"

"I lied about Cathy and me. I had sex with her the night of her party. I had too much to drink."

I couldn't talk. The paralyzing news was as if I got hit in the gut, taking the wind out of me.

"How did you find out she's pregnant? Who told you?"

"Her mother, Sharon, called me to their house to deliver the plants the night you were all worried about me. I thought it was safe because Cathy was in Paris.

"Sharon called me into the den and Cathy was sitting on the couch. This is when she made the announcement. I felt like you that she was trying to trap me knowing we were getting married."

I looked at him, hurt. "It's bad enough you cheated on me but you lied when I asked you. For weeks, I have been going around feeling terrible not trusting you."

"I felt horrible. I couldn't tell you. I never expected her to come home again. It was a mistake and I hoped it could be buried. I never thought she'd get pregnant.

"And you're taking this tramp's word; you're the father? What makes you think she didn't fool around in Paris?" I could feel my hate for Cathy bursting out of me.

We went for a paternity test at the hospital and I'm ninety-nine percent the father."

"You went to the hospital for a test with her! How sweet, Todd."

He looked up at me. "Please, don't look at me like that. I made an inexcusable mistake. Jenny, I don't love her. It's a moment I wish I could take back."

"We're supposed to be married on Sunday next weekend and I hear this monster, Cathy, had sex with you. Now, she's carrying *your* baby."

My world collapsed. How could this be? I was sick hearing Cathy had the most precious part of Todd growing inside her. She had Todd emotionally where she wanted him. I was losing Todd without doing anything wrong. Those knot in my stomach that I had carried for weeks with doubt something had happened between them had been there for a reason. The signs were in front of me. I had pushed them in the back of my mind. I didn't want to deal with the reality of Todd still having feelings for her.

My mind was filled with the fact that he loved me that little that he cheated. Panic overcame me being pregnant. I had to hold back my words from making a decision from anger. I had to think this through carefully for a few days giving the shock time to sink into me. Maybe Todd's parents could help us deal with this madness.

"Take me home, Todd. Don't bring this issue up in front of your family. Your parents will be coming home to find a surprise 25th-anniversary party."

My world, as it had been with happiness and feeling loved, was over.

"Jenny, I can't stand you hating me. We need to talk this out."

"I don't want to get into this nightmare until your parent's party is over. I need time to think of what you did to me. By then, maybe I'll have time to decide if we're going to have a wedding."

"Please, don't make a decision tonight."

"Todd, let's get home and help Rita. I'm not up to talking."

We drove back as strangers. I couldn't fathom how love as strong as ours could suddenly have a black cloud hanging over it.

Cory and Judy's Day

Cory drove with his truck window down and grabbed his wife's hand. "Isn't this great, Judy? What do you want to do?"

"I thought you had something planned."

"I'd like to head for the Fish and Crab Shack in Orleans. We can celebrate our anniversary with a good lobster. "

"A lobster! I can't remember when we had one."

"You deserve whatever you want." He looked over at her with the feelings of a teenager in love.

They pulled up at noon in front of the shack and the place was starting to fill up fast being a Friday.

"Suppertime must be wild in here," Cory said, as he pulled the chair out for Judy to sit.

She smiled, looking up at him. "Thank you, sir."

They sat across from each other on the outside deck. It was the last week of September and the weather was still in the eighties. The outside exterior wasn't closed for the fall season.

The boats were tied up at the docks. They could see the late fishing boats coming in with their catch for the day. The seagulls chattered loudly circling the vessels while they went into their slips.

"Maybe our lobsters are on that boat," Cory said, laughing.

"Look at the seals at the end of the wharf sunbathing. They're not scared of people walking near them."

"They're here so often, they must overlook humans."

The waitress came out. "Good afternoon. Can I start you out with a drink?"

Cory looked up at her. "I'm going to have a tall glass of cold beer."

"Which one, sir?"

"I'll have a Bud, please."

The waitress looked at Judy. "I'll start with water, lots of ice, and a lemon."

Cory had already made his mind up with the appetizers. "Bring us a plate of littlenecks to start. Give us time to finish them, and put an order in for two baked lobsters, a baked potato, and coleslaw with extra tartar sauce on the side."

"That sounds heavenly, Cory." Judy took in the smell of the saltwater air. "We have to do this more often."

Cory looked at Judy's hair hanging straight down with the sun hitting directly on it. Her strands sparkled with different tones. "You look stunning right now, Judy. I never saw you with makeup. Where have you been, my darling?" He smiled and touched her hand on the table, looking straight into her eyes.

"Jenny took the time to try to make me look young again. She insisted I needed a different look for you."

"She was right. You could pass as a model."

"Flattery will get you everywhere, Cory." She gave him a loving smile.

Their ice water and cold beer came out along with the little necks. Cory took a long swallow of the cold ale. He had foam on his upper lip. "Ah, there's nothing more refreshing on a hot day than a cold beer." He wiped the dripping from his mouth with the back of his hand.

They dug right in with the twelve little necks on a bed of lettuce with spicy cocktail sauce in a tiny steel cup. Judy wanted to explode with the news of Jenny being pregnant but decided to enjoy their meal first and go for a ride to be alone.

The lobsters came out, and as they ate, there wasn't much time to talk from concentrating on cracking the shells. Cory helped Judy break hers. They took the fresh, soft meat pieces and dunked them into the hot, melted butter.

"Oh, Cory, this is so delicious." Judy was using her fingers to get every piece of lobster meat hidden in the shell. The tails were like a piece of steak with their thickness. They laughed at the crazy things their kids had done growing up while enjoying the meal.

The waitress came to clear-off their dishes full of shells and dirty utensils. She placed two warm, wet towels on the table. "Any room for dessert?"

"I think we're going to walk this off and get ice cream later," Judy replied.

Cory paid the bill and they walked out to their truck. Two rugged-looking men were by their pickup; one looking it over, while the other was bent down feeling a tire.

"Can I help you?" Cory asked.

"We were just looking at your truck. It's in good shape. Any chance of selling it? I'd be interested in buying it."

"Not in your life. Too many memories."

The two men walked away. "Thanks!"

"That was odd," Judy remarked, getting into the passenger side.

"Everything's odd or suspicious. You should have been a mystery writer. You would have written great stories."

****

They drove to a festival being held in Orleans. They knew Rita was at the one in Barnstable. Cory took Judy on the Ferris wheel. As they went high, Cory studied the grounds below them.

"Look at all we can see up here," Judy said.

Cory started to rock the seat. "Stop that, Cory. You know I hate shaking the seat this high up." Her fingers dug tighter onto the bar going across.

They acted like teenagers walking around holding hands. Cory went to the booth with the rifle to shoot. "Let me see if I still have my shooting skills. Remember that Teddy bear I won for you?"

"We were so young, Cory. I kept that huge, stuffed animal in my bedroom…on the floor. It was too big for my chair."

Cory paid for five shots and won. "I still have the aim, honey."

"What would you like, Miss?" The man behind the game stand waited for Judy to choose.

234

She looked the gifts over, and her eyes came upon a doll with a white bonnet, and a red and white flare printed dress. "I'll take that doll."

The man walked over to the toy section and handed her the prize.

"Here you go." He gave her a smile.

Judy got excited thinking if Jenny had a baby girl, this could be the perfect gift with memories of Cory winning the doll.

The man behind the booth then proceeded to call out, "Someone just won this pretty little doll for a special person. Come on over and try your luck." The noise of the rides over-rode his voice.

"A doll out of all the prizes! How did you end up with that being your choice?"

"You never know if Jenny or Faith will have a daughter in the future."

"What if they have sons?"

"Could happen. I'm sure they'll bless us with many grandkids. As long as they're all healthy."

They walked away with Judy keeping a hold on the doll. They sat and watched the crowd stroll by them. People were rushing to get on the rides and the loud screams filled the area from the thrill-seekers. The atmosphere was dusty from the dirt flying. The smoke from the engines running the excursions was thick carrying a strong smell of gasoline.

They got up and walked around the park until they came upon an ice cream stand.

A man behind the counter with a large, white bib apron looked down at them. "What can I get you?"

Cory looked up at the list of choices on flavors and then asked Judy, "What do you like?"

"I'm going for a real treat. If I'm going to cheat, my choice is definitely going to be a high-calorie dessert. Give me a hot fudge sundae with vanilla ice cream and tons of whip cream topped with a cherry."

Cory laughed. "I'll say that's a treat! I'll have a large chocolate in a cone."

"You're going to make me out to be the pig," Judy said, giving him a teasing shove.

"This is our day to do anything our hearts desire." Cory gave Judy a warm hug.

The ice cream cone came out first, and Judy grabbed her sundae as if it was the last one she would have for the year. They sat on a bench near the roller coaster holding onto a handful of napkins.

"How can anyone go on that monster ride?" Judy asked. "I'm petrified of speed and sudden drops. I think I'd pass out with the first plunge."

She dug her plastic teaspoon into the paper cup coming out with a glob of chocolate drippings and vanilla ice cream. "Hum—this is so good, Cory. Worth every high and dangerous calorie." Her eyes closed with contentment as she swallowed.

Cory looked at the roller coaster. "I loved that ride when I was younger. Don't think I'd go now. I'm too old." Cory wiped his chin with a napkin. "Boy, once ice cream starts to melt, it's a race keeping up with licking the drippings. I'm trying to figure out if I'm enjoying the ice cream or hating the work to keep it from melting on my fingers."

"Anything you have to work for is usually worth the fight to achieve the win. Also, you'll never be too old for me, darling." Judy leaned over and kissed him.

"Hey, watch it. I know you're after my ice cream on my lips."

"That was a tasty kiss, but my flavor is more delicious. Let's end the day by going for a walk on the beach. We'll take our shoes off."

"Sounds like fun?" Cory said as he sucked the last blob of ice cream out of the bottom and bit the end of the cone.

"I swear the first lick of ice cream and the last piece of the wafer is the best. Not sure which I enjoyed more today, the lobster or the ice cream cone."

Judy scraped the bottom of her container with the spoon until nothing was left. "I wish my tongue could reach the bottom to get the last melted drop."

Cory laughed because he knew she wasn't joking. They threw their wastes into the barrel and walked to the truck.

After a long drive, they pulled into a parking spot near the sand dunes. The seashore went for miles stretching right down to Provincetown. The sand was soft with no stones or rocks.

Cory and Judy held hands again with a rhythm stride and traveled a good mile walking the beach. They walked barefoot in the warm water. Their conversations touched the memories of their youthful times with dating and having blessed moments when their three children were born.

"I love the water and Cape Cod beaches, Cory. We've had a great life here."

"Remember all the trips to the beach with the kids, Judy? We'd wait for the tide to be low and bring their pails to catch the crabs left behind with the receding water."

"We still have those colorful, shiny stones they collected since they were babies in the living room in five jars," Judy remarked. "The two of us sat for hours on the beach blanket to let them run in any direction chasing each other or being splashed in the water. The best times were when we helped the three of them learn how to build sandcastles. Todd always cried when the rising tide came and destroyed his hours of hard work."

"Where did the years go, Judy?" Cory put his arm around her shoulder. They continued to stroll with the remembrance of being young, having their family, and building the business was a feeling of satisfaction with what they had accomplished together.

"Do you know that we must have walked for miles without thinking we had to walk back?" Judy laughed.

"Well, let's turn around while we have the energy. We'll take our time. I'm not young like I used to be, my dear," Cory admitted.

When they got close to their truck, both were short-winded from not getting out more often with walking.

"We need to rest before we go home. Let's sit on the stonewall over there." Judy led him by the hand.

They sat down and Judy looked at Cory. "I have been holding in the greatest news all day. I think this is the time to tell you."

"You...Judy Costa....held a secret all day? I don't believe it."

"Jenny told me to tell you this secret when you weren't driving."

"Really. It must be a whopper if I have to be sitting," he laughed.

"It's the opposite. You, Cory, are going to be a grandfather."

Cory looked at Judy with panic. "Jenny's pregnant?" It was asked in a whisper.

"Why do you look upset? Aren't you excited?"

Judy couldn't have told Cory anything more disastrous. His mind was in fast mode. Cathy was pregnant carrying Todd's baby and so was Jenny. How could his son have been free with himself?

"Todd never told me and I was with him yesterday afternoon. Why would he tell you and not me?"

"He didn't tell me. Jenny told me just before we left. Todd doesn't know. She's going to tell him today while they're getting the furniture. It won't be long; they'll be looking at baby furniture. I think we have the baby cradle in the barn stored up top. Once she tells everyone, I'll clean the bedding, and we can give the bed to them. I might even have a trunk with the kid's infant clothes. You know me, I saved everything. Do you think we have more clothes hiding somewhere?" She kept rambling on and on with excitement, not realizing the catastrophe.

Cory got up from the stonewall. He paced around looking up at the sky. "This can't be happening."

"Honey, what's the matter. I thought you would be thrilled out of your mind. If you're upset, please, don't show them. Your disappointed expression will make Jenny feel horrible. She was afraid you would be displeased.

"She's not sure how Todd will take the news either. At least they're getting married next weekend. In fact, Todd was trying to get her to marry him this Sunday without knowing about her condition. I would have been upset if they ran off and eloped."

Cory sat again on the low, stone barrier and looked at Judy but no words could come out.

"Cory say something. This was supposed to be a happy moment for us. It doesn't matter if she got pregnant now or after the marriage. This doesn't mean that Jenny's not a good girl."

"Judy, I have some terrible news, and I was hoping to hide this from you until Monday."

"When have you ever hid something from me? Don't start telling me and then stop."

"Remember, your uneasiness with Todd leaving the other day and not stopping in to tell us where he was going?"

"Yes." Judy was glued to Cory's words waiting for his information to hit her.

"Sharon called him to deliver some shrubs and Todd didn't stop in to tell us because he didn't want to listen to us getting upset with him going there after the raid. He had no idea at all that Cathy was home."

Cory moved closer to Judy. "Yesterday, I took Todd down by Lover's Lake to talk to him. I felt like you that something was wrong. When he finished dropping the shrubs off to the Greco's, Todd had been called into their house."

Judy listened bracing for the bad news.

"You can imagine how shocked Todd was to see Cathy in her father's den sitting on a couch. She didn't come home because of her father's trial coming up. Cathy's pregnant and claimed Todd's the father."

Judy wanted to block her ears. "Please, tell me this isn't real. This can't be. You mean Todd did fool around with Cathy that night coming home late from her party? He lied to us?"

Judy stood up with tears flowing down her face. "What's he going to do?"

"He's in bad shape with all this. To top this news of Cathy, I know Todd doesn't know about Jenny. I hope she doesn't tell him before we get home. I'm not sure what he'll do. He thought this fling with Cathy would blow over," Cory said.

"Jenny doesn't know about Cathy, and Todd doesn't know about Jenny! Talk about two destructive storms coming together. What will he do?" Judy was frantic.

"It gets worse, Judy. Can you handle hearing more?"

She sat back down on the wall. "I'm not sure. How bad can this get?"

Cory told her about the threats towards Todd if he didn't marry Cathy on Sunday. "He was told to confirm the marriage today. That's probably why he wanted to marry Jenny right away."

"Well, Jenny isn't marrying him before the scheduled date. They're crazy about each other and you know it. Tony Greco isn't going to get away with this. What kind of threats did he make?" Judy was wild with the thought of Cathy being pregnant by her son. Of all families; a mafia one!

"He swore something painful would happen to his family."

"They threatened all of us? My God! How does Todd know if the baby is his child?"

"He went that day for a blood test, and he's the father."

"No one gets results that fast. They're trying to scare him. That woman has been running around for years."

"Judy, Tony's a mob boss. He sent one of his gangsters with Todd and Cathy and ordered the lab to give him an answer within an hour. That's why he was late coming home."

"What's he going to do, Cory? I can't believe they threatened him—us! What's Jenny going to do? What if she finds out about all this? Once she does, the news could end their upcoming marriage. I don't think Jenny can handle this. I can't!"

"I don't know what will happen when Jenny tells him they're having a child?" Cory said.

"What do we do about the threats, Cory? Do you think they mean them?"

"I told Todd that we'd call Carl Monday. He's on vacation. This man never takes time for himself, and he's out of town when I never needed him more. Let's see what Carl says. I'm sure he'll tell us all the legal ways to handle this. If Cathy's willing to be paid off, I'll do it."

"You think she cares about money? She's filthy rich. She's *Nina Mae*, remember?"

"I told Todd that Jenny will have to be told. We need this all cleaned up before the wedding. We'll worry later on how Jenny handles the news. Meeting Carl will give us time to respond to this situation. Carl's the person we need to reach as soon as possible. He'll have the answers for us.

"Cory, this is scary."

"Let's head back home. After this conversation, I don't think we can do anything else that will give us pleasure. We need to talk directly to Todd and see if he knows about Jenny. If Jenny told him, he's going to be out of his mind."

"I honestly believe this will cut Jenny's heart out. We have always helped the kids, Cory, but this is the worst situation facing us."

Cory and Judy got into their truck and started heading back. Judy sat close to Cory, but no words were passed back and forth. They were both glad the conversation of Cathy and Jenny's pregnancies, and the threats against Todd, all came out at the end of their day and not in the beginning. Otherwise, they would have missed a special day with each other. Both of them were in shock and wondered how to help Todd and Jenny fix this problem and save their wedding day.

Judy picked up the doll and held tight to her trinket. "Please, Cory, slow down. You're going too fast down this long hill. I want to get back alive. Things will work out. Speeding home won't solve them faster."

The truck traveled down the road, faster than normal, picking up speed.

The wind started to blow forcefully in Judy's face and hair from the open window.

"I said, *SLOW DOWN!* You're not funny. You're frightening me."

"Something's wrong with the brakes! They feel soft." Cory had a terrifying look on his face.

"What do you mean? You have no breaks going down this slope? Cory, be careful, there's a curve up ahead!"

Quickly, their pace was at lightning speed.

"Oh my God, Judy! Hold on! We're going off the embankment!"

"NO!" Judy screamed, holding Cory's arm and the doll for dear life.

The Celebration Ends

Rita finished her interview earlier than expected at the Barnstable Fair and went to the bakery to pick up their parent's 25th Anniversary cake.

The baker opened the cover showing a three-layer cake. "Do you like it?"

The cake had all-white frosting displaying silver letters standing on the top and a silver ribbon around the bottom. The base had an oval plate facing the front with a white design around the rim. In the center of the oval was written "Happy 25th Anniversary" with a silver background. It was plain but simple.

"Oh, Mr. Lewis, you did a wonderful job. Thank you."

He closed the cake up and Rita took the pastry with excitement.

She was happy to get home earlier than planned so she could start the surprise anniversary supper. She wanted something special. Cooking wasn't a talent of hers, but she was going to give it a try. Rita decided on roasted chicken with stuffing, mashed potatoes, and fresh string beans. She wanted to prepare the meal in a short time.

After placing the spiced chicken in the oven, she grabbed a book and sat outside on the porch swing to enjoy being alone for a few hours.

The family had been disappointed that Sam and Faith couldn't make the occasion. They were saving their vacation time for the wedding.

****

As Todd entered the driveway, I saw a strange look on his face.

"What's the matter?"

"Sam and Faith must have gotten the time-off to come to the anniversary dinner. Dad and Mom will be thrilled to see them. There's his Auburn Model 8-98 Brougham Chassis. Come to think of it, he was supposed to give me a ride in the car before they left last time. He won't get away this time. Let's go inside and join the family. We don't want to be walking in when my parents arrive."

I took a deep breath holding back anger. Todd acted as nothing happened between us.

He stopped walking once he spotted a squad car. "What would a police car be doing here?"

"I hope they're not going to question you for Mr. Greco's court case. It'll ruin your parent's night."

We opened the front door and saw Rita, Sam, and Faith sitting in the living room. Two cops were standing by them writing something down on a pad of paper. They turned toward us.

"Hi. What's going on?" Todd asked walking into the room.

I noticed the girls were crying.

"Who are you two?" One of the cops asked.

Sam stood-up. "This is my brother, Todd, and his fiancée, Jenny. I think you two should sit down. There's no gentle way to tell you both this. Dad and Mom were in an accident this afternoon. They were going around the corner on Route 6 by the Ocean View Cliffs and came down the hill too fast and went off the embankment."

"*OH, MY GOD!* Were they hurt? Did the ambulance take them to Cape Cod Hospital?" Todd was moving in circles trying to absorb the horrifying news.

Sam's eyes filled up. He went up to his brother and put his hand on his shoulder. "Todd, they were both killed."

Todd became hysterical. "No, I don't believe you." He tried to block the terrible news out. "It can't be true. We were with them this morning. They can't be dead."

Sam led his brother to an armchair. "Todd sit down for a minute."

He didn't answer. Anger erupted and he threw a book from the couch into the fireplace. He was trying to grab anything in sight to destroy.

"Todd, stop it." Sam latched onto his arms.

Todd fell down to the floor on his knees sobbing. "It can't be true. How could this have happened? Dad was an excellent driver."

Todd looked at the cops. "Did someone hit them to push them off the cliff?"

"A driver behind them stayed to give us a report. They stated that your parent's truck started slowly down the hill and developed into a tremendous amount of speed around the curve. Your father lost control, and they went off the hill."

"They didn't deserve to die like that."

"We're doing all we can to investigate this accident, Mr. Costa. There's a chance the brakes might have given out."

"That's absolutely impossible."

"Why would you say that? Anything is likely," Sam replied.

"I'm positive because Bob checked Dad's truck out completely this morning before they left. He put brake fluid in, added water, and checked his oil. He's a mechanic and knew what was supposed to be inspected for their trip. Dad had new brake shoes installed a month ago. Why would they give out?"

"That's good to know. Is Bob around so we can question him?" The cop asked.

"They should be here any minute. Are you looking at Bob as a suspect?"

"With an investigation, everyone is a suspect," Mr. Costa."

I heard a scream come out of me. "I can't handle this. I loved them. I hugged and kissed Judy this morning." Faith put her arms around me, and we both went to pieces.

"What are we going to do? Look at the kitchen decorations. They would have been so thrilled to know we gave them a party," Sam said.

I walked into the kitchen and looked pale. Rita came up to me. "I think you should rest on the couch with your feet up. I'll get you a pillow."

Rita took me by the hand and whispered. "You can't take a chance and lose this baby. I'm telling you to rest. Does Todd know?"

244

"No. I was getting ready to tell him when he gave me some shocking news."

"What news?"

"We can talk later."

"I can't imagine waking up or doing anything in this house without hearing or seeing your parents. Your mom was always here to talk to us. Your dad was a rock for Todd and Sam. The world has stopped. I want to wake up from this nightmare." I didn't want to handle any more deaths.

I laid down on the sofa while Rita adjusted the pillows under my knees.

A knock came on the front door and Bob and Ray entered.

"The food sure smells good in here," Ray said walking into the living room. He didn't see the cops in the corner. "Why's everyone sitting in here? I thought this room was for special occasions?"

Bob walked in behind him. "Well, we're about to have a wonderful celebration. When is the happy couple due to come home?"

Todd walked up to both men. "We have some tragic news. My parents were killed."

Bob and Ray were frozen in place with no reaction. "Oh, my God, Todd."

"Which one of you is Bob?"

Bob turned around and looked surprised to see the police there. "I am." He stepped in front of Ray.

"We heard that you worked on Mr. Costa's truck this morning before they left."

"I gave the truck a full inspection. I always do when he travels, but it's rare they go out of town. Cory wanted me to go over everything."

"Did you work on the brakes?"

"I looked at them, sir. They didn't need any work, they were in perfect condition. In fact, we installed new ones a month ago. Why do you ask?"

"We're looking at this accident from all angles. The witness who saw the car go over said he didn't see any brake lights go on when they went down the hill."

"What did they hit?"

"They went over the embankment."

Bob made the sign of the cross. "Those poor souls."

"Did Mr. Costa look at the brakes after you checked them before leaving?"

"Why would he? Cory trusted me. Are you accusing me of doing something to his brakes?"

"If you are, get the idea out of your heads," Todd interrupted getting angry. "He has been a devoted friend and family member for twenty years. He and Ray worked by my father's side every day since they graduated from high school."

"We have to ask these questions," Mr. Costa."

"I don't like you hinting at such an accusation," Sam stated. "I can't remember Bob and Ray not being family."

Officer Ferreira went up to his partner. "I think this family has had enough dreadful news. They need to absorb what has happened. Will you all be available if we need to ask more questions?"

"Yes, but we need to plan two funerals and would appreciate our privacy. If you have any questions, please save them until this is over."

"Thank you for your assistance and patience with us at this sad time. Here are our telephone numbers if you need to call us at the Chatham Police Department. Again, we're both sorry for your loss. Hopefully, we'll find no foul play."

"Why would you say that?" Todd asked.

"Because, until it's proven to be an awful accident, we check everything out," officer Justin remarked.

Officer Ferreira spoke next. "Their bodies were taken to the Cape Cod Hospital in Hyannis. At least one of you will have to go to the morgue and legally identify the bodies. Our deepest sympathy to your whole family."

As they started towards the door, Officer Justin turned and grabbed a bag he had placed on the chair. "I forgot there was something on the seat in the truck. He walked over to Rita. "We found a doll. Looks to be a gift you'd get at winning a game at a park fair."

They walked towards the front door and closed it behind them.

"What an adorable doll." Rita looked at the white bonnet, and the red and white flare printed dress.

I jumped up. Let me have the doll." I held it tight. I had no doubt that Judy wanted the prize for my baby. I only hoped Judy told Cory. I cradled the doll with more tears running down my face. I wanted the last remembrance of them knowing that I had shared something private with Judy about her future grandchild.

****

The seven of us sat in the living room traumatized. The tears became dry after hours of crying.

"This doesn't seem real," Rita said staring straight ahead. I picked up their cake and was excited about making the meal and setting the room up. Four hours later, we're mourning their deaths."

I sat up. "God, two more burials!"

I think Todd and I should get to the morgue at Cape Cod Hospital." Sam looked at him. "Do you think you can handle everything here, Rita?"

"If you don't mind, Bob and I would like to go with you for support."

"That would be comforting, Ray. We can talk over what might have happened. I'll take my car," Sam said.

The four men climbed into the car and disappeared down the road.

Rita looked at Faith and me. "I don't know what I'm supposed to do next. My legs don't want to move. Maybe I should shut down the oven before the roasted chicken is overcooked."

I felt like I walked in slow motion as Faith and I followed, not knowing what to do to help.

"I hate to take down the decorations you put up," Faith said, looking around the kitchen. "What are we going to do with all this? Removing them seems so final, and yet, there's nothing to celebrate."

"They were happy about leaving the house. They never went anywhere, and the one time they wanted to go out, they got killed. I can't believe they'll never be here with us. It's too overwhelming." I shook from distress.

Rita sat at the table. "My parents put all of us before their own needs. Mom devoted her whole life to the family. How do we come down the stairs in the morning and not smell her homemade blueberry pancakes, muffins, fried eggs, and toast that never once got burnt? She was an expert in cooking.

"Two days ago, she had a cold working at the stand and never complained. Then she ran up to the house to start supper. No wonder my father loved her so much. She could never be replaced. He idolized her and I can see why. He was always gentle, and at the same time, strong.

"Dad taught Sam and Todd everything on how to run the businesses and care for the farm animals. Because of him, my brothers know how to build homes with their own hands, grow plants, and shrubs to have a side business. When they have to care for their own families, they'll have all the knowledge from Dad being smart and patient to teach them the same trade. He taught them to be men, fathers, and husbands."

Rita looked at Faith and me. "You're both getting great men. They will carry on the part of their father with his gentleness and love. You won't have to worry about a man who'll hurt you."

I choked holding back the pain Todd caused me with Cathy.

Faith couldn't hold back the tears. "I want to go outside by myself for a while. I hope you don't mind." She walked out wiping her face with a tissue.

"How're you holding up, Jenny? Are you going to be okay?"

"Their deaths hit me harder than my own mother's. I truly felt blessed having Judy as my future mother. I loved her so much, Rita."

Rita came over and held me in her arms. She kissed me. "I know you did, and she adored you. What a shame they'll never know you're giving them a grandchild."

"They do, Rita."

She looked at me. "You told them?"

"I told your mom when I was fixing her hair and putting makeup on her. Rita, she was ecstatic. I asked her to tell your dad when he wasn't driving." I smiled. "I told her not to congratulate Todd today until she found out I told him. I bet they won the doll for our baby."

"They died knowing you were pregnant. I'm sure Mom couldn't hold the news from my Dad for too long. She had a hard time keeping secrets. Her famous words were, 'Don't tell them I told you—but.'" We laughed through tears thinking of her weakness.

"Todd still doesn't know you're pregnant?"

"I asked him to pull over by the beach. I felt it was a romantic location. He wanted to tell me something first. Todd admitted cheating on me with Cathy the night of her going away party. Rita, Cathy's pregnant and Todd's the father. They went to the hospital for blood tests."

"Pregnant! He never told me."

"You knew about this?"

"Todd told me he had sex with Cathy the night before she left for Paris. He has regretted it since."

"You never told me?"

"It was Todd's place to tell you, Jenny. I knew you would be upset with me as you are now. I had nothing to do with Todd's actions."

"I'll talk to Todd later but we have to concentrate on your parents right now."

****

The four men pulled up to the hospital. Sam opened his driver's side and everyone followed him into the entrance. They walked in the front doors to the receptionist's desk.

"We'd like to know where the morgue is located." Sam choked on the word.

"I have to call the pathologist to let him know who you're going to see. The name?"

"We're here to identify the bodies of Cory and Judy Costa." Sam thought he was going to lose control of his emotions saying his parent's names associated with death.

"Have a seat."

"This isn't going to be easy," Sam said in a weak voice. My God, Todd. How are we going to look at them?" He started to fill up.

The receptionist called them over. "You can go down to the basement floor. It'll say Morgue on the door. The elevator is on your right down that hall in front of you."

Bob and Ray stood up. "Want us to go with you?"

Sam gave a look for support. The four men went to the basement.

The pathologist met them at the elevator. "Mr. Costa?"

"I'm Todd and this is my brother, Sam. We're the children of Cory and Judy Costa."

"My name is Dr. Robert Conti. I'm sorry for your loss. Losing one parent is painful enough, never mind both of them."

He turned to look at the other two, "I gather you two are friends."

"Yes," Bob said.

"You can have a seat in my office on the right. Todd and Sam follow me."

They went into a dark, depressing room that had a freezing atmosphere. Dr. Conti rolled out two draws containing bodies.

"I'm sorry. If I had known you were coming, I would have had them placed on a table." He uncovered their faces.

"Yes, those are our parents." Sam felt nausea rise in his throat. Their faces were recognizable but destroyed.

"Do you want me to do an autopsy on them?"

"No. Let them be at peace. We know what killed them."

"Please, I have to get out of here." Todd felt faint and broke down.

Dr. Conti took them down the hall to his office. "I need you to sign this form. I'll notarize your signatures identifying their bodies."

After they both wrote their names, the doctor brought another paper out. "This is giving me the authority to notify the funeral home of your choice."

Todd filled in their information for the Nickerson Funeral Home.

"They'll call you for further instructions."

"Sorry to say, we know the procedure." Todd walked out of the room with the other three following him.

They got into the car, and Sam sat for a few minutes in the parking lot. "I can't believe they got killed. Our parents are gone forever. He pounded the steering wheel and released his anger. Why, why, why?" There wasn't a dry eye in the car.

Another Funeral

"The guys are back," Faith said. Sam parked the car and the men walked onto the porch where the girls were sitting on the swing; their usual spot after supper."

"How did you make out?" Rita asked, looking washed-out.

"Everything's scheduled, papers signed, and the dates and times. We don't think you need any details."

Todd sat in the lounge and patted the cushion signaling me to join him. I hesitated because I didn't know how I felt with us. My life and feelings were hanging with Cathy being pregnant.

"I know no one's going to have an appetite, but let's not waste this meal. Dad and Mom wouldn't want that to happen. Bob and Ray, please stay."

Bob looked at Rita. "Do I have to vote on the meal? If I see anyone drop from their seat after the first bite, I'm out of here."

Everyone laughed. Rita's remarked, "You better lie if it's bad."

The three women had taken down the balloons and decorations. Rita tried to make the atmosphere into a normal mealtime at the kitchen table. The only thing missing was their parents to share family conversations. It was eerie, sad, and emotionally draining as everyone kept their feelings hidden.

"Who wants to say the prayer?" Rita said.

I stood up. "God, have Cory and Judy at your table. Let them no longer feel pain, but peace. Have them always by our side to watch over us."

Todd came over to Rita. "I called Nickerson Funeral Home to take care of the upcoming wakes.

"I don't know if we should have a private vigil. How do you all feel?" Sam asked.

They looked at one another and Todd spoke. "We have all been through a lot with the loss of Jenny and Kathleen's family."

"I vote that we have a wake for the public with Dad and Mom's friends but a private funeral for the family."

I spoke next. "Why don't you think of putting your parents to rest with my family at the St. Teresa Cemetery, and then have a Mass for the public at St. Teresa, The Little Flower chapel."

"A good idea, Jenny," Todd said. Does everyone agree? I'll call Fr. Rick and see if we can have the funeral Mass on Monday afternoon at 1 o'clock at the chapel. We don't need to have a wake. We'd have to have closed caskets."

Oh, my God. They were injured that bad?" I cried.

"What do you expect when your truck falls off a cliff?" Sam walked away.

"I'll call the *Nelson News* for the obituary as soon as we all confirm the hours and day," Rita added. "I'll also call the Chatham Chronicle. Those two newspapers should reach all their friends.

After supper, everyone made the funeral arrangements. We all felt numb going through emotions with planning two more funerals. Within an hour, all the plans fell into place.

"We'll have no gathering after the funeral. That way, we don't have to worry about food or entertaining people at the barn," Sam said.

Rita looked at everyone. "Is that what Mom and Dad would have wanted?"

"What do you mean?" Sam asked.

"Would they exclude friends and neighbors from saying goodbye to any of us? People would come to support us, not our parents."

"Before I put this in the two newspapers, I say we invite the public for the Mass and burial. Bringing them to the chapel might be God's way of pulling people to bury their loved ones in this beautiful location.

"Let's take money out and pay our caterers to do the whole brunch. We do nothing. If we do the planning this way, we wouldn't have any regrets. We need to give our parents the celebration they deserve,"

Rita suggested.

I spoke up. "Rita, if Faith's willing, we can both run the garden stand, and Bob and Ray can handle the carpentry businesses. Both places will only be open on Saturday and Sunday. We'll close Monday and leave a sign up due to the deaths of your parents. This way you'll lose business for only one day, which is slow. It'll give you and your brothers a chance to get the funeral arrangements made for Monday without worrying about the business end."

Todd came up to me. "That's sweet of you to offer to do that."

I wanted to respond to his remark but I kept my feelings hidden. Todd and I still had a serious problem to talk about with saving our relationship.

Sam looked over at his brother. "Todd, can you and Jenny handle your wedding so soon after another loss? Will the celebration be too soon? Right now, you may say it's okay, but you might feel differently when the wake and funeral are over on Monday. It takes a while for reality to sink in after death. You'll all be handling the death of both parents. I want you two to think about this with your wedding plans. You can always postpone it for another week or month."

"We'll talk about that later," Todd said.

I sat quietly wondering if we were going to be married. As far as I knew, no one knew about Todd's news with Cathy, except Rita.

Arrangement Planned with Their Lawyer

Sam scheduled the wake at 8 am until noon, followed by the funeral at 1 pm at the St. Therese The Little Flower Chapel. Fr. Rick would be saying Mass and having the burials at the St. Teresa Cemetery."

The family decided to bury Judy in the cream-colored dress she had picked out for our upcoming wedding. Cory would wear the dark navy suit he had picked out for the special day.

Sam and Todd discussed the situation with Bob having worked on their father's truck.

"I can't believe Dad's brakes on the truck gave out. Bob's excellent with fixing things. I don't like the idea that the cops are actually thinking he had something to do with this accident. You know the police. They want to solve a case and get someone blamed for the crime so the people in town will think they're doing their job," Sam replied upset.

"Maybe we should call Dad's lawyer, Carl Miller. Why wait for him to be accused. At the same time, I don't want him to look like he's guilty looking for a lawyer?"

"You're right, Todd. It's smarter to have a lawyer on standby with the facts in case he's blamed."

"This day has been depressing. It's bad enough losing Dad and Mom and now Bob is looked at as a possible suspect. Today, I got up to care for the animals and had coffee with Mom. A normal day. Jenny and I laughed with her and Dad, as we watched them kiss each other with the excitement to a day by themselves. The four of us were in the same town of Orleans but in different sections.

"Dad was a super driver. How could he have lost control of his truck? Sam, I get sick thinking how frightened they had to have been with the steep drop off a cliff for God's sake."

"Todd, I think it's too soon to marry. Jenny isn't over losing her whole family. That was a few months ago. You have to be excited, Todd, on your wedding day. You won't be doing Jenny any favor by just going through the motions. She'll know it. Women feel more deeply than us men.

"Every person would understand. Do some deep talking with her and come to an honest decision. If you wait another month, maybe you'll be in a better frame of mind. You have a lifetime together. Don't rush and let our parent's death interfere with your happiness. Dad and Mom wouldn't want that to happen."

Todd held back on the incident with Cathy. He was too ashamed to tell his brother.

"Sammy, what are we going to do with the house, our land, businesses, and the animals?"

"Why don't we wait until the funeral's over and we get this behind us. Don't jump ahead. After things calm down, we'll talk again.

"Calling Carl Miller is a good idea because we have to know what our parent's Will consists of with all of us. We can ask him about Bob's situation with the cops and see what he thinks."

"Sounds good," Todd said.

****

Monday morning arrived with another wake and funeral. This time, Sam, Rita, and Todd were going through the emotions Kathleen and I had experienced with loss. God seems to block out the events when we lose a loved one. We smiled at friends, people we knew, ones we didn't, when we really didn't want to be there in the first place. The family worried more about making the guests comfortable before their own sadness could be felt. The family was surprised to see so many attending on a weekday.

Why not? Their parents were loved by all. Their food stand, shrubs, and carpentry business were known by families for miles in multiple towns over the Chatham line. People bought from the Costa family because they were honest people. Extra apples, tomatoes, and leafy greens were thrown in their bags without buyers noticing until they got home. An extra shrub or boxes of flowers with bright colors were added in their orders and put on their trucks.

The three siblings stood in line greeting and thanking the people for coming to support them. I didn't see too many coming by without tears. They were gentle and loving souls, good parents, and loved each other beyond anyone's imagination, even their own children. Cory and Judy's deep, long stares into each other's eyes, held secrets only they would have known through the years.

Nothing was ever going to be the same. Each sibling would be lost and devastated. Their lives would take a long time to be carefree and fun again without them. There would be an empty void.

The house Cory and the men built for us would be an everyday reminder. Something we never would have been able to afford without years of saving.

Todd looked over at me in-between talking to a friend. I wanted a penny for his thoughts.

"How are you holding up, Todd?" He came back to reality by Bob's voice.

"The best I can. Thanks."

"Don't thank me and Ray. We're here because this is where we belong. This is our second family. We both never found that special girl. Your Mom filled our hearts. Her cooking and bringing us cold or hot drinks, depending on the time of the year, will be remembered. She'd tell us to dress warmly during the freezing winter. When we got sick, she insisted we stay in your guest bedroom, and she nursed us back to health.

"Your father gave us bonuses for no reason. He built my shed for no cost. He gave us wood for our stove in the winter. He put a few bucks into my pocket when my truck broke down. He was a father to Ray and myself."

"Don't worry, Bob. You and Ray will always be family. When the funeral's over, Sam and I will be able to talk about business. We want a meeting to decide how to handle the farm. Don't panic wondering if you'll lose your positions."

Bob filled with tears. "Your parents did a super job bringing you three up. A person can't miss you're all Cory and Judy's children. They left you with morals and honesty."

Todd didn't feel that way with what he had done with Cathy.

The wake ended with more people attending than the family could have believed. Fr. Rick said the closing blessing over Cory and Judy. The procession of cars and trucks headed to St. Teresa Chapel for the Mass.

"Look at the people here. I hope the chapel holds everyone." Rita said looking at the crowd.

Flowers filled the altar and their fragrances surrounded the walls. The two caskets were rolled down the aisle. There wasn't an empty seat in the church. Many stood up against the inside structure.

Fr. Rick said the Mass and gave a special eulogy for both Cory and Judy. He knew them well. At the end of the Mass, he blessed the caskets. The pallbearers from the funeral home pushed the caskets to their gravesite.

There were ten seats available for family and others. It was the beginning of October and the leaves were bright gold, deep reds, and orange blended into the surrounded burial area.

Cory and Judy were going to be buried in front of Mary, Dorothy, and Joe's grave.

"How can so many good family members be gone within months of each other?" I asked. I started to feel the loss of my family all over again. It was still raw.

The wake and funeral were over. Flowers were placed on the two caskets. Tears flowed from the loss of two wonderful people.

The caravan of vehicles drove to the farm for brunch. The caterers did a great job setting everything up for the family. Colorful, cut flowers were placed in the center of each table. Todd and Sam had put them together before going to bed.

Friends came up to the Costa family to talk about the shock of Cory and Judy's deaths. Todd noticed Attorney Carl Miller and his wife, Carolyn, walking towards him.

Carl took Todd's hand firmly. "I'm shocked beyond words from your parent's accident. I can't believe they're gone. They were not only clients but close and dear friends."

"Thank you, Mr. Miller."

"I'd like to set a date up for you all to come to my office. I have your parent's Will to read with instructions. Call me in a few weeks when things have settled down."

"We'd like to come by next week, Mr. Miller. Would that be too soon?"

"Call my office when you're ready."

"Thank you both for coming."

By the middle of the day, everyone felt exhausted. They continued to mix in with neighbors and friends who they hadn't seen in years. Exhaustion was kicking in from the stress.

The catering workers sensed the family had a long day and started to clear food and dishes off the tables. They hoped the guests would see it was time to say goodbye and let the family rebound.

There are always stragglers. I saw a couple keep a conversation up with Todd for a half-hour, and he seemed to stare into space.

Taking matters into my own hands, I walked over to him. "I don't mean to cut into a good conversation, but Todd, Sam needs your help in the house."

"Well, guess we should be getting home," the guest remarked. "Todd, we're sorry for the loss of your parents. We'll keep you in our prayers." The couple turned and left.

"Thank heavens you came over." Todd took a deep sigh of relief. "They kept rambling on and on until I was looking at them with a blank expression. I can't tell you what they said to me."

"It's been a long day, Todd. Everyone's still in shock. I think that's the last of our friends. Why don't you go and relax at the house? I'll thank the caterers."

"What would I do without you?" He kissed me.

"I've been there. Go inside."

I watched him disappear through the backdoor and knew that this catastrophe was going to stay with Todd and me for years. All of us lost our parents. Whoever heard of that? Todd looked lost without them.

Newspaper Headline

"Where's the newspaper? I haven't read one in days." Cathy Greco looked all around the kitchen for the paper.

"I haven't seen today's." Sharon took a sip of morning coffee.

"Dad always has the paper on the table."

"Your father went to court this morning for his hearing. They're having the testimonies from the people who came to the house. He'll get his sentence today."

Cathy walked into his den and saw the publication laying on her father's desk. She picked the paper up and read the headline: *Funeral today for a couple from Chatham killed on Friday.*

She walked back out to the kitchen with the journal in her hand. "How awful!"

"What?" her mother asked, as she stopped drinking and glanced back at her daughter.

"A couple was killed in our town going off an embankment. Let me read more of the article. I hope we don't know them."

"Give me the newspaper." Sharon grabbed it out of Cathy's hand.

"What's the matter with you? Let me read this." Cathy pulled the newspaper back. "Oh, my God! It's Todd's parents!" Cathy looked up at her mother, who said nothing while looking back at her.

"Did you know about this?"

"Your father told me this morning."

"You were trying to hide this from me."

"It was a horrible accident."

"Accident, Mother? Four days ago, Dad threatened Todd with harming his family, and by coïncidence, Cory and Judy are dead. Are you serious?"

"Calm yourself down, Cathy."

"Calm down?" By now she was screaming. "They were the most loving, decent people I have ever met. How could Dad have killed them?"

"Don't say such a thing." Sharon got off her chair and looked out the kitchen window.

"Oh, let me see—Dad doesn't kill, he pays his gangsters to do the dirty work for him."

Sharon turned to face her daughter. "Stop it, Cathy."

"Are you this desperate for a marriage that you close your eyes to Dad's criminal acts? He works with thugs and murderers, and people who rob families who are struggling. He's corrupt. Now, you're trying to convince me that he had no part in this?"

"Oh, that's right—I remember. Dad wanted an answer by Friday. It's Monday and Todd, Rita, and Sam are burying their parents. My God! I have no respect for you two."

"Don't let your father hear you talking like this about him when he comes home."

"Did you ever stand up to him? Are you happy with all the material things you have, Mother? Do new cars, maids, Chauffeurs, cooks, a two-million-dollar home make these crimes worth turning your eye?

"I found out that material things mean nothing. In two months in Paris, I became so filthy rich beyond my own dreams. Look inside my bag, Mother." Cathy dumped the items out onto the kitchen table.

Money flew everywhere. "Look! I have so much cash being Coco Chanel's model; I'll never have to want again. The green comes in so fast, there's no time to bank my checks. I kept getting richer and richer, but I'm lonely.

"I came back after doing runway shows multiple times to an empty suite and had no one to tell me how proud they were of my accomplishments. Not even you or Dad took the time to call me. I was used by Coco, although I knew she didn't need me. We're as good as the moment until someone better comes along to replace us.

"When you get rich and are naturally a beautiful woman, no one wants you as a friend and fears you being around their boyfriend or husband. Where are your friends, Mother? I never saw one person come into this house knocking on the door uninvited. They all came by invitations to the Greco's private, fake parties. I earned my modeling talents by working hard. I was born with the looks. Didn't you use all your talents the same, Mother?"

"What are you talking about, Cathy."

"You were just as beautiful and stunning as I am. It's painful to see your youth starting to disappear, isn't it? In ten years, I'll be considered *Over the Hill* in the modeling business. As young as I was, I remember watching you dress up for Dad's house parties. You were gorgeous, Mother. The men flocked to you."

Sharon got up from the chair. "You don't know what you're talking about."

"Oh yes, I do. I remember at ten years old looking in the peephole in Dad's office to see you letting men have sex with you. Being young, I wasn't certain what they were doing with you, but I knew it was wrong. I feared Daddy would be mad."

"You were too young to know what sex was, Cathy." Sharon poured another cup of coffee.

"No, I wasn't. By twelve years old, I had been broken in by Jim Angeletti. Remember him, Mother? All those times he took me for rides wasn't because he was being nice to me. He taught me to be a desirable woman to men, how to please them, how to win them over. By fourteen, I was a pro at sex. That's when I met Todd."

"What has gotten into you?" Sharon was shocked.

"I learned a lot watching you, Mother. I watched you pull men in with your beauty and your money. We both used our bodies for anything we wanted.

"Your father has always treated me with respect."

Cathy laughed out loud over and over again. "All my years watching you two, I never saw him put his arm around you, give you a secret look of admiration, or show an ounce of love towards you. Not even a kiss. No flirting. Although, he had no problem with the other woman coming to your parties.

"You both gave your attention and sexual advantages to others, not each other. Then you wondered why I grew up with no real, loving feelings for a man. I never saw love in this house. I never had a father who hugged me. I was lucky if he was home, and if he was, he'd disappear in this den.

"Todd was right. I deserve to be pregnant. I passed out sex like candy. I shouldn't have this innocent child in me. I don't know how to give love to this infant. I'll be looking at my baby as someone holding me back from being famous. I had it all in Paris. I can't give 24/7 to one person, Mother. I'm selfish. Todd knows me better than I do myself."

"Now, I have to live with the fact Todd and his siblings were punished for my mistake with throwing myself at Todd in the barn. I didn't love him, Mother. I wanted him to crumble in my arms so I could hurt Jenny.

"You defended your mafia husband with whatever he did. I loved Todd's family. I respected them and was jealous of the love they all had for one another."

Cathy looked at her mother and sobbed. "My God, Mother. Dad killed two innocent people. Todd's family has to be devastated by both your actions. I'm seriously thinking of having this child and giving the baby up for adoption. This way I can go back to Coco, and Todd can marry the girl he loves.

"For once, I should show I'm decent and let Jenny and Todd get married Sunday. I pray Todd never finds out my parents took the lives of his—for nothing!"

Sharon went up to Cathy and held her two shoulders, and shook her. "You'll not give this child up for adoption. You may never give me another grandchild. I'll do better with this baby."

"What, Mother…love it? Do you know how?"

"Don't become a sassy bitch. I'm your mother and watch your mouth. You'll marry Todd. He had a choice last Friday. We won't have you walking around town with a big belly being single. You don't have to prove your looseness with men. I may end up taking this baby away from you."

"Over my dead body. I may have a future with Todd. I have to be careful of what I say because maybe my own father wouldn't think twice of dropping me in some ditch to save his face. You're not going to take this baby. It's ours. Start living your own life, Mother. Stop living it through me."

Cathy started to walk out of the kitchen, and Sharon stepped in front of her. "Don't you dare call Todd? You'll open a can of worms. He may not even put it together that we were the cause of his parent's accident."

"I'll never want a thing to do with this family again. You're as low as he is. He picked a good mate. You have become a person with no morals or have a conscience when someone disappears. You play the part well not knowing a thing. How can you look yourself in the mirror? I never should have come home. You murdered Todd's parents because of my pregnancy. Something they had nothing to do with for them to die."

Cathy started towards her bedroom and stopped to look back at her mother. "Todd and his family don't deserve what you did to them. You ripped their parents out of their lives. You're evil. I'm sick to know that I belong to this racketeering family. I pray Dad's put away for life."

Court Hearing

"Attorney Souza, please come to the bench." Judge Spooner wanted a private talk with Tony Greco's attorney before sending down a verdict. Tony didn't want a jury to hear his case. Witnesses from other mob members, who wanted amnesty, were called to testify against Tony for his past and updated actions. The hearing lasted four hours.

"Yes, your Honor." Phil Souza had defended Tony on all his cases and was known by the underworld organized crime families as the best criminal lawyer.

"You do realize that your client has given no excuses for his actions facing this court with harboring and abetting criminals and murderers in his home?"

"He wanted to stay with pleading the 5th, your Honor. I'm hoping to get him off with a light sentence."

"You think this mob boss deserves a light sentence?" The judge looked discussed. "Go back to your seat."

The judge looked over the police reports for a few minutes reading each crime.

"Mr. Greco, stand up."

Tony did as he was requested. He felt sure that there would be a small punishment of maybe six months, which he had served numerous times.

Tony stood straight waiting with a frustrated look while balancing himself from one leg to the other. He was anxious with the judge taking so long to get the penalty announced. Judge Spooner continued to go over the statements. Tony assumed this was going to be a simple, non-proving arrest.

The other criminals arrested in Mr. Greco's home were already sentenced one by one. Their jail punishment went from twenty-five years to life in prison.

"Mr. Greco, you have been known as a gangster way back as a teenager, and then you became a mob boss. In-between the advancement, should I call it, you have had twelve sentences, and with good counseling. You got off all of them with a light sentence."

His attorney looked at Tony wondering if it had been a smart move not to have had a jury. Tony kept refusing one. Phil wasn't feeling comfortable with the judge's attitude.

"I'm sentencing you for hiding criminals and murders in your home. I'm not blind to the involvement you have with each member's group. I just went over their testimonies from the other cases involving you that have been heard last week and yours today.

"You're not innocent of their crimes. You have chosen actions to take against other members and innocent people causing their deaths. You have been taken in and arrested countless times from 1921-1934 working under two mafia bosses.

"There's a question of you being a suspect with murder two years ago. The FBI's still investigating this open case. I can't sentence you for that criminal action.

"Four people, who were arrested from your home, testified that you were a partner in the position of a mob boss with Charles "Lucky" Luciano and John Joseph Gotti, Jr. They're the two most powerful and dangerous crime bosses in America.

"The evidence in last week's court case showed that you and Giuseppe Morello ran the New York organization as a conglomeration of various smaller mafias that allied or merged under both your leadership. The decision-making came with numerous meetings in your home in Chatham, Massachusetts. The FBI has been watching your home for two years.

"Al Mineo and Steve Ferrigno were ambushed and killed Nov. 5, 1930, in the courtyard of a Bronx apartment building at Pelham Parkway. This order was founded by the FBI unit. The gang members of Mineo and Ferrigno testified that you and Morello gave those orders. You were arrested in the area at the time of the crimes.

"I sentence you, Tony Greco, to thirty years behind bars with no parole. You're to go directly to the federal prison of the United States Penitentiary in Leavenworth, Kansas.

The judge slammed the gavl down on his desk showing his authority and power over Mr. Greco. Judge Spooner waited for Tony to be taken away.

Before leaving, Tony looked at Phil. "You've got to get me out of this!" Tony looked shocked as two court officers came to put handcuffs on him.

"Phil, appeal this judgment," Tony yelled, as the officers took him out to a parked transport vehicle to drive him to Kansas.

As they took Tony out of the court, his attorney stood motionless. Phil always got Tony off, but this time was different. Between being caught red-handed with the mob members and bosses, and the court cases heard a week before, Tony was being put in the slammer. He was his forty-seven years old. Thirty years was a life sentence, getting out at seventy-two.

Tony had no time to call Sharon. He had told Phil to call her after his sentencing thinking he would get a few months. To his surprise, he was never going to be home again.

****

"Hello?"

"Sharon, it's Phil."

"I've been sitting on pins and needles. How much time did Tony get?"

"Sharon, Tony was sentenced to thirty years with no parole. They took him out of court handcuffed and taken directly to Leavenworth, Kansas."

"Phil, tell me this isn't true."

"Sharon, I can't even appeal this case. Tony's in so deep, I can't find an excuse to get him out of jail. The judge had too much evidence against him in the last court session with the FBI agents, State Police, and the Chatham Police Department.

"With all the gang members as witnesses, they hung Tony. Four got immunity for talking. I'll put in for another hearing, but I'll tell you now, the request won't go over with this judge."

"Will Tony call me?"

"He may be allowed one call. You'll have to wait and see."

Sharon hung up dazed. Tony was finally behind bars with all his years of sneaking and blaming others for his actions.

Sharon went to talk to Eddie. He was sitting in Tony's den. "Tony was sentenced to thirty years with no parole. They took him directly to prison."

"I'm going to head back to New York and see Giuseppe."

"You have unfinished business. Tony wanted you to take care of Todd and Cathy's situation. Do you think you can finish this job? He didn't have the Costa's killed for you to forget about the main purpose of forcing Todd to marry Cathy."

If Sharon had said nothing, Eddie would have walked away without any other punishment to Todd, other than his parent's death. Sharon wanted more thrown at Todd.

"I'll take care of it, Sharon." Eddie wasn't too comfortable with taking orders from Tony's wife. She wasn't the one in charge. He was going to follow through because of Tony's orders, not hers.

"This Sunday is his scheduled wedding day with Jenny. Give him a deadline on the same Sunday. See how Todd feels with us taking his day away from him and Jenny. I'm firm on it Eddie."

Sharon felt freedom for the first time in years with Tony put away. She was now in control, or so she thought. She was determined that Todd was going to pay for getting Cathy pregnant.

Decisions with the Farm

Sam and Todd met with Bob and Ray to discuss how the business was going to be run with the deaths of their parents.

"I'm going to have to step in and take more responsibilities," Todd said. I'll never be like my father, but we can all run this business together. My parents would be sick if we let our livelihood go under. They worked too hard for years. It's now our job to keep getting bigger. We can always hire other people.

Sam cut in. "I graduate this week. I have to look for a steady job. Faith will be working with a veterinarian for a year to get her degree to open her own animal hospital. In the meantime, I can work here."

Todd took a deep breath. "After our parent's death, I have come to realize that work is a necessity, but couples need time together. We can't live and breathe just to make money. This was the first time that my parents got away by themselves. They'll never do it again.

"Sunday, Jenny and I will be married, and we'll be in our home on the hill. I'm sure Rita will live here, but we won't be able to count on her to cook and clean for all of us like Mom. She has a demanding job as a reporter. Mr. Nelson can call on her to go to a location anywhere within hours. That leaves the house empty.

"Bob and Ray, the three of us were wondering if you would consider moving in and living at the house. This way you could also watch out for things when we're not here. I'll still be up before dawn to take care of my normal chores, feeding the animals, and running the stand. You two will be in the same position as you have been with running the carpentry side of the business."

"I don't know about Bob, but I'd love to live on the farm. I'd be interested. Todd, do you think you can teach me to care for the animals? I have always wanted to do that watching you."

"That's great, Ray. Teaching you would be a help. We can fall on each other if something comes up and one isn't able to be here."

"Don't leave me out." Bob looked excited. "Who wouldn't want to be part of this farmland and family? Knowing Jenny, she'll be down here helping out. That's if you don't have a family right away." The guys laughed.

"If you two can move in before the wedding, that would be great to be all settled by then," Todd asked.

"I have Wednesday off with no classes so I can help you guys," Sam replied.

"We'd love your help, Sam. We don't have much to move." We rented an apartment and we don't have a lot of furniture. I'll bring my shed your dad bought for me."

"I'm glad because there isn't a lot of room adding more items in the house. Our parents have everything you will need. Your personal belongings would be enough. If you want to use your own beds, we can put the others in storage in the barn."

The three of us have a meeting tomorrow with our parent's lawyer reading the Will. Can you both be here early? I'll feed the animals and get them out in the fields before we leave.

"Todd, I can be here at 4 am to help you. There's no reason for me to wait to learn this job," Ray said with enthusiasm.

"Okay. We're settled. You boys move on Wednesday with Sam's help. I'll teach Ray animal care. See you early tomorrow. Oh, yes, ten windows came in for a job in Sandwich. Bob, schedule a date to get them installed."

****

Morning arrived, and I was up early to try the responsibility of taking over Judy's job making breakfast. Todd and I had not discussed the situation. I had no solid decision with our marriage. I started to panic knowing it was six days away.

I started out with a few pieces of burnt toast. As the charred bread's scent started roaming through all the rooms upstairs, I could hear the windows being opened. I lost points with the comparison of Judy's perfectly golden toast. My try with cooking was getting worse when one egg broke in the frying pan and one fell on the floor. I cleaned the mess up before anyone came downstairs. I acted as if no mistakes were made.

"Well, Jenny, how's breakfast going?" Todd asked.

"It's not your mother's breakfast," I replied.

Rita and Sam came downstairs and sat down in front of their plates.

"They say that breakfast is the most important meal to start the day. I was hoping everyone was hungry enough to eat anything," I announced.

The bacon was darker than normal; but crunchy. It showed between their teeth while they talked. The pancakes didn't rise but were cooked. The ham was a little overcooked and slightly dry.

While I was getting my coffee, I heard them laugh. I turned with my hands on my hips facing the three of them. "First of all—I hate getting up early, so know this action was done from love. If you're all still alive by tonight, I may try another entrée. I might become what you consider a cook."

I laughed at myself. "Wasn't this horrible? Maybe I'll be better at feeding the animals. They eat anything, even if it's spoiled." I took one look at their teeth. "*Please*, to save you embarrassment before going to see Attorney Miller, brush your teeth. Don't ask why. You'll know when you look in the mirror. By the way, be prepared tomorrow morning. I may plan on serving cold cereal. How can I kill that?"

Rita got up roaring. "Make sure you check to see if the milk hasn't gone sour first."

"Maybe we should warn Bob and Ray. They may change their minds moving into the house. I think they're excited thinking everyone cooks like Mom," Sam teased me.

"Todd, since you're all going with Sam in his car to the lawyers, do you mind if I drive yours to go to work?" I asked.

"Why don't you take today off?"

"I can't. There's so much work piled-up. Besides, tomorrow's

Saturday, and I'll be off for the weekend. I have a lot of last-minute details. Can I have the keys to your car?"

"I'd rather you stayed until we got back. I can drive you."

"Todd, you know I can't take advantage of Mr. Nelson with him giving me more time with all the funerals. I'll give your keys back at supper."

When the three left to go to their meeting with Attorney Miller, I took Todd's car keys. I had my father's 1930 Buick back home but had to change the registration over to my name. It was time to bring the car to Todd's farm. It was kept in the barn, but I knew the car should have been used or mechanical problems would start from sitting.

I had a lot of work at the office with editing. With so many deaths in our families, I had taken more days off than I had in the past two years. Getting behind the wheel of Todd's car felt like something foreign since everyone had been taking me places.

I loved the windows open and letting the wind gently blow through my hair. The breeze wasn't strong enough to mess my style, but the warm air felt good. Being alone for the first time in months made driving relaxing.

As I cruised down the road, the reality of Judy and Cory's death engulfed me. Tears surfaced. I had dreamed of the security with Judy replacing my mother. I remembered back to Judy being excited hearing that she was going to be a grandmother. The two of us had shared a special moment. I wondered if she told Cory the news before they died?

I knew with all the love I had for Todd that we couldn't get married with Cathy's situation. Todd gave me no confirmation he wanted me, not Cathy.

Judy and Cory weren't going to see me all dressed up at my wedding and give me hugs as parents do. I wouldn't hear the words that a mother says, *'You look beautiful!'* I would crave Cory's look of approval for Todd's choice.

I suddenly felt empty and wanted to wake up from this horrible accident. The reality was painful. I missed and needed my cousin, Kathleen, to come home. If Cory and Judy were alive, they would help

Todd and I make a decision with Cathy's pregnancy. Judy and Cory were my future. My outlook without them was depressing.

Driving along, I noticed a black car that had been following me for a long time, until I got to the company, and they rode by me. I drove up to the *Nelson News* and parked the car. The loneliness was felt without Rita by my side. The love and warmth I had found with all the Costa members hit me. They gave me a reason to get up. What would I do alone if I left Todd?

Reading the Will

A buzz came on Attorney Miller's intercom. Carl had the new system installed. Allan Charles Bernstein, a former Tamarac City Council member, had invented the machine in the 1930s for the inter-office communications systems.

"Yes?"

"The Costa family's here to see you."

"Tell them to come in, Janet."

"Good morning," Mr. Miller said, welcoming the three of them. Have a seat. Get comfortable. First, I'm sincerely sorry for your loss. Cory and Judy were the dearest friends of ours. I never thought I'd be talkin to their children about their Will for another thirty years.

"The Will's really a simple one. In fact, your parents came in here two weeks ago to update the documents.

"Let me start with Todd Costa's section: The house that had been completed last week on Lover's Lake, along with five acres, is left to you. Whatever's in the house or on the property is yours."

"Under Samuel Costa's section: Your parents left you five acres to build your home across from Todd at Lover's Lake. The Federal Housing Administration will provide insured loan funding to build if you require more money than what your parents left you.

"You're in luck, Sam. Just two years ago, the F.H.A. allowed homes to be designed how a person wanted them to be designed, but the major stipulation is that each home has to be built in a way the building would blend in with the rest of the homes in the surrounding neighborhood. Todd's home is top-notch, and having been built near the lake, your parent's investment for you to build on your property will be worth every penny.

"Under Rita Costa's Section: This had been a hard decision for them since you have a job that keeps you moving and not settled in one area. The house is left to you, Rita. At any time, if you decide to move out-of-state and want to sell the house to your brothers, they'll have to buy you out, including the business side.

"Each of you was left $20,000 in cash. They did hope you'd put aside an account for your children if you're blessed with any. As for the farm, you're all co-owners. If at any time one of you wants out, the rest have to pay the sibling their share. Do any of you have questions?"

"I can't believe my parents had this much money." Sam sat in shock.

"Your parents worked for a future for all of you, not them. They both had a decent inheritance from their parents and banked the profit.

"I wanted to give you solid advice. Do not, under any circumstances, tell anyone that you inherited this amount of money. It's no one's business. If you do, there might be bitter feelings from friends and neighbors, who had gone through the Great Depression and had the banks clean their savings out. I'm including Bob and Ray who work for you. No one!"

"My parents lived their lives struggling. I'd never have thought that they were actually rich." Todd kept shaking his head.

Carl looked at all of them. "I would say you were close to one of the wealthiest families. They took all their savings and hid it when the Depression hit. Not knowing their money situation, you turned out to be better children. You worked hard and built an enormous business and the townspeople respect you for having had that success.

"People are funny. They're happy for you until they learn you have money. Money's a root of evil." Carl took out a pen for each one to sign their documents. "This doesn't have to go to court. You're all free to collect your inheritance.

"Your parents didn't want anyone at the bank to know about their savings, so they put the money in a safety deposit box in my bank under my name, although, it's legally in your names. I don't want you to deposit a check this high so I cashed your share under my name. The bank's used to me having a large balance and may not think

276

anything of the tremendous withdrawal.

I suggest you all get your own private deposit box and get your money in there today. This

way, if the banks fail again, you will still have access to money on hand. Remember, the IRS has a lot of power over your assets. They can put a total freeze on your money. Make a smart decision about what to do with this inheritance. Don't keep this amount in the house.

"I'm sure you'll each make your parents proud. Todd and Sam, I wish you both all the happiness with your upcoming marriages. My wife, Carol, and I look forward to Sunday."

"Before we leave, I'd like to ask you something. Bob Taber, who has worked for my father since high school, is being investigated for meddling with the brakes on my father's truck." Todd replied.

"Why's he being blamed?"

"The police thought my father's brakes just gave out until they heard Bob had worked on them and the car's function before they left. Dad had new ones put on a month ago."

"Bob may have a problem here. That's going to be hard to prove that he's innocent when he admitted to checking them before your parents left. Are they certain it was the breaks that caused the accident?"

"A couple in the car behind them said that they didn't see Dad's brake lights go on when the truck was traveling too fast down the hill."

"I think Bob needs a lawyer. We have to figure out why the lights didn't work or the breaks when your father had Bob put new ones on a few months ago, especially, when they accelerated with that kind of speed. What an awful experience for Cory and Judy. Have Bob call to make an appointment to see me."

They thanked Mr. Miller and walked to Sam's car. For a few minutes, they sat jolted by the surprise with such an inheritance from their parents.

"Can you believe this?" Rita asked. "We're rich within seconds."

"I'm glad I didn't know. It was such a unity feeling working together all the years growing up. If we save like our parents, our kids can have security when we die. We have to keep the business going."

Todd was determined.

Sam started the car, and drove off slowly, taking the ocean view road home to relax. He opened the windows to get the fresh air. "Cape Cod is cold as hell in the winter. I don't think any place can beat its beauty during the rest of the seasons. There's so much to do and see. How people can be bored staying anywhere from Bourne to Provincetown is beyond me."

"We better enjoy the rest of the fall. Todd, you and Jenny should have great weather for the wedding next weekend. It's supposed to be another Indian summer in the eighty degrees."

Rita put her arm on Todd's shoulders leaning forward from the backseat. We have to make this day for Jenny and you. Mom and Dad would want that.

More Threats

The family pulled in the yard after seeing the attorney. "That's odd; I thought Jenny wasn't going to put a full day in with work. It's 6 o'clock," Todd said, looking at the clock walking into the kitchen."

"Maybe she stopped for something. Like…a cooked meal from one of the restaurants!" Rita said laughing.

"Stop being so hard on her," Sam said. "It'll take years for either of you to come close to Mom's cooking. Maybe never. God, there wasn't a thing she couldn't tackle. I don't remember one bad meal my whole life."

"I miss waking up smelling the coffee along with a full course breakfast frying. How did she have everything placed on the kitchen table at the same time? Every item was on the counter ready to serve. She was remarkable," Rita said, looking out the window hoping to see Jenny coming in the driveway in Todd's car.

The phone rang. "I'll get it," Todd yelled out walking into the living room.

"Hello?"

"Hi, Todd."

He didn't recognize the voice. "Who's this?"

"Forget my voice already? It's Eddie—you know, Mr. Greco's employee."

"What are you doing calling my home?"

"I was calling to say how sorry I am for your parent's accident."

"I don't want your sympathy and don't call here again. Do you hear me?" Todd was in a rage trying to keep his voice down.

"Don't hang up, Todd. We had a deal. You didn't meet your end last Friday. You have until Sunday, six days from now, to confirm marrying Cathy or else."

"Or else what? I have a date Sunday to marry Jenny, and no one's going to take that away from us."

"Really. I would hate to see Jenny end up like your parents. Accidents happen every day. It's hard to prove they weren't a twist of fate."

Todd was speechless for a moment. "What did you say?"

"Tony told you before that you'd feel pain like never before if you didn't marry Cathy. You wanted to be a smart ass and not give Mr. Greco an answer? How would you like to find Jenny dead in the woods? And by the way, your sister, Rita—she's some looker."

"You son of a bitch. You killed my parents?"

"No, Todd, you killed your parents. If you had married Cathy, they would be alive today. Do you want Jenny to end up like this? Don't think this is a threat. We proved what can happen if you ignore us. The mob doesn't screw around with their threats.

"Call Sharon with your answer. No second chances on this. And, if you let anyone know about our conversation; family, a lawyer, or a friend, including Jenny or Rita themselves, you won't have a farm or them. The mafia has no problem with sleeping after leaving families devastated; nothing's going to shake us. If we get arrested for your parent's accident, our gang members will finish the job." Eddie hung up.

Todd put the phone down on the desk and sat in the chair traumatized. His parents were killed by the mob because he wouldn't marry Cathy. Now, Jenny and Rita's lives were in jeopardy. His head was spinning.

He got off the chair and walked outside towards the barn. Todd didn't want anyone to see his uncontrollable emotions. Having his loving parents killed because of his mistake with Cathy made him ill. He was hyperventilating feeling like a caged animal in the barn.

He wanted to get his hunting gun and go to the Greco's and blow each one apart. Todd ached for his father. Now they threatened Jenny. Todd sat paralyzed being on the edge of everything and everyone he loved to be taken away from him. He had no one to confide in with this situation.

****

I walked in the door at six-thirty. "Sorry, I'm late. I had two reporters come in at five with their stories. I had to edit their reports for the next day. I stopped and got pizzas. I hope no one ate yet."

Rita walked up to me and took the three boxes to the oven to heat them up. "I was starting to go through the refrigerator to see what I could throw together. You're a lifesaver."

"Where's Todd?

"He took a telephone call in the parlor and then disappeared," Sam answered.

"Maybe he got a call for work and went to the shop," I said.

"Jenny, can I talk to you?" Rita asked, going into the living room.

We both sat. "Have you told Todd yet?"

"Do you think Todd can handle hearing I'm pregnant right now, Rita? Losing your parents is painful enough. I don't know what to do about the wedding."

"You can't ignore this problem. A decision has to be made today."

"I'm going to settle this right now, Rita."

I got up from the couch and walked out the backdoor. I had to tell Todd. The excitement and closeness were gone. Cathy had won him over with fathering her child. We were both pregnant by him. I hoped it was me he loved and wanted to marry.

I couldn't find Todd inside the shop. I walked into the barn. He was sitting on a haystack. Todd looked up and saw me. He wiped his eyes with the back of his hand and tried to smile. I knew his world had collapsed after his parents died.

I sat next to him. "Todd, we have to make a decision. I can't hide that I'm hurt and angry with you lying about Cathy. Cheating on me was one thing but you fathering a child with her is unimaginable. I'm sure she's delighted knowing I'd be devastated. How could you do this after our moment together? Did our love mean that little? I have to know."

"Jenny, I have hated myself since that night."

"I'm not sure if I can ever forgive or trust you. It's a slap in the face. I'm in a rage that she's going to have a baby with you."

"I knew you were going to be traumatized. I didn't know how to ease my actions."

"You threw a knife into my heart."

By now, my tears surfaced. "Are you sure you're the father? Could the lab tests be wrong? After all, I'm sure she ran around in Paris? What if you weren't the only man she had been with before leaving for France? Anyone could have been with her. Are you going to believe her?"

"I felt like you that she had to have taken up with someone over there. That's why I agreed to go for a paternity test. I swore the test would prove to be someone else, Jenny."

"I get sick picturing you both going together as a happy couple to see if you were having a baby together?" By now I was yelling. "And how did you feel with this wonderful news, Todd?"

"We weren't a happy couple. I was in torment thinking what I did. Jenny listen…"

Todd was trying to hold me. I pushed him away. My mind was running in circles. I had been holding off for the right moment to be beautiful telling him I was pregnant. I couldn't swallow my pride and except Cathy winning him over. It was a nightmare. I was a respectable girl in town, and Cathy was a whore. The loving feeling of sharing my news with him was gone. I didn't want him from pity.

"I'm madly in love with you, Todd."

"Jenny, I love you from the bottom of my heart." His eyes filled.

"When were you going to tell me? After we were married, and she couldn't hide the pregnancy? I'm surprised you had the decency to tell me now. Do her parents expect you to marry her?"

Todd looked drained giving me a blank look.

"What are you going to do, Todd? Are you going to marry her?"

He didn't say anything.

"Oh my, God—you are! A few days before our supposedly wonderful wedding, you tell me your streetwalker is pregnant by you, and you're marrying her. You're tossing our love aside?"

"No, Jenny. I want to marry you. I'm asking you to forgive me. We can put this behind us."

"Really? I have to live with the fact she'll have your child. How do I get excited if I become pregnant?"

"Honey, I know I took something very special away from us. Please, Jenny, don't leave me. Let's work this out."

"Are you serious? You expect me to be excited taking our vows Sunday and to begin a life together knowing that woman's having your baby."

"Don't say that Jenny. I never stopped loving you."

"You stopped when you touched Cathy. A girl I feared you were still in love with and you swore I had nothing to worry about with the two of you. Don't come near me, Todd. You just crushed me." I ran out of the barn down towards the lake.

****

Rita looked out the kitchen window towards the shop. "Jenny and Todd are taking a long time coming to eat."

"Do you want me to go get them?" Sam asked, putting down the newspaper.

"That's okay. I feel like going for a walk. I'll be right back."

Going by the barn, she noticed Todd sitting on a haystack.

"What's the matter, Todd?" She looked around, "Where's Jenny?"

"I did a horrible thing, Rita. I didn't know how else to handle this than be honest with her."

"What did you do?"

Todd told her about marrying Cathy, and he watched the same hurt and shock on his sister's face.

"Oh, God! No, Todd. Where's Jenny?" Rita got up. "I have to find her, Todd."

"I'll go with you."

"No, stay here. She can't be in a good frame of mind after hearing this wonderful news days before her wedding. I'm sure the confession cleaned your soul and put a knife in hers." Rita ran out the door leaving her brother alone.

Todd walked out of the barn to his carpentry shop. He sat and looked at the tools with edges to do serious damage to oneself; a hammer, a utility knife, circular saw, drill presses, and other pieces of equipment facing him. He noticed his rifle used for hunting on a hook hanging off a shelf in its case.

Maybe they would all be better off without me, he thought. *Cathy would have my baby. Jenny would meet another man.*

His parents left them enough money to be comfortable. Todd's thoughts went to signing his whole inheritance over to Jenny. She could live in the beautiful home his father had built for them. He wished Jenny would have been the one pregnant with his child. What a wonderful gift that would have been for him.

Todd grabbed a piece of paper, dated it, and wrote his request to name Jenny to receive his endowment from his parents. He felt defeated and could feel all his energy and desire to live, go out of him. He became separated from his surroundings.

He walked over to his rifle and loaded the gun. He wanted to place the firearm in his car before going to see Attorney Miller in the morning. Once he signed the transfer of his share over to Jenny and had it notarized, he would go to the Greco's and kill Cathy's mother and the gangsters. He wanted her to feel the pain they gave him. It didn't matter if he went to jail for the rest of his life or got killed. He had nothing to lose. The Greco family won.

****

"Jenny, Jenny? Where are you?" Rita was in a panic searching down by the water.

Rita loved her brother but was angry he was in this ghastly situation. She knew Todd loved Jenny with his whole heart but had allowed a one-night stand to give her a reason to leave him. Since high school, Rita loved Jenny as a sister. We were inseparable. She felt sick that this situation was going to change everyone's lives.

Rita continued to yell for Jenny. Sam came running down the path from the house. "What's going on? What happened to Jenny?"

"Todd told Jenny the most devastating story that crushed her and she ran off."

Sam grabbed his sister by the arm. "What did he tell her?"

"Sam, Cathy Greco is pregnant. Todd's the father."

"You're joking?"

"I wish I was. I can't find her. I'm scared to death she's going to do something to herself."

Rita wasn't sure if I had the chance to tell Todd my news before he jolted me with some horrible events. The only people other than herself that knew were, Judy, and possibly Cory, and they were dead.

"Where's Todd?" Sam looked around searching for him. "Why isn't Todd looking for her?"

"I left him in the barn."

"I'll go get Todd and we'll both come back and help."

Rita continued down towards the lake while Sam ran up to the barn.

Sam found the barn door wide-open, but Todd was nowhere to be found. He noticed a light on in the shop.

"Todd? Todd? Are you here?" Sam was looking between the lumber piles. "If you're in here, for God's sake, answer me." He was now aggravated.

Finally, he saw Todd's boots sticking out from a stack of planks. He wasn't moving his feet. He found his brother sitting on the dusty floor, just staring into space.

"Why didn't you answer me? Todd, did you hear me?" He still didn't answer or look up at his brother.

Sam walked over and pulled Todd up onto his feet and shook him. "What's the matter with you? Do you realize Jenny's missing? Rita's searching for her by the lake?"

He shook him by the shoulders harder. "Get a hold of yourself, Todd."

He looked at Sam. "I have nothing to live for now."

"Of course, you do. Getting a girl pregnant doesn't mean your life is over. We'll work this out. The important thing now is to find Jenny.

Are you going to help?"

"I can't face her. I broke her heart. She's going to leave me. I lost Mom and Dad and now Jenny."

"This isn't the time to feel sorry for yourself. If you love Jenny, you'll help us look for her."

"She had every right to be raving mad at me. You don't think she'd do anything, do you, Sam?" Todd was slowly coming back to reality.

"I don't know. What can be worse than hearing a few days before your wedding your future husband got someone knocked-up? It's enough to make any woman get hysterical."

"Let's take my car down." Todd got his keys out.

****

I sat on a log at the water's edge that Todd and I had shared many times holding hands after swimming in the lake. We had spent hours laughing and talking about our upcoming marriage.

I could hear my name being called from a distance up the hill. I didn't want to be found. From crying nonstop, I felt numb. My wish was to be left alone to deal with my anger and hate.

I tried to put the situation in perspective. *Todd gave his heart to Cathy, whether his actions were from lust or love. How do I go back knowing he had those sexual feelings for her? Why would he choose to be with her with us being engaged? Do I mean that little, and she means that much?*

Rita stopped halfway down the dirt path and saw a figure sitting on a log. "Jenny?" She ran up to me and wrapped her arms around me crying. "Oh, my God. I thought you did something terrible when you weren't answering me."

"I want to die, Rita."

She looked straight in my eyes. "Don't you ever say that again. Do you hear me? I love you and so does our family, especially Todd."

"No, he doesn't. If he did, he never would have made love to Cathy." The tears started up again, rolling off my cheeks. "How could he have done that to me—to us? That lousy tramp's carrying his

286

baby."

"He told me. It's an awful situation. Did you get to tell him about your pregnancy?"

"The situation wasn't wonderful anymore. I'm in a horrible situation being single and pregnant. I'll have a bad name like Cathy. What man will want me? What do I do with all these feelings for Todd? He's the love of my life. How could I have been so blind? I knew deep down that he was with Cathy at her going away party. I was scared that my fears were true and blocked the truth from my mind. I didn't want to deal with the possibility. This situation is worse. A baby's in the picture with Cathy and I'm having one at the same time. He may think he has a problem with only Cathy? What if he knew I was pregnant? Who would he marry?"

"You've got to tell him, Jenny."

"I can't marry him. He lied, saying I had nothing to worry about with her."

"Jenny, men don't think before they act. When they're drunk and have a chance for sex, and it's in front of them, they go for the taking. Men aren't emotional as women. They're animals."

"Are you saying that I should accept that remark, and just pick up the pieces with what he caused? Cheating on me is bad enough but Cathy's pregnant by him. Do you know what that's doing to me?"

"I don't know what to say, Jenny. I'm in shock like you, but don't make a decision when you're in this terrible mental state. Let's all talk things over, when we get to the house."

"I'd feel like a fool with all of you trying to persuade me to forgive him. Why are women the ones who have to hide their hurt and live with their man's mistake just to make *them* feel good again after *they* caused the pain? WHY?" I wanted to tear apart anything within arms-reach.

The lake area lit-up with headlights and we were spotted by the men. Sam got out of the truck and walked over to me. "Are you okay?"

"No, I'm not." I burst into a sob in Sam's arms.

Todd approached to hold me. "Don't touch me, Todd." I pushed his arm off me.

"Please, let's go up to the house and talk this out." Todd seemed desperate.

Sam went up to Rita. "You and Todd go home. I'll walk Jenny back."

They disappeared up the path in the car.

"Come here, Jenny." Sam took my hand and we sat on the tree limb. I curled in his arms.

"Did you know about this, Sam?"

"Jenny, I'm shocked. Todd never told anyone."

"I can't handle this, Sam. It's too painful and I can't forgive him."

"You can't overlook what he did. No one would. Todd's a good, loving, and honorable man. I'm not trying to excuse what he did, Jenny. I do know he's madly in love with you. He made a horrible decision that will cause a child to come into this world. I can't imagine doing that to Faith.

"My brother got carried away. I do know Cathy's waiting to grab Todd. I don't believe she's in love with him. It's a challenge. She probably enjoys watching you suffer. I know, because I fell for Cathy before my brother. He doesn't even know. Cathy just hops from one man to another."

"In other words, men expect their women to forgive them."

"I was lucky. I had no woman in my life back then."

"Would you have had sex with her now dating Faith?"

"I can't picture doing that to her. I'm saying that sober. Men never know what we're going to do until the time comes for us to make a decision, especially if you're drunk."

"I can't talk about this anymore. All I'm hearing is poor Todd for being weak and I'm supposed to forgive him. Cathy's carrying his child. I want this to all to go away. Let's go up to the house. I can't talk about it, Sam. Let's go."

We walked up to the path with few words between us. I was too hurt and angry to have small talk.

Rita had coffee brewing on the stove, and the aroma filled the air when we walked into the house. The familiar setting brought me right back to expecting to see Judy in the kitchen. The loss overwhelmed me with my own private pain with Todd. Meeting in the kitchen was a daily routine hearing everyone laughing and joking, but tonight was different. You could sense the stress and tension.

As soon as I entered the kitchen, Todd took my hand. "Let's go outside. I want to be alone."

"I'd rather sit here at the kitchen table."

"Jenny, go and talk this out. Don't bury it, because the situation won't go away. You two have too much love to let pride get in your way," Sam looked upset, as he poured his coffee into a mug.

Todd and I sat on the porch, which had always been a comfort zone for us, but not tonight. At the moment, I didn't want any part of Todd. I felt forced to be in his company. I never thought I'd feel this way with Todd over anything.

"Jenny, I can't take back what I did or the lying. That was inexcusable."

"Is that supposed to make me feel better? Do you think I'll feel secure when you're late coming home?"

"My fear is losing you, Jenny. We have too much love to throw this away."

"You mean what we had."

"Don't say that, honey. I didn't know Cathy was back home from Paris. I would never have gone to her house."

All the muscles in my body felt tight. Talking about Cathy in any form made me angry to the point of wanting to walk over and slap Todd hard in the face. It was the first time I had any desire to hurt him. I wanted him to suffer like I was from his actions.

"I'm going to ask you again, Todd. What are you going to do with Cathy and this baby? Are you going to marry her?"

Todd acted like he wanted to say something but held back. I knew in the depth of my heart he loved me.

"You better give me an answer, Todd. I don't like waiting." I sat sideways facing him on the swing.

"Jenny, I have a baby to think about who's coming into this world. It's innocent of my wrongdoing. I can't live with myself walking out on the responsibility of caring for the child? It doesn't take away my love for you."

"I'm going to make this easy for you, Todd. I'm leaving as soon as I get my parent's farm sold. That ends our life together. There will be no wedding. You cancel the plans."

I stood up. "Tomorrow, I'm quitting my job and taking my things out of your home. I have my Buick and can get around without depending on anyone."

"Please, Jenny. I love you."

I stood up. "What do you want me to do, Todd? Attend your wedding and watch you and Cathy bring up a child? Why don't you stick a knife in my heart? After all, I don't want you to marry me and live with guilt over leaving Cathy. I see no future with us."

I looked at him feeling tears forming. "I loved you, Todd. I can't believe all our dreams are gone because you spent one time with Cathy. If she wasn't pregnant, I might stay. I didn't do anything wrong and I lost you. I'm not sure if I will ever get over this."

I walked into the house and up to my bedroom without talking to Rita or Sam sitting in the kitchen. I could feel their eyes on me as I passed. I held the tears back long enough to get to my bedroom.

I sobbed my heart out questioning if I was right walking away. I started to gather my small items and clothing that I had accumulated living at the Costas. I wanted to run into Todd's arms. Was I giving him up too easily? Pride makes us take the wrong path. How long will I be able to hide my own pregnancy?

At this point, telling him that I was pregnant wouldn't bring him or myself joy. It would put more burden and stress on him. I decided to keep my pregnancy a secret. The pain was unbearable leaving him. I had no doubt that I loved Todd or would ever feel this deeply for another man. At the moment, I couldn't live with him, but knew I couldn't live without him at the same time.

A knock came on the door. "Jenny, can I come in?" It was the first time Rita knocked since I came to live with them.

"Come in, Rita."

"Did you tell him?" She had hope in her eyes.

"Rita, sit down on the bed. I made a decision. Tomorrow, I am quitting my job, putting my parent's house up for sale, and then moving. I'm leaving the Cape."

Rita grabbed my hands. "Please, don't leave. You're making the wrong decision from being hurt. You want to strike back at my brother. That's normal, but don't give all this up. My father worked his fingers to the bone to give you and Todd that beautiful home."

"Good, he can have the place with Cathy." I continued to fold my clothes.

"If you walk, Cathy has won. You'll be doing what she wanted you to do. Giving Todd up will make no sense. Within months or years, Cathy will meet someone else. Do you really think a baby will make her fall in love with Todd and stay with him? Todd will be bringing this baby up alone."

"What do you all want me to do, Rita?" I turned facing her mad as hell. "*Tell me!* Do you want my soul? He already admitted he can't leave this baby. Do you want me to sit and watch all this while I'm showing?"

"He didn't say that he can't leave the baby."

"Oh, yes he did." I continued to fold my clothes.

"Jenny, that's why it's so important that you tell him you're pregnant."

I leaned over the bed and looked her in the eyes. "Promise me, you'll never tell him. *EVER! DO YOU HEAR ME?*" I grabbed Rita by the arm. "Say it. Under no circumstances will you tell him."

"Please, Jenny, don't ask me to keep such a treasured moment from my brother. He would be sick knowing you left carrying his child. He loves you, not Cathy. He'd hate me more for not telling him."

"That's my decision, Rita. I'll have to live with the secret."

"What are you going to do? I have to keep in touch with you. How will you bring a child up alone?"

"I'm thinking about giving the baby up for adoption. If my mother or yours were alive, I'd rethink this. I can't take care of a baby and work at the same time. Love's not going to put food on the table, or buy diapers for the baby, or pay for doctor's appointments."

"You can't give this child up. This will be my nephew or niece. My parent's grandchild! The baby will be part of Todd."

"You can have that with Cathy's baby."

Rita cried with her arms up in the air. "What's happening to this family? We were all happy a week ago. Our parents are dead and you and Todd aren't marrying. To top it off, you're leaving Chatham for where?"

"I was thinking of New York. I can disappear. I lived in Manhattan before moving here. I know the area. My past can stay hidden. I don't have to see Todd walking in town with his child— the child that should have been ours."

"You can still have this infant. Please, Jenny, I am begging you. It's a horrible decision to live with the rest of your life. Somewhere, somehow, you'll look back regretting giving your child up. You'll always wonder about the baby. I know you. You're a warm person with a lot of love to give to a child, especially Todd's. Your love for Todd will go into the baby. God will help you."

"I'll have time to decide before my delivery date. I'm really tired, Rita. I'd like to be alone and try to unwind from this gruesome day. I'll see you in the morning." I kissed Rita like I had every night. "I love you. Goodnight."

****

Rita went down to the kitchen to join her two brothers having coffee. She interrupted Sam talking to Todd. "Did I come at the wrong time?"

"There's no good time with this," Sam remarked.

After pouring her own coffee, Rita sat across from Todd. "We all have to talk about this. Every one of us is involved. Jenny's part of this family. What are you going to do with Cathy being pregnant?"

Sam got in a rage and stood over Todd. "How could you have done something this stupid and irresponsible? You couldn't keep it in your pants? What did you think this half-hour or so of pleasure with getting Cathy laid would do to Jenny? Did she ever come to your mind? You didn't think your actions would tear Jenny's heart out? Was the piece of ass with the biggest town tramp worth it?"

Rita grabbed her brother's arm. "Sit down, Sam. Yelling and making him feel worse than he does isn't going to get this solved."

Rita faced Todd. "Jenny told me you're going to marry Cathy. Is that true?"

Todd knew he was going to be hated by his siblings and by Jenny no matter what he said or did. How could he tell them he was the cause of their parent's deaths? Now, there were threats against Jenny and Rita if he didn't marry Cathy by this upcoming Sunday? A day that would have been the most wonderful and blessed day for him and Jenny. Their wedding plans were all set. He had no idea how to live without her. If he took the steps down the aisle with Jenny, she'd be dead within the week.

He knew, if Sam heard the truth, his brother would be in his car within minutes with his rifle, like he himself wanted to do. Sam would be behind bars and Faith without a future husband.

Todd had to be the bad guy who had to prevent everyone's lives from ending. He knew because of his irresponsible actions with Cathy that every person's life would never be the same. He felt hate for the Greco family. Just their names made his skin crawl.

"Todd, your sister's waiting for an answer." Sam looked at him wondering where his brother's mind was traveling.

Todd turned and looked at them. "I love Jenny beyond anything in this world. I have to marry Cathy for the baby's sake."

"Are you *insane*?" Sam was back on his feet with his face in Todd's. "You're giving up a woman you adore, one who worships the ground you walk on, a lady in every way, a scheduled wedding in days, a home that Dad worked his heart out for the two of you, all because Cathy Greco is pregnant? She'll survive, Todd. Stop feeling guilty. Don't throw your love and a wonderful life with Jenny away for someone who'll never love you. Cathy's not capable of caring for another human."

"My child shouldn't grow up with the Greco name. I won't do that to one of my children. This baby didn't ask to come into this world.

It'll have my name, especially if it's a boy. I'd rather die than see a son carrying the Greco's name and watch him always defending himself his whole life with the reputation of having had a grandfather who had been a mafia boss and put away for his crimes. Tony was put in the slammer where he belongs with his killings, criminal activities with bootlegging, fraud, extortion, and blackmailing families, you name it. I hope he rots there!"

Rita walked over to Todd. She put her hand on his arm resting on the kitchen table. "Is that what this is about…blackmail? Is there more going on than we know?"

She looked up at Sam. "This makes sense. Why would Todd leave Jenny? We know how much you both are in love. Todd, are you being threatened?"

He panicked. Rita discovered the truth. If either of them knew the truth, they would be on the hit list with every gangster entering Cape Cod.

"You know, Rita, for a girl who doesn't believe in relationships, stop trying to make this situation into something that isn't. What are you writing a mystery book? I'm doing what any decent man who's about to become a father should be doing.

"I'm sorry if you're both upset. I have to live with hurting Jenny, and the decision isn't fair to her. I wish this all came out after Jenny and I were married. The situation would have been different, but it isn't. I have to deal with what's facing me."

"Todd, if Tony's threatening you, tell us. We'll get Carl to help. If you marry that girl and put Jenny in a frame of mind of not being able to deal with this, I will never speak to you again. I'll disown you," Sam said, getting angrier by the second.

Rita came between them. "Don't you ever let me hear you say that again. Either of you. Dad and Mom never would have allowed us to become enemies. I'm not going to let Cathy tear this family apart. We may never agree on what one of us is doing, but we're all old enough to make our decisions with our lives. If this is what Todd wants, we have to back him up and try to figure out what to do without pushing Jenny out of our lives. I can't live without her. She's been my dearest friend since high school. You do realize that, Todd?"

"She'll never forgive me, and I don't blame her. Rita's right. Jenny lost her family and has no one. She needs us."

"Jenny needs you!" Sam said. "How can you live with yourself doing this to her, Todd? Cathy deserves any bad thing that comes her way because of who she is and how she destroys lives."

"Yes, she does, Sam, but my child doesn't. I want this discussion to stop. Bob and Ray are due here anytime to move into the house. They don't need to be dragged into this family problem."

Rita jumped into the conversation. "Everyone in town will know what's going on, Todd. By tomorrow, people will have to be told the wedding is called off. Luckily, it's just family and a few close friends who were coming to the event. We have to call the caterers and the band. What do we tell them? It's well known what a special couple you and Jenny are and how happy everyone was with this time coming up Sunday.

"What do we say? I never thought ahead of calling people," Sam said. I don't want to be involved."

"You realize the truth will come out later, and Jenny's going to feel like a fool. Don't be surprised if people treat you differently, Todd." Sam looked disgusted with his brother.

"We'll tell people we decided to hold the wedding off because we felt it was too soon after our parent's death." Todd felt worse knowing he had to lie to his closest neighbors and friends.

Rita looked at the invited guest list. "We have thirty-two on the list. I'll start calling tomorrow. I can't believe we're doing this. I hate picking up the phone."

Rita never lied to anyone and was upset she had been put in this position. She wanted to knock sense into Todd and Jenny. How could a normal day have turned into such a heartbreak?

Kathleen's Rehabilitation

Dr. Blair sat at his desk when his nurse, Debbie, walked in to see him.

"This is the day we move Kathleen to the rehab," Debbie said.

"I feel bad for her. My hopes were high I'd bring back her facial features. She would have been a beautiful movie star. It had been her dream. I heard she was a great actress. How many people have David O. Selznick requesting a meeting with you for a part in one of his upcoming pictures next year?"

Debbie took his hand. "Miracles are wonderful. Sometimes they happen. Remember, Kathleen has years facing her with healing. Each year, new technologies come out. You might have another promising surgery to perform on her. She's young. That's on her side."

"Let's get this over with and move her to the second floor. Are all her papers in order?"

"Everything is set. She lucked out with a private room that opened last night."

Knock, knock. Kathleen turned and saw Peter and Debbie in the doorway.

"Kathleen, you're finally leaving this old room after six months. Happy?" Debbie pulled a wheelchair up near her bed.

Peter held her hand. "Time to take your bandages off, Kathleen. I accomplished a lot with the damage you had, but you're going to have scaring, redness, and your face will be swollen. What you're going to see isn't the final you."

"Will it be noticeable?" Kathleen asked.

"A lot is going to show for months. There are some spots that will fade in time, but the final finish may take a full two to three years.

Remember, Kathleen, you're lucky to be alive."

Debbie and Peter slowly unwrapped the bandages. Once they finished, they stepped back.

"I want a mirror."

"I don't think you should, Kathleen. Wait until we get you settled in your room."

"It's my body and I want to look at myself. Now!"

Debbie got a hand mirror. "Remember, you're not looking at what you'll look like later."

As Kathleen took the mirror in her hand, her heart raced. Anxiety caused her to hyperventilate. Taking a deep breath, she slowly brought the reflector up to her face.

"*Oh, God—no!*" She started to cry. "Who wants to see this ugly face on a movie screen or walk by me on the street?"

Debbie let her cry. It was a normal reaction from patients for the first time. "Kathleen, give yourself three years and the medical field is always improving. We may have another kind of surgery to diminish the scars. Don't give up."

"I want to be left alone."

Debbie and Peter walked out and saw Kathleen laying back in bed glaring up at the ceiling. The mirror laid on her lap.

Kathleen was moved to the rehab section a few hours later. For the next two weeks, she only said a few words when someone spoke to her.

****

Three days later, Debbie walked into Kathleen's room with a wheelchair. "Hi, Kathleen. How are you feeling?"

"What's the wheelchair for?"

"I'm taking you to your first appointment with Dr. Barbara Lyons."

"Why?'

"She's a psychologist, Kathleen."

"They're for people who are nuts. I'm fine."

"No, you're not fine and you're not nuts. You're depressed. What you're going through is normal. Every single person with damage to their bodies goes through shock. You're looking at a complete stranger."

"I'll get over this in time. I don't need to see someone to talk this out."

"Kathleen, you have no choice. This is a required step to recovery. Dr. Lyons is a trained professional with clinical skills to help you learn to cope more effectively with the life issues and mental health problems you'll be facing when you leave here."

Debbie gently pulled Kathleen's blankets back. "Let me help you."

"I can get into the wheelchair myself." She put her hospital robe on and sat in the chair.

Debbie pushed her down the hall and knocked on Dr. Lyon's door. "Come in." Kathleen had her chair placed in front of the doctor's desk.

"I'll return in an hour to bring you back." Debbie put her hand on Kathleen's shoulder. "Relax, Kathleen. We're all here to help you." She walked out with the sound of a click from the door closing.

Kathleen faced someone she felt was her enemy. *They must think I'm crazy. God, why did you do this to me?*

"Hello, Kathleen. I'm Doctor Lyons, but please, call me Barbara. I have all your records since your accident and during your stay. First, I'm truly sorry for the loss of your parents."

Suddenly, Kathleen choked up. She hadn't talked about her pain losing them and had kept the event buried deep within her soul. Tears were fighting to surface.

"There's no need to talk about the accident or your surgeries. We know why all this happened."

"No, I don't know why all this happened." Kathleen was emotional. "I had two parents I loved, a home, a future with being an actress, and I was beautiful." Tears flowed. I've been locked up in a hospital for six months with one surgery after another suffering from pain. Now I have no future. Maybe I should join a circus."

"You have every right to be angry, Kathleen. You're here for us to deal with your change physically, which affects you emotionally. This is an everyday topic I have with patients. That doesn't mean you don't feel alone with this tragedy.

"You're dealing with a life that has been taken away from you through no fault of your own. There are multiple conditions for you to face. Let's start by dealing with the new look of Kathleen. You're still the same inside.

It's terrifying to see a stranger looking back at you in a mirror. It's a mental adjustment. Some people don't adapt because they can't deal with the transformation. You have to desire the hard labor with what's facing you. These catastrophes are real. No one goes through them without having anguish dealing with what was taken away from you. We all have choices. You're the only one who can decide if you want to move forward with living.

"For you to progress, Kathleen, you have to open up with all your feelings, whether it's done through anger, yelling or crying. That'll help you break the barriers. The great thing is, Kathleen, you're truly going to heal better than what you see when the bandages come off. The first time seeing yourself is horrifying. Slowly, the changes will help you go through every month ahead."

Kathleen put her head in her hands and sobbed while her whole body shook.

Dr. Lyons got out of her chair and took her hands. "Kathleen, get out of your wheelchair and sit in this armchair. Let's get a healthier atmosphere where you can feel relaxed."

"Thank you." Kathleen let her paralyzing, damaged body fall on the cushion. "I don't know where to start."

Barbara waited patiently for her to begin. "How do you feel?"

"I feel alone. My happiness with life had always been surrounded by Rita, my dearest friend, and my only family member left, my cousin, Jenny. I feel that I can't turn to them because they don't know what I'm feeling. We were inseparable. I'm jealous they have no changes to adjust to, although, I wouldn't want them to be in my shoes.

"I feel sorry for myself and I know that isn't going to change my situation. I get angry at God, and yet, I know He's loving and merciful. I fear what's facing me. Six months ago, I had my loving parents."

Kathleen cried again and couldn't continue talking.

Barbara gave her a Kleenex. "From as early as I can remember, I wanted to be an actress." She turned to the doctor, "Sounds childish, huh?"

"No, it doesn't, Kathleen. We all need dreams and goals. Being angry with people who had no tragedy is also normal. It doesn't mean you want them to suffer."

"I had an appointment with David O. Selznick from Selznick International Pictures. Can you imagine!"

"How sad to lose that opportunity. How long have you been acting?"

"Does a five-year-old wearing her mother's clothes and almost killing myself in her high-heels count?" Kathleen laughed for the first time since the accident. "I put on shows for my parents and friends constantly."

"Do you know how to direct plays?"

"I know you have to be creative. For directing the acting, you have to portray the story as a whole and know the whole script. You can't fear to face the audience. Being a director, you have to develop a good relationship with the actors; you have to spend hours with rehearsals. I guess you'd call a director a team leader."

"Why don't you think about it, Kathleen. The work would keep you active in the field you love. By then, maybe more surgery can be done."

"I'll think about it. Thank you for mentioning the idea."

After Kathleen's first hour talk with Barbara, she left the office losing the resentment she came in with feeling sorry for herself. She had hope.

In the following months, Dr. Blair and his nurse, Debbie, went to court and helped Kathleen win her case with a jury getting money from the train accident that caused her loss of parents and disfigurement. The settlement would support her for the rest of her life with no worries.

Kathleen had two more months in therapy with Dr. Lyons. When her rehabilitation was over, Rita would return to bring her home for support.

Selling the House

As soon as I dressed and ate, I called Carl's office. I wanted a new life.

"Hello?"

"Is this Mr. Miller?"

"Yes. Can I help you?"

"Mr. Miller, this is Jenny Rossini."

"Why, hello, Jenny."

"Are you in real estate sell homes or know of someone?"

"My wife, Carolyn, is a real estate agent. Are you thinking of selling your parent's home?"

"Yes. I'd like to get the house and property on the list as soon as possible."

"I hear Cory built a beautiful house for you and Todd on the hill above Lover's Lake. I don't blame you wanting to unload the other property."

I didn't want to tell him what happened. I avoided talking about the marriage completely.

"What do I have to do to show the house?"

"I'll have Carolyn call you. The both of you can decide on a sale price and when you want to put a date on selling. She'll be fair with you, Jenny."

"I don't doubt that, Mr. Miller."

"I have Todd's telephone number."

"I have moved back to the house until it's sold. Leaving the property alone this long was taking a chance of being broken into or coming home to damaged things."

"We'll never sell the property three days before your wedding.

Carolyn sells fast, but not that fast," Carl laughed. "It would be a great business if we did."

I gave him my home telephone number. "She can call me anytime tomorrow. I'd like her to come over and look at the place."

"I'll give Carolyn the information today, Jenny."

****

They hung up, and Carl sat stunned with the conversation he had with Jenny. *It doesn't sound like she's getting married.* He couldn't figure out what happened. He knew Todd was madly in love with her.

Jenny had called when Carl was ready to close the door to his work. He arrived home earlier than normal walking through the backdoor.

"Well, I'm having a husband home early for dinner. How did I get so lucky?" Carolyn was happy to see him.

"Caught up with everything. I'm all yours." Carl had that professional, mature look with lots of thick, wavy, gray hair, clean-shaven, a terrific warm smile, and hazel eyes. His navy two-piece suit with a red and blue tie against his white shirt made him more handsome.

"Would you like a highball?"

"I can't remember when I had one during the day. That sounds good, Carolyn." He kissed her on the cheek going by.

"Let's have the drinks outside in the lawn chairs." She put the drinks on the tray with a few crackers and cheese before supper. They sat outback on a patio facing the riverbank. The drinks were placed on the courtyard table.

"This is relaxing. I should get out early more often." They both chuckled.

"I had a strange telephone call today."

"Aren't all your calls strange?" Carolyn asked as she grabbed a few crackers with cheese slices.

"Jenny Rossini called me wanting to put her parent's house up for sale. I told her I'd have you call her. In fact, she wants you to go to the location tomorrow and look the property over with her."

"I'm free tomorrow. I'll call her. Too bad the wedding has been called off for a few months."

"I *knew* something was wrong. She didn't want to talk about Sunday at all. Who told you?"

"Rita Costa called. She said Todd and Jenny wanted to wait a few months with the death of Cory and Judy. They weren't comfortable with celebrating."

"Something's wrong, Carolyn. I wouldn't think his parent's death would stop them. She didn't want to discuss anything with the marriage that was supposed to take place in three days. Not even that the marriage was canceled."

"Maybe she felt disappointed the wedding wasn't going to happen this weekend. That's a blow to any bride who was planning on being married in two days. Everything's planned and gowns are bought. She's a sport in my books agreeing with Todd to hold their day off for a few months.

"Cory gave them a beautiful home to move into on their wedding day. I don't know if I could wait to move into that place. Canceling and holding off longer isn't going to bring Cory and Judy back. They were our dearest friends, and we both know they wouldn't want them to wait."

"That's what I mean, Carolyn. It doesn't make sense."

"Unless we hear something different with their reasons, we'll have to go along with their broken plans."

"I wonder if I should talk to Todd?" Cory asked.

"Why would you do that? We have to respect their wishes. If they're comfortable with the decision, we should keep our nose out of their plans."

"There's something not right."

"Let's go into the house. Dinner's ready. We should enjoy a nice quiet evening together. I pray no one calls you tonight."

****

Friday morning arrived, and Carolyn called me. "Hi, Mrs. Miller.

I'm glad you had time to call. Yes. I'm home all morning. See you then."

Yesterday, Ray had driven me back home. I wasn't sure if he and Bob knew the wedding was off. I didn't want to mention it or I'd have to deal with explaining why. I was hoping Todd would tell them.

I couldn't understand how the deep love Todd and I had for one another had fallen apart so easily. I never saw the breakup coming. *Why wasn't he fighting for me?* I walked around in shock, trying to wake up with the fact that Cathy was still in Todd's life.

What am I going to do with our child? There would be no way Todd could be active in our lives while being married to Cathy.

I felt unimaginable stress with not having my mother or Judy to talk to about this situation. I had lived through losing my parents, aunt, and uncle, and the deaths of the Costas. I was bracing myself for Kathleen's changes in her appearance. Rita was going to bring her home in a few months. I couldn't wait to see her. As painful and heartbreaking the events were, losing Todd was pure hell. He was the reason I got up to face the day.

I prayed the right decision had been made to leave Todd without sharing my news with him. Todd didn't say when he was going to marry Cathy. I wanted out. I never could deal with the humiliation of him choosing a loose woman. The situation overwhelmed me.

"Knock, knock!"

At 11:45 am, I opened the door to see a tall, distinguished-looking woman in her late thirties with long, black hair, and green eyes looking at me.

"Hello, Jenny. I'm Carolyn Miller."

"I'm glad to meet you, Carolyn. Please, come in. Thank you for coming."

I led Carolyn over the creaky floors to the kitchen table. I had a platter on the table with homemade sugar cookies. The teapot started to whistle.

"Have a seat, Mrs. Miller."

"Please, Jenny, call me Carolyn."

I poured the hot tea in the kettle in our cups on the table. The milk, lemon slices, and sugar were placed in front of us.

"How many rooms do you have here?" Carolyn asked as she added a few lemons pieces to her tea. She grabbed a cookie.

"There are three bedrooms and my Uncle Joe put a new updated three-piece bathroom down the hall. After my father died, my uncle was a great help to my mom and me being alone.

"There's a large barn where we kept five horses; four worked the land, and one was my own to ride. Dad surprised me and brought home a white mare for me. My father was a farrier, who worked for a man across the fields, placing the shoes on the horses and did anything else around his farm needing repair. We had plenty of room for a few goats, cows, one large boar, and a female pig who had piglets yearly. The male was quite lazy. You name it; we had all kinds of animals."

"Are they still here?" Carolyn asked.

"I had them moved to Todd's barn when I stayed there."

"The tea hit the spot, Jenny. Thank you."

"Would you like another one?"

"If you don't mind, I'd like to take a look around the house."

I took Carolyn through each room. It wasn't modern but had all the conveniences that were needed. I assumed a new buyer might renovate the home. A wringer washing machine was in the kitchen, a small refrigerator with an icebox on the side, and a potbelly stove. The pantry was large where we kept our cans of food, sugar, flour, and baking needs.

The bedrooms were not fancy. Old curtains were hung from the last time my mother put them there before her death. She had done all she could with the little we had. My father never had any interest in updating anything to keep up with modern designs.

"Why don't you take the curtains down, Jenny. They would bring in a lot of light."

"I can do that."

I walked Carolyn out to the barn. It was a good size with ten stalls. The top floor had room to store the hay. No more animals roamed that area. There was no reason for them to be kept here, except my desire to have White Christmas returned to me. I hoped in time, I could take my mare back if I found a place with a lot of property.

Showing Carolyn around our property only made me feel emptiness. My past memories were pushed out of my life. The home, barn, and land felt like a ghost town. My reasons to live here were gone. I was moving, but I felt no emotions.

"You have a great piece of farmland, Jenny. How much?"

"Dad bought twenty acres off a family who lost everything with The Great Depression. It was the best investment he ever made. That's when things were good for us."

Carolyn added, "Massachusetts has about 125,000 pieces of farmlands. The bad part is that the reports show a decrease in New England at 15.9 percentage. The Great Depression hurt the sellers. Great for the buyers who had money to hold out for a better future. At this moment, some families are getting $65.86 an acre which would give us an asking price of $1,317.20. Your property goes down to a brook, which can supply water to the farm and the animals. That's a plus.

"I'd say we can start at that price, but I doubt you'll get the asking amount due to the fact that people are struggling to survive. I'll start at the value, but don't get your hopes up. I'm going to call a family who has been looking for months to get farmland in the Cape Cod area. Do you mind if I show them around if the interest is there?"

"Anytime, Carolyn. I want to sell as soon as I can."

"Be careful not to spread those words around or mention the need to move fast, or the buyers offer a low price thinking you're desperate. I'll call you tomorrow."

"Thank you, Carolyn, for coming to see the place."

"It was nice meeting you, Jenny. I'll try to get top dollar for your property. If we're patient, the price may happen, but I know you don't want to sit on selling too long. Many people are hurting. It's 1939, and we're at the stage of another war outbreak. In fact, last month, on September 1st, the Germans began an invasion of Poland, while Britain and France declared war on Germany two days later. Things aren't looking good.

"That's why I want to jump right on this property before people stop investing. The family I have in mind will like the brook. The waterway may be a big selling point. Not many properties offer water."

"I appreciate what you're doing for me. I'll look forward to your call."

Carolyn walked to her 1938 Bentley 8 Litre. It had a rich, deep green body with a black top, fenders, and stepping boards. I knew the Millers' were doing well.

I walked into the house, put my head in my hands at the kitchen table, and sobbed. *Oh, Mom. I wish you were here. All my dreams have faded. I have no future with Todd. I lost the love of my life. Cathy's carrying Todd's baby and so am I. How could Todd have done this to us? I need you so much. I miss you. I don't know what to do. I feel so alone.*

A Police Report

Saturday morning, a police car pulled into the driveway. Bob, Ray, Sam, and Todd were working in the lumberyard.

"Wonder what they're doing here?" Ray asked.

The two officers, who had come to their house when their parents died, got out of the patrol car.

"Hello. I hope we're not disrupting anything important."

"No, Officer Ferreira," Todd said. "What can we do for you?'

"I'm glad you're all here. We could have called on the phone but we wanted to share the update with your parent's investigation in person."

The men looked at each other.

"Do you know Claire Dutra? She owns the flower shop in Orleans."

"Oh, yes, *The Flower Bell*. She buys a lot of our annual and perennials for her business. Is anything wrong?" Todd questioned.

"She came to the police station to explain what she saw in front of her store the day your parents had their accident. She claimed two men, who looked like hoodlums, were looking over your father's truck. One seemed to be bending down checking under it and the other examined their tires. She claimed to have seen the one with wire cutters in his hand went under the truck. Our mechanic looked your dad's truck over from one end to the next. He found a wire had been cut to the breaks."

Officer Justin finished the details. "Mrs. Dutra saw your parents coming up to their truck while she was on the phone with a customer. She put the phone down and ran out to talk to them. She called out your father's name a few times, but he took off. We gathered he didn't hear her.

"Claire had to get a delivery out within twenty minutes and figured she'd call your parents when she got back. When she saw their accident in the *Nelson News*, she called to come in and speak to us about the incident. We have a description of the two men and the department's investigating this further."

Officer Ferreira came up to Bob, "We want to apologize to you Bob, and your whole family, Todd. We put you through a lot of worry at a bad time." He put his hand on Bob's shoulder, "You're no longer a suspect in this case. We do know, Todd, that your parents were killed by someone. We have to find out who and why. We'll investigate who those two men were at the truck. Claire couldn't give a good description.

"I don't think a person in town hated your family. All we could come up with was that many families during the Great Depression lost everything they owned. We hope no one planned their deaths from being jealous of all you had with the three businesses. This case is going to be hard to solve, but we will keep looking."

The two officers shook their hands before getting into the police car and left.

They all stood shocked. "My God, someone murdered them!" Bob was enraged. Todd and Sam, I'm truly sorry for all of you. Who would ever do that to the most giving people I know? I hope they find the bastards and hang them. I'll be the first in line."

Todd got panicky wondering if the investigation would lead to Eddie. If so, the family would learn the truth about why they died.

Todd's Decision with Cathy

The next day, Todd was working in the greenhouse dividing the different plants and shrubs. Bob and Ray were at the carpentry shop next door, measuring lumber for two wooden doors. The two men had moved into the main house. Having two extra people living in the house kept conversations going instead of the constant silence.

Rita had been asked by her Mr. Nelson to cover a story with the new movie *Gone with the Wind* in New York. It was the best film of the year produced by David O. Selznick. The scenes were set in the South against the backdrop of the American Civil War. The story was about Scarlett O'Hara, the strong-willed daughter of a Georgia plantation owner, from her romantic pursuit of Ashley Wilkes, who was married to his cousin, Melanie Hamilton, to her marriage to Rhett Butler. The leading roles were portrayed by Vivien Leigh, Clark Gable, Leslie Howard, and Olivia de Havilland. Rita was excited to be among the stars of the year.

Rita slipped her camera into her suitcase hoping for photos to be taken with all the actors. She couldn't wait to meet Mr. Selznick knowing Kathleen had scheduled an appointment to visit with him and discuss a future in acting. She prayed Kathleen was healing well.

Sam left for the day to go back to his college dorm. He was graduating next week with Faith. When he got home, he told Faith of the canceled wedding. She had been asked to be Jenny's bridesmaid and couldn't wait for Sunday. She was heartbroken and shocked when she heard the reason.

"I can't believe Todd would cheat on Jenny. Oh, that poor girl!"

"Let's not discuss it, Faith. I'm sick over it. Jenny left the house to go back to her parent's home."

The family was traumatized by canceling the wedding. It had been an event the invited couldn't wait to unfold. All the guests were notified they were holding off the wedding until a further date. The family would handle the truth later. Their special day had been stopped.

****

Todd was carrying a tray of yellow roses from the stand to put out front when the phone rang.

"Hello?"

"Todd, my friend. Todd's skin crawled hearing Eddie's voice. Todd listened and didn't reply.

"Sunday's around the corner. We haven't had an answer from you about Cathy. She's waiting for you to walk her down the aisle. You see, Todd, we know Jenny's back in her parent's home—alone. I have one of my men in the area waiting for my call on what your answer will be. The cops would have a hard time finding her body in the thick woods in the back of her home."

"You son-of-a-bitch! If you harm her, I'll blow your frigging brains out. No matter where you go, I'll find you."

"I have someone who wants to talk to you."

A moment passed with the phone exchange. "Hello, Todd, it's Sharon."

Todd felt smothered with no defense to stop this planned death threat.

"Are you there, Todd?" Sharon was being sarcastic. He could tell by her tone that she was now his attacker and enjoyed the control with Tony in jail.

"I know you're listening. If you don't answer me, Todd, Jenny won't be breathing much longer."

"What do you want, Sharon?" He choked knowing he had to answer her. What he wanted was to slam the phone down loud enough to deafen her.

"I have a minister scheduled for Sunday to be here at 1 o'clock so you and Cathy can say your wedding vows. It would have been nice to have a large wedding and put the announcement into the newspaper, but we want to keep your marriage quiet so the public doesn't know that she's knocked-up by Todd Costa, who was due to marry Jenny Rossini on Sunday."

"You have to demand this Sunday."

"Yes, this Sunday. The day you and Jenny were to be married. Funny how things work out. I hope you're as excited as if it were Jenny."

"You know, Sharon, I don't need you being a wise-ass to me. I'll be there." He hung up.

"Oh, my God, how did this happen? All from being selfish and wanting a piece of Cathy. How could I have been so blind? She wants us married on Sunday, he thought. *Sharon knows that would give me unbelievable pain. I don't want to live through that day. It was supposed to be Jenny and me. Jenny, I love you so much. I can't tell you the truth about why I'm hurting you. Life without you will be nothing. I'm going to have to live for my child. Why couldn't the baby have been ours? I'd be marrying you with such pride.*

Being forced to marry Cathy was making Todd sick. His father's help would have been the best action to take to stop this from happening. The more Todd absorbed his loving parent's deaths from his mistake with Cathy, the more he felt he would lose his mind. Todd couldn't share the horrible truth with his siblings. He had no feeling for this woman. She came back from Paris to destroy him. Todd didn't feel Cathy was worthy to have the honor of carrying his baby.

****

By Saturday afternoon, Todd couldn't erase the thought of this blackmail ceremony. He couldn't imagine even standing next to Cathy saying vows. Sunday, Rita and Sam were going to be gone for the day, so he planned to sneak away from the house.

Todd didn't know how he was going to go on living without Jenny. He spent the full day working to keep himself busy.

"Todd, why are you killing yourself with work? You've been out here since 4 am." Ray questioned him as he walked into the large, glass-enclosed greenhouse nursery carrying plants.

"I have a lot to do. I meant to tell you I'm going to take the day off tomorrow."

Ray laughed his head off. "Of course, you're taking the day off. It's your wedding day. By the way, where's Jenny? She's not planning on staying at her home until you two get married, is she?"

Todd had been in such turmoil he realized no one told Ray or Bob the wedding had been canceled.

Ray was a short man with dark, brown hair and a wide build. For his small size, he had the strength to lift lumber like a giant.

Bob had two large scarlet-blue Hydrangeas in his hands. "I thought I'd give you a hand bringing some plants in before dark. In two months, winter will be upon us again. I hate seeing the snow and ice. The season can't leave fast enough.

"I guess we'll all be putting our time into the carpentry shop. I love the idea we don't have to travel far now to get home, except down the driveway to the shop. Think we can handle it, Ray?" They both grinned and looked at Todd.

Bob was tall with dirty blond hair. A man's man, you would say. Handsome in a rugged way. Always in a good mood and willing to help. A big guy with a huge heart.

He laid the plants down. "What time's the catering company coming to set the tents up? Aren't they usually here the day before early in the morning? Did we scare Sam and Rita out after moving in yesterday? No one's around, including the future bride. Where's everyone?"

Todd stared at them. "I have something to tell you." He put the plants down he had been holding and turned to them. "Tomorrow, Jenny and I won't be getting married."

Bob and Ray looked at each other with their mouths open.

"Tell us your joking, Todd," Bob asked.

"I'm ashamed to tell you why. I don't know if I can get the story out of me."

Ray went over and tapped Todd on the shoulder. "Come on, Todd. We're all like brothers. We've been together for years. There's nothing you can't say to us."

Todd looked at them with tears in his eyes. The men never saw him show emotions to the point of almost weeping. His voice was breaking up.

What's wrong, man?" Bob was now concerned.

"I had a one-night fling with Cathy Greco before she left for Paris. She came back pregnant claiming me as the father."

They stood there motionless.

"Todd, are you telling me Cathy has been gone three months, and she's naming you as the father—and you're falling for that? You stopped your wedding because of this lie?"

"I went for a paternity test and I'm the father."

"God, no, Todd. Poor Jenny. That's why she's asked us to help her move back home. That's why no one's here."

"She went back to her parent's home because we broke up. She's selling her house."

"I can't believe you two are throwing your lives away over Cathy. What are you planning on doing?"

Todd turned his back to them. "I'm marrying Cathy to give the baby my name. I don't want my child to have the Greco's name with all the crime in the family. I want to bring the child up the right way."

Ray went in front of him. "You left Jenny for this woman? With all, you two shared and loved, this relationship has ended?"

"Look. I made my mind up."

"Why are you marrying someone you don't love?" Ray was stunned.

"I told you why."

Bob grabbed Todd's shoulders and faced him. "I woke up this morning and felt a coldness in the air. No one was in the house and the aroma of breakfast was gone, along with the laughter downstairs. At first, I thought you were all out helping the catering company set-up, or the girls were running around doing the last-minute things that women do the day before a wedding.

"But, I never thought I'd hear this. I feel the pain in my bones. You two will never get over the love you have for each other. Both of you will be married to another person with nothing but emptiness."

Bob continued. "I know, Todd, because my girlfriend cheated on me, and my life has had a void ever since I ended our relationship. She begged me to forgive her, and I was too proud to take her back. Now, I can't find the feelings to look at another woman.

"Two years ago, I saw her in town with her husband walking with their two sons. Children that could have been mine. When she looked at me, I felt her love still in her eyes. Our expressions locked as if time stopped.

"Was the decision worth me not forgiving her? I'd give anything to take that moment back and stand by her side. We all make mistakes, Todd, but taking the easy way out isn't the answer. You have to want what you're deciding on with your life. Cathy Greco isn't your dream girl.

"You'll have loneliness and hurt the rest of your life. On top of that, you'll watch Jenny marry another man, have his kids, and have the sight eat at the bottom of your soul. The pain will make your relationship with Cathy worse because you'll hate her for doing this to you.

"I pray your child doesn't grow up in a loveless atmosphere and listen to parents hating each other. No one's going to come out being happy, Todd. I'm telling you this because I love you like a brother. Re-think what you're doing!"

Todd's expression showed a broken heart beyond repair. "The sad part is, Bob, you're right. I'll love Jenny until I take my last breath."

Todd slapped the dirt and mud off his hands onto his dungarees from the plants. Bob noticed a tear come down Todd's cheek as he turned not wanting them to see his emotions and walked out. The two men watched as Todd got into his car and drove off.

The Final Sale

I took out the vacuüm cleaner to give the house a deep cleaning when Carolyn left. I had done the top surface. It had been a year since I last did the hated chore of cleaning windows, polishing floors, and cleaning cabinets. The dust had collected, but the small touchups made the house shine. I wanted to be prepared in case Carolyn called to say someone wanted to look at the property.

I was washing the kitchen floor when I noticed Rita pull up in front of the house. I rested the mop handle against the kitchen wall.

Rita knocked. "Come in."

"I have to go cover the new movie, *Gone with the Wind*. I leave this afternoon. I wanted to stop by and talk before I left."

I cleared the kitchen table removing the cleaning items. "Have a seat. I'll make tea for us."

"I have news from the police department regarding my parent's accident."

"Good, I hope."

She told me all the information the policemen found on the two men at Cory's truck. "Who would ever want them dead? I can't sleep thinking about this, Jenny."

"Oh, poor Judy and Cory. They never hurt anyone. I'm so sorry, Rita. I hope they find out who did this heartless killing. How can anyone feel they can take a person's life for nothing? All of you must be sick over the findings."

"They are and Bob and Ray are ready to go hunting for them."

"Let the police do their work."

I placed the cups of tea down on the table.

"With you gone from our house, I don't enjoy tea by myself

anymore. In fact, I don't enjoy anything. The house is dead quiet. It's a death-zone. There's this horrible vacant feeling in the house since my parents died. The gap is painful. I want to see and hear them. It's making me sick knowing that will never happen. Their deaths were too fast and unexpected. I keep waking up waiting to hear them down the hall talking in their bedroom. I used to fall asleep listening to them having soft conversations.

"I can't wait for Kathleen to come home. The loss of you and Todd have added to this emptiness. Instead of sharing and supporting our losses, we're all going separate ways. I don't want to come home after work. Are you coming back to your job? At least, we would be with each other during the week.

"I called Mr. Nelson and gave my resignation Friday. I'm leaving town. I'll miss everyone. Life's not going to go back the way it was, Rita. At least you have Bob, Ray, and your brother at the house."

"What are you going to do, Jenny?"

"Yesterday, Carolyn Miller came over and I showed her the house and property. She knows of a family that might be interested, especially with the brook attached to the sale."

"You're serious leaving Cape Cod? I hope you thought about the Great Depression going on and the war in Europe. We were both lucky having jobs. What if you don't get one in New York?"

"Rita, with the sale of the house, I can live on that until I decide what to do with my life and where to work. Every part of my body wants to stay, but I couldn't survive mentally living in Chatham knowing Todd was married to Cathy.

"I don't know how I'm going to function tomorrow knowing that was supposed to be our wedding day. It's hard enough trying to deal with your parent's deaths. I'm stuck in a situation I can't change. I feel like I'm being sucked into quicksand. How am I going to make a new life when I lost the one I wanted with Todd?"

I started to cry. "I love Todd and I don't know what to do with these feelings. I'm in shock. I sit here alone and wonder, why?" I screamed from anger. "I can't sleep. Last night I walked the floor until four this morning. I fell asleep from mental exhaustion."

"Jenny, I don't like you being here alone, either does Todd."

"What does Todd expect me to do? Stay with all of you knowing he'll never be mine? He's going to marry Cathy. The thought of her having his love drives me insane. She wasn't in his life, and then suddenly out of nowhere, I'm hit with this dilemma. I wasn't prepared. Four days before my wedding, I found out I lost him…us! I never got to tell him about our child."

"Jenny, don't ever think Todd will love Cathy."

"Rita, knowing or thinking it's me he loves, doesn't help the fact she'll be Mrs. Costa, living and sleeping with him… and bringing up his child. That doesn't help me to go on with my life thinking at least he loves me? It's not enough."

"I can't help wondering, Jenny, if Todd had been threatened in some way by Tony Greco. None of this makes sense. Mr. Greco would do anything for Cathy."

"Todd has a mind of his own. He can walk away."

"What if he can't?"

"What do you mean?"

"Jenny, we're women. We know these inner feelings we get…our gut instincts! There's something wrong with this situation. Cathy popped up out of nowhere being pregnant. Once she left for Paris, she had no interest in Todd, not even to keep in touch with him. I mean, if she loved him, don't you think she would have called him? Todd had no connection or desire to be with her."

"I don't care how she popped up. Todd's the one who's throwing away our life together for whatever reason. He's putting her above what we had and that's enough to end our relationship. I'm not going to sit and go crazy trying to analyze a reason for this breakup. I need to get on with my life. I'm carrying a baby."

"Do you love him, Jenny?"

Of course, I do, but he's not mine anymore? I will never stop loving him. He chose Cathy, now I have to choose my life. End of story, Rita!"

I got up to put the cups in the sink when the phone rang.

"Hello?"

"Hi, Jenny. It's Carolyn. I spoke to Manny and Julia Keene. They would love to see your place sometime today. They're very interested."

"Sure. I'll be here. Is one o'clock okay for you?"

"That will be perfect. We'll see you then."

"Thank you, Carolyn."

I hung up and looked at Rita. "Boy, that was fast. One day the house is up for sale and a couple wants to see the property."

"How am I going to get up every day, Jenny, and not be able to talk to you? We have shared everything. It's bad enough we're separated from Kathleen."

"There's no reason for us not to stay friends, Rita. You go to New York all the time. If you don't want to be at a hotel or be bored all alone, stay with me."

"I don't want to visit you in Manhattan. I want you here."

I was drained talking about something I couldn't change. "Well, I have to finish cleaning the kitchen and bathroom. Carolyn will be here in two hours. Send me a picture of you with Clark Gable. You're a lucky girl!"

Rita hugged me tightly. "I'll be gone for three days. I'm sure the house won't be sold until then. I'll stop by and see how you're doing. For you, I hope the sale goes through."

"Thanks, Rita. Have a safe trip."

I walked Rita to the front door and waved until she disappeared down the dusty, dirt road. I closed the door and gathered the cleaning solutions off the top of the kitchen sink and washed the tub and toilet. Everything was presentable.

I took the kettle to heat some water for another cup of tea. Being alone, I didn't know how to occupy myself after being surrounded by the Costa family. It had been a wonderful life, and I was lost being torn away from them. I now faced the world alone and pregnant at eighteen.

****

I walked into the bedroom and took down my wedding gown. I took the dress from Todd's house that had been covered with a black, heavy plastic bag. I had to take one more look knowing that Judy and Cory bought it for me. I remembered the shopping day filled with fun with Judy, Rita, and Faith looking for our gowns.

I thought about taking the dress back to the store and giving the money to Todd's family, but I couldn't part with it. I slipped the bag off the top of the gown. The dress was perfect. My eyes filled while I wrapped my arms around the garment. I fought the temptation of trying the gown on again.

How beautiful, I thought, as I spread the dress out to unfold the train. *I would have made a stunning bride.* I wanted to see Todd's expression as I walked down to him. Cory was going to give me away. Judy was a replacement for my mother. I lost everyone in a few weeks. *Why?* That's all I kept asking. With all Cathy's money, why didn't she give this child up in Paris?"

I thought back to Rita's remark. Threats from Tony Greco. Did it make sense or was it because I wanted to believe the reason? I knew deep down in my heart what Todd and I had together. We knew each other inside and out. Todd was not himself. One time, he seemed like he wanted to say something to me and then clammed up.

Now, I was questioning myself on leaving. He was being decent by taking responsibility for what he caused. *Should I have told him I was pregnant?* I didn't want Todd from pity. *Would he leave Cathy if he knew?*

If my mother or Judy were alive, I wouldn't be thinking of adoption. How was I going to take care of an infant and work to make money to survive and pay all my bills? No man would want me knowing I was pregnant and unmarried. Men didn't think much of a single woman in my condition. My list of why not to keep the baby went on and on. I could only see the decisions to give our child up.

Panic set in with my thinking about what I had to do by myself. The reality started to hit me with being totally and completely alone. The fact overwhelmed me. I was going to be nineteen in a month and had no direction.

All my confidence in leaving Cape Cod was starting to scare me. Telling Todd off, leaving their home, the people I loved, were making me feel insecure. I reacted to the shock and hurt. The situation was too much for me to handle.

I pulled the heavy plastic over my gown and hung the dress up. I was happy Todd and I decided to leave the gowns for the girls at his house. I didn't have to deal with seeing their faces taking them back to the store.

Within a few minutes, there was a knock on the front door. Carolyn was standing with a couple.

"Hi, Carolyn."

"Jenny, this is Manny and Julia Keene."

"Welcome," I said, opening the door for them.

Manny was short and stout with a full black beard and bushy hair. Julia was short and heavyset with gray hair. Julia's eyes roamed all over the kitchen while the three of us talked. She was forward and walked down the hall to open the bathroom door and look into the bedrooms without waiting to be shown.

Manny was more interested in seeing the land outside and the barn. "Where's the brook to the property? I have a lot of cows to take care of if we move here.

The water would be a great advantage to the farm."

Julia came out of the third bedroom. "It's a nice clean home. I like the bathroom being updated." She looked out the kitchen window that faced the pastures and barn. "This is a peaceful setting."

"Let's take a walk outside." Carolyn led them out the backdoor.

I put the coffee pot on in case someone wanted a cup on their return and placed the leftover sugar cookies in the middle of the kitchen table. I looked out the window and watched Carolyn taking them in the barn. Manny stayed longer than his wife.

Carolyn then walked them down the path towards the brook. I got in a state of panic knowing I'd have to move if they bought our place. Everything negative was happening too fast. I felt there was no time to make a good decision. The thought raced through me to stay and see if things would fall apart for Cathy and Todd, and I'd be there to pick up the pieces. I'd swallow my pride to keep Todd in my life.

The more I looked at my options, the more I knew staying was impossible. I wouldn't be able to hide being pregnant. What would the townspeople think of Todd? I loved him too much to have him face our friends and community fathering two babies at the same time. I took another deep breath. *Stop doing this to yourself. You have to leave the Cape. There's no other solution.*

It took Carolyn an hour to show the Keene's the land. They came in with wet, muddy shoes from being down at the brook. I looked at each step they took with the dirt being left on my clean floor.

"You have a nice place here, Miss. I'm sorry to hear your parents died. I can't believe your father didn't do much with this land. There's a lot of room open to broadening this farm."

"He wasn't home much, Mr. Keene. Guess our place needs someone like you with the interest to make the place grow."

"We have two teenage sons and the three bedrooms here are nice and big. Love the porch swing you have out front."

"We did, too. After supper, we sat on the seat almost every night. It's very peaceful watching the sunset."

"I don't like playing real estate games jumping back and forth with a price to see who wins. I'd like to buy your place, but I can't offer the full price. We have a lot to do getting the farm up and running it our way to perfection. I'll offer you $1,000.

"Wow, that's $300 less than the asking price," I said. "I was depending on the full price." I knew Manny was taking advantage of me.

I looked over at Carolyn. She looked back. "That's still a good offer, Jenny."

"Timing's everything. I guess it isn't a profitable one. I know you're taking advantage of me, Mr. Keene. Yesterday, I had another couple with two small children come after Carolyn left to see the place. They plan on giving me an offer late this afternoon. I'd like to wait and see what they present."

Carolyn looked at me with a surprised look.

"I'll go as high as $1,200, Jenny, but that's our limit. The land with the stream of water is rare to find on a piece of property."

"Since you're here and giving me an offer, I'll accept it. I'm glad you went back to the real estate game, Mr. Keene," I remarked. We all laughed.

"I would like to move in within two weeks. Is that unreasonable for you?"

"No. By then, I should know where I'm going."

Manny walked over to me and reached his hand out. "It was a pleasure meeting you, Jenny, and I wish you the best. Again, I'm sorry for your loss. Now, I think Carolyn and I have papers to sign."

"I can come back here Monday, Jenny, for you to sign papers."

"Carolyn, I have a car. I can get to your place. It's easier than dragging everything here. What's a good time?" I asked.

We all agreed on 10 am on Monday morning. "I need to get all the paperwork together. We'll see you then, Jenny."

I tried to get them out fast. Tears were surfacing. I closed the door and put my head against the glass panel. *Thank you, Dad and Mom, for the gift of this house. The money will help me start over.* I couldn't share the excitement of the sale with anyone. I could only think about what this money would have meant to Todd and me getting married.

Todd's Marriage to Cathy

On Sunday morning, Todd woke up at four o'clock to a perfect, warm day. It was early but the sun was supposed to come out and reach eighty. Ideal weather that he and Jenny would have welcomed on their wedding day. He faced a threat to marry Cathy on their day. This would finalize the end of his future with Jenny. He couldn't tell her he loved her from the bottom of his heart. He had to take this step to save her.

Todd sat on the edge of his bed looking out the window. His parents had saved every penny to leave this farmland for their children. They struggled during the Great Depression to survive.

His dad was going to help him out with the Greco's threats. There were no solutions in Todd's head on how to get out of marrying Cathy without putting Jenny and his family in danger. The anger rose in him knowing they killed his parents. Where was justice?

The police had the reputation of working with the mob over the years. The cops would eventually inform Tony about Todd's accusations with filing a complaint, which would lead to the future death threats that would be carried out as promised. He had to worry the police department wouldn't find Eddie with Mrs. Dutra's description. Eddie would think Todd went to them with all the intimidating scare tactics. It would be suicidal.

He decided to get into his farm clothes and feed the animals. Bob had coffee brewing in the kitchen when he came downstairs. The emptiness in his gut came from not seeing his parents' and his dad reading the morning newspaper at the kitchen table. He ached for their lives to be back before their deaths. Bob and Todd had small talk until the coffee was done. Todd poured a cup.

"Thanks Bob. I'm going to get the animals fed."

Bob knew this was supposed to be one of the biggest days in Chatham with Todd and Jenny being married. The house was dead quiet. Ray was taking advantage with sleeping late.

"Why don't I help you, Todd." Bob grabbed the hot pot of coffee to heat up the rest of his at the halfway mark in his cup.

"Bob, you do something for yourself. Enjoy the time off. I need this time to think alone. It's not the day I had planned."

Todd couldn't share the event ready to unfold with Bob. At 1 o'clock, he would be marrying Cathy against his will. "Think I'll sit on the swing on the front porch and drink my coffee before I go to the barn."

Bob wanted to talk to Todd. He could only imagine the torment he was under knowing how important this day was supposed to be for him. They had been friends for over fifteen years and talked about anything. For the first time, Bob didn't have an answer. This was something Todd had to do completely on his own.

Todd sat on the swing and swayed back and forth in a slow rhythm touching his hand on the spot where Jenny used to sit next to him, while he drank his coffee. The memories flowed through the years that he and Jenny had shared. He wondered how she was this morning after he put a knife into her heart. He let her walk out to handle the pain that she didn't deserve.

This was the day he dreamed of making Jenny his wife. They would have been married at two this afternoon. He imagined seeing her in the wedding dress she had been excited to wear going down the aisle in the little chapel.

His parents died from the hands of the mafia months after Jenny's mother, along with her aunt and uncle put to rest. Todd was fortunate to have a brother and sister. Poor Jenny was in isolation with no siblings. Her dearest cousin, Kathleen, was in a hospital in Detroit struggling her own battle getting better in the rehabilitation center to save her identity.

Todd wanted to go to Jenny. He was tempted to ask her to run away with him. No matter what he was feeling or wanted, he knew his decisions would be playing with Jenny's life. In time, the mafia would find them.

He took the last sip of his coffee and left the cup on the porch. In a depressed state, he walked to the barn. The sign on the business door announcing they would be closed on Sunday due to their wedding had been taken down.

He took the feed out. His first trip was to the cows in their stalls, and then one by one, he milked them. The barn door was opened and the goats, sheep, and hens were let out in their penned area. The cows were placed in the pasture when he finished. He went up to White Christmas, Jenny's mare, and brushed her down until her coat shinned. She was a beautiful animal. He then went to his stallion, Midnight, to do the same chore.

The daily task took an hour. He saddled up his horse and rode down the paths through the woods where he and Jenny had found pleasure being together. The enjoyment without her was gone. Todd realized nothing was ever going to complete his life. The void was so deep in his soul he couldn't imagine living another day without her. He had no doubt they had a deep, rare love. It had been so comfortable.

Todd came back from the run and put all the horses out in the field and walked back to the house. The clock showed 12:30 pm. Todd decided not to act like he was excited about marrying Cathy. He stayed in his dirty, animal-smelling clothes, and muddy boots. He covered his driver's seat with heavy pad to sit on and drove up to the path to the main road.

****

He arrived at 1 pm and knocked on Cathy's backdoor. He rubbed most of the dry mud off his clothing and shoes. Sharon opened the door. "What are you doing?" She was insulted.

"I'm here to marry your daughter. I didn't have time to freshen up after feeding the animals and getting them ready for pasture. I had chores to do."

Cathy came out in a white, straight style dress, wearing a white hat and white gloves. Knowing Todd, she laughed. "Leave it to you. I can see the excitement you're having today, Todd."

"I find this a cheap shot. How dare you come to this house dressed like this. Go home and change. You smell!" Sharon was wild.

"This is who she's marrying, Sharon. Don't ask me to be phony. If I was getting married for love, the event would be different. You made me lose Jenny. This was supposed to be my day with her." Todd was getting furious thinking about what he had to do. "How dare you ruin my life and Jenny's and take part in my parent's death." Todd was bottled-up with anger, hate, resentment, and heartbreak.

"Mother, go into the house and leave us alone."

"Who are you to tell me to go into the house?"

"You're not making the situation any better. We're getting married. It's my place to talk to him."

Sharon walked past her daughter with red in her eyes.

Cathy asked Todd to come into her father's office. "Todd, I love you. I always have and I'm thrilled about having your baby."

"Please, Cathy, don't over-do the words on how thrilled you are after giving up your fame with modeling for Coco Chanel. This wasn't your choice. If it had not been proven that I was the father, I would have left you in the dust.

"I'm not marrying you because I love you. I want you to know before we start the wedding. I'm doing this to keep my baby from having the Greco's name. I'm doing this because your father and his gangsters threatened the rest of my family and Jenny. Why would you think I'd be coming here happy to marry you?

"You know your father killed my parents. How can you live with this fact and face me? I thought you had some decency in you, but I guess not. Right now, Cathy, I have a deep hate for all of you for taking my wedding day away from me. Jenny and I are in love, and you know it. How can you be this desperate? You have money from your fame that I will never see in a lifetime."

"You have every right to be mad at me—and hate me. I'm not proud of my parents, never have been, Todd. I'm threatened as much as you, believe it or not. I want you to know, I have loved you since grammar school. I never should have cheated on you when we were a couple. I know, when you see and feel what I have for you, you'll not be sorry we married. I can love you enough until you get over Jenny."

"I won't get over Jenny. You can't understand that because you have never loved."

She went up to Todd, wearing her white gloves, and held his hands. "I swear to love you with all I have until I die."

"Don't promise something you're not capable of doing, Cathy."

Sharon came into the den. "The minister's waiting outside under the gazebo. Why's Todd in this house with all the dirt on him? I'll never forgive you for wearing those filthy clothes. Get out of this house."

"He doesn't need you to forgive him. He needs me, Mother."

"Be there in ten minutes." Sharon walked away steaming mad.

"Todd, I know you love Jenny. I'm not stupid. My father has gone too far with threatening you, even from prison. He won't let this go if we don't marry. You don't know him. He's worse than you think. He's serious with the attempts that would carry them through with the rest of your family.

"I didn't know anything about your parent's deaths until I saw the accident in the newspaper the next day. Marrying me keeps your family alive, including yourself...maybe me. Our baby, their grandchild, is going to be our weapon to use against them."

"Don't ever let me hear you say that again. My baby will not be used as a weapon for anything. If this is your plan, I'll walk out on you now. I don't care if I'm killed."

"You get killed, Todd, and no one will be there to protect your child."

"Your family has me just where they want me."

Cathy tried to get close to him. "Todd, remember how we used to be together? The wild sex between us? We'll have that again."

"No, we won't, Cathy. There's more to love than just wild sex. What you and your family have done to me has stopped any feelings with memories that used to be there for you."

Cathy walked closer. "There's going to be many cold nights, and you'll look for warmth. You're a man, and sooner or later, you're going to want what's lying next to you. I promise you won't be disappointed. I know how to make you happy. There was a time we had been wild about each other. She took his hand again. "Now, let's get married. The longer we wait, the more it'll upset my mother."

****

Todd walked with her to the minister. The area was decorated beautifully with flowers. A perfect wedding if you were in love with your partner. Todd's soul was with Jenny.

The minister studied Todd from head to foot and didn't dare say anything about his dirty clothes. Todd felt frozen in time and too depressed to say a word. He thought of the beautiful St. Thérèse Chapel where Jenny and he said their own vows after giving her an engagement ring.

Todd could feel the love for Jenny flow through him. He remembered her hands that reached out to hold his when she said vows to him the chapel. He had noticed all the freckles on her arms. He loved the light-brown spots on her face, telling her many times that she had been kissed by the sun. Everything about her excited him.

This moment with Cathy was a show. He loathed the idea he was cornered into this charade. He felt this was all a bad dream and he'd wake up. He lost Jenny forever.

"Todd." He heard his name called and came back to the minister looking at him.

Cathy started her vows.

"I promise to love who you are now and who you are yet to become.

I promise to listen to you and learn from you, to support you, and accept your support.

I will celebrate your triumphs and mourn your losses as though they were my own.

I will love you and have faith in your love for me, through all our years, and all that life may bring us."

Todd felt her lies. *Mourn your losses!* He felt grieved knowing how his parents would feel seeing him standing in front of Cathy instead of Jenny. They would have refused him to do this. His dad might have had a rifle in his hand.

"You can put the ring on him." The minister smiled.

She put the ring on his finger, and then secretively, slipped her ring in his hand.

How could he return those vows? He already said his to Jenny in the chapel. He knew Cathy meant what she said at this moment, but had no doubt the promises would fade through the years."

The minister looked at Todd waiting for him to say his words to Cathy.

Todd looked at her.

"I promise to love and care for my child and be a devoted father through the growing years. I will care and shelter you the best I can until that moment arrives."

Todd slipped her ring on without looking at her, while Sharon and Cathy were stunned with his vows.

Hesitation came from the minister, who wondered if this was a joke. "I now pronounce you man and wife. You can kiss the bride."

Todd stepped down from the platform without offering a kiss. He held his hand out to help Cathy down the few steps. She looked at him knowing there was going to be a challenge with this marriage but she was determined to make it work. Patience was going to be needed with nightly touches to bring his skin alive and bring back what they once had between them.

Sharon walked right up to Todd. "This isn't over with us. You're lucky we had no guests. I would have had someone blow your head off and take your baby."

"You would have to blow my head off, Sharon, to get my child. I'll do everything in my power to keep the infant out of your care. We don't need you."

"Enjoy your buffet alone." Sharon walked away.

Cathy stood in the middle of the yard. "What do we do now, Todd? Do we fly off to some tropical island for a honeymoon or do we go to a motel?"

"I have no idea, Cathy." Todd looked down at her. "I can't see running off alone and celebrating this day after we had sex in your barn. We already got a prize from that night. Right now, I want to go home, Cathy. I'll let you know my plans. Right now, I'm numb with this event. I can't even call this moment a wedding. You're now married with the name of Mrs. Cathy Costa. I wanted to go to bed tonight with Mrs. Jenny Costa."

"Todd, I have it written in our marriage papers that my name stays Nina Mae so that I don't lose my famous status that I worked hard at gaining fame in Paris."

"That's security for you, Cathy. I can only guess what you have planned in the future with this child. I have to get home and feed the animals."

He started to walk away and Cathy grabbed his arm. "You're not going to make a fool out of me any longer. I'll take just so much. I put up with your sadness and heartbreak, along with today's embarrassment. Tomorrow, I expect you to come here to get me. I'll be packed. We can live here and put up with my mother every day or find us a home."

She walked into the house, dreading she would have to explain to her mother why he left without taking her.

Todd got into his car and drove off. On the way home, he pulled over to Nantucket Sound Beach located on Cockle Cove Road in Chatham. He got out of the vehicle. He walked up to the edge of the saltwater and watched the small ripple of waves hit the shoreline.
He looked at his ring and felt the urgent need to get the band off his finger. The trickery to this union disgusted him. Todd pulled hard to get the piece of jewelry off and flung it as far as he could into the air towards the ocean. He watched as the ring plopped with a slight splash entering the sea. Having the band off made him breathe again. It was as if he took something dirty off him. He swore to never wear a ring for the rest of his life unless he was married to Jenny.

Jenny Facing Reality

At 7 am, I woke up to the bright sun coming through my window. I couldn't get out of bed. My eyes filled knowing this was supposed to be my wedding day with Todd. There would be no vows being said between us in the Little St. Thérèse Chapel in Chatham.

I forced myself to put my feet on the floor and walked to the closet door and pulled my wedding dress down off the hook. My fingers slowly pulled the thick, black, plastic covering off the gown. The sequence beads on the dress sparkled with the sun hitting on them.

How beautiful. I had to put the gown on, even if the action brought sadness. *Judy and Cory would have loved to see me in this wedding dress.* I wanted to see the gown on my body for the last time.

I slipped out of my pajamas and put the undergarments on before sliding the wedding dress over my head. The back buttons had to stay open since I couldn't reach them. Maybe Rita being my maid-of-honor would have snapped them closed for me. My shoes had been in a box in the corner of the room. I opened the cover, took them out, and slide my feet into them. My matching hairpin was sitting on the dresser. I clipped it to my hair to pull the curls off my face. To complete the outfit, I gently took the headpiece out of the box and connected the comb into my hair.

I stood back and looked in the full-length mirror. *Todd, look at me, honey,* I whispered under my breath. *I'm beautiful.* I twirled around and around holding the train up off the floor.

There was one more thing left to do. I went to the tiny box in my nightstand drawer and pulled the item out. There was Todd's wedding ring that I had engraved *My dying love forever, Jenny. October 10, 1939.*

I placed his ring on my left finger and stood in front of the mirror saying the vows I planned to recite to him today in the St. Thérèse chapel.

"I take you, Todd, to be my partner for life,
I promise above all else to live in truth with you
And to communicate fully and fearlessly,
I promise to be your lover, companion, and friend,
Your partner in parenthood,
I give you my hand and my heart
As a sanctuary of warmth and peace
And pledge my love, devotion, faith, and honor
As I join my life to yours forever."

I took the ring off and placed the band back into the small box in the drawer. I took one more look in the mirror at my wedding dress and accessories on me and then put them away, while the tears flowed. My heart was broken. I had pains in my chest, shortness of breath, and felt overwhelmed being traumatized. Never would I have thought I'd be standing here alone on my wedding day. I still couldn't absorb what happened.

The idea of never having Todd in my life stopped me from wanting to take a step in any direction. I never felt isolated as I did at that moment. After losing my whole family and Todd's parents, and him, I had no will to live.

My house had dead air. There was no human presence or the sound of the animals that had once filled our barn and fields. My mother had kept the house alive and loved me freely without any boundaries. The silence overtook me. I felt like death faced me.

My other love, White Christmas, was in Todd's barn. I wished I could have saddled the mare one more time and ride her through the woods that Todd and I had traveled with his black stallion, Midnight. I wanted to connect to Todd's soul.

I needed to get away from the house. It was too empty. I put my bathing suit on and slipped my summer dress over it and put a towel and beach shoes in a tote bag. I grabbed the keys to the car and decided to go to the beach.

Please, God, get me through this one day that was supposed to be the happiest day of my life. I wanted to erase Sunday and get to tomorrow without living it.

Being abandoned with my nerves on edge and my body shaking, I decided to stay close to home. I went to Orleans. The town is referred to as the "elbow" of Cape Cod since this is where the peninsula takes a 90-degree turn to the North. Going to Provincetown would have taken a full day. I didn't want to travel that distance.

I pulled over to Skaket Beach since the area had calm waters and a warm wind compared to the other waterways. This was the gentle side of Orleans. I put on sandshoes and walked with my bundle to the beach. The towel was large enough so that I didn't have to lug a heavy blanket.

I took my wrap-around dress off, revealing my black one-piece bathing suit, and sat in the sun. I slipped the beach shoes off and dug my toes in the warm sand and laid-back and listened to the distant caws of seagulls flying above me. Sunbathers were already swimming in the water and leaping over the waves crashing onto the shore.

I started to remember back to Todd and me watching the sunsets at this location that threw unbelievable colors across the sky with their reds, yellows, pink, and purple which all blended together at sunset which attracted locals year-round.

Since it was low tide, the water enabled me to walk for a long stretch on a sandbar. Coming back, I stayed knee-high in the water while the high tide was arriving. I walked out further and went in for a swim. The water felt warm and relaxing. Coming out, a few people passed by starting conversations with me. It took my mind off my heartache. We shared a few laughs.

Hunger started to hit me. I sat long enough to dry off and then put my wrap-around dress on again. I carried the items to the car and drove to the center of Orleans. I saw the Ocean Grill and went to get a bite to eat. It felt odd without Todd.

A tall waiter, looking to be in his early twenties, with black, messy hair came over to me. "Can I help you, Miss?"

"I'll have a cup of your clam chowder and a plate of clam cakes."

"Anything to drink?"

"Oh, yes. A hot cup of tea."

"A hot day like this and hot tea hits you?"

"Odd, huh? I love hot tea. It relaxes me."

"I'll put the order in."

I loved Cape Cod for its fresh fish. If I was with Todd, I would have ordered a full meal with swordfish. I sat next to a large picture window facing the piers in the old shack next to the boats that were in their slips on the dock. The waves from the passing watercraft caused the tied boats to sway, keeping me mesmerized.

I looked around and saw couples holding hands or giving each other a fast kiss. At that moment, I felt completely separated and out of place. Laughter filled the room from the people at the bar having drinks. I felt like a small dot in a huge space.

The waiter brought the cup of chowder and I watched the hot steam rise. My appetite faded. I could hardly swallow the small cut-up pieces in the chowder. My throat felt like it was closing. A panic attack was rising within me, causing me to feel the need to run. The air felt thick with no oxygen to breathe. My hands felt sweaty, my heart started to race, and my hands shook.

The waiter returned. "How's everything?"

"I've changed my mind. Could you cancel the tea and make my clam cakes to go?"

"Certainly."

When he brought a food container over to me, I threw money on the table giving him a big tip so I didn't have to wait for change. "Thank you," I said.

He looked at the tip. "No. Thank you!"

I couldn't wait to get in the car to drive home and hide. How could I have been so stupid to think I was able to handle this day? Why did I go out by myself acting like I was so independent not needing Todd?

I felt as if the car wasn't going fast enough to get me back in a safe haven at home. I came to a sharp bend in the road on a high cliff and tried to slow down. It was a dangerous curve, and I came close to going off the edge on the turn. I pulled over to the soft shoulder and realized this dangerous curve was where Cory and Judy went over in their truck. I remembered reading about the event.

I walked over to the perimeter of the area and looked down at the deep drop. *How awful! Oh, my God, Cory, and Judy. You didn't deserve to die like this. I loved you both so much.* I sobbed my heart out with no control as if someone reopened a wound in me. My shoulders shook and my face was wet from tears. A passing car braked going by the loop seeing me standing there.

The darkness of night started to take over the sky. I got back into my car and drove straight home with no stops.

I got into the house, locked the door, and my body trembled. All my security was gone. I felt the terrifying separation from Todd and his family. The loss made me start losing touch with reality.

I don't think I can do this, Lord. I'm going to swallow my pride and talk to Todd. I need him in my life. I'll do anything to get him back. Please, God, help me get back to a normal life. I'm starting to unravel.

I went into the bedroom. I felt something was going to happen to me. The fear had kept me from getting into pajamas. I curled up in a ball above the covers with my clothes still on me. I pulled the comforter over my head. Somehow, I passed out into a deep sleep.

****

Monday morning, I woke up with my clothes damp. I must have had night sweats from the physical, paralyzing fright that I tried to deal with from everything closing in on me. I wanted to wake up from this horrible nightmare. Thank God, I lived through Sunday. It was over. Gone.

I took a fast shower to get ready for the appointment to meet Carolyn at her office to sell the house. It was a blessing my home sold in two days. *Todd, you would have been happy to hear the money we could have had*, I thought as I got dressed. I planned on telling him after the legal papers with the sale were signed.

I arrived at 10 am at Carolyn Miller's office.

"Hi, Jenny, come on in.

As I entered Carolyn's office, Mr. and Mrs. Keene were sitting at the roundtable.

"Hello, Jenny." Manny welcomed me.

"The weekend went fast. We're here to sell and buy a house," Carolyn said. She went to her desk and got all the legal paperwork. One by one, she had the Keene's and me sign the official papers which we individually needed to do. Within minutes which felt like hours, the sale was completed.

"Jenny, your house is now sold," Carolyn said.

"Mr. and Ms. Keene, I wish you the very best. I loved my home and hope you feel the same," I said shaking their hands.

Manny came over to me. "Come by for a visit. In a few years, we'll have the farm in full force making money. We wish you the best."

Mrs. Keene gave me a long hug. "You take care of yourself, you hear?"

It had been so long since anyone wrapped an arm around me, that the warm action from a stranger made me fight back tears. "Thank You."

Fear took over my every action knowing I stood without the man I loved and wanted in my life.

Carolyn came over to me with a check. "Make sure you keep this in a safe place. I hope you're going straight to the bank with this money?"

"I'll wait to see if I'm going to New York. If not, I'll deposit the cash in the Chatham Bank."

"Are you moving?" Carolyn asked.

"I'm not sure." I was upset I made the statement.

"Don't carry that check around too long, Jenny, and don't let anyone know you have the funds or you could be robbed. People are desperate with the Great Depression. That can be a lifesaver to a family. Would you like me to come with you to the bank?"

"I'll be alright."

I walked out of Carolyn's office with a spring in my step. My mind was made up to go see Todd and talk about this situation with Cathy. I felt a ton of stress and pressure come off me.

Maybe things could be worked out for us.

If Cathy didn't want her baby, I was willing to raise the child with Todd, and Cathy could go back to her modeling. She could come anytime to see her child. Once Todd and I worked a date out to get married, I would tell him about our own baby on the way. Cathy's child would be part of Todd. That was all that mattered. I loved him enough to bury my pride.

My first stop was to go home to hide the money. My father had a safe under the pantry floor. He never told me, but I saw him stash money in the spot many times. Opening the top, I found a roll of bills. I counted it. He had $550 dollars. It was half of the sale of the house. It wouldn't take long for someone at the bank to spread the rumor that I banked an unbelievable amount of money. I wanted to wash up and change into dungarees before seeing Todd. I couldn't wait to hold him in my arms.

Why didn't I think of this in the beginning? I knew Cathy wanted to go back to her fame in Paris. Her secret of having a baby would stay with us.

Searching for a Home

Todd spent the day riding to see "For Rent" signs in front of homes. He needed a rental for him and Cathy. He made no mention of it to her. He rode by properties in Chatham. Nothing was available. He didn't want to be too far from his business so he could work the farm with Bob and Ray.

He stopped at the corner grocery store to see Mr. Judd. "Hi there, Todd. How did the wedding go yesterday?"

"We decided to hold off a while from the loss of both our parents."

"That's too bad. I know Jenny was all excited when she was in here last week."

Todd didn't want to get into the subject. Mr. Judd was a talker. He knew everything a person was doing in town. Being an owner of a grocery store, he had people opening up to him with their lives —and others!

"I have a friend who's looking to rent. Do you know of any family that's looking for tenants?"

"Well, the O'Donnell's have a house they want to rent down on Stanley Lane. They do the farming there and don't want the house empty. It might be worth your time to check with them."

"Thanks, Mr. Judd. Have a great day."

He watched Todd go out the door trying to guess who really wanted a rental. He was told Cory had built his son and Jenny a beautiful home on Lover's Lake. Why would he be looking for a rental?

Todd knocked on the O'Donnell's door. A husky, tall man in bib-dungarees came to the door.

"Can I help you?'

"Hello, my name is Todd Costa. I'm looking for a rental place, and

Mr. Judd said you may be thinking of renting your home."

"Why, yes, we are. You're Cory's son?"

"Yes, I am."

"We were so sorry to hear about their accident."

"Thank you." Another topic Todd wanted to avoid. "Can you tell me what you want for rent?"

"We're asking $40 a month. Heat and utilities would be included. It has three bedrooms and one bath. The location is down on the farm about another mile. I'll take you down there if you'd like to see the farmhouse."

"Yes, I would be interested."

They drove in separate cars, so Todd could leave when he wanted. Todd looked the farmhouse over and was surprised with the clean condition the place was in and a bonus of being partially furnished.

"My wife's very particular and comes every week to clean the place," Mr. O'Donnell replied.

"It's a comfortable looking place. I'd like to rent the house."

"Well, that's great. When do you want to move in?"

"Now."

Mr. O'Donnell laughed. "My wife's going to be happy to hear this. We still plow the fields and care for the animals in the backlands so you may hear some noise now and then."

"I'm used to a racket. I run our business with carpentry equipment and care for the animals myself."

"Would you care to do the chores for the animals here? I'll take another $10 off the rent."

"I'll think about that after I see how things go back home."

"When you're ready, you can come by the house and get the key."

Todd thanked Mr. O'Donnell and started for home. He felt like he was hit with a ton of bricks. *What am I doing renting a house with Cathy? My home is at Lovers Lake.*

****

Todd pulled up to his family farmhouse and saw Rita's car in the driveway. He went into the kitchen and she was making a Hamburg casserole with potatoes and fresh corn.

"The aroma's good in here."

Rita walked up and hugged him. "How are you doing?"

"When you have time, we have to talk."

"I always have time for you."

"Where are the boys?"

"Bob and Ray took a truckload of lumber to someone who's having a new porch added to their home. They'll be gone most of the day. So, what's up?"

"Rita, Cathy and I got married today."

Rita looked at him. "Today!"

"I wanted to get this agony over with marrying her for the baby's sake."

"You're married. Why so fast?"

"When did you think I would?"

"I honestly hoped you and Jenny would work things out."

He told her about renting the house and having to move out.

"I'll put up with Cathy living here just to have you home." Rita was holding back the hurt from the loss of Jenny and with the emptiness of Kathleen. She didn't want to lose her brother.

"I can't live with her in this house or the one Dad built. That was a place for Jenny and me. I'd give anything to live here. If I didn't find a place today, Cathy was going to have us live with her mother. I can't picture putting up with her."

Rita shook her head. "Look what's happened to all of us in two weeks, Todd. Kathleen's in the hospital, Mom and Dad died, Jenny's gone, Bob and Ray are living here, and you're married to someone other than Jenny, and moving out. There's no family anymore. It's like our lives stopped. You gave me a reason to come home from Detroit. Now, you'll be gone." She started to cry.

Todd put his arms around his sister. "We have to move on, Rita."

She looked back at him upset. "That doesn't mean I'm happy."

Todd looked in the oven. "When's it going to be ready?"

"It should be done in a half-hour," Rita said, wiping her eyes.

"I have to get some things together, and then I'll eat with you."

Todd packed a few clothes and felt like his shoes were in tar and couldn't move. Every part of his body wanted to stay in the house he grew up in with all his memories.

Rita and Todd ate, and he listened to her stories about meeting Clark Gable and the other actors in *Gone with the Wind*. He was impressed. Conversations flowed, but no laughter.

"I have to leave. Cathy has been fair with me being open about not wanting this marriage."

"I don't understand, baby or not, how you're going into this with not one ounce of desire to be married to her. I can see you dread leaving here."

"I'll have to see how this marriage works."

"And what if it doesn't? You would have thrown Jenny out of your life for nothing. You could have had a baby together. Cathy isn't the only one who could give you children." Rita was fighting not to tell him Jenny was pregnant.

"It's too late, Rita. I'm married."

Rita grabbed his left hand. "No ring?"

"Cathy bought me one. I threw the band in the ocean on my way home. I swore to never wear another one unless the ring was from Jenny.

Rita couldn't believe his remark. He admitted openly his love for Jenny. What was going on with him?

He got up and hugged Rita. I'll be working here. I can't give you any of my plans yet because I don't have any. It'll be day by day. I won't leave the business."

"I'll be leaving for work every morning without seeing you. It's so dead in this house. It seems odd having Bob and Ray walking around our house. I love them, but they're not Mom and Dad. I miss Jenny."

"I may be here. Let's wait and see what happens."

Todd went to walk out the door and turned back. "Have you seen or heard from her?"

"I saw her yesterday. Jenny's selling the home. Carolyn Miller might have a buyer today. Her next plan is to move to New York."

"Move! She's leaving Cape Cod?"

"She doesn't want to, Todd. Jenny can't live in the same town as you. She'd be watching you and Cathy bringing up a baby—yours. That's asking a lot out of her."

"I thought Jenny would always be close to me."

"How could she, Todd? Those chances are gone since you got married."

Rita could see Todd was hurting. "Jenny has to move on with her own life. She can't stay around hoping for you to come back to her. There's no hope at all. Your marriage to Cathy really ended any future with Jenny."

Todd opened the door depressed. He feared another man was going to love Jenny. A stranger will get what was intended to be his—Jenny. Rita heard the click to the backdoor closing.

She started to clear the kitchen table and felt a sadness beyond anything she could have imagined. The house used to be so alive with happy times and love. She ached for her parents to be alive and home. She missed seeing Todd and Jenny sitting on the front porch. The world they all knew stopped.

****

Todd arrived back at Cathy's. Each step he took getting to the door made him want to leave the property. He knocked. Cathy stood there with a smile letting him enter.

"Nice to see you, Todd."

"Yesterday, I found a house that we're going to rent. It's on the outskirts of Chatham ten miles from here. It has three bedrooms, a bath, and a kitchen. The home is partially furnished. It's in A-1 condition. A good start for us. I have to pick the keys up. If you want, we can go now and you can see the place."

"Yes, I'd like to see the house. If you wait, I'll get my purse."

"Cathy, I think we should take your bags to move in today. I have mine in the car. We can come back at another time when your mother isn't home for whatever else you find important to take with you."

Sharon came out of the kitchen.

"Well, you decided to come back…and you're clean."

"We can keep this wall up between us, Sharon, or actually become civil to each other."

Cathy came out of her room lugging her large bag.

"Where are you going?" Sharon asked her.

"I'm taking my things, Mother. I'll be back for the rest."

"You're leaving?"

"We'll be back, Mother. Todd and I are going to look at a place to rent."

"Renting? After how you lived in Paris, Cathy. Why aren't you looking at buying a house? You can live here with me? There's plenty of room."

"We want our privacy, Mother, like any married couple."

Todd and Cathy went out the door, leaving Sharon floored that she would have no control over Cathy's decisions and whereabouts living elsewhere.

They reached Mr. O'Donnell's house. "I'll get the key from him. I want to give him the first month's rent and security."

"I haven't seen the house yet, Todd. Don't you think we should wait until I approve of the place?"

He leaned in the driver's open window. "Cathy, we need to be out of your mother's home—today. I'm not living with her for one night. This is going to be our home until we find something else." He left Cathy sitting on the passenger side and walked up to the front steps and knocked.

"Well, hello, Mr. Costa."

"I'd like the key to the property. I have the rent money."

"Come in, Todd. I have a renter's agreement for you to sign. I'll give you a year lease."

"Is it possible to go monthly? We may want to buy a home."

"That will be okay. Sign and I'll give you a copy along with the rent deposit. Let's see…today is October 12, 1939. Mr. O'Donnell gave him his copies. "We'll talk later."

"Thank you, sir. We appreciate this opportunity to be here." Todd

345

closed the door. He got behind the wheel and started to drive down the street.

Mr. O'Donnell was straining his eyes to see the passenger. This woman had blonde hair, while he knew Jenny had red. He wondered if this had something to do with them canceling their wedding.

"As long as I get my money, Todd can do what he wants," he mumbled to his wife, closing the door.

****

They pulled up to the house, and Cathy's expression wasn't showing acceptance to the location. "This is a cute house, but not what I expected."

It had a front porch with gold paint on the outside and black shutters. You couldn't miss it coming up the street. Todd opened Cathy's car door.

"There's a lot of property here." Then, Cathy noticed the hundreds of cows roaming in the pasture. "Are we supposed to care for them?"

"No. Mr. O'Donnell has hands to do that, but he did offer to cut our rent down $10 if I took over."

"You're not thinking of doing that, are you?"

"Right now, I have a farm at home to run with our own animals."

"Maybe I can help you."

"We have two men doing the work. That's enough."

"Here's the key. You can officially open the door." Todd's hands were full.

"Isn't the bride supposed to be carried over the threshold?" She gave him a smile. "I know you don't feel the urge, Todd, but you can make me feel good for a minute, can't you?"

Todd put the bags down and lifted her over the doorsill entrance. She shocked him with a long kiss before he put her down. Without waiting for his reaction, she said, "Thank you." She immediately looked around the house. He picked up the bags to put them in the bedroom.

"Wow, we have three bedrooms. She looked out the kitchen

window. "Look at all the cornfields. Maybe we can collect ours early in the morning next year when they're ready," she laughed.

"This is great, they have furniture. We don't have to run around looking for any," Todd remarked.

Cathy looked over the sofa. She sat on the chair and bounced. "All of this will have to be replaced. It's old. I was hoping we'd decide on a home together. This isn't my style."

"I found it with luck. Mr. Judd from the corner grocery store told me about the place."

"It's far from what I had in Paris. Guess this would be considered low class living. Maybe poor," Cathy replied.

"You're not going to be a queen anymore."

"Can you sit down a minute?" Cathy patted the cushion next to her.

Todd sat opposite in the armchair facing her.

"You said you were still going to work your farm at home. What am I to do?"

"Take care of yourself and our baby. I don't want you working."

"I'm not going to fall apart moving around and doing things. It keeps me in shape and healthier than sitting around all day. I was thinking of maybe going to the modeling shop in Orleans and getting a job helping with the fashion designs.

"There's a designer who has been advertised a lot in the Cape Cod magazines. The stores are owned by Karol Richardson. I think she has one boutique in Newport, Rhone Island. Karol's a British-born designer who completed her art school education at the London College of Fashion, specializes in great style as well as comfort.

"She's been featured in WWD, LA Times, Soho News, and Cape Cod Magazine. Her stores have been voted "Best Women's Boutique" on Cape Cod many times over. My background being a model for Coco Chanel should be impressive."

"How are you going to get there?"

"I have a car at home, silly. We'll have to pick it up tomorrow. My mother will be gone to one of her tea parties. We can gather the rest of my clothing. After that, I want no reason to go back to the house."

"Don't you think being on your feet all day pregnant will be too much for you?"

"What do you think other women do in a family way? Stay-at-home moms do more than working ones. They have to clean, cook, and do anything else the family needs, although, I have never done a thing for myself. I had maids. In Paris, I also had no responsibilities with cleaning or cooking. I had servants who waited on me for everything."

"Are you telling me, Cathy, that you're afraid to dirty your hands and try cooking?"

She went up to him and sat on his lap, wrapping her arms around his neck. "I'll do anything for you. In fact, I'm excited knowing it's just you and me, and we're going to have a family."

Todd didn't believe Cathy. He knew "motherhood" was new to her and the so-called responsibilities would overwhelm her. Cathy liked being the one catered to, not the one taking care of others. She lived in wealth and fame. He knew in his heart this would not last. Changing dirty diapers and feeding a child was out of her personality. He feared Cathy would go back to Coco for modeling and leaving Jenny would have been for nothing. Cathy never did anything without a plan.

Todd nudged Cathy off his lap. "I have to get back to the farm."

She ran up to him. "Oh, please, let me go back with you. I'd love to learn how to help you."

"You can't do that kind of work expecting. When we get your car, you can go to the

Boutique and see if they need someone. It's less work. For now, why don't you put your things away. We'll plan on getting your clothes and other items tomorrow. I'll be back in a few hours."

"No kiss?"

"See you soon," he said, closing the front door.

She watched Todd get into his car and drive off.

What have I done? Look at this filthy pigpen! How can I live like this after being catered to with everything? After all, I'm Nina Mae. All I had to do was model. I don't want my stomach getting out of shape? What if I never get my figure back? I don't want to lose my fans in Paris! Why didn't I recognize the signs of being pregnant? I would have taken care of this problem fast. I need my fame. This house is low-class. I'm a star!

I should have thought this over before getting married. Now that I think of it, I could have gone in hiding in Paris and put the baby up for adoption. I'm never going to bring up a child. I'm not the motherly type. I can't care for a baby full-time. I don't even like them. Maybe I won't carry full term. I've got to find a way out to get back to Paris.

Todd's Decision with His Home

Todd thought of the possibility of Cathy bringing up the topic of moving into the new home his father had built for him and Jenny. He was getting nervous about her legal rights being his wife. He had to do something fast.

He called Mr. Miller. "Hi, Carl. Can I come in to see you today?"

"What's the problem, Todd?"

He opened up and told Carl about his marriage to Cathy and why, leaving out the threats. He explained his fear of her ownership rights to the house.

"Cathy has every right to the property and can insist on moving in there, Todd."

"What can I do?"

"Well—your brother, Sam, was given the lot across from you as an inheritance from your parents. Why don't you give him the house your dad built, and have Sam pass his property to you? Put it just in your name. Don't let Cathy know you own Sam's lot. You can build another house anytime in the future on that piece of land.

I can get a Property Sales Contract made up showing you both signed it on the day I read your parent's Will giving all legal rights to Sam for ownership. This will be an action passed to Sam dated before your marriage. Being your wife, Cathy has the legal power to anything you own, unless you had a written prenuptial agreement."

"Carl, I never thought of it. I'm not the one who's rich, it's Cathy. Let's face it, she's known all over the world as *Nina Mae,* the famous model for Coco Chanel."

"You may have rights to what she owns if she didn't have you sign her prenuptial agreement."

"I don't want anything from her."

"I'll make the papers up with the date of that Friday. You have a serious problem also with your property and business. She can also claim that ownership."

"You have got to be kidding me?" Todd broke out in a sweat. "Rita and Sam would kill me! Including Bob and Ray."

"Can you talk to Rita and Sam tonight and bring them with you?"

"Oh, my God! My family will be wild."

"They have to come tomorrow, Todd. I'll try to set these property exchanges as an inheritance transfer on the Friday before your wedding to Cathy. If you go by your Catholic religion, not being married in the Catholic Church, the ceremony will not be accepted legally in their eyes. It's legal in the eyes of the law.

"I'll make another legal paper showing you own Sam's lot but will file it away until you need it papers in the future. I want you all here by 10 am.

Todd called his brother, Sam, at his dorm. Todd explained the legal work and the conversation with Attorney Miller.

"Would you be interested in doing this? If so, we have to do it tomorrow."

"Are you serious? Faith and I loved that house."

"Carl's getting the papers in order now."

"See you two tomorrow at Carl's office."

Todd got to his parents' house and packed his car with more belongings. He went down to the lumberyard and landscaping business and grabbed his sister, Rita, Bob, and Ray into the barn to talk about what Attorney Miller wanted to do to secure their family property and business.

They all looked dumbfounded but the three agreed.

****

Todd hopped into his car and drove back to Cathy before she had time to think of what he owned and how she could get her hands on his ownership.

He pulled up to the house and decided to act more civilized with her so she would stay in a good frame of mind until tomorrow.

Todd walked into the bedroom. Cathy went to pick a box up. "I don't want you lifting heavy things. Take care of yourself. I'm capable of doing the work. It smells good in here. What are you making for supper?"

"I'm making something easy for the first time. Spaghetti and meatballs.

"You have one thing on your side. I'm hungry so anything will hit the spot." He turned giving her a smile.

Cathy hoped he had a change of heart and decided to give the marriage a try. *Maybe he'd forget Jenny.* She was feeling warm inside with the hope that her husband was going to fall in love with her again.

In an hour, they ate supper. "How was it?" Cathy looked over at him.

"I think there's hope for you. I actually liked it. The meatballs were tender and moist. I'll give you ten points on this supper."

Todd wondered if this Cathy could possibly have emotional feelings. Maybe the pregnancy changed her. He had to keep his mind in one place and not look at the captivating woman he married.

"I should get some sleep. I have an early start in the morning. Let me help you with the dishes," Todd said. After cleaning the kitchen together, he went to take a shower outside. Cathy went into the bathroom for a bath and came out in her nightgown.

She suddenly thought back to that night they made love in the barn. Cathy got chills thinking about their sexual encounter. It had been wild. She wanted that same experience. It was amazing she had not had sex since that night.

When Todd came in, he saw Cathy standing in front of the bathroom door. The light was behind her and he could see her bare body through her nightwear. She looked sexy with her blonde hair falling around her shoulders. He could see her once flat, tight stomach, now slightly bulged. His child was in her. How he wished his eyes were on Jenny in that condition.

She dimmed the bedroom light and pulled down the covers on

Todd's side of the bed. He climbed in and rested his head on the pillow. Her body powder had the fragrance of roses and her body curved in the right places. He gave her a fast peck on the cheek. "Goodnight, Cathy," and turned over.

She pushed onto his side of the bed and put her warm body against his back and pressed her frame into him. He felt her belly on his lower back. She started to kiss his neck. He felt her firm breasts rubbing against his shoulder blades.

He loved Jenny, but Cathy was right about him being a man. Todd wanted her body all over him. He desired a sexual encounter. It had been too long.

Even being pregnant, Cathy was hot wanting him inside her. Her hand traveled down the front of him until she reached his erection. The touch made him moan. There was no way of acting like he didn't want her. Nature showed differently.

He wanted to keep her happy. At the same time, he wanted contact with a woman. When their lips met, he sank into a burning desire.

Through the years, Cathy knew all the arousal spots to make Todd go wild. If they had nothing else, the sex drive between them was a hunger that drove them both crazy. He gave in to her teasing and touched the areas she craved from his hands and mouth.

"Love me, Todd." He never heard her say those words. She was confusing his mind. This didn't seem like the usual wild, untamed sex they shared for years. It was lovemaking for the first time. He felt his betrayal of Jenny. With guilt, he pushed the emotions aside and continued the foreplay until they had long internals of intercourse. This wasn't the selfish Cathy going only for what she wanted. She was gentle and became a partner with the union. He felt her heart was involved along with passion.

After they were satisfied, she curled under his shoulder giving him a fast kiss. "That was wonderful, my husband." Cathy closed her eyes with contentment. Todd kept his arm around her waist and they slept in the spoon position.

Signing Papers

The morning sun rose and Cathy found Todd gone. He left her a note on the nightstand. *Sorry, I had to get to work early to feed the animals. I didn't want to wake you. See you tonight. Todd.*

Hum, no words of love. I guess this note and last night's lovemaking is a start. He didn't hold anything back, she thought. Cathy started to feel emotions that she never had in her life. Getting up for a cup of coffee, she anticipated his return for supper. The thought of his presence gave her an electrifying stimulation.

Her past intimacies with other men were cold with no emotions to protect her from connecting to the man. *This is different,* Cathy thought as she sipped her coffee. She couldn't wait to see him. His walk, smile, and touch woke up her sexual hunger. She wanted the night to come so they could get into bed again. Her body shook with the thought of them locked together. Pregnancy didn't stop her desires.

****

By 6 am, Rita and the men were up ready to do their jobs. Todd rushed to the house to join them for breakfast.

"Hi, Todd." Rita came over to give him a kiss. "I'm glad you're here before we go see Attorney Miller."

She placed the hot breakfast on plates and served the meal individually. The aroma of freshly made coffee filled the air.

"We have to discuss what we're faced with to save the possibility of Cathy getting her hands into our farm."

Rita felt strong resentment. His choice of marrying Cathy caused this commotion and insecurity to their possessions, not just his. She wasn't over the fact that Jenny was out of their lives. She was stunned with her brother hurting Jenny and marrying this run-a-round tramp.

Sam and Faith pulled into the driveway. She had worked with the veterinarian before they arrived. Her animal hospital would be open in six months.

"Let me get two more plates before we continue." Rita went up to the stove and grabbed two cups and filled them with hot coffees and filled their plates with scrambled eggs, bacon, and home fries with toast.

Todd started with information on why they were all together. "As soon as Cathy and I said our vows, I started to think of the home that Dad had built. Cathy may want us to move into it."

"We wouldn't be in this mess if you didn't screw around with her," Sam added, lifting his coffee to drink. "It's your mistake by choice and we might lose our money and property that Dad and Mom worked so hard all their lives to give us because of your actions. Dad and Mom are probably rolling in their graves knowing you married Cathy. I can't sit here and not let you know that I'm burning inside. We loved Jenny and she was crazy nuts about you. It's all gone."

Faith cut in putting her hand on Sam's arm. "Let Todd finish. This isn't going to get any of us anywhere."

Everyone looked at each other knowing deep down Todd was the one who lost the most. The prize was Jenny. He wasn't the same man without her.

"Let's get back to the meeting coming up. First of all, Carl's dating all our legal papers with the house, property, and business from the Will to the Friday we met with him before Cathy and I got married.

"To start, the papers will look like I signed the house Dad built to Sam on that date. Sam, in turn, would have signed his property across Lovers Lane to me. This transaction of ownership is never to be discussed with Cathy. She's to know nothing about my piece of land. Otherwise, she gets half.

"Bob and Ray are now living in our parent's home. Rita, maybe you should think of having a sale's agreement with our house being sold to them on the same date. You travel sometimes for months and it's going to be hard to keep up with the place. I don't want Cathy to get any of this real estate.

"The property, farm, animals, and both businesses will be legally in Rita's ownership. As far as Cathy will know, Bob, Ray, Sam, and I will be hired workers on a monthly paycheck.

"This is what I would like to get done legally if you all agree. Carl will have a separate legal paper showing our inheritance with these changes from the original wishes of our parents before I married. Rita, you'll still have the right to stay in this home in-between your job assignments.

After listening to what Todd and Attorney Miller plotted, they all agreed that it was the right move. Everyone's lives were going to change. Falling into this plan with property ownership made sense. This way, all the property and businesses, along with the farm and house, are going to be in the right hands with Rita with no possibility of Cathy getting anything.

****

The family rode to Attorney Miller's office and the paperwork was printed and signed by everyone under the date of Friday, two days before Todd's marriage.

"This should be legal where no one can fight this in court," Carl explained. "If Cathy sees these papers with the agreement signed by the siblings before her marriage, she will realize she has absolutely no ownership to any possessions. She can't claim the businesses because I listed them in Rita's name, and she'll be giving you all a paycheck as her employees. Cathy's entitled to nothing because it's legally worded that way.

They each received a signed copy.

"Thank you, Mr. Miller, for helping us with this matter."

"You're very welcome. All of you are now protected."

They drove home and sat at the kitchen table. Todd went to the office and came out with papers to give to Sam and Faith. "Here's the invoices with the furniture Jenny and I had picked out. I put a down payment on them. If you like it, you can pay the balance." Todd walked over to Sam. "It's now yours. Enjoy what Jenny and I wanted. Live in that house for us. I'd rather see you and Faith living there."

Todd filled up with emotion. He could have been married to Jenny and living in their perfect home. He realized that he had been trying to bury his love for Jenny by not having a conversation about the loss of their separation.

Bob and Ray were already talking together about going to the bank first thing in the morning to take a loan out for Rita with the sale of the house passed to them. It was a steal with what Rita charged them for the purchase.

Rita now felt relieved to be able to travel with no responsibilities with the dwelling. The boys would take care of the farm and the two businesses, with everyone getting a paycheck monthly. She had a place to lay her head down coming home from a job from wherever, unless she decided to move out for good.

Conversation and laughter started to fill the house for the first time since their parent's accident. No one approved of Todd's marriage to Cathy, but they decided to pull together as a family to support him. Everyone finally knew what they owned and how to move ahead with no more fear of Cathy getting her hands on anything.

****

Five o'clock arrived and Todd was ready to end his day. Bob and Ray continued stacking the lumber on the piles. Now, the two friends only lived up the dirt driveway to their farmhouse. They had to stop saying *the Costa's* since they would be the owners the following day. The farm and businesses were still the Costa's.

Todd drove to Lovers Lane to see his home. He took one last look at his beautiful house by the lake. He swore never to come back. He felt lost and defeated. Todd couldn't hold back the tears from his loss. He lost Jenny. Being a man crying didn't bring any shame to him. His heart was broken. He and Cathy would be going through the emotions of a married couple and nothing else.

Cathy waited by the front door with a smile. "I missed you." She gave him a long kiss.

"Had a long day," Todd said as he flopped down onto the sofa.

Cathy had made a casserole made with meat and vegetables along with baked potatoes. Todd was hungry and sat at the kitchen table. "It looks good."

"Hope it tastes good." Cathy could see a change in Todd. Last night, he came home in a happier mood. Today, his mind seemed miles away.

They ate in silence. He helped clear off the table again; a habit of his for years helping his mother. I'll get the keys to the car and we can bring yours back." He walked out the front door.

She got her purse and joined him. They drove a while and she looked over at him. "Are you okay?"

"Tough day."

"Do you always come home this way—having a *tough day*?"

"I'm sorry."

"Do you think we can take a ride to the home your dad built?"

"Why?"

"It's new. Our rental is okay, but since you have a home sitting there with no one living there, we might as well move into the place. Let's face it; Jenny won't be living there so why keep the house empty? It's not a shrine. I'd like to see the property."

"Cathy, I can't live there. I passed it over to my brother, Sam, since we were getting married. In fact, I think it's this weekend they're moving into it. It's no longer mine."

"When did you do that?" She became angry.

"Friday before we got married."

"Were you afraid I'd grab it from you?"

"Cathy, my parent's Will was read to the family before we got married. My siblings and I needed to get things in order. We couldn't leave things hanging with everyone going in different directions. There were no plans of you being in my life. I will never live in that house without Jenny so I gave it to Sam and Faith. My father built it."

"So, your newly built house overlooking Lover's Lake will never be ours?"

"Not now." Todd felt a ton of stress and relief come off him knowing he gave the home to Sam. What a safety net from Mr. Miller.

"What about the business and the farmhouse?"

"Why are you so interested in what my family owns? We can't compare my things to your parent's possessions with your millions. My things are small."

"What are you planning on doing for work?"

"Working where I always have been—on my family's farm. That's my life, Cathy. It was what my father and past generations have done."

"That's not a living." Cathy was upset, folding her arms across her lap.

"What do you mean—not a living? Have you plowed a field? Do you get up at 4 am to feed animals, clean out their stalls, milk them, or make the cheese? Have you run a landscaping business and a carpentry shop? Do you grow and sell vegetables from the fields to the public to put food on their table or grow plants to help people have beautiful landscapes, like the ones your family bought from us? Do you hammer away for months on end to build a home or do repairs to someone's building? You think I'm not working for a living?" Now Todd was getting angry. "This is our life now, Cathy. I'm not going to change for you. It was a life Jenny and I were looking forward to with a family.

"All your life, you were spoiled walking around looking beautiful. Daddy gave you whatever you wanted, and you got big bucks walking down a runway with designer clothes. No wonder you always had beautiful nails. You never worked!

"You might as well know now, Cathy. I don't own anything. Rita sold the house to Bob and Ray because she's never home. I planned to move out once we got married. Rita and everyone figured Jenny and I were going to get married and move into the house built by my father. Sam and Faith wouldn't be living there. No one was going to be home. We all didn't want it to be empty when Rita had to travel."

"Are you kidding me? Your sister got it all?"

"Things were different when my parents were alive. Something your parents took from all of us. We had to make decisions for our best security. My parents worked their whole lives to give us what was theirs."

"I don't believe you have no money invested in your farm or lumber company."

"Bob, Ray, and I will be working for my sister. I will be getting a paycheck from her like any employee. It's a steady job."

"We have nothing?"

"We have each other and a baby on the way. Isn't that what you wanted? Being filthy rich, you never mentioned you wanted your hands on the little our family had for years. You sound like your father, Cathy. Do you want to give me some of your millions? I don't see you wanting to share your possessions with me. If I want to be forceful, I could claim your millions. I didn't sign your agreement. You just wrote it up. Legally, it's mine.

"I thought you had something to fall back on with your living. My money's all in a bank."

"I'm sure in a bank located in Paris, in your name only."

The conversation stopped since the tension was rising.

They got to her parent's mansion and Cathy went straight to the garage to get her car. "I'll meet you back home." She was in a rage.

Todd watched as Cathy drove out the circular driveway in a mint-green 1939 Chrysler Imperial Custom Parade. She drove in style. Todd couldn't picture her staying in the old farmhouse they were renting.

He drove off behind her. It was hard keeping up with her speed. She disappeared on the main road heading towards town. He had no doubt that Cathy wouldn't be back early. She probably was going out on the prowl, pregnant or not.

Todd got on his knees and thanked God that all the paperwork went through the morning before this argument. He knew this side of Cathy; she wanted the best, but the farm-life wasn't the cream of the crop. Cathy had a taste for men and money. Paris only put the frosting on the dream. Todd knew sooner or later, she would return to *Nina Mae*.

Visit to the Costa Farm

A few days after signing papers selling the house, I knocked on Rita's front door.

"Hi, Jenny. Since when do you have to knock?" Rita asked.

"Since I moved out. I came to tell you that I sold my home. I had to share the news with someone. I have all the security I need to take care of myself."

"You seem on a high from the last time I saw you."

We sat at the kitchen table. "So, Jenny, what's your next move?"

"Rita, I'm not mixed-up with a decision anymore," I said excitedly.

"Well, that's great to hear."

"I'm not moving. I'm going to swallow my pride and take a chance on being rejected."

"I'm thrilled you're not leaving the Cape. What do you mean by rejected? From what?"

"I'm going to tell Todd that I want to work things out. I'm going to offer to bring Cathy's baby up. If she agrees, I'm going to tell Todd that I'm pregnant. I feel good about this. It's the right thing to do. It's the answer we needed. Why didn't I think of it sooner?" I smiled being delighted solving our problem with Cathy.

Rita put her head down and then looked up at me. "Jenny, that's going to be impossible. It's too late."

"It's not too late. They haven't got married yet."

"Todd and Cathy got married, Sunday. I didn't know myself until Monday."

I sat in shock feeling nauseated. I couldn't react for a few minutes.

Rita continued. "He rented a house down the street. I think he said the farmhouse owned by Mr. O'Donnell. He doesn't want her here, or especially in the new house Dad built for you two." Rita saw Jenny's expression change. "Say something, Jenny."

"I guess you saved me from making a fool of myself." All the air was taken out of me.

"Don't feel that way." Rita's eyes filled.

"Todd married Cathy on *our* scheduled wedding day. What a nice slap in the face. While I was coming apart, he was holding her hands saying his vows to her. The next day, he rents a house. That takes care of my stupid, romantic thinking."

"Jenny, I wish I could change this mess."

"I'm back with my first plan, but I have to admit, this insult has made me stronger to leave Chatham and get on with my life without shedding another tear."

I stood up. "Sorry, Rita, I won't be staying for tea. I want to go back home and pack."

"I have to know where you'll be."

"I'll call you when I get settled. At least this money will give me time to think about getting a job and move right into a place without wondering if I can afford the tenement. Tell Todd that I wish him the best and thanks for the good times and fond memories."

I got up and walked out the door. I felt the separation from my best friend. I couldn't be nice to her, although, Rita didn't deserve me being nasty. This pain wasn't caused by her. I was hurt, angry, and absolutely heartbroken. I had the right plan but it was too late by one day.

Todd's Return to the House

Twenty minutes later, Todd's car pulled into the family's driveway. He opened the door and walked into the kitchen seeing his sister in tears.

He ran over to her. "What's the matter?"

"I'm sick of being between you and Jenny."

"What do you mean?'

"Jenny rode in hoping to see you. I had to give her the news of your marriage on Sunday. You know—the day you two were to be married?" Rita was angry and couldn't hide it.

"What did she want?"

"She wanted to work things out with you. Jenny was willing to offer to take Cathy's baby and you two could bring the child up. That was until she heard you got married. I never saw her so hurt and mad.

"Don't get me involved anymore, Todd. You should have been the one to come to a conclusion with Jenny, not me. You left that poor girl hanging after bringing Cathy into our lives from nowhere. I wonder how you would have felt if she announced being pregnant by another man?"

Todd sat down at the table. "She wanted to work things out?"

"Yes. Jenny shouldn't have been the one trying to work your problems out with Cathy. You caused this turmoil. It was your place to solve this situation with her instead of letting her run off heartbroken. You can't imagine what you did to her. Jenny's packing and leaving Chatham for New York. By the way, she also sold her home and thought the money would have been a great start for the two of you."

"What have I done? I never would have thought of Jenny and I taking Cathy's baby and letting her go back to Paris."

"Why did you marry Cathy two days after telling us about her pregnancy? If you waited, you would have given Jenny time to let the shock sink into her and us. Maybe the two of you might have come up with this offer to Cathy. We all know she's going to return to Paris. It's only a matter of time. Instead, you married her. Now you have to live with it." Rita got up and walked out the kitchen door.

Todd's family would never know he caused their parent's death or that he was blackmailed. If anyone did anything against Cathy or her mother, Jenny and Rita would be killed. How do you tell the people who you love that story? They would have gone after them. No one would be alive.

My Final Decision

I drove home devastated. Thinking about Todd being married drove me crazy. There was no way left to bring us back together. It was final.

How could he marry that tramp on our scheduled wedding day? I hope he drowns in misery.

I didn't mean the thought, but I wanted to hurt him. There was no way to punish him. I was completely shocked he left me that easily. Was I feeling his love for me or was it because I wanted him to love me that much. I knew there would be no other man like Todd in my life.

The next morning, I left a note on the table for the Keene's. I set the keys to the house and barn next to the letter.

I had to leave more quickly than I thought to get a new job. There was no time to sell my furniture or find a way to move the pieces to New York. I wish you both happiness in your new home. Jenny Rossini

I took the envelope of money my father had hidden and the check from the sale of the house and walked out leaving the door open. I had no other spare key. The car was packed with all my clothes that could be squeezed into the backseat and trunk along with special keepsakes from my mother and a few from Todd. If my pain eased, I might have wished to keep what Todd had given me. For some reason, I took my wedding dress, accessories, and Todd's wedding ring I had inscribed.

I stopped at the end of the driveway and looked back at my home. The memories held good times, well others were hardships my father caused me and my mother. My past was gone. My parents and our home were frozen in time. It was a hollow feeling.

The most painful decision was leaving Todd. There was no doubt that I loved him, but I couldn't stay and deal with him married to

Cathy and watch his excitement having a baby with her. Leaving Cape Cod for Manhattan was the only way out I could see. Now, I had to face the agonizing decision to either bringing our child up alone or to give the baby up for adoption.

~~~~

BIO OF THE AUTHOR

Alberta Sequeira

I guess you could say that I was an Army brat. My father, Albert L. Gramm, Sr., was a retired Brigadier General in the Army. Dad had been one of the commanding officers in the 26th Yankee Division during WWII, fighting in battles like Lorraine, Metz, and the Battle of the Bulge.

I have two beautiful daughters, Debbie (Lopes) Dutra of Berkley, MA, and my deceased daughter, Lori (Lopes) Cahill of North Dighton, MA. Lori died in 2006 at thirty-nine years of age from alcohol addiction. She's buried with her father who fought the same disease.

I was born in Pocasset, Massachusetts, on the outskirts of Cape Cod. I live in Dartmouth, Massachusetts with my husband, Al. I graduated from Dighton High School in Dighton, Massachusetts and belong to the St. John Neumann Church in East Freetown, Massachusetts.

I'm an educational instructor for three-hour workshops titled *Bring Your Manuscript to Publication, How to Publish Your Own Book with*

Create Space, and *Writing Memoirs."* I'm also a co-founder of *Authors Without Borders (www.awb6.com)* and a director, producer, and co-host with the NBTV-95 Cable TV show out of New Bedford, Massachusetts. I've written for the Cape Cod Today blog for seven years.

The Rusty Years is a book written for the reader's imagination to fantasize how in the 1930s three friend's destinies got twisted from wrong choices in life to prevent them from moving forward. The story had allowed me to fabricate multiple character's individual lives and allow the reader into the world of Jenny Rossini.

Hopefully, this book will pull readers away from their stress in life, and encourage them to grab a cup of coffee, a soft pillow, a couch to relax on, and enjoy my second book in the series. Let's say...like eating potato chips...once you read *one,* you can't stop, until you have read them all.

Other Books by Alberta Sequeira

Upcoming:

The sequel: *The Rusty Years; Secrets Revealed (Fiction)*

The Mindset of the Alcoholic and Addict (Narrative Non-Fiction)

A Sample of Heaven: Our Last Call (A Christian Memoir)

From War to Flashbacks (Non-Fiction: History of Brigadier General, Albert L. Gramm's Military Status)

Published:

Someone Stop This Merry-Go-Round: An Alcoholic Family in Crisis

Enter behind closed doors of a family's private life of hardships and struggles with alcohol abuse. People living in the same atmosphere will relate to the constant confusion, disappointments, broken promises, and fear. Family members become enablers only bringing the abuser, Richard Lopes, deeper into his addiction. This memoir was nominated for the "Editor's Choice Award 2009" and for the "Dan Poynter's e-Book Award 2011." It's a highly recommended read for the alcoholic and drug users, family members, counselors, doctors, and anyone wanting to learn what goes on in an alcoholic family.

Please God Not Two: This Killer Called Alcoholism

This powerful sequel to *Someone Stop This Merry-Go-Round* is an emotional, touching story of the daughter, Lori Cahill, following the same path as her father. The merciless demon returns making the mother watch the same horrible tragedy unfold for the second time. There are many lessons in this memoir. I guess one could call it a "What Not to Do" book. Nothing is held back from the reality of the devastation that this disease leaves behind.

Handbooks:

Bring Your Manuscript to Publication

Do you have a story but don't know how to go about publishing it? You may ask: Do I call on agents or publishers; what is a query letter, synopsis, book proposal, media kit? Look no further. This is your handbook.

How to Self-Publish Your Own Book with Create Space

Are you tired of paying a publisher to print your book and coming out with everyone else getting a huge part of your royalties? Here is a handbook to help you take the leap and publish your own book through Create Space and come out way ahead. Print for free with no hidden costs. Easy steps to follow. The instructions will help you correct mistakes, learn about embed fonts, hard keys, margins, see the difference between page breaks and section breaks, inserting headers, footer and page numbers, hidden text, deleting asterisks, publishing a paperback and an e-book with Kindle, and much more.

Writing Memoirs

Welcome to the world of writing memoirs. It all starts with the desire to share an event in your life. Do you wonder if you can use someone's name? Can you write by giving yourself another name? This is a handbook taken from Alberta Sequeira's three-hour workshops on teaching memoir writing.

I'm thrilled when a reader leaves a review on Amazon for me. Good or bad, they help me to grow as a writer.

All books in paperback and Kindle are available.

All my published books are available at
www.amazon.com/author/albertasequeira

Email at alberta.sequeira@gmail.com

Website for Substance Abusers at
www.albertasequeira.wordpress.com

www.ingramcontent.com/pod-product-compliance
Lightning Source LLC
Chambersburg PA
CBHW071155020726
47502CB00002B/413